The Greek Holiday

Maeve Haran is an Oxford law graduate, former television producer and mother of three grown-up children. Her first novel, *Having It All*, which explored the dilemmas of balancing career and motherhood, caused a sensation and took her all around the world. Maeve has written fifteen further contemporary novels and two historical novels, plus a work of non-fiction celebrating life's small pleasures.

She lives in North London and a much-loved cottage near the sea in Sussex.

Maeve Haran

The Greek Holiday

PAN BOOKS

First published 2020 by Pan Books
an imprint of Pan Macmillan
The Smithson, 6 Briset Street, London EC1M 5NR
Associated companies throughout the world
www.panmacmillan.com

ISBN 978-1-5098-6653-3

1 3 5 7 9 8 6 4 2

A CIP catalogue record for this book is available from the British Library.

Typeset by Palimpsest Book Production Ltd, Falkirk, Stirlingshire
Printed and bound by CPI Group (UK) Ltd, Croydon, CR0 4YY

Visit **www.panmacmillan.com** to read more about all our books
and to buy them. You will also find features, author interviews and
news of any author events, and you can sign up for e-newsletters
so that you're always first to hear about our new releases.

For Georgia, Holly and Jimmy

One

'Remind me why I'm here, in the boiling heat, about to spend ten days with women I've hardly seen for years and might not even recognize?'

Nell glanced at Dora, who, despite her protestations about the heat, managed to look cool and elegant in a bronze off-the-shoulder dress more suited to a cocktail party in Canary Wharf than a ten-hour ferry trip in the blinding heat.

'Because it's an adventure,' Nell replied, grateful that she was wearing serviceable cotton. 'Because we're going back to the magical Greek island we fell in love with when we were eighteen. We used to be inseparable, remember? We were going to be friends forever – except maybe Moira. And then life got in the way. Husbands. Children. The demands of domesticity.' She paused, embarrassed, remembering that Dora had neither husband nor children. 'And in your case, your big job,' she added quickly. 'I think it's a lovely idea getting together. Even Moira. And also it means a lot to Penny, and Penny's an exceptionally nice person.'

'How unfortunate for her,' Dora drawled.

Nell looked round the dock at Piraeus, the port to the Greek islands, for any sign pointing to the terminal where the four of them were supposed to meet but could see nothing useful, and certainly no sign for Zanthos.

The truth was, they'd all been surprised when Dora had suddenly agreed to come. Dora had a glamorous life in public relations. Once Nell had seen a gossip piece in the paper with the headline 'Pandora Perkins, the scariest PR in London'.

Nell consulted the email from Penny again, feeling grateful she didn't have a life like Dora's. Working as receptionist in a GP's surgery couldn't remotely be called glamorous ... The shock hit her that, actually, she wasn't. Three weeks ago she'd opted for retirement after that last run-in with the new practice manager from hell. She was now an ex-doctor's receptionist. 'Oh look, there's a sign saying Passenger Terminal,' she pointed out. They rounded a corner away from the line of huge ferries, each with its aft end open like a gaping mouth for all the cars and container lorries to drive in, and almost tripped over a red-faced man pulling two vast suitcases plus an overnight bag while his wife strode insouciantly ahead.

'I wouldn't mind one of those,' Dora remarked, looking after them.

'What, the suitcase?' Nell glanced at the bags to see if they were made by Louis Vuitton, Dora's usual taste.

'No, the husband. I always wondered what they were for. Now I can see.'

They both giggled. Nell looked at her watch, grateful they had left plenty of time to find the terminal and buy their tickets. To be honest, Nell always left plenty of time for things. She thought people who were late were selfish and rude.

'I don't see why we didn't buy the tickets online,' Dora pointed out. 'Queueing for tickets feels like masochism in this day and age.'

'Penny said it would be cheaper.' Nell realized that Dora probably couldn't imagine a world where counting the pennies mattered. 'You know your problem?' She tried not to sound sharp. 'You're too used to turning left on aeroplanes. Experience real life for a change. We're retracing the holiday we all shared when we were students. It's significant. A milestone.'

'I hate milestones. They remind me how many miles I've come.'

Dora's attention was suddenly grabbed by two Orthodox priests who were walking past them swathed in black, with tall black hats and beards that would have made your average Shoreditch hipster choke on his sourdough sandwich. 'Look, they'll know, they're Greek and it's their duty to be helpful to strangers.'

Dora strode forward and shook the hand of one of the priests enthusiastically. He blanched with shock and stepped backwards, as if Eve herself had materialized on the smelly dockside, the fateful apple in her hand, ready to bring about man's eternal fall from innocence.

'Excuse me, but do you know where Terminal P1 is, to the Cyclades Islands?' Dora enquired.

He shook his head violently and scuttled off in the opposite direction.

'That was helpful,' Dora complained. 'To think I assumed meeting at the terminal would be like catching the Eurostar and I could buy a cappuccino and a copy of *Grazia*.'

'Come on, it must be round here,' Nell said. Even though it was so early in the season, the sun was beating down and Nell found she was sweating profusely. There were people everywhere, pushing and shoving. Apart from two little boys sitting on the harbour wall fishing, it was more a scene from hell than a Greek holiday fantasy. She'd been told you could see the Acropolis once you were on the ferry, but at the moment all she could see were angry-looking people shouting at each other and a row of smokers sitting puffing away next to a heap of suitcases. They rounded another corner to find a bright-red-painted building with 'Passenger Terminal' written above it.

Not only was it closed, but chained and padlocked. They plonked themselves down on the bench outside and leaned on their pull-along bags. 'Oh, bloody hell.' Nell wiped the sweat out of her eyes. 'I know. Why don't we ring Penny? I bet she's found it.'

She delved into her backpack just as a curious figure came into sight, wearing a long dress in a rather unfortunate shade of purple, embroidered with the kind of key patterns you find in Greek temples, and reading a book as she walked along, apparently oblivious of the chaos around her. Her hair was an untidy birds' nest that made Nell think of the Edward Lear poem about the old man who found two owls and a hen, four larks and a wren had all made a nest in his beard.

Nell suddenly realized who it was. 'Moira!' she greeted the third member of their little troupe. 'Have you found the right terminal yet?'

The newcomer closed her copy of Robert Graves' *Greek Myths and Legends* and looked round hazily. 'Sorry, no. I've just come from the Archaeological Museum in Piraeus. You really ought to go.'

Dora lifted an eyebrow just enough to imply that archaeological museums were not exactly on her list of essential activities.

Moira taught classics at one of the most famous colleges in Cambridge, and lost few opportunities to remind you of it. 'I'm so excited,' she announced, staring off into the blue distance

4

of the sea. 'Our ferry stops at Ios, where Homer was buried, and I want to get off and at least offer some kind of libation. The only thing is you only get six minutes.'

'I hear Ios is a party island now,' Dora pointed out bitchily. 'Vomit in the streets and twenty-four-hour booze cruises. What would Homer think of that?'

Moira shook her head in horror. Nell watched, fascinated, hoping no larks or wrens flew out.

'Though in the Odyssey he does talk about the wild wine that leads men on to sing at the top of their lungs,' she informed them, 'and to dance and blurt out stories better not told.'

'I've had some of that,' Dora agreed.

'Me too,' agreed Nell. 'Though not for far too long.'

'We'll have to put that right,' laughed Dora. 'Do you remember retsina?'

'The one that tastes like Dettol?'

'The very same. We'll see if they have some on the boat.'

'When we find it,' Nell sighed, her usual energy beginning to deflate in the heat. 'Oh yes, I was going to ring Penny.'

'Hang on,' Moira pointed behind them, 'isn't that her now?'

Dora and Nell turned round just as a smiling figure bore down on them about twenty feet away, looking almost the same as she had when they first met as students – frumpy clothes, straight fair hair, freckled face and an air of almost desperate eagerness.

'My God,' whispered Dora. 'She's wearing an Alice band! At our age! I gave up those when I was twelve. And she looks so keen to please, just like this spaniel we had when I was a kid that never stopped wagging its tail. Even at burglars.'

'Not a spaniel,' Nell found herself whispering back. 'A golden retriever. Dora,' she added guiltily, 'you're a bad influence. Behave yourself. Hello, Penny,' she greeted her friend with a smile. 'What's that you've got there?'

'*Spanakopita!*' Penny announced proudly.

'Is that "good morning" in Greek?' Dora enquired, trying to suppress a giggle.

'That's *kalimera*,' Moira corrected repressively.

'Don't you remember, girls?' Penny gushed. 'When we caught the boat last time we were starving and this is what all the Greek people were eating. They're spinach and cheese pastries.' She held out four greasy triangles.

Nell was the first to take one. 'Delicious!' she pronounced.

Moira ate hers in one bite and almost choked while Dora screwed up her face, reluctant to risk getting grease on her unsuitable outfit.

'Well, here we are,' Penny was almost bursting with excitement. 'The adventure begins! The terminal's just round that corner.'

They lined up for their tickets, which turned out to be very easy to buy once you found the right place, and just as Penny had said, considerably cheaper than pre-ordering online.

Tickets in hand, they went off to look for the ferry, pulling their bags behind them, a strangely assorted group: Nell pretty and neat in beige cotton shorts and crisp white shirt, her dark hair in a bob; Moira looking like a member of the Bloomsbury Group on holiday; Dora rich and glamorous, looking as if she might own the ferry line rather than being a foot passenger; and lastly Penny, who did indeed rather resemble a retriever eagerly chasing a ball.

'Thank goodness for pull-alongs,' Penny grinned round at the others. 'Do you remember last time we had to carry our suitcases right across Athens because we couldn't afford the bus fare?'

They reached the water's edge, where a row of ferries was lined up.

Dora's gaze fastened on a small, sleek vessel called *Sea Cat 3*, which was clearly built for speed. 'I don't suppose we're going on that one?' she asked longingly.

'I think that's ours there.' Moira pointed to a large, lumbering vessel with a yellow funnel. 'It stops at six different islands, and one of them is definitely Ios. I really will be able to get off and make my libation!' She could hardly contain her classical joy. 'And we should see the sun set over some of them.'

'Terrific,' commented Dora.

'Try and view it as a mini-cruise,' Nell suggested pacifyingly.

'A cruise without a four-star restaurant, a spa, or even a swimming pool?' Dora replied waspishly. 'I'm going to sit over there in the shade.' She pointed to the bright orange waiting area.

When she was out of earshot, Moira raised her copy of *Greek Myths* and whispered to Nell behind it. 'I have to say, I do wonder why on earth Dora is joining us.'

Nell glanced over at Dora, who was elegantly raising a real old-fashioned cigarette to her shimmering bronze-lipsticked lips. 'Yes,' she replied calmly. 'The same question had occurred to me.'

To add to Dora's annoyance, the boat was packed with people returning home for the festival of a local and much-revered saint. The green fabric banquettes had been instantly colonized by entire families, the children sitting on their parents' knees or running up and down screaming with joyful exuberance; the passageways were choked up with suitcases and baskets full of food being taken home for the festival. The only available seating was in the cafe area.

Nell went off to inspect the menu. 'Well, basically, girls,' she reported cheerily, 'it's moussaka and chips or moussaka and chips.'

Above their heads an enormous TV screen relayed a football match at maximum volume. 'Time to resort to the grape,' Dora announced, plonking down a bottle of retsina and four glasses. 'Let's see if it tastes as bad as we remember.'

Moira rather primly put her hand over her glass. 'I don't really drink.'

The others looked at her in amazement.

'Euch!' winced Dora. 'It really does taste like Dettol!' But she drank it all the same.

After they'd finished, Dora went off to explore whether there was any chance of a cabin, announcing that it was the only way she could survive the night.

'There must be some reason she's come,' Moira insisted. 'I mean, slumming it with the likes of us is hardly her scene.'

'Of course she came!' Penny replied, shocked. 'It's a reunion. I'm sure she wouldn't have missed it for the world.'

Outside the cafe window, the sky was turning apricot with streaks of magenta. 'Come on.' Moira grabbed her rucksack. 'We'll miss the sunset.'

'But what about the seats?' Nell asked, panicking at the thought of a whole night sitting on the crowded and none too clean floor. 'Why don't I stay here and keep them?'

Their dilemma was solved by the return of Dora, announcing she had secured a cabin with four bunk beds. 'Imagine – the purser said we could have it cheaper if we let a stranger have one of the bunks, but I couldn't see who would agree to sleep on the floor.'

'I would have,' instantly volunteered Penny.

'I know you would, Penny,' replied Dora, who seemed to

have softened somewhat now she had the prospect of a cabin. 'But I was only joking.'

'Come and see the sunset before you go to bed,' Moira suggested.

'Yes, come on Dora,' Nell seconded. 'It's your first night in Greece! Enjoy it! You don't have to stay up late.'

It was a glorious evening on deck. The wake of the ship seemed to be made of liquid silver and the wind that blew through their hair was warm and caressing. Nell stared up at the stars. She thought she could see Orion's belt but didn't dare point it out for fear of a half-hour lecture on the other Greek-myth-inspired constellations from Moira. She hadn't seen so many stars since she'd taken Willow to the London Planetarium. She wouldn't think about Willow on this beautiful night. She'd accepted Penny's invitation because it had felt like getting away from what she knew was becoming an unhealthy obsession with the daughter who wouldn't talk to her. And surely it would be fun to spend some time with her three friends from college, ill-assorted though they might be? Wasn't that part of the fun? She certainly hoped so. She made herself concentrate on the thousands of stars and planets above her, sharp as jewels in the blackness of the open sky.

'I wonder what the weather's like at home? Horrible, I hope.' This mild statement seemed almost blasphemous on Penny's lips.

Towards the stern on the top deck, a group of lively young people sat on their bags drinking wine and playing guitars.

'Do you remember how incredibly bold it was, going to Greece when we were young?' Nell's voice seemed to hum with pleasure at the memory. 'Not like now, when they all fly to Bali or South America. The Greek islands were the height of adventure. An unknown frontier!'

'And no hotels or Airbnb!' Penny laughed. 'Just a little Greek lady dressed in black waiting at the dock to offer you a room.'

The group of young people were clearly in Sixties nostalgic mood. 'If You're Going to San Francisco' segued into 'Leaving on a Jet Plane'.

'Do you remember the cafe in Zanthos that had the only jukebox in the village?' Penny asked them. 'And the one record it had was "Black Magic Woman", and we played and played it? I'm going to ask them if they know it.' She jumped to her feet.

'Oh, God, stop her, someone,' Dora begged, but it was too late. In five minutes they were all joining in the chorus.

It was too much for Dora, who got to her feet and made for the cabin, where she sank gratefully onto the bunk bed, trying to ignore the smell she hoped wasn't carbon monoxide and deafen herself to the clanking and clattering of the ramp going down at the first island to let off cars, vans and loud, excitable pedestrians. She stopped herself thinking about how many years it had been since she'd last heard that song.

At least, she comforted herself, things couldn't get much worse than being below the car deck in a two-foot-wide bunk bed in thirty-degree heat.

Moira announced she was going to find the purser and ask when they would dock at Ios, while Penny and Nell went into the bar and bought a bottle of wine to share with the singers on deck. They were an assorted bunch who had met each other at a hostel in Athens and decided to travel on together to Ios, where apparently the party never stopped.

They ranged in age from about seventeen to thirty, the girls mainly in tiny shorts and tank midriff tops, the men in Lycra and t-shirts, as if they might be about to jump onto a bike and join the Tour de France.

'They're like a modern version of us,' Nell laughed.

'Without the Afghan coats and hippie shawls,' Moira agreed. 'Do you remember that Berber wedding dress you found in Kensington Market and wore for about two years till it smelled worse than a camel?'

Nell laughed at the memory. 'I loved that dress. It absolutely appalled my mother. Which was part of the charm.'

'Do you think they mind having us oldies sitting with them?' Penny asked anxiously, suddenly reminding Nell of a gun dog who has dropped its master's pheasant and fears an angry reprisal.

'I doubt they've even noticed,' Nell replied. 'And if they have, we probably remind them of their parents.' She stood up, holding out the bottle. 'Anyone for a top-up?'

'Ooh, Demestica,' said a pretty girl with a mass of dark curls. 'We're going up in the world!' She made a place for Nell to sit next to her. Nell beckoned Penny and Moira to sit down too.

The moon began to rise. 'Look, it's almost full!' Penny pointed out with satisfaction, as if she'd ordered it from Harrods. The warm breeze felt like being wrapped in the lightest of silk scarves.

Penny laughed happily. 'Do you remember that fringed shawl of mine? The one with the embroidery that we kept over a lamp when I wasn't wearing it?'

'The black one with red and pink roses on it?' Nell replied. 'Whatever happened to it?'

'I left it in my parents' car and Mum put a pack of paté down on it. Deliberate sabotage. She said I looked like Gypsy Rose Lee and everyone was laughing at me. They were good days, weren't they?' She took Nell's hand for a moment and squeezed it. 'Thanks for coming. To be honest, I'm not sure what to expect.'

Nell squeezed back. 'I jumped at the chance! Living on your own, you don't get too many opportunities for adventure. The thrill of being a Single Lady on Saga cruises can definitely wear off, I assure you!'

Whether it was a tribute to the presence of Nell and Penny, they didn't know, but one of the guitarists began to play Bob Dylan's 'The Times They Are a-Changin''.

Nell sang along with the bit about your sons and your daughters being beyond your command, and felt a lump come to her throat. Willow was certainly beyond her command. She was only in Weybridge, but still Nell hardly ever saw her – or her baby granddaughter. Willow: the only known example of a daughter who preferred her mother-in-law to her own mother!

Maybe she had no one but herself to blame. She had been the one who'd had the affair that ended the marriage all those years ago. And Robert, her ex-husband, had wasted no time in reminding their daughter of it at every opportunity. Grudgingly Willow had stayed with her, but she'd spent half her time with Robert and his new wife. And now, since she had married and had a baby of her own, Willow seemed to spend every free moment with Marigold, her husband Ollie's ghastly mother.

Nell had to stop herself reaching for her phone and checking the latest Happy Family photographs on Instagram.

Opposite them, a young woman in the tiniest shorts Nell had ever seen began to furiously scratch a mosquito bite. Without really meaning to stare, Nell noticed that her legs were covered in them. 'Our campsite turned out to be in a swamp,' she explained.

Her boyfriend leaned across to examine them more closely. Hopefully he would reassure her a bit.

'Christ, you look awful,' was his only comment.

Nell shook her head and shrugged at Penny. Bloody men.

Next to her, Penny felt the carefree moment drift away. That was just the kind of remark her husband Colin would have made. She really ought to ring him.

Deep down in the recesses of her mind the connection between Colin and the nasty comment reverberated, but Penny stowed it safely away in the hidden place where she kept anything that might threaten her marriage.

'Shall we go to bed?' She pulled Nell to her feet, realizing how late it was getting. 'I wonder what's happened to Moira.'

'Probably tucked up in her bunk by now, dreaming of nymphs and satyrs.'

'I hope she doesn't miss Ios. Or get stuck there with all the party people.'

'Dora would probably be delighted if she did.' They exchanged a telling look. 'I hope Dora's going to be OK in Greece. She seems to have such different standards to the rest of us.'

'I'll look after her, don't you worry,' Nell promised.

'Nell, you are a star.'

As if prompted by her comment, they both looked up at the amazing velvet blue above them, studded with stars that seemed so much nearer than they were at home, and couldn't help smiling. For the first time, it really was beginning to feel like an adventure with no responsibilities. They could forget supermarkets, and parking, and whether the washing machine was working.

'When we wake up we'll be in Zanthos!'

The last thing Penny did as she climbed into the bottom

bunk, her large feet sticking out the end as she stretched, was to open her wallet and take out a blurred photograph of a small Greek village with a blue-domed church and bright white cube-shaped houses climbing up a steep hillside, above a ridiculously blue sea.

There was silence in the cabin apart from Dora's gentle snoring. Penny put her head down on the pillow, trying to do her mindfulness exercises to help her sleep and not think of Colin's last words to her. That he certainly felt sorry for her friends if she'd organized the whole thing. That she couldn't even put a sandwich in a paper bag without screwing it up.

But sleep wouldn't come. Colin's words kept going round and round in her head, until she sat up and fumbled in her backpack, checking the printout of their accommodation for the twentieth time. Her daughter Wendy laughed at her for relying on pieces of paper instead of her phone, but Penny found paper reassuring.

There it was. 'Traditional Greek house with four bedrooms and sea view.' It had been surprisingly good value. Probably because it was early in the season.

Penny tucked the confirmation into her handbag, and finally fell asleep.

Two

_____

Nell woke up with a jolt. They had docked already. Penny and Moira were still asleep but Dora stood looking into the small mirror on the wall, perfectly made up at six in the morning.

Nell closed her eyes again. She had gone to sleep with Zanthos so clear in her mind. In some ways it was still the biggest adventure she'd ever had. On the night they'd arrived all those years ago their ferry had been delayed, and it was much too late for the little Greek ladies who waited on every dockside offering rooms for about five pounds a night to foreign visitors. They certainly couldn't afford a hotel and there didn't seem to be any sign of a hostel.

That was when Nell, to her eternal shame, had sat down on her suitcase and wept.

It had worked, too. A young English guy had materialized out of the dark and offered them all somewhere to stay for the night. Nell would never forget the moment she'd woken up the next day, sharing a bed with Penny, Moira sleeping on the floor on one side of the bed and Dora on the other in sheets thoughtfully provided by their host, in a dazzlingly bright white house, a Greek blue sky blazing outside and the smell of patchouli joss sticks mixed with a sweet, pungent scent she didn't recognize. 'The Dawning of the Age of Aquarius' from the musical *Hair* had been blaring up through the floorboards.

'What's that smell?' Nell had asked shyly. 'Is it a scented candle?'

'Haven't you ever smoked a joint before?' asked Dora, breathing the smoke in deeply.

Nell hadn't wanted to say no, that she'd led a sheltered life in Sevenoaks.

It had been too late the night before to unpack nightdresses. 'Shall we all wrap our sheets round us,' Dora had suggested with a laugh, 'and appear as Greek goddesses?'

And so they had.

Rather unromantically, their host's name was Geoff and he lived in South Kensington, a trustafarian no doubt. He had rented the house for the whole summer. He surveyed them all, a libidinous glint appearing in his eye even though it was eight in the morning: 'Well, girls, I see you're dressed for an orgy.'

Through a subtle system of antennae they all agreed it was time to go and edged towards the stairs, threw on their clothes and bade him farewell. His face as they waved goodbye had been a picture. Clearly, he'd expected to sleep with at least one if not all of them.

Laughing, they'd bumped their suitcases down the steep and narrow cobbled street, narrowly avoiding donkeys carrying huge loads and interested old men with caps and huge moustaches sitting on wooden chairs outside their homes, until they found what seemed to be Zanthos's only cafe.

They had ordered thick Greek yogurt with honey that tasted like the food of the gods and played 'Black Magic Woman' on the jukebox, not yet knowing it was the only pop music track the establishment possessed.

Nell had looked at the others and sighed with happiness. 'I have definitely woken up in heaven. I don't care if I never see Sevenoaks again. One thing – ' she paused before demolishing the last spoonful of her yogurt – 'where are we going to sleep tonight?'

It was Moira who had surprised them all.

She had been on the same landing as they had at college, but not really part of their friendship group. Coming as she did from the wilds of Lincolnshire, she lacked the sophistication of the townie. And then there was her problem with kilts. Her wardrobe seemed to possess no other type of outfit. 'Probably her school uniform,' said Dora, who was already flirting with the outrageous fashions of Zandra Rhodes.

Moira was also a lot more dedicated to her studies than the rest of them. Their goals were more to do with having a good time than getting a First. But, as usual, it had been kind-hearted Penny who had included her in the invitation all those years ago. 'Three is never a good number, and anyway how can we not invite her when she's studying classics and we're going to Greece? Besides,' Penny had added unconvincingly, 'she'll be able to fill us in on the Greek myths.'

This, they had discovered, had turned out to be only too true.

'I have a good feeling about this place,' Moira had announced. 'I think we should sleep on the beach and save our money for food and travel. The gods will look after us.'

And so they had. And the gods had done their bit. No one stole their luggage or paid them any unwelcome attention. And they had agreed on one other thing.

'Basic rule of adventure,' Dora had grinned round at the other three. 'Never tell your parents. At least, not until you get home!'

'Can you imagine what my parents would say if they knew I was sleeping on the beach?' Penny had giggled.

Nell had only met Penny's parents a few times, Dora maybe once. They were the backbone of the tennis club, the golf club and the church flower rota.

None of them knew Moira's parents – a housewife and a father who was an evangelical preacher. 'My dad would have me crucified,' Moira said.

'I hope that's a metaphor,' shuddered Dora, who came from Wembley, which although suburban was close enough to London to have some of its reflected gloss.

'I just won't ever tell mine,' Nell had announced, and ditched Sevenoaks and all it stood for forever.

'Oh my God!' Moira woke up with a start. 'I slept right through Ios!'

'Maybe just as well,' consoled Penny. 'It might have been a big disappointment.'

'Yes,' seconded Dora, 'it's probably more stag night from Basildon than jolly nymphs and shepherds.'

As they fought their way up the stairs through the throngs of heavily laden locals and stood on the deck in the pale morning sunshine, they were stunned to find a giant cruise ship moored in the harbour behind them.

'Look at the size of it!' Nell marvelled. 'We never saw any of those before.'

The harbourside was almost as packed as Piraeus. Huge groups of Chinese tourists thronged all along the quay deciding which boat trip to take, and behind them a row of about thirty cafes were all full to bursting.

None of them spoke as they looked round, trying to get

their bearings and see at least something they recognized from their original visit.

Dora, eager to unpack and have a shower, hailed one of the larger taxis, and Penny gave the driver the address. Only she noticed the slight raise of the eyebrow as he registered the location of the house where they were to spend the next week. '*Endaxi*, ladies, OK, OK. No problem if you lose your handbag there. You are next to the police station.'

Moira thought this a strange comment, but decided to let it pass.

'How has the weather been?' asked Nell. The quintessential holidaymaker's first question.

'Too hot, *kyria*,' the man replied over the sound of all his religious symbols knocking together as they dangled from the rear-view mirror. 'Easter wet. Processions all happen in the rain and then the heat arrive and not go away.'

They all smiled at each other. This was just what they wanted to hear, coming from a long, cold English spring.

'Look at all the tiny roadside shrines,' pointed out Nell, fascinated by the plethora of crosses and painted icons, often with jam jars of flowers in front of them. Moira began explaining that Christian shrines had often been converted from earlier ones to Apollo or Athena.

Ten minutes later the driver negotiated his way into a huge car park, packed with cars, taxis hooting and coaches disgorging large groups headed by umbrella-wielding guides.

'Can this really be Zanthos?' Moira stared out of the window, for once struck by no appropriate classical quotations. 'I mean, it was *tiny*! There can't have been more than five hundred people living here.'

'Zanthos very busy now,' endorsed their driver. 'Season starting very early. Was week after Easter, now big ships come from beginning of March.' He drew up in the far corner of the car park. 'This address you give me.'

He pointed to a house down a narrow turning. It was a charming house – dazzlingly whitewashed with the classic bright blue painted windows and front door, the exterior covered in pink and purple bougainvillaea. It had just one obvious drawback: it was only yards away from the fume-filled pandemonium of the car park.

'Good God.' Dora shook her head. 'It's like bloody Piccadilly Circus!'

'There was supposed to be a sea view!' Penny blurted, on the edge of tears.

'There probably is, from the roof,' Nell, ever the diplomat, reassured, a skill honed over many years of dealing with angry patients and harassed doctors. 'Come on, let's go and see inside. Is the owner meeting us here?'

They started to unload their bags from the taxi. 'Zanthos quiet place in evening,' the driver informed them. 'Go to Lefkas for having fun!'

Dora shuddered. At that moment, the front door opened and a smiling Greek lady appeared on the doorstep. 'All the single ladies!' she greeted them, in what Nell supposed was a tactless reference to Beyoncé's megahit song. She led them into an interior courtyard with a pebble mosaic floor, fashioned at one end into the shape of a fish. 'Is very old way of making floor,' their new landlady informed Nell, who was studying it and wondering if it would work on her small patio at home. 'Is called *hohlaki*. Need great skill.'

'I'm sure it does,' agreed Nell.

As promised, there were four bedrooms and two shower rooms, one on the ground floor and one upstairs, and a roof terrace which did indeed have a view of the sea – if you could mentally blot out the row after row of cars and coaches in front of it.

'Oh dear,' Penny sighed, Colin's words about her inability to organize anything ringing in her head.

'Not OK?' asked the landlady, visibly disappointed.

They all looked at Penny, who burst into tears and rushed downstairs to her bedroom.

'It's fine,' said Nell firmly.

'Good. Good. Two keys on kitchen table. Here my number in case of emergency. You want I bring breakfast?'

'No. No. We'll go out for breakfast. Thank you.'

Their host backed away, still smiling until she finally disappeared down the narrow staircase to the floor below.

'It is *not* bloody well all right,' flashed Dora as soon as she'd gone. 'It's in the middle of a sodding car park for a start! There are probably cockroaches underfoot, and the whole place is more basic than a boarding house in Blackpool!'

'The location leaves something to be desired, I grant you,' Nell conceded, 'but it's clean and comfortable and extremely good value, and to some of us, Dora, that happens to matter. Besides, Penny's been to a lot of trouble setting it all up. If you need five-star luxury, quite possibly there's somewhere in the village where you can find it. Otherwise, just shut up, will you, and make the most of it. A skill you've probably never used before.'

Tension crackled between them as they contemplated ten days in each other's company.

Moira put down the guidebook she was holding and tried to say something positive. 'It says here there was a temple to Apollo on top of the hill just behind us. Did you know the Greeks believed he pulled the sun across the sky every day with his fiery chariot?'

21

'Oh good God, Moira.' Dora slumped down on a chair. 'I think you're mistaking me for someone who actually gives a fuck.'

'That's your problem, Dora,' Nell turned to the small fridge and examined its contents. 'You don't seem to give a fuck about anything. Except possibly yourself. Glass of water, anyone?'

Penny sat down on the bed next to her bag, trying to work up the courage to go back downstairs. Almost without thinking, she'd checked her phone. There was a nice message from her daughter Wendy. Nothing from Colin. She'd already left three messages, but possibly he'd hardly noticed she was away. In fact, he'd looked quite gleeful when she'd first told him she'd be going. And of course she'd filled the freezer. It was probably only when he ran out of food that he'd notice, and then no doubt he'd go and stay in that club of his, ridiculous outdated institution that it was, and be fed nursery food by subservient waiters and drink too many gin and tonics with the other old bores.

Oh God, this was so different from her fantasy. On the internet it had looked like a lovely village house and she hadn't thought to ask how far it was from the beach. Typical. Colin sometimes told her she was a waste of space, and that was exactly what she felt like today.

There was a knock on the door, and Nell's face appeared. 'Come on, we're all going down to look for the beach and have some breakfast. So stop looking like a squashed plum and let's go out. It isn't the end of the world. It's a perfectly nice house apart from the unfortunate location.'

She held out her hand to Penny. Penny willed herself to take it.

'Look, you did all the work while the rest of us sat back and let you. Maybe it's a lesson to us all.'

Penny allowed herself to be led downstairs, where the other three were waiting. 'Why don't we try and find our cafe on the beach?' Nell suggested. 'I mean, the village may have changed but at least they can't have moved the beach!'

They made their way through groups of tourists in the steep narrow streets, all dutifully looking up at carved doorways and glimpses of the blue-domed church.

'Look at that,' Moira pointed to what was obviously a bar, called The Sunburnt Arms. 'That's quite witty.'

'And look at all these cash machines,' Nell marvelled. They stopped and studied the bank of three ATMs. 'Do you remember how long it took to cash a traveller's cheque when we were here? About half an hour in a stiflingly hot bank? I wonder what happened to traveller's cheques. Do you think anyone still uses them?'

'And poste restante,' chimed in Dora. 'I was really impressed by the cool guys with dreadlocks and dark brown tans who were eternal travellers and picked up money and letters from their poste restante addresses. Like something out of Graham Greene or Hemingway.'

'Probably cheques from their parents in Tunbridge Wells,' Nell pointed out laconically. 'OK, what's happened to the main square?'

When they'd last seen Zanthos it had seemed to consist only of the main square plus a few vertiginous side streets leading up to the Acropolis.

'Isn't that where Penny attacked the donkey man for being cruel?' Nell asked, pointing at a small side street.

'Doesn't seem to have done much good,' Moira commented as a donkey passed them carrying a vast air-conditioning unit.

'And no, Penny, you are not allowed to have a go at him.' They passed a dimly lit interior from which the aroma of coffee drifted enticingly out. 'Come on, let's look for the beach in a minute. I'd kill for a coffee.'

'Do you have any yogurt and honey?' Nell asked the waiter, and tried to hide her disappointment when he brought not the delicious home-made Greek yogurt they remembered with a pot of honey and wooden swizzle stick to serve yourself, but the kind of pre-mixed carton you could buy in Tesco.

'Look,' she suddenly remembered. 'See what I found in my impenetrable filing system.' She held out a photograph of them all at eighteen, on the beach where they'd slept for a week.

Penny, tall and flaxen-haired, smiled out shyly from the picture, her skin reddened from the sun. 'Oh God, look at me, I always go the colour of a ripe tomato!'

Moira wore an embroidered peasant top with blue jeans; Nell was in the famous Bedouin wedding dress. 'They must have thought I was completely barmy!' she laughed. Finally there was Dora, in a tiny miniskirt and camisole top. 'I'm surprised you didn't get arrested,' Nell laughed.

'Or cause a riot!' Moira seconded.

'I do remember being followed by some old guy who kept jabbering on about free love. I told him he could pay like everyone else, but fortunately he didn't speak English and had no idea what I was saying.'

'I remember trying to communicate with my *kalimeras* and *kalisperas*,' Penny laughed. 'Not like now, when everyone speaks English.' They finished off their coffees. 'Right,' Nell announced, 'to the beach!'

There was only one way to the sea and they picked their way down the narrow path, laughing and teasing each other, realizing with relief that by bringing back the past they had started to enjoy the present.

At the bottom of the street they stood and looked around, stunned. Their little beach with its tatty cafe was now a St Tropez-style enclosure with row after row of spanking new sunbeds and colourful striped umbrellas. Instead of the wooden cabana cafe, there was a large glass-enclosed restaurant.

'Bloody hell!' Moira squawked. 'Twenty euro for a sunbed and umbrella! We didn't have that much to spend in a week!'

'Come on, we deserve it,' Dora decreed. 'It's only early and we can stay all day.'

They all plonked their bags down on their chosen sunbeds – except for Moira, who, as a point of principle, insisted on putting her towel down on the sand.

A sleek middle-aged man in chinos and a white t-shirt approached them for payment. Nell had a sudden brainwave. 'Hello, aren't you Yorgos? I remember you when you were about six!'

Yorgos stared round the group. '*Po po po!*' he exclaimed. 'You are the English girls! We never forget you here! You came early to Zanthos, long before all this!' He gestured round to the smart surroundings. 'When my mum cook on an oil barrel and my dad have only old – what is English word – deck chairs on the beach!'

'How is your dad? Takis, wasn't it?' They all thought of the charming Takis, who, despite a face that looked like a Greek Mr Bean and his habit of wearing crumpled linen shirts and shorts, had won them over at once with his friendly hospitality.

Yorgos grinned like a madman. 'Takis! Yes! He has gone to Kyri. My brothers and I run this place now.'

'Where is Kyri?' Moira asked.

'A dot in the ocean, full of goats and relatives. Best to keep far away. Where are you staying?'

Penny started to look anxious again. 'At the back of the town. A nice house big enough for four,' Nell supplied swiftly.

'Have you been to Lefkas? Is entirely new part of Zanthos. Not enough room in the town for tourists, so they develop Lefkas. For the young people. Now, you must stay here for the day as my guests!'

'Well . . .' Penny began.

'Brilliant,' interrupted Dora. 'We'd love to.'

'And you must eat with us also. I will tell my wife to let my brothers know. She will cook you a wonderful lunch! *Yassas*, famous English ladies.'

'Did you hear that?' Moira commented. '*Tell* his wife to cook. Some things don't change.'

'Don't complain,' Dora reprimanded her. 'This is a definite improvement. Lunch here with Yorgos and his brothers, back to the house for a siesta, and then tonight let's go and see this Lefkas place.'

'Didn't he say it was for young people?'

'Come on, Penny, we're only going to look at it,' Dora said. 'A couple of cocktails and you can be back in bed with a nice cup of cocoa.'

Penny settled back on her sunbed under an umbrella, refusing to rise to Dora's comment. She wasn't as silly and naive as Dora was making her out to be. And anyway, maybe now they'd met Yorgos, things weren't so bad after all.

'Do you have a changing room?' Dora asked him.

He nodded enthusiastically. 'Not like when I was a child and we had to lock the toilet to keep the hippies out!'

Dora strode off to put on her bikini. No unseemly messing

about with towels in the great British holidaymaker tradition for her.

The individual changing rooms were clean and well lit. They even had locks. As Dora stripped off her dress and delved into her bag for her bikini, her eye was caught by a copy of *Vanity Fair* left by a previous guest. She sat down as if she had been suddenly winded.

On the cover was a large photograph of Venus Green. Venus Green, blonde and beautiful winner of a reality TV show, budding megastar with a voice and personality like a young Kylie Minogue.

Venus Green, whose PR, best friend and mentor Pandora Perkins had been for the last five years. Until the little bitch had dropped her three weeks ago and appointed a rival thirty years younger.

Later that evening, the taxi dropped them at a rank in what seemed to be the middle of nowhere about two miles from Zanthos. 'Excuse me,' Nell asked an old man sitting by the side of the road with an equally ancient dog. 'Where is Lefkas?'

He pointed down the road.

They walked for about a hundred yards until they turned a sharp corner revealing an entirely new town like something from a futuristic film. Down one side of the road, giant screens seemed to be showing football games or pop videos at maximum volume under flashing neon signs offering slot machines or cut-price cocktails.

'Oh my God!' Moira clutched Nell's arm. 'Look at that aberration! How could anyone create such a monstrosity?'

There, in front of them, in shiny plastic bricks, was a miniature version of the Acropolis, so brightly illuminated they had to shield their eyes.

At the end of the newly created road was a beach. Gratefully they made for the shore, where they hoped to sit and have a quiet drink. There seemed to be a small crowd of people standing in the sea, chatting and drinking bottles of beer. As they approached Penny let out a muffled shriek.

Mainly over sixty, the men were round and pot-bellied, the women leathery and tanned. And they were all entirely naked.

'What do you know!' Dora shook her head in startled disbelief. 'I think we've discovered Lefkas's nudist beach at happy hour. What a very edifying sight.'

In the end they bought a bottle of wine and took it back to the house with some hummus and olives. Thankfully all the tour groups had returned to their ship, and the car park was quiet and empty.

They settled themselves into comfortable chairs on the rooftop terrace and Nell opened the wine just as the cruise ship turned round and began to depart from the harbour, making way for another two ships which had been waiting for entry.

As they watched, a terrifying flash of blue lit up the horizon, followed by a deafening and almost instantaneous crash of thunder. After that, the whole sky seemed to erupt in a kaleidoscope of colours and sounds so dramatic that they had to run for cover, just as the heavens opened and sheets of driving rain swept across the patio.

'Do you know, girls –' Dora held up her glass towards the multicoloured sky from the shelter of the nearest bedroom – 'I think Zeus is sending us a message. Time to abandon your lost dream and return to Athens, where people wear clothes and the Acropolis is made of real stone. As it happens, there's a boat leaving tomorrow, and I vote we get on it. What do the rest of you think?'

For a moment no one broke the shocked silence, interrupted only by more cracks of thunder. Then Moira turned almost apologetically to Penny and Nell. 'As a matter of fact, I'm really longing to see the new Archaeological Museum in Athens. Everyone says it's even better than the BM.'

Nell shrugged, mystified.

'British Museum,' elucidated Dora.

'But what about the money?' Nell demanded, although she was also thinking of Penny, whose idea it had all been, and how disappointed she was going to be. 'We paid for the whole stay in advance.'

'I'll cover it,' said Penny, quietly determined. 'I didn't tell you the reason I planned all this. I had a legacy from my dad. My parents had saved all their lives so they could travel when they were older, and then they never did. "Don't postpone your dreams," Dad told me when he was dying, "because that's what we did." So I decided to spend some on coming back to Zanthos – because maybe you'll think I'm a suburban saddo, but that holiday was one of the happiest times of my life. I felt young and daring, as if everything in life was going to be wonderful.'

She didn't mention the fact that she hadn't told her husband about the legacy. This was going to be *her* money to spend the way she wanted to. Colin had been so rude about her dad's little investments, just because he saw himself as a big-city whizz; but as it happened, they'd come good in the end.

But now the holiday was collapsing, and he'd find out anyway. He'd say she was a failure, and he'd be right.

'I know,' Nell suggested, sensing some of Penny's anxiety without needing to be told. 'Why don't you and I go to another island? There were six on the way here, remember. We could even go to several.'

'Be island hoppers!' Penny's sad spaniel face visibly brightened.

'Real jet-setters,' Nell laughed.

Dora tried not to smile. It was hard to imagine two more unlikely members of the international rich. 'I'll deal with the landlady,' she volunteered. 'I'm sure she won't charge much if we say we're leaving because of the noise from the car park that she happened to forget to mention in her ad.'

As good as her word, she went off to find their landlady. Half an hour later she returned, smiling broadly. 'Result! She says if we don't make a big noise about it in our review, she'll let us off the rest of the stay. Lucky for us it's so early in the season.'

She slipped a small package quietly into Penny's hand.

'What on earth's this?' Penny asked.

'Just a little thing. I seem to remember you bought one when we came before.'

Penny undid the tissue paper to reveal a silver snake bracelet, with glowing eyes made of blue glass, that you wrapped round your upper arm.

'Oh God,' Penny bit her lip. 'I really did have one just like this! I bought it from a street vendor and couldn't eat for a day because it took all my money. Thanks, Dora.'

'Now you can feel young and daring again. Sorry for being a party pooper.'

'Maybe not young.' Penny slipped the bracelet onto her arm. 'But certainly daring.' Something about the snake armband already made her feel a little more fearless. And if she and Nell went island-hopping, she wouldn't have to let Colin know it had all gone wrong.

'Tell you what,' Dora suggested. 'Why don't we all go out for a last blowout dinner together?'

Three

Penny touched the talisman of her new bracelet for courage as they climbed on board the ferry next morning. She hadn't even called Colin to tell him of their change of plan, and he certainly hadn't got in touch with her. 'I think I'll stay on deck,' she said to Nell. 'Which island do you think we should go to?'

'Moira thinks definitely Ios,' Nell grinned. 'She slept through it on the way out so she's going to make a dash to Homer's tomb when we stop. She says we can go with her. Lucky us.'

'OK, Ios it is!' Penny agreed. 'But didn't Dora say it was the party island?' she added dubiously. She didn't want to find herself on another Zanthos.

Nell waved her guidebook. 'This says Ios is the prettiest island in the Cyclades. Has anyone seen Moira, by the way? Lost in her guidebooks as usual?'

Penny looked round the deck. Moira was usually at the front of the boat, eager to point things out to them. 'Oh, I know,' she suddenly remembered. 'She said she was going for a little lie down in Dora's cabin.'

'That's not like Moira. Too much retsina last night?'

They smiled conspiratorially, imagining that with their new plan there would be plenty more carousing to come, as they watched Zanthos gradually receding beyond the frothy white path of the ferry's wake.

'I hope you don't mind too much?' Nell asked Penny. 'About Zanthos not working out?'

'Not since you came up with your brilliant suggestion. Zanthos turned out to be a big disappointment. Unless I romanticized the place in the beginning.'

'No you didn't,' Nell reassured her. 'It was amazing back then. Friendly. Unspoilt. Genuinely Greek.' They remembered the sight of the overweight nudists, and began to laugh. 'I wonder if it's what the locals wanted: to be invaded by cruise ships and Russians drinking beer for breakfast?'

'I suppose once you invite mass tourism in, you don't get much choice.'

They sat down and sunned themselves on a varnished wooden bench, and before long they had nodded off in the warm and soporific wind.

'Nell! Penny! Wake up!' They were roused from their slumber to find Dora, barefoot and anxious and wearing just her slip, standing in front of them. 'It's Moira! She's been really sick and I don't know what to do!'

Nell, with all her years of dealing with demanding patients at the surgery, snapped into action mode. 'Let me have a look. What's the cabin number?'

They followed the panicking figure to find Moira leaning out from her bunk, white as whey, noisily puking into a plastic duty free bag from Athens airport. She was so desperate that she hadn't noticed it contained Dora's new perfume.

Nell sat on the end of the bed. 'Has she had diarrhoea as well?'

Dora nodded, unwilling to go and look at the devastation in the toilet.

'I can see you make a natural nurse,' Nell commented wryly. 'Anyone got a thermometer?' Nobody had. She laid a hand on Moira's damp and sweaty forehead. 'Yes, she's got a temperature all right.'

'I bet it was that octopus we ate at the harbour last night. Do you remember, we couldn't resist because the fisherman said it was caught that afternoon?' Penny blurted. 'Moira liked it so much she ate mine as well.'

From the bunk, Moira groaned at the memory.

'I'd better go and look for someone in authority.' Nell jumped up. 'Give her bottled water, and if anyone's got Dioralyte, give her that too to rehydrate her.' She disappeared towards the stairs, leaving Dora and Penny in charge of the patient.

Nell seemed to be gone an inordinately long time. Moira continued to puke while Dora looked on, horrified. Penny tried to hold back their friend's tangled mass of hair.

'It looked like a bird's nest before, so God knows what it's like now,' Dora commented unsympathetically.

'Shut up, Dora,' Penny surprised herself by replying, 'and go and look for some bottled water.'

Grateful to leave the war scene of their cabin, Dora pulled on some jeans, tucked her slip in as if it were a camisole and scuttled off. Just as she got to the staircase, the ferry juddered to a halt.

Nell reappeared, accompanied by a white-clad official with epaulettes on his shoulders. 'This is the purser. They're sending a small boat from the island we were passing and they want us to get off. They've phoned a doctor, who'll be waiting for us on the quay.'

'What, *all* of us?' Dora asked, horrified.

'Come on, Dora,' Nell replied. 'You wouldn't like it if we abandoned you with food poisoning in some godforsaken place, would you?'

'*I* wouldn't have had second helpings of undercooked octopus,' Dora stated.

'Oh for God's sake, stay if you want!' Nell had no time for this diva-like behaviour. 'Penny, can you get Moira's things?'

Penny almost skidded across the puke-sodden floor of the cabin and gathered up all the stuff she could see.

'Hey, that's mine,' protested Dora, when Penny picked up a Prada rucksack.

Penny threw it at her. 'And good luck if you come down with salmonella in Sloane Street.'

The purser and one of his underlings carried Moira up the steps and across the deck to the lifeboat area. A small Greek caique was bobbing up and down beside the ferry like a duckling next to its mother. Moira was laid inside its small wheelhouse with Nell, Penny and the luggage following. It had almost started to pull away when a tall figure in a sick-smeared white top, looking more like Medea or one of the Maenads than a smart London PR, half threw herself into the boat. One of the ferry passengers chucked the Prada rucksack down after her, then handed her her suitcase rather more gently.

As they headed through the choppy, white-horse-crested waves towards the shore they could hear Dora throwing up over the side. 'Oh my God,' Nell half-laughed. 'She's being seasick. I hope the wind's not blowing the wrong way.'

Eventually Dora sat down, looking pale and undignified. 'So where the hell are we going?'

Nell asked the captain for the answer in halting Greek.

'He says the island's called Kyri. It has only five hundred inhabitants.'

'Oh, brilliant. Nightlife central, then,' Dora commented grudgingly. The others ignored her. 'Isn't Kyri the place Yorgos was talking about – where Takis went? A speck of land full of goats and relatives, to be avoided at all costs?'

'We don't have much choice, as you may have noticed,' Nell pointed out crisply.

As the small boat buffeted its way towards the shore, they could make out a neat harbour with the usual jumble of bright white cubes climbing up the hillside towards a tiny blue-domed church. A row of cafes lined the quayside, one of them decorated with streamers of bunting. 'For the saint's day,' the captain informed them, without elucidating which saint. Every island seemed to have its own special saint, quite often mummified, which they carried round on high days and holidays.

Nell kept stroking the groaning Moira. 'Nearly there now. You're a VIP. They've made a special stop for you. Look, there's the doctor standing on the quay. And an old Greek lady swathed in black, just like the old days. She's probably come to offer us rooms.'

'And I can imagine what they'll be like,' muttered Dora.

'Isn't this what we wanted?' Nell threw at her. 'A genuinely unspoiled island just like Zanthos used to be?'

Dora had been about to reply 'Not this unspoiled,' but in a rare moment of tact, thought better of it.

'You can sort out payment for the boatman,' Nell told her as the small boat pulled in and the captain and his sixteen-year-old assistant helped Moira onto dry land.

Dora reached for the Prada bag, hoping it hadn't got completely soaked.

'*Ochi, ochi* . . .' *No, no.* The captain shook his head vigorously, as if being paid was almost an insult. 'Four beautiful ladies coming to our island is enough payment,' he announced with a bow. 'The saint requires us to do good deeds.'

The doctor was indeed waiting for them at the quay and had enlisted two youths with a makeshift stretcher. Moira was duly carried off to the surgery, still holding onto Nell's hand as if her life depended on it.

'*Kalimera, kalimera*,' the old lady greeted them. 'My son has beautiful rooms in his hotel over there on the side of the water, if you need somewhere to stay.'

At the word 'hotel', Dora visibly perked up. She followed the black-clad figure, while Penny went off in the wake of the doctor. Not looking where she was going, she walked slap-bang into what seemed to be a washing line draped with huge orange rubber hanging out to dry. Stepping back, Penny took in the suckers, pale and menacing like something from a horror film.

'Oh my God, it's octopus! Quick, don't let Moira see. She'll probably have a relapse!'

When they were finally in the doctor's surgery and Moira was laid out on his couch, he asked what they thought she had eaten.

'Octopus,' replied Nell. 'But it was freshly caught. We saw the fisherman bringing it in.'

The doctor nodded curtly. 'Probably cooked it on his engine. They all do. I keep telling them it's not a good idea.'

'Oh my God, you're not serious.'

He smiled, feeling Moira's pulse and popping a thermometer into her mouth. 'The fishermen think it tastes best that way.'

'I am never, ever going to eat octopus again in this country,' Penny muttered.

'Somebody ought to give them a few cooking lessons,' commented Nell, who had done a Prue Leith course with some of her divorce money in the hope of either a new career or a new man to cook for. Unfortunately neither had materialized.

'Leave your friend here with us,' the doctor offered. 'My wife and I will look after her while you find somewhere to stay. There is not much choice on an island like Kyri, but the hotel is good.'

'Will she be all right?' Penny asked anxiously.

'She needs rest, and little food. I will give her antibiotics also. These things are very common on holiday.'

'Oh, thank goodness,' Penny breathed. 'Our other friend has gone to check out the hotel.'

'That is good. It is only the other side of the harbour. You will like it, I think.'

They left Moira sleeping under the peaceful eye of the doctor's wife and headed for the hotel, looking around them for the first time.

The town was indeed very small, arranged along the two extended arms of the harbour. Three or four narrow streets stretched up the hillside, lined with purple bougainvillaea. None of the buildings was above three storeys high. They had elegant curved entrances, first-floor balconies with iron railings and doors in the usual bright blue.

'What an elegant little place,' Penny admired.

'Probably the Venetians,' Nell commented. 'They seemed to get everywhere round here.'

Cafes and small restaurants lined the waterfront, in front of which stretched a horseshoe-shaped fringe of beach lined with tamarisk trees. The beach seemed to be full of laughing children playing a game with bat and ball attached by stretchy string.

'We used to call that Jocari when I was growing up,' Penny laughed. 'I was a bit of a Jocari queen.'

They stopped to watch, struck by the simple beauty and peace of the place. The weather was perfect. Even though it was midday the sun was kind and generous, no rays to blind and dazzle, so they were able to look round even without sunglasses.

Penny noticed a butterfly land on the nearest tree and to her amazement she could hear a bird singing. 'Do you know,' she pointed out to Nell, her voice ringing with pleasure, 'I don't think I've ever heard a bird sing on a beach before.'

'Watch out!' shouted a voice from the hotel balcony above. 'She's going to have an orgasm! Stand back.'

They didn't need to look up and see who it was.

'So what are the rooms like?' Nell enquired.

'Surprisingly good,' was the reply. 'Especially mine.' This was at least said with a certain self-parody. 'And that's not the only thing.'

Nell shrugged and walked towards the hotel entrance. The lobby was light and airy, with a plain white-tiled floor, paintings of seascapes adorning the walls, and several model boats made of driftwood arranged on the window sill and reception desk.

Opposite the desk was a carved mahogany day bed with cushions in different shades of blue. Behind the desk stood the ancient lady who had come down to the quayside to meet them.

'*Kalimera*,' she greeted them. 'My name is Cassandra.' She reached out a gnarled hand the same deep-hued tint as the mahogany bed and squeezed Nell's, then took two old-fashioned keys from the rack behind the desk. 'Two rooms are on the harbour – your friend has one – and two at the back. Good things with both. Back is quieter, good for sleep. Front has sea view but near to men sitting in cafes, drinking too much and making stupid arguments about things they know nothing about!'

A second later Dora appeared, skipping down the stairs. Behind her, in the same crumpled linen (well, perhaps not the *actual* same crumpled linen), came their very good friend Takis from so many years ago.

'Dear, dear ladies!' The face, wreathed in smiles, seemed just the same, dark-browed and deep-furrowed and with the same enchanting smile they remembered so well.

'Takis!' screeched Penny. 'You haven't changed at all!'

He jumped forward and kissed her hand. 'My English ladies! It is a miracle! Yorgos he called me to say he had seen you and then *pfaff*! –' he snapped his fingers – 'here you are in our island of Kyri!'

'It *is* a bit of a miracle,' Nell agreed, 'if you can call a dose of food poisoning a miracle. We were on our way back to Athens when Moira – do you remember Moira?'

'The clever girl who know more Greek myth than me?'

'That's the one. Anyway, Moira came down with some horrid illness and they had to drop us off here.'

'Your bad luck is my good luck,' he replied gracefully. 'And is she recovered, your clever friend?'

'No, not yet. The doctor says she must rest for a few days and has given her antibiotics.'

'Doctors!' Takis shrugged dismissively. 'You should ask my daughter Ariadne. She is the expert on herbs that grow on our hillsides.'

'OK. How old is Ariadne?'

'Fourteen? Maybe fifteen?'

'Goodness! She must be clever.'

'We must make the most of our miracle. If your friend is being looked after OK, I will take you round our island.'

Penny and Nell looked at each other guiltily. 'That sounds wonderful, but we'd better check on her first.'

To their astonishment they found Moira sitting up in bed, clearly feeling much better, cosily tucked up with a huge volume the doctor's wife had found for her from his library. 'Did you know,' she asked them instantly, 'that it was Hippocrates who said doctors should help, but above all, do no harm! I've always thought that was the most brilliant thought and I had no idea it was his.' She smiled bravely. 'He also said "food be thy medicine", but I don't think I'm ready for that.'

She did still look pale and in need of rest, and declared herself more than happy to stay in bed for a few days with Hippocrates while the rest of them went off exploring the island.

'If you ask me,' she announced with a deep look, 'it seems a lot more than coincidence that we fetched up here, don't you think? Zeus has something in mind for us. We just have to find out what it is.'

Penny and Nell exchanged glances, neither of them sure they were up to doing the bidding of the king of the gods.

When they got back to the hotel, Takis declared that the only way to see Kyri was by boat. An hour later he was waiting for them at the harbour jetty in a dark blue boat, with a small cabin and lots of deck space to lie out on and admire the scenery.

'Is it your own boat?' Penny asked as she climbed aboard.

'It belongs to my friend, though here most people have a boat,' Takis grinned. 'People still live by farming and fishing.

We don't have much tourism. That's why all the young people are leaving. There's no jobs they want here, so they all go to Santorini. There is an airport there, you see.'

'And do you want more tourism?' Despite herself, Dora was becoming interested.

'Of course! Tourism is what keeps the Greek economy going,' he shrugged. 'Or almost going. The other islands have much more than we do. And yet we have ninety beaches!'

Nell stared out across the deep blue of the Aegean Sea. She could feel the sun warming her pale English skin and a delightful feeling of well-being began to spread through her. She glanced across at Penny, hoping she too was sharing it.

She worried about Penny. It was clear her husband was a deeply unpleasant man, and yet for some reason she put up with him. Of course, there was an old-fashioned argument that said any husband was better than no husband, as long as they didn't beat you. That's what her mother's generation would have said. In fact, that was what her mother *had* said when she and Robert split. Not that she'd had much choice in the matter. As soon as he'd discovered she was being unfaithful, he'd left at once.

For the five hundredth time, Nell thought about why she'd had an affair all those years ago. In some corny sense it was like that Abba song where the wife thought she was a 'concealed attraction' being kept from the excitement by a dull husband. Robert had been such a predictable man, a man of habit; and Francis, a drugs rep of all things, had been charming and full of fun. Looking back, she was amazed she hadn't recognized that these were qualities that probably went with the job, but at the time she'd been bowled over by him. And it had been enjoyable. And exciting. But like the wife in the song, she'd certainly paid the price.

'Are you OK, Nell?' Penny broke into her thoughts. 'Only you looked a bit sad, somehow. I was hoping you weren't regretting not just going home?' Penny fixed her anxious gaze on Nell.

Nell burst out laughing. 'Actually, Penny –' she leaned back on the boat's cabin, where they were all sitting while Takis steered, and stretched luxuriously – 'I can't think of anywhere I'd rather be.'

'Really?'

'Really! Look at us, going on a boat trip with the sun shining, and the sea a hundred different shades of blue.'

'And no Moira to lecture us about Homer,' Dora offered with a grin.

They listened, enthralled, as Takis took them right round the island with its tiny bays, long sandy beaches and crystal waters so clear you could see down fathoms deep to the rock formations on the sea bed below.

Towards the south they passed a large boat, painted dark red, with a beautiful figurehead of a dark-eyed woman, her white breasts bare, holding a seashell in her hands.

'Goodness,' Dora exclaimed. 'That looks like a pirate ship! What is the significance of the topless lady?'

Takis laughed. 'Kyri was once a pirate lair. The French corsairs stole from the Turks and hid their plunder here. But in fact the boat belongs to our mayor, an interesting man. He allowed the first gay marriage here on the island. You can see how that would have got up the nose of the priests!'

'And the maiden on the figurehead? Is she a pirate's moll?'

'More likely a nereid, the nymphs of the sea. There were fifty of them.'

'I thought those were sirens?' Dora said.

'Sirens were bad, luring sailors to their death. The nereids were helpful to sailors.'

They rounded a headland to where a row of small buildings, each with a huge wooden door in the lower floor and a large balcony above, seemed almost to be built into the cliff face. 'Are they garages?' asked Dora.

Takis laughed. 'You are almost right. Garages for boats! They are called *syrma*. The fishermen park their boats inside in the winter. As a matter of fact, our mayor lives in the two at the end, round the next headland in the bay.'

'But it's so remote!' Nell protested. 'Is there even a road?'

'A bit of a lone wolf, our mayor. But he has his boat.' He grinned at them, a gold tooth flashing in the sunlight. 'And also a motorbike.'

'What's he like, your mayor?'

'Depends if you ask a man or a woman,' Takis grinned.

'He sounds like my kind of man,' Dora replied archly.

'I'm sure you will meet him soon.'

Half-listening, Penny was conscious of a feeling of disappointment. Another macho man. She went on staring at the row of buildings that clung to the shoreline, intrigued. 'They could be so stunning. Imagine if you painted all the wooden doors in different colours.'

During Colin's long absences travelling or staying in London, Penny had dabbled in interior design, painting furniture and picking up clever finds in junk shops. A couple of friends had even asked her to do up their houses. She had actually made a bit of money out of it – 'your pin money' Colin had called it dismissively.

'I mean, think of the peace of living here,' she continued, pushing Colin firmly from her mind. 'It's an amazing spot. You'd almost feel as if you were part of the sea yourself!'

'Watch her,' Dora teased. 'She'll be turning into one of these nereids!'

It was true that Penny, looking happy and relaxed with her long hair escaping from the Alice band and the first freckles beginning to dot her face from the Greek sunshine, did have a faint air of the sea nymph about her.

'And now,' Takis announced, 'we will stop at the little bar I have on the next beach.'

They rounded a bend to find another small beach nestling in a cove, with a tiny church on the hill behind. A row of cheap plastic sunbeds lined the water's edge with the occasional umbrella advertising ouzo dotted between. Behind them was a small cabana with a top that flipped down to create a bar, in front of which five or six tables with blue-and-white plastic tablecloths were ranged invitingly. A young girl of fourteen or fifteen stood behind it, waving.

'My granddaughter Ariadne.' Takis waved back. She ran down the beach and waded in, catching the rope he tossed and fixing it to a buoy floating in the shallow water.

'These are the famous English ladies: Nell, Dora and Penelope.'

Penny smiled at hearing her full name. 'Penelope was a very famous Greek lady, after all,' Takis shrugged.

'I know.' Penny nodded. 'Moira has often told me. Patient Penelope, wife of Odysseus. She waited ten years for him to come home after the Trojan War.'

'Typical bloody man,' interjected Dora. 'He probably stopped at the pub.'

'She's the archetype of the faithful wife,' Penny added, sounding suddenly sad. She waited for somebody to say 'Just like you,' but no one did.

Nell looked around, taking in the lack of customers. 'Well, I suppose it's early in the season.'

'It doesn't matter what time it is in the season,' Takis sighed. 'Hardly any customers.'

They sat down at a table, and Ariadne brought the menus.

'Do you do the cooking as well, Ariadne?' Nell asked the girl.

'No – I do.' Cassandra's wrinkled face popped out from behind the door of the cabana. 'I prepare it at the hotel and we bring it here every day. If it doesn't sell, we take it back to the hotel. It's never wasted.'

They studied the menu.

'I know it's an odd thing to ask,' Penny apologized. 'But could I possibly have yogurt and honey?'

'You should really try our calamari,' Takis suggested. 'My mother's calamari is the best on the island.'

They all shuddered, thinking of Moira.

'Maybe next time,' Nell replied. 'I would love the lamb souvlaki.'

'Me too,' seconded Dora.

'And just the yogurt for you, *kyria Penelope*?'

Penny nodded.

'And a bottle of that wine Nikos, the mayor, brought.'

'Does he grow grapes too?' Dora demanded.

'He has a small vineyard in the centre of the island.'

'There seems to be no end to his talents. How old is this paragon?'

'About the same age as you ladies, I would guess.'

'Not a toyboy mayor, then?' Dora pursued. 'Oh well, nobody's perfect.'

Ariadne arrived with the wine and they sat for a moment in companionable silence, listening to the small waves lapping on the shore and feeling the warmth of the afternoon sun on their backs.

Nell let out a long sigh of contentment. 'Takis, this place is magic. In fact,' she looked round at the others, 'it's just like Zanthos when we first went there all those years ago, isn't it?'

'All we need is a jukebox with "Black Magic Woman",' agreed Dora.

Takis got up and went inside the cabana. A few minutes later, he emerged with a battered tape machine.

'Good God!' Dora shook her head. 'I didn't think those still existed in the age of downloads and Spotify.'

He pressed a button and a halting version, not helped by the tangling of the tape, of Carlos Santana's voice crackled out of the loudspeaker. '*Don't turn your back on me, baby . . .*'

They all sang along, laughing with remembered delight, until Penny's yogurt and honey arrived.

'I have added a few of our own walnuts, *kyria*,' Cassandra said as she put the bowl down. 'Tell me what you think of them.'

Penny took a mouthful and closed her eyes. A look of bliss suffused her entire face.

'Even better than I remember,' she announced. 'Takis, I have died and gone to heaven.'

Takis smiled back. 'No you haven't, Penelope. Your friend ate undercooked octopus, and you were taken off the big ship and left on an enchanted island called Kyri. It's just a pity that no one else has heard of it!'

Four

Back in their simple but pleasant hotel rooms, Nell got out her phone. This time, she couldn't resist checking Instagram and looking at what Marigold had posted. She'd been amazed they had wifi, but according to Takis, this was another masterstroke by the lone-wolf mayor.

Sure enough, there was the ghastly Marigold, beaming out with baby Naomi, Nell's granddaughter, in her arms, and looking deeply pleased with herself as usual. Nell was honest enough to admit that she probably overreacted to Marigold, but it was very hard to accept that your own daughter seemed to prefer her mother-in-law to you. Admittedly Marigold and her henpecked husband Ted had a lot more to offer. While Nell had to watch what she spent, Marigold lived in a mini-mansion with swimming pool and tennis courts, and was eager and willing to have them to stay whenever Willow wanted. In fact, Nell, suspected, she'd quite like to have them full time.

She checked Willow's feed and felt a pang of thwarted love at seeing her beautiful daughter, long fair hair falling about her lovely face with her big eyes and high cheekbones, softened by her characteristic sweet smile. Nell was a pretty woman herself, but Willow had almost model looks. She was creative, too, always with a new scheme or interest. 'Hello, darling,' Nell murmured to the picture. Maybe she should ring her and say hello properly.

But Willow was always in the middle of something – and usually in Marigold's company.

Nell put her phone firmly back in her bag. Penny had slipped over to see Moira, and then they had planned a quick dinner before an early night. So much had already happened today. She surveyed her neat array of clothes and chose a simple linen dress. It was crumpled, but what the hell; if Takis could get away with permanently crumpled linen, so could she.

Dora was already downstairs, sitting outside the hotel at a harbourside table with a bottle of white wine. She had changed too, into a sleek gunmetal number that covered her up while somehow emphasizing her large breasts and gently swelling stomach in an extremely sexy manner. That was what you got for spending the kind of money Dora habitually shelled out on her wardrobe, Nell decided as she walked towards her.

Moments later, Penny came into view. 'Hello girls – oh, you've both changed already.'

'You were the one doing a good deed,' Nell reassured. 'How is the invalid?'

'Much better. And she's really hit it off with the doctor and his wife. She's called Eleni, and she studied classics too, so they're in seventh heaven deciding whether the Trojan War actually happened or was based on a series of different sieges altogether, chronicled by some chap called Eratosthenes – or was it Aristophanes? I'm not very hot on the classics.'

'Sounds bliss,' Dora grinned. 'I so wish I was there to give my opinion. Anyway, you look fine.' It had been on the tip of

Dora's tongue to say that all Penny's clothes looked the same anyway, but a rare moment of tact prevented her. 'Sit down and have a drink.' She began pouring the wine, then suddenly slopped it onto the table.

The others glanced round to see what had provided the sudden distraction.

A tall, elegant newcomer with a long, aristocratic-looking face, high domed forehead, slightly drooping moustache and greying but otherwise copious hair had come out of the hotel and seated himself at the last table.

'Do you think that's the mayor?' whispered Dora, hastily putting down the bottle.

'Maybe.' Nell tried to stare without appearing to stare.

Penny, not experienced in the art of subtlety, turned round to give him serious consideration. The man smiled as if this were only his due, and raised his eyebrow in acknowledgement. '*Kalispera*, ladies.'

'No,' whispered Penny with unusual certainty. 'He doesn't look like a lone wolf. He's too smooth to live on his own in those remote fisherman's cottages. He's more of your hot-and-cold room service kind of chap. In my view, that is,' she added, suddenly surprised at her own self-confidence.

The newcomer looked around him as if he were waiting for someone, consulted his watch and got up. Not the kind of man who liked to be kept waiting, clearly. He nodded in their direction and strolled off.

'Hmmm . . .' began Dora, just as Takis appeared with some menus. 'He looks rather intriguing.'

'I see you've met our rich Athenian,' Takis grinned as he handed them a menu. 'Alexandros Georgiades. Calls himself Xan. He's a property developer with fingers in a lot of dubious pies in Athens.'

'I can tell you're not a huge fan,' Nell laughed.

'I hate Athenians. They laid waste to our island in 400 BC because we refused to give them tribute, killed all the men and sold the women and children into slavery.'

'And it's not as if you're one to hold grudges,' Dora commented. 'So what is the rich Athenian doing here?'

'He's bought a tumbledown house near the beach from old Yannis, and he wants to bulldoze part of an olive grove for his holiday home.'

'And you don't approve?'

'It's a beautiful spot. Olive trees are sacred in this country. Sophocles called them "the trees that feed the children". And it happens to be next door to my beach bar. Not everyone likes the idea. Fortunately it needs official approval.'

'And you don't think he'll get it?'

'There is a big meeting coming up. It will be interesting to see.'

They ate a simple but delicious supper of lamb cooked on hot coals, with a Greek salad of tomatoes and black olives on which a huge slab of feta cheese took pride of place.

'Do you remember when we were in Zanthos and shared one of these between all four of us?' Penny reminded.

'And they wouldn't give us any more free pitta bread because we ate so much of it!'

They all laughed at the memory. 'Oh dear,' Penny admitted, 'I feel guilty having such a good time when Moira's ill.'

'I am one hundred per cent sure that Moira will not be thinking about you. Moira is quite selfish in her monomania about ancient Greek culture,' Nell corrected. 'And anyway, it sounds like she's having a whale of a time proving the Trojan War never actually happened.'

'And it does mean we can have another drink without Moira

being holier-than-thou about hating the taste of alcohol.' Dora poured them a second glass.

Penny, who had been about to cover her glass with her hand, decided against it. Her phone suddenly beeped beside her, making her jump so much that the others stared at her.

'Sorry,' she apologized. 'I just wasn't expecting a call.'

She looked at her phone. There was a WhatsApp message from Colin: *I had some people round and now there's no more food in the freezer. How the hell long are you going to be away?*

Penny put her phone in her bag in case the others saw the message. No *Hello, hope you're having a good time*; just, what was he going to eat when she was away? She took a deep breath to hide the tears that threatened to start. How could he even upset her so much when he was two thousand miles away? She sighed. Maybe she ought to get in touch with her daughter Wendy, and ask her to sort it out.

As they drained their wine and hugged each other good-night, Penny felt a sudden impulse to tell Nell what her husband was really like. But if she did that, she realized with a painful insight, she might have to do something about it.

And the pathetic truth was, she wasn't brave enough.

Next morning, over a delicious buffet breakfast of fresh fruit salad, the wonderful yogurt and cakes with syrup and fresh plums buried in them like a sponge clafoutis, Nell and Penny decided they should drop in on Moira and try to get some kind of idea how long she would be ill.

Cassandra appeared with a pot of thick Greek coffee. 'I hope you ladies like proper coffee. It is *poli kalos*, very good. All these young people, they like frappés!' She pointed at an unfortunate girl in the next cafe, drinking a beige concoction in a glass with foam on top.

'They use Nescafé! It is an outrage! It isn't even Greek!'

'Do you remember when we were here before, if you ordered a coffee they proudly brought lukewarm water and a sachet of Nescafé?' Nell whispered.

Penny tried to think of a way of soothing Cassandra's wounded national pride.

'How silly of them. I just wanted to say again how wonderful your yogurt is!'

'It's because of my goats,' Cassandra beamed. 'They wander on the hills behind the beach cafe. My granddaughter Ariadne makes sure they don't fall into the sea.'

'Goodness,' Penny replied, thinking of her own children at Ariadne's age. 'As well as minding the cafe? Doesn't she have schoolwork?'

'What is the point?' Cassandra's whiskery chin rose defensively. 'She is going to work for her father anyway. What does she need to know about biology and chemistry, except to mix these silly cocktails the young people like?' She became suddenly philosophical. 'If only he had more customers. Why do you tourists go to the other islands and not here?' she accused.

They all shook their heads and replied that they had no idea, except that none of them had heard of Kyri before.

After they had finished the extremely strong Greek coffee Dora decided she would leave the others to their Florence Nightingale mission and head for the beach cafe, where she could have a cappuccino. 'Your cake was delicious, by the way.'

Cassandra softened. 'I get up at six to make sure the baking is fresh.'

'It certainly tastes like it,' Dora smiled.

'Then you must take some with you!' Cassandra disappeared briefly, returning with a huge slice of cake wrapped in a paper napkin.

Dora mentally calculated the calories, but couldn't resist. 'Thank you. *Efharisto*.'

'*Parakolo*,' beamed Cassandra. 'As I said, it is very good!'

Dora waved the others off and went to find some suitable footwear for clambering down the steep path to the cafe, with or without goat companions. The trouble was, Dora didn't believe in trainers. The young ones in her office often walked to work in them. A sudden wave of panic at the thought of her office made her stop for a moment and stare fixedly out to sea.

She wasn't going to think about the horrible thing that had happened. No doubt everyone in the PR world was chatting and tweeting about it, but she wouldn't even go there. She had left her phone firmly in the drawer in her bedroom. It had been like tearing her heart out of her chest, but it had to be done.

She'd just have to buy some suitable shoes from one of the small shops that lined the harbour. After trying two different places that sold only hideous plastic shoes to protect against sea urchins or jewel-bedecked sandals, she hit upon the idea of the supermarket, which turned out to have a supply of inoffensive plimsolls stacked between the enormous red tomatoes and the plaster statues of the Sacred Heart. Dora selected a pair in white that made her think of gym lessons at school, which she'd hated so much that she'd pleaded a permanent period.

Back at the hotel, she picked up a tourist map from the reception desk. Kyri was so small that it looked as if you could cross it in a couple of hours if you were an enthusiastic walker, which Dora wasn't. She studied the map. Takis had taken one look at her unsuitable shoes and recommended a bus from outside the hotel. With the new plimsolls she could probably walk quite easily, but decided to take his advice anyway.

The bus was full of old ladies with laden shopping baskets who all made room for her, offering impenetrable greetings.

'*Kalimera*,' Dora nodded round at them – a mistake, as they grinned and replied with a flood of incomprehensible Greek to which she could only nod and smile. She was relieved when after one stop she recognized the tiny church above the road that led down to the beach. She could easily have walked it, she decided as she waved goodbye to the enthusiastic gathering of grannies – pushing away the uncomfortable thought that they were probably not much older than she was – and started down the overgrown path. If she had known or cared about nature, she might have appreciated the yellow broom growing all round her, the thyme-scented hills behind her or even the lavender she bruised underfoot as she made her way along. Suddenly she felt the touch of rough fur, and shrieked loudly to find she had almost been bulldozed by a goat.

Quickly she stepped out of the way as two more followed. Behind them was Ariadne, Takis's daughter, presumably on her way down to the beach bar.

'Hello Ariadne, are these your goats? They gave me the fright of my life!'

Ariadne nodded. Her pale face with its thick black eyebrows and slanted almost-black eyes reminded Dora of a young Frida Kahlo. 'They are my grandmother's. She keeps them for the yogurt.' She shrugged irritably, and Dora glimpsed the strength of character beneath her smile – also not unlike Frida's.

'Shouldn't you be at school or something?' ventured Dora, realizing as she spoke that actually she had no idea how long Greek children had to stay in education.

'My grandmother says I don't need to pass exams to work for my father.'

'And you have other ideas?'

'I would like to study plants, the pharmacy of nature.' She

54

gestured around her. 'We have so much here – oregano for sore throat, fennel for bad stomach, orris root for when you are . . .' She squatted down and scrunched up her face in a gesture of such expressiveness that Dora had to laugh.

'Constipated!' replied Dora.

Ariadne gestured at a clump of young green leaves, just unfurling in the morning sun, with a white flower-like stem emerging from the centre. 'Holy basil,' pronounced Ariadne, 'blessed by the saint.' She didn't expand as to which saint, but Dora assumed it must be the one with the unpronounceable name who was paraded round on his feast day each year.

'Is that why it's holy?' enquired Dora.

Ariadne looked shocked by her ignorance. 'Holy basil was found around the tomb of Jesus Christ after the Resurrection. That is the greatest feast day of the year in Greece. The church uses basil with their holy water, but if you have a cough –' again she staged a demonstration, this time of a coughing fit – 'a tea of holy basil is the best cure for it.'

'What else is medicinal?' Dora was surprised that she, the arch-sceptic about all things naturopathic, was actually interested.

Ariadne pointed out a cluster of large red berries. 'We make these into bread. Also a strong drink. I am not sure of the word.'

'Liqueur?'

'Yes. Mastiha liqueur. The island of Chios is famous for it, but ours is better.'

'And is that good for something too?'

'For getting drunk,' grinned Ariadne, as Dora jumped again at the sudden touch of a rough-furred neck. 'That is Juno. She is my favourite. I think she likes you.'

Maeve Haran

Dora found herself being playfully butted, and almost tripped. 'If that's liking, I wouldn't want to meet her angry.'

They continued down the steep path, with Juno the goat still breathing down Dora's neck in a disconcerting manner. Soon they came to a small clearing full of bright pink oleanders and wild rose bushes. Dora stopped to pick one.

'*Loulouthia!*' Ariadne shrugged in disgust. 'Flowers. They are a waste of the good soil.'

Dora stuck the rose behind her ear. It made her feel like a hippie, and she laughed out loud.

'Sssh!' Ariadne quieted her, looking round.

'Why?' asked Dora, intrigued. They seemed to be in the middle of nowhere. The path had veered left through what seemed to be a large olive grove that led directly down to the beach. The beach bar was five minutes further along the sand.

Ariadne didn't answer immediately. They climbed further down, Dora following in the girl's footsteps. They were nearly at the bottom when Ariadne took her hand and led her through the ancient trees to where two or three of Juno's fellow goats were rooting around, hunting for tufts of early grass.

It was an extraordinary place. Dora looked around, trying to get an idea of how many olive trees there were. Fifty at least, she guessed.

'My favourite place,' Ariadne whispered. 'Sacred to the goddess.'

'Which goddess?' Dora enquired. Like saints, there seemed to be so many.

Ariadne cast a withering glance in her direction. 'Aphrodite, of course. The one you call Venus.'

At the word Venus, Dora felt a tiny arrow of panic pierce her consciousness. None of her friends here had the slightest idea who Venus Green was, and they probably cared even less. But Dora knew how quickly word would have spread in London's smart restaurants and the latest hip wine bars that she'd lost her major client.

She closed her eyes, telling herself she wouldn't think about it.

Ariadne clutched her arm. 'You feel it also!'

Dora opened her eyes again, momentarily disorientated. What was the girl talking about?

'I always know when she is here.'

'Right. OK,' Dora replied doubtfully. 'When does she usually come?' She decided it would be unfair to challenge Ariadne directly. The young liked to believe in things.

'Sometimes at noon when it is so hot, the sea has a mist over it. Or it might be in the dark when the land is still and quiet.' She suddenly stopped, holding her body dead still. 'There. Breathe in. That is her perfume. The goddess must have been here!'

Dora, repressing a tolerant smile, took a deep breath.

There was a definite fragrance – fresh and green, with a strong overtone of pungent eucalyptus. She tried to place it but decided she couldn't recognize the aroma.

'It is myrtle, what we call *myrtia*. The plant is sacred to Aphrodite. They used it at all her rituals. Often her statues had a garland of myrtle round their neck.' Ariadne paused dramatically, puffing herself up with pride. 'And yet there is none growing near here.'

Beyond her, Juno the goat tossed her head in apparent agreement.

'Look around you, Do-ra.' Ariadne had the secret smile of a high priestess or a vestal virgin. 'And show me where the *myrtia* is growing.'

Dora stared around her. Ariadne was right. There was no myrtle.

'It must be hidden somewhere,' she almost snapped, feeling as if she'd wandered into *The Magus*. Any moment now, some fake priestess would appear wearing a scary mask.

Ariadne maintained her faintly irritating smile of superiority. 'Maybe she is angry.'

'So will I be, if I don't get that cappuccino.' Dora took Ariadne firmly by the arm. 'And why should she be angry?'

Ariadne walked ahead, clicking at the goats to follow. 'The rich man from Athens . . .'

'Xan something . . . ?'

'Yes, him. He has bought this olive grove so he can build his stupid house in her special place.'

'I see. And that will be quite near your bar.'

Ariadne shrugged. 'We have hardly any customers.'

'What will happen to the olive grove?'

'He wants to chop down the part next to the house – to build a swimming pool! When the beach is only five minutes away!'

'No wonder the goddess is angry.' Dora looked across at the sun sparkling on the shallows in the perfect horseshoe bay. It really was a beautiful place. A thought suddenly struck her. 'How do you get supplies to the beach bar? By mule?'

Ariadne smiled at this old-fashioned idea. 'In his friend's boat. My father drops what we need every day from the hotel.'

That was a relief.

'I hope he's dropped some of Cassandra's delicious cake. She gave me a slice and I left it in my room.'

They walked together for the final five minutes along the white sand beach. With its backdrop of pine, wild mastic and locust trees, the occasional sudden clump of pink oleander or wild olive, it was indeed a magical spot.

Magic. That word again. For God's sake, pull yourself together, woman, Dora told herself sternly. You're getting as bad as Ariadne.

Moira was sitting up in bed when Nell and Penny arrived at the doctor's house. Eleni, the doctor's wife, had lent her a fetching bed jacket with lacy arms, not the sort of garment they normally associated with Moira.

'You look like a Jane Austen heroine,' Nell teased her.

'These people are so kind!' said Moira. 'I keep offering to join you lot in the hotel but they won't hear of it. Apparently this bug was really lethal. He says I've got to stay in bed or anyway on a sofa for a week! They have agreed at least to let me pay them. And thank God the doctor has a wonderful library stuffed with history books, especially about this island.'

'Really?' Nell was genuinely surprised that any books had been written about tiny Kyri. The island was so small and inconspicuous that it was hard to imagine it had much history. What had Takis's son called it? 'A dot in the ocean, full of goats and relatives.'

'The archaeologists have dug up loads of shards of Minoan pottery, but that's not the fun bit.'

'Oh?' Nell's interest was beginning to wane.

'Pirates!' Moira sounded as if she'd won the lottery. 'There's so much been done on classical civilization, but hardly anyone knows about the French Corsairs who ruled this coast. Pirates were masters of the sea here for two hundred years! They used to rob the Turks and hide their booty in the caves.'

'It all sounds wonderfully Johnny Depp,' Nell nodded, recalling that Takis had mentioned pirates too.

'Listen to this!' Moira picked up an ancient-looking tome and read aloud: "'The island of Kyri was for many years the pirates' place of rendezvous, where they spent in terrible debaucheries the booty they robbed from the Turks – to the great advantage of the ladies, who are none of the coyest nor the ugliest . . .'"

'Translation, please,' interrupted Penny.

'It means,' supplied Nell, laughing, 'the local girls were both good-looking and up for it!'

'And listen to this,' Moira added enthusiastically. "'The ladies of Kyri had no other employment than making love or cotton stockings . . ." Don't you adore that? Which would you choose? To make love or cotton stockings? I know which I'd do!'

'Make cotton stockings, obviously,' Penny teased.

'And the best thing of all, a real mystery –' Moira was getting so excited, they thought she'd have a relapse – 'was the statue!'

'What statue was that?' asked Penny.

'One of the pirates, Olivier de Menton, found this incredible statue of a reclining Venus. She was lying on a day bed, holding the apple she'd been handed by Paris – the one that started the Trojan War.'

'I'll take your word for it,' Nell replied hastily.

'De Menton told the French king about the statue, and was offered a pardon if he brought it to Paris.'

'And?'

'He discovered the king was going to hang him for treason anyway, so he hid the Venus somewhere on the island. And no one's been able to find it since!'

'That does sound rather amazing,' conceded Penny.

'And the other amazing thing,' Moira enthused, 'is that five thousand people lived on Kyri then. Now it's about five hundred.'

'Goodness.' Penny looked anxious on behalf of all five hundred residents. 'No wonder they're worried about all the young people leaving. Do you think there's anything we could do to help?'

'Like what?' Moira asked sceptically.

'Well, there's hardly anywhere to stay apart from the hotel. I wondered about those fishermen's cottages we saw on the boat. Just imagine if we could do up the empty boat garages. We could paint the huge doors all different colours and do up the rooms with the balconies above. I bet they'd be snapped up on Airbnb!'

Nell looked at her, impressed. 'Maybe my daughter Willow could help. She's the queen of Instagram. She uses it all the time.'

Moira was too busy thinking about her pirates, but Penny noticed the wistful tone in Nell's voice when she mentioned Willow, and wondered what the story was about her daughter. She didn't talk much about Willow.

'Why don't you talk to Takis?' Nell suggested. 'He seems to know everything and everyone. The only thing is, you wouldn't want this island to get like Zanthos, full of fat nudists drinking beer, would you?'

As they said goodbye to Moira, Penny was conscious of a sense of relief that the doctor wanted Moira to stay in bed. That meant they needed to stay on the island too.

Back at the hotel, she approached Takis straight away about the feasibility of doing up the boathouses.

'Some of them will agree, but others will ask how much it will cost them when maybe no one will come. Shall I fix for us to meet them and maybe have a look round?' Takis enquired.

'That would be brilliant. Would tomorrow be possible, do you think?' Penny asked, conscious of time passing. It was probably mad to get involved, but maybe they could just start the thing off.

Takis replied with one of his rubbery Mr Bean smiles. 'I'll see what I can do.'

Nell and Penny sat down at their usual table on the harbour-side. 'I wonder where Dora's got to. She said something about going to the beach bar. Maybe she's stayed and had a swim and sunbathe.'

'Hello girls!' They turned to find Dora emerging from the hotel in another of her unsuitable outfits, a cocktail dress in red velvet which would have been ideal at a film premiere but seemed a tad overdressed on the quay in Kyri. She sat down and ordered a strange-looking liqueur called Mastiha.

'It's made from mastic berries,' she informed them gaily. 'I've just had a seminar from Ariadne on how to use every plant from sage to rosemary and thyme! You'd be amazed at how useful they are.'

'Sounds like something from Scarborough Fair,' grinned Nell, picking up the drink to have a sip.

'Sorry?' Dora looked mystified.

'You know – *parsley, sage, rosemary and thyme* – that's the chorus to "Scarborough Fair". I thought you were in the music business. Don't you know your Simon and Garfunkel?'

'I have very little to do with the music business, actually,' Dora bristled.

'What about that singer . . . what's her name?'

'Venus Green,' supplied Penny surprisingly. 'My daughter and I were addicted to the show she won. We never missed a single one.'

'Actually,' Dora lowered her voice, 'I wanted to tell you about an amazing experience I've just had with Ariadne.'

'Goodness.' Penny leaned towards her, all eager retriever.

'Let's just get a glass of wine,' Nell suggested. 'I'll listen better then.' They tried to find the young boy who was serving, but there was no sign of him. In the end Nell went to the reception desk to ask, almost tripping over the long, aristocratic legs of Xan Georgiades.

'Have you seen the waiter, by any chance?' Nell asked him, taking in that he was wearing a tweed suit of the type you normally saw only on racecourses in England – except for the cut. His suit managed to look stylish, rather than like something out of P. G. Wodehouse.

'Sorry, no,' he replied languidly. 'I'm trying to get hold of a gin and tonic myself.'

The waiter suddenly emerged, and Xan bowed to let Nell place her order first.

'A bottle of white wine, please. And three glasses.' Dora might well feel like one after her Mastiha.

Xan ordered his gin and tonic and followed her out, politely sitting down two tables along from Dora and Penny.

'Right,' Nell announced once the wine was poured. 'We're sitting comfortably, so why don't you begin?'

Dora sipped her drink, not noticing the new arrival sitting slightly behind her.

'I was in this olive grove with Ariadne,' she began. 'It's an amazing place – right on the beach down by Takis's other bar.'

Almost imperceptibly, Xan's back stiffened, and he leaned subtly towards them.

'Ariadne's often down there. She's an amateur botanist, always collecting herbs and berries and things. It was her who recommended this stuff.' Dora raised her glass of transparent liquid. 'It's actually made from resin.'

'You were going to tell us what happened when you were down there.'

'Right.' Dora banged down her glass with a slight flounce at being interrupted. 'Ariadne says the grove is sacred to the goddess . . .'

'Which goddess is that? There seem to be an awful lot.' Nell tried not to giggle. Dora seemed so serious.

'Aphrodite . . . or Venus to the Romans.'

'The goddess of love,' Penny smiled.

'Anyway, Ariadne is convinced she comes to the grove.'

'Right,' Nell nodded, deadpan.

'The thing is, she said you could tell she'd been there when there was a scent of myrtle, and while were standing, it suddenly came. An overpowering scent of myrtle! Right out of nowhere.'

'But surely that's not so odd,' Nell pointed out. 'Wasn't there myrtle growing there?'

'That was the thing,' Dora looked from one to the other and shrugged. 'There wasn't any myrtle anywhere.'

Nell and Penny glanced at each other, unsure how to react. 'So what you're saying,' Nell attempted, 'is that this goddess was really there?'

Dora shook her head. 'I don't know what I'm saying. I'm just telling you what happened.'

Behind them, Penny caught a look of intense irritation on Xan's face, covered almost instantly by a patronizing smile. 'I hope you don't mind me interrupting, ladies.' He looked straight at Dora. 'But I think your imagination must have been in overdrive. There's nothing in that grove except a few goats. It was probably cliff rose, which can smell a little like myrtle. It grows everywhere round here at this time of year.'

He drained his drink and bowed, then began to stroll along the harbourside towards the other end of the town.

'Well, what do you make of that?' Nell asked.

'Didn't Takis say he wants to bulldoze the olive grove for his holiday home? I don't suppose he wants any inconvenient goddesses hanging about and getting in his way.'

'But you can't actually believe there was a goddess there?' Nell was sceptical.

'I don't know.' Dora looked thoughtful. 'But tomorrow I'll go and see if there are any of these cliff roses nearby. Do either of you want to come with me?'

'We can't,' Nell replied. 'We're going to meet the owners of those boat garages on the beach. Penny reckons she can turn them into star Airbnb attractions.'

Penny and Nell looked at each other.

'I feel I just want to help,' Penny said with sudden determination. 'It's such a beautiful place. Takis says people go to Santorini and even Sifnos, but not to Kyri. It's time people knew what a lovely island this is.'

'Good for you,' Dora replied, looking at her thoughtfully. 'But I thought we were only here for a short holiday.'

Five

Back in her room, Nell decided that this time she really would call Willow. It was ridiculous that she should feel nervous of ringing her own daughter. But she did.

As usual, the phone rang out and didn't even go to voice-mail. Willow hated voicemail. She said it was stupid, because she could tell that the person had rung anyway. Only old people left voicemails, she said. So it had to be bloody Insta-gram.

Sure enough, there was her darling granddaughter nestling in Marigold's arms, smiling boldly straight at the camera. She was the prettiest baby. Green eyes full of light, a tiny nose and a shining cap of chestnut curls. For one delirious moment Nell thought the little dress Naomi wore was one she had sent her, and then she looked more closely. No, the material looked thick and expensive, whereas Nell's had come from Next. No need to wonder who the source was. Willow hated shopping and lived in vintage creations which she threw over faded blue jeans, so it wouldn't be her.

Nell looked again into the sweet, loving little face and ached to be acknowledged as her granny. Instead of which, the

66

photos spelled out as clearly as could be that she was Not Wanted on Voyage.

Penny, on the other hand, was clearly being missed – not because of her sweet and generous nature or even her undoubted household efficiency, but because there was no food in the freezer.

For a few seconds she was tempted to ignore Colin's latest message altogether, but then the marital guilt that he had cleverly managed to exploit for decades made her reach for her phone and send a message to her daughter. Could Wendy could just pop round and put some supplies in, and Penny would reimburse her as soon as she was home?

She had hardly put on her nightdress before a pithy reply arrived with astonishing speed as well as evident enjoyment.

Forget Dad, was Wendy's response. *He exploits you because you let him. If he's that starving he can always go down to the pub. Now go and enjoy yourself. That's an order!*

Penny couldn't help smiling. The truth was, she *was* enjoying herself. What had seemed like a disaster only days ago was turning out to be fascinating.

And then, without her even noticing, Penny the Worrier morphed out of the ether, like some evil genie – only, as far as she knew, she hadn't even summoned it.

What the hell would the locals make of some interfering Englishwoman who didn't even speak Greek telling them to paint their boathouses and do them up to go on Airbnb?

She finally stopped worrying and picked up her book. For some reason, Agatha Christie always got her to sleep in five minutes.

The next morning Penny was woken by the sun streaming in directly through her shutters and a strange sound, almost like the beating of a drum, repeated hypnotically until she had to throw open the window and peer out. Nell was doing exactly the same thing.

'What on earth is going on?' Penny enquired sleepily.

'No idea. I wondered if it was one of these endless feast days they seem to have here.'

To Penny's surprise, Nell was wearing glasses. 'I didn't know you wore specs.'

'Since I was eighteen. The optician said I was studying too hard.'

They stared down from their windows until they found the source of the drumming. It was Takis, and he was banging squid against the harbour wall.

'What are you doing?' Penny called out, horrified.

'This is how we tenderize them,' he shouted back. He took in Penny's alarmed expression. 'Don't worry, Penelope, I know you care for living creatures but they are all dead!'

Penny couldn't help laughing at the reputation she seemed to have acquired so quickly.

'Sorry,' Nell apologized, 'that's probably my fault. I couldn't resist telling him the old story of you hitting the donkey man in Zanthos with your handbag.'

'That donkey was skin and bone. It could hardly stand up!' Penny replied, sounding as angry now as she had then.

They smiled at each other and stood for a moment looking out at the village below. Beyond the row of cafes and restaurants was the small beach, fringed by tamarisk trees, where the sea sparkled in the morning sunshine and the white sand made you want to run across it barefoot.

'It's probably raining in England,' Nell commented smugly.

'Why don't we go for an early morning swim?'

Five minutes later they hurried past a group of old men in

caps and berets who cheered at the sight of the two English ladies stripping off to their swimsuits and running, laughing, into the waves.

'*Daxi! Daxi!*' they congratulated, as Nell and Penny splashed each other out of sheer physical delight at being in a warm Greek sea with the sun beating down and the air already hot at nine in the morning.

'I could get used to this,' Nell sighed, feeling the water envelop her in its comforting embrace.

'Bliss!' pronounced Penny.

'Bliss!' agreed Nell.

'Breakfast ready!' shouted Takis, who had come to watch them with the old men.

'Have we died and gone to a heaven where the men make the breakfast?' Nell demanded, laughing.

Colin flashed into Penny's mind, but for once she refused to let him take over her thoughts. He couldn't be allowed to spoil everything.

'I hate to disillusion you,' she called to Nell as she reached for her towel, 'but I think Cassandra's the one who's been up since six making yogurt.'

'Well then,' Nell shook out her wet hair, 'we'd better not disappoint her and go and eat it!'

Moira was feeling distinctly better. She didn't know whether it was the antibiotics, the enforced rest or the amazing care from the doctor and his wife, but whatever it was, she was almost herself again. And with that came a feeling of restlessness.

'Eleni, do you think we could at least go for a little stroll? Just ten minutes? I will go mad otherwise!'

Eleni smiled indulgently. 'I will ask my husband.'

She disappeared off downstairs to the surgery, and returned ten minutes later nodding his assent.

'We must go only just round our garden and a little of the lane beyond. And then back to the bed. He says your entire system will have been knocked out and you must only return to your life very slowly. But a little walk is a good thing, he says.'

Moira brushed her bird's nest of hair out as best she could, while Eleni watched with mixed fascination and horror.

'I know, I know,' conceded Moira. 'I need to do something about it.'

'I will do it if you want,' Eleni offered shyly. 'I was a hair-dresser before I married my husband.'

Moira pulled on her curious assortment of clothing, which was looking very much the worse for wear. 'You weren't a fashion buyer as well, by any chance?' she joked with Eleni.

'No, but I do have the clothes that belonged to my mother. I couldn't, how do you say in English, bring myself to throw them away.'

'OK,' Moira replied dubiously. Being dressed like an old Greek lady didn't seem a vast improvement on her current image.

'She was very fashionable,' Eleni smiled. 'I will show you later.'

As she walked via the stone staircase to the upstairs floor, Moira suddenly realized what the doctor meant. She had better use the handrail and take it gradually.

'Are you feeling dizzy?' enquired Eleni anxiously.

'Not really,' lied Moira, calling her distant farming ancestors to mind for some inherited stoicism, but holding tightly to the banister at the same time.

Fortunately the dizziness passed, but it made her realize the doctor was right about her system being affected. This was going to take longer than she'd thought, but there was no need for the others to spoil their holiday by staying with her.

The garden was surprisingly green in the shadier areas, and Eleni insisted on showing off her one rose and a hollyhock. 'This is my English garden!' she announced proudly.

'Very nice,' replied Moira, who had zero interest in gardens or gardening – as the fellow don at her Cambridge college who'd made the mistake of asking her to join the garden committee could endorse.

At the very end of the garden there was a small gate. Moira went through, and stopped as if she'd just seen a vision. 'What on earth are those?' She pointed at some large pieces of stone with carved facia.

'Oh, those are pieces of column. They are everywhere on the island.'

Despite her condition, Moira dropped reverently to her knees and began to stroke the smooth golden stone. Even though the column was in pieces, it was just as it would have been thousands of years before. 'But they could have come from a temple to Apollo or some such thing!' she exclaimed finally, almost overcome.

Eleni smiled tolerantly as if Moira had just praised the quality of something completely ordinary, a slice of bread or a cup of Greek coffee.

'There is a whole theatre carved from the rock on the other side of the island. You can almost walk past it without noticing it. You will have to get better, and we can go and see it.'

Moira sat down on another lump of carved stone, looking as if she'd accidentally landed in paradise. And she still had the pirate caves to explore, too. Maybe her stay in Kyri was going to be longer than she'd planned.

*

Takis stepped forward to address a dozen or so people – mainly grizzled and tough-looking men who were eking out an ever-decreasing income from fishing. Their wives stood in a row with folded arms and the kind of battle-ready expressions Penny had seen before on the first comers at the start of a jumble sale. They clearly thought they were somehow going to be cheated.

'*Yiassas*, neighbours,' he began, speaking at first in Greek. 'You know me well, but let me introduce these two charming English ladies – Penelope and Helen – Greek names, you see. They have a plan to make some money for you all by renting to tourists in summer these boathouses which you only use in winter anyway. Penelope is a famous decorator of rich people's houses' – he smiled at Penny, who would have challenged this outrageous lie if she knew what he was saying – 'and Helen also will be helping her.'

Turning to Penny, he addressed her in English. 'So, Penelope, explain to my neighbours what you want them to do and how such an idea will work, and I will translate to them.'

'Come on, Penny,' whispered Nell. 'Imagine you're Dora instead of you. She's got the confidence of Boris Johnson and skin as thick as an old walrus.'

Penny tried to remember the two things she'd been told were important when public speaking: be confident from the beginning, and make eye contact with one person in the audience. Unfortunately, the woman who was right in her eye line was the scariest-looking of them all.

'Right.' She forced her usually soft features into sternness. 'I'm sure you've all heard of Airbnb? The company that has revolutionized staying in private houses and brought an income to people in places like Kyri – and really annoyed the

72

hotel trade by undercutting their rates by a mile.' She gestured towards Takis, who shrugged and looked comically mournful.

'I think your boat garages are perfect for renting to tourists.' There was a murmur of interest at this. 'But we need to make some improvements. To begin with, we will have to paint the boathouse doors in wonderful bright colours so that they look good in photographs. I suggest we have a painting party and do it together – we might even be able to do it tomorrow? If everyone could bring a lot of sandpaper and brushes . . .'

'And who will pay for the paint?' demanded the scary woman who Penny had been addressing eye-to-eye. She waited with a stern expression while Takis translated.

'I will,' announced Penny, surprising herself. After all, she still had a bit of money left from her legacy. 'And Helen here will provide lunch for everyone.'

Nell blinked. Penny knew she'd done a catering course, and now she was sunk in it whether she liked it or not.

'And who are you to tell us what to do?' suddenly demanded one of the old ladies, swathed entirely in black to proudly proclaim the status of her widowhood. 'Incomers who don't even know Kyri!'

Various others, especially the men, murmured in agreement.

On her own, Penny would probably have agreed with them, but fortunately she had Takis on her side. Before there was time for the rebellion to catch on, he spoke up. 'Listen, my friends. You all know what is our problem? Eight out of ten new jobs are in tourism. How many of them are in Kyri? None! Will your children become fishermen like you, and brave the winter sea to catch a few fish? No, no and no!' He turned to a grizzled old man at the back. 'Apostolis, where are your grandchildren?'

'In Athens,' conceded the grizzled gentleman.

'And your daughter, Irene Papadopoulos? Where is she?'

'In Santorini. Married to an Albanian.'

They all shook their heads in sympathy at this Greek tragedy.

'Takis is right,' said Apostolis. 'We must stop all our sons and daughters having to leave Kyri. We will come with our paintbrushes and make our island even more beautiful than it already is!'

Nell, sensing the change of mood in the room, smiled to herself. Through a combination of threat and charm, Takis had won them over. As her mind flipped through possible options for feeding a small Greek army tomorrow, she noticed a newcomer making his way through the crowd.

He was tall and well-built, with greying black hair and a moustache to match, and his deeply tanned skin provided a dramatic contrast to the faded blue denim of his shirt. He looked round at the gathering with a detached amusement until his eyes fixed on Penny. He seemed mentally to take a step back and look again, as if he were seeing something he couldn't quite believe to be true.

'Nikos,' Takis greeted him enthusiastically. 'Nikos, my friend. I doubt that you will want to rent out your house on Airbed . . .' Nell laughed at this approximation of Airbnb. 'But this will affect you also. You are going to be No. 1 tourist resort on Kyri.'

The man called Nikos laughed. 'Just as well my house is round the corner. I wouldn't want to wake all your guests with my noisy motorcycle.'

'Ladies,' Takis smiled broadly. 'This is Nikos Dukakis, my very old friend, as well as esteemed mayor of the island of Kyri.'

The meeting broke up with a muted air of excitement as

everyone departed in twos and threes discussing where the sandpaper should be bought, who had paintbrushes or rollers, and whether the men or the women were more competent to actually apply the paint.

'I think that went rather well,' Penny grinned as the last person left.

'Fandabidozi!' said Takis, and spun round on his heels.

'Is that Greek for brilliant?' asked Nell, fascinated.

'Glaswegian,' explained Takis improbably. 'Enthusiastic endorsement by Wee Jimmy Krankie. I worked in Glasgow many years ago.'

'Do you think the people were convinced about doing it?' Penny asked anxiously. 'There was quite a lot of hostility, I thought.'

'Not surprising, is it?' Nell shrugged. 'I mean, we've only been here five minutes and here we are interfering in their way of life.'

Takis shook his head vehemently. 'No. OK in the end. You have to put a bomb under these people. They don't even like to change a light bulb. That is why we are so stuck in the past.'

'All right,' Penny grinned. 'We'd better deliver on our promises. I'll have to go and take a proper look at these boathouses. There's only so much tourists will take in the name of folksy interiors, but I've done quite a lot of stuff for friends with no money, so it should be OK.'

'You just have to persuade people they need to spend a lot of money to get serious simplicity,' Nell laughed. 'By the way . . .' She looked at Penny curiously. 'Have you ever met that man Nikos before?'

'The hunky lone-wolf mayor of Kyri? Can't say I've bumped into him in my local Waitrose, no.'

'Only he seemed to know you. He stared at you as if you'd just stepped out of a dream.'

'Oh for goodness' sake, Nell!' Penny shook her head at the ludicrousness of such a suggestion. 'How could I know the mayor of a tiny Greek island, especially one who's approved gay marriage? They've only just allowed blessing of divorcees in my church at home.'

'Hmmm.' Nell looked unconvinced. 'Well, I suppose only time will tell, won't it?'

Dora picked her way along the path from the bus stop to the beach cafe in her new plimsolls as carefully as Joan Collins in stilettos navigating the red carpet. She didn't like to admit it, but falling over was no joke at their age, especially when your phone might be out of signal to summon immediate assistance.

She almost did fall when Juno the goat, white and shaggy with long cream fur and curly horns, came up and nuzzled her. The animal's extraordinarily human face almost seemed to be smiling at Dora.

'You wouldn't look so happy if you knew I was picturing you as a nice furry rug by the side of my bed,' Dora informed her.

The goat kept smiling.

She looked up the hill behind her, wondering how long it would take to walk here via the path over the hills from the harbour. The route didn't look that steep. She'd ask Ariadne. She was almost at the beach bar when she got an overwhelming temptation to check out the olive grove and see if she could still smell myrtle. Dora couldn't tell a pine from an oak, but she stood among the trees looking round her intently.

There were about fifty trees, many with amazing gnarled and knotted trunks, fanning out like umbrellas, their silvery leaves rustling in the breeze, their tiny berries pale now but starting to ripen into the familiar black. Many of them seemed to be dead or dying as Xan had said. She suddenly felt ashamed that she had hardly even known olives grew on trees instead of coming ready to use in a tin or supermarket container. She was like one of those deprived kids they had on the news who'd grown up in environments so urban they didn't know milk came from cows.

It was so silent here, you could almost imagine nymphs and satyrs playing hide and seek behind the massive tree trunks and falling together in a lascivious heap amongst the fallen berries.

Dora breathed in deeply, but there was only the smell of the sea and a faint apricot scent coming from the pink oleander bushes that had seeded themselves here and there. They really ought to be the national flower of Greece, since they seemed to grow in every garden and on every motorway reservation, gaily reminding people their holidays had started.

Today there were no nymphs or satyrs or goddesses; only the goat, and absolutely no scent of myrtle. She glanced round for any sign of the cliff roses Xan Georgiades had claimed were growing here. Zero.

She turned round to head back to the path when another, more daring idea occurred to her: she would just have a glance at the existing house he had bought from old Yannis.

It was more of a cabin than an actual house. The sides were built of what looked like driftwood, and the roof of corrugated concrete. It was certainly not a place of beauty, except for its amazing uninterrupted views of the dazzling Aegean Sea below. Dora could see the arguments for demolishing and rebuilding. She started to laugh at the idea of the louche and aristocratic Xan living here.

'I'm glad you find my humble abode so entertaining.' The voice behind her made her jump and step backwards onto the goat, who protested loudly.

She willed herself to keep her cool. She had addressed conferences full of tough ad executives – she could handle one posh if extremely angry Greek.

'I was on my way to the beach bar,' she said coolly. 'And I thought I'd make a detour to look for these cliff roses.'

'Maybe they're not cliff roses.' Xan's eyes narrowed nastily. 'Flowers aren't exactly my special subject.'

'I'll ask Ariadne,' Dora smiled sweetly. 'She knows more about plants than David Attenborough does about sperm whales.'

'Who the hell is Ariadne?' he asked irritably.

'Takis's granddaughter. She looks after the goats and runs the beach bar.'

'Then she's not doing a very good job, is she? Kindly remove that animal from my property before it shits all over my olives.'

'Certainly,' Dora smiled again. 'But I thought shit was good for growing things.' She turned towards the beach path, the goat following her, her heart beating fast and her breath quickening, but maintaining the superior and slightly scary expression that made journalists quake and her clients feel grateful she was representing them and not their rivals.

She shrugged on her Prada rucksack and continued on the path to the beach, not looking back to see if he was still watching her.

When she arrived at the beach bar she found, to her irritation, that it was closed and there was no sign of Ariadne or – much worse – the cappuccino she was longing for.

She took off her plimsolls, rolled up her jeans and walked along the white sand fringed by deep turquoise sea, letting the water lap against her ankles, soothing her irritation. She closed her eyes. Somewhere further along, a lone bird sang in a tamarisk tree. The peace here was like nothing she had ever encountered before. London seemed a lifetime away. She'd always been impatient with all that mindfulness crap, but standing here alone in the landscape, breathing in the clear air, she could for the first time see the point.

Reluctantly, she turned and made for the path.

Half an hour later she plonked herself down next to Penny and Nell, who sat busily writing in a new notebook they had just bought from the little supermarket. 'I've just had a rather angry encounter with that man Xan in the olive grove.'

'And what exactly were you doing in his olive grove?' Nell asked, trying not to smile. 'Checking on the myrtle count?'

Dora gave her a quelling look. 'I went to see if there were any of these cliff roses he was talking about.'

'And were there?'

'Of course not.'

'Why did he get angry? Because you were trespassing?'

'Nonsense. I had to get Ariadne's goat out of there, anyway.'

'The one that follows you everywhere?' Penny added innocently. 'Ariadne was telling us it has fallen in love with you.'

'That would be just my luck.' Dora tossed her perfect bronze hair. 'To be adored by a goat. And she's even female.'

'Tsk, tsk,' Nell reprimanded her. 'Nothing wrong with that in this gender-fluid era.'

'So why did he get so angry?' Penny enquired. 'Does he

think your goddess is going to get in the way of his planning permission?'

'Can goddesses get in the way of planning permission in the modern era?' asked Dora.

'Well, this is Greece,' Nell replied, laughing. 'They still take their gods and goddesses very seriously.'

'Odd, given that it's a Catholic country,' commented Penny. 'Well, Greek Orthodox anyway.'

'We need Moira to put us straight,' Nell said. 'Do you know, I'm beginning to rather miss her.'

Dora looked appalled.

'Anyway, what were you up to?' Nell asked her.

'Well,' Dora admitted, 'I was just glancing into his house. It's very ramshackle. He obviously doesn't live there.'

'Of course he doesn't,' Nell said. 'He's staying here, isn't he?'

'I'd forgotten that. What's all this, then?' She indicated the notebook. 'Late spring resolutions? Is that wine in the bottle?'

'No,' snapped Nell, 'surgical spirit! Why don't you have some?'

'What's eating you?'

Nell thought for a moment and wondered if she should tell the truth. Why the hell not? Though Dora, committedly single, would probably think she was certifiably bonkers.

'OK . . . I just looked at my phone. Look.' She handed the phone to Dora, who passed it to Penny.

'It's a baby's birthday party.' Dora shrugged.

'Yes,' nodded Nell. 'My granddaughter Naomi's first, as a matter of fact. I think my invitation must have got lost in the post. OK, girls; the honest truth is, I have a serious case of The Other Granny Syndrome. In this case, perfect Marigold. My daughter prefers her company to mine.'

'I'm sure she doesn't,' attempted Penny, picking up how deeply hurt Nell sounded.

'She certainly does. Marigold who buys baby clothes from Gucci and gives her stuff from Baby Einstein.'

'You're kidding me,' Dora objected. 'There's no such thing!'

'There bloody well is,' insisted Nell, warming to her theme. 'And baby massage, and baby yoga. Marigold takes her to the lot.'

'Thank God I haven't got children! But isn't it great that this Marigold does it all? No granny duties for you. You're free to travel, go away for weekends. No ghastly standing at the school gates in the depths of winter. Brilliant.'

'Except that I want to,' Nell confessed. 'I really, really, really want to.'

'And what happens if you offer?' Penny asked gently.

'She never says no,' Nell replied, her voice fraying at the edges. 'There's just always some reason why it falls through. And then I go on Instagram and there's Naomi with bloody Marigold! In her bloody swimming pool, or wearing some expensive clobber Marigold has bought her.'

'Oh, Nell, what a drag for you.' Penny instantly understood. 'The woman sounds really insensitive.'

'Anyway, look, it's quite a big deal for me to admit it,' Nell shrugged. 'Let's have a drink and get to work on that note-book.'

'Thank you for trusting us,' Penny said quietly, raising her glass and thinking about how she hadn't been brave enough to share the truth about her own marriage.

'Yes,' Dora added, obviously much struck. She hadn't got many close girlfriends. In fact, this holiday was the longest period she could remember spending alone with other women. For a fraction of a second she thought about confessing that she'd lost Venus Green, her biggest client, and that everyone in the PR world was probably gossiping about it; but no, she didn't do all that Oprah stuff. Her technique when faced with pain or failure was to wallow in guilt and self-indulgence, drink too much wine and then pretend nothing had happened. It had worked so far.

She decided to swiftly change the subject before it got too dangerous. 'What is the notebook for?' she enquired. 'Haven't you heard of new technology?' Actually, that was a bit rich; she was hardly a tech queen herself.

'I prefer good old pen and paper,' Penny insisted. 'We're making a to-do list for converting the boathouses. We're going over there tomorrow to assess them properly. Fancy joining us?'

'I don't think I will, thanks. Any news of the classical invalid?'

'Champing at the bit,' Nell replied. 'She wants us to go and explore pirate caves once the doctor allows her.'

'Not long now till we're due back in Athens,' Dora reminded them. 'Don't want to miss those flights, do we?'

No one answered. Dora looked at them searchingly. 'Do we?' It might be all right for a housewife and a retired receptionist to stay on indefinitely, she thought irritably, but she had a life. A sliver of panic chipped its way into her mind about what would be waiting for her.

Nell looked at Penny. They had just arranged to paint the boathouses a few days before they were due to fly back. Surely that was a problem?

Penny studiously avoided her eye.

'Of course we do,' replied Nell briskly. 'Now let's get back to that list.'

*

Penny had left her phone in her room, and when she got back she heard it ringing. Panic felled her for a moment – could it be Wendy or one of the children? But Wendy always used WhatsApp. She looked at the caller. Colin. She nearly answered it, then stopped and stared at the number. It would, as usual, be a complaint.

When they'd first got married, she'd wondered why someone as ambitious for money and success as Colin had chosen her – rather plain, unsophisticated and totally unmoved by status symbols of any sort. He didn't seem to value the attributes she did have – kindness, empathy, a kind of bohemian creativity, the skill of making a lovely home. When other people had asked her to do their rooms up for them he'd laughed. He took all that for granted as the minimum qualifications for being married to Colin Anderson, and just saw her flaws. She wasn't glamorous like the other wives; didn't shop in the places they did or want to meet for coffee in Caffè Nero. Her dinner parties lacked their style and panache. That wasn't a word he'd learned in Dagenham when he was growing up. He seemed almost to resent her for knowing about his humble origins.

Penny sat down hard on the bed, struck for the first time with a stunning revelation: she didn't actually like her husband, let alone love him.

The admission was horribly painful. It meant that years of her life had been wasted – except for producing her daughter Wendy, lovely, bouncy, down-to-earth Wendy. She seemed, despite the example of her parents, to have made a happy marriage to an ordinary, kind, likeable man and had ordinary, likeable children who Penny utterly adored. And then there was Tom, who lived halfway across the world and seemed half in love with money, like his father.

She fortified herself with a glass from the bottle of wine she'd stored in the fridge, and played back the message on her phone.

Colin's irritated tones invaded the calm of the sunny bedroom. As ever, no 'hope you're having a lovely time', but straight into a complaint. He'd run out of clean shirts and apparently it was in some way her fault. And when the hell was she coming back, and didn't she remember they'd been invited to drinks with his partner and his partner's wife?

Penny looked out of her window at the village below. The sun was a blaze of colour as it disappeared below the horizon, dipping the sails of two small boats in molten bronze. A group of elderly men argued and laughed on a wall. Children played football on the beach under the tamarisk trees. Two old ladies in black stood chatting. A comforting buzz of conversation rose from the harbourside cafes. The cicadas sang. Everywhere was the sweet, waxy smell from the tiny white flowers that Cassandra said were called *angeliki*.

Penny came to a decision. She wasn't going to answer that message, or any other messages from her husband.

A dizzy sense of light-headed liberation overtook her. She had never made a decision just for herself in her life. Was this selfishness? She didn't know, but whatever it was, it felt very good.

She tended to avoid mirrors, but now she deliberately crossed the room and stared at her own face. Why did she still wear this silly schoolgirl hairband? With a sudden surge of joy, she tore it off and shook her hair out.

Tomorrow was another day, as Scarlett O'Hara said in *Gone with the Wind*. From now on she was going to be a bit more like wilful, selfish but somehow admirable Scarlett.

*

'What's happened to Penny?' hissed Dora to Nell the next morning, as they sat in the pretty breakfast room with its nautical paintings and doors open to the sunny harbour. 'She's ditched the hairband and suddenly seems full of the joys of spring. Any minute she'll start singing that Kyri is alive with the sound of music.'

'Maybe she's excited about the boathouses,' Nell shrugged. Penny did seem somehow happier. 'She told me she's done a bit of interior design at home, but never had the chance to take it seriously. Perhaps we're going to witness the flowering of her talent.'

'It must be bloody boring being a housewife, being dependent on someone else and not having any freedom,' commented Dora, secretly feeling she would love someone else to run her life just at the moment.

'Especially with a husband like Charmless Colin, who manages to attractively combine being rich and mean.'

'He can't be that mean, if he paid for Penny to come on this little jaunt to Greece without him,' commented Dora.

'Don't you remember, she paid for this herself? A legacy from her dad, I think she said. Anyway, shh – she's coming.'

Penny sat down with them, her tray loaded with yogurt, honey and walnuts, a baklava and a large glass of freshly squeezed orange juice. 'The breakfast from heaven,' she announced. 'And all thanks to Ariadne's goats. Do you meet them on your daily trip to the beach?'

At that moment, the elegant Xan Georgiades emerged from the tiny lift in the lobby like some god appearing out of Zeus's head.

'Good morning, ladies,' he said stiffly, his eyes fixed on Dora. 'Are you doing any exploring today?'

'As a matter of fact,' Penny answered gaily, 'we're having a painting party down at the boathouses. We're going to help the owners get them ready to rent on Airbnb.'

'Indeed?' he replied frostily. 'Then I sincerely hope you have the right building permit.'

He swept out and hailed a taxi from the rather ramshackle taxi rank on the quay outside the hotel.

'Oh dear,' Penny asked, losing her carefree gloss of happiness for a moment. 'Do you think he's right about the permit?'

'*Malakas!!*' exclaimed a familiar voice from behind the counter. 'Athenian asshole.' Takis's rubbery features appeared. He was holding a pack of bottled water. 'What does he know? The fishermen used to sleep there, so you are not changing the usage. He is scared because he knows I am on the committee that will decide about his holiday house.' He smiled impishly and tapped the side of his nose. 'What food are you taking to the party today?'

This time it was Nell's turn to look smug. She reached under the table and produced two large bags of vegetables and other groceries. 'Would you mind if I used your kitchen for a bit of preparation?'

Takis bowed. 'My kitchen is your kitchen.'

'I thought I might introduce them to a bit of Ottolenghi.'

'What is Ottolenghi?' demanded Takis enthusiastically. 'Is it is some kind of pasta?'

'It's the name of a chef,' Nell laughed.

'But isn't he Turkish?' Penny asked. 'Is that a good idea? You know . . . the Greeks and the Turks . . .'

'I thought he was Lebanese, actually,' Nell challenged.

'Yotam Ottolenghi,' announced Dora, reading from her phone, 'born Jerusalem. English-Israeli chef.'

'Well, there you go. Do you think the Greeks are ready for

all that chopping?' Penny teased. 'It drives me mad. Give me good old Delia any day.'

'Come on, girls,' Nell encouraged them. 'We're going to show them there's more to life than moussaka.'

'Rather you than me,' Dora commented. 'Anyway, I'm going to the beach.'

'Via the olive grove?' Nell raised an eyebrow. 'Let's hope Mr Georgiades doesn't catch you.'

Dora ignored them, and picked up her beach bag. 'Good luck, one and all,' she waved as she headed up the hill away from the village.

It was another glorious morning. The sea sparkled enticingly through the olive trees, and there was a scent of pine that reminded her of holidays in the South of France before her parents got divorced and Dora was left with her increasingly bitter mother. She made her way through wild oleanders and scented yellow broom. In the distance she could hear goat bells from Ariadne's goats and soon Juno, her devoted admirer, appeared on the precipitous path next to her. Somewhere in the distance she heard the distinctive call of the cuckoo, one of the only birds she could actually recognize.

Ariadne's sweet and eager face appeared over the next ridge.

'Is that a cuckoo?' Dora enquired. 'Or don't you have them in Greece?'

Ariadne looked shocked. 'Of course we do. Cuckoos are famous here. Do you not know that Zeus, the king of the gods, pretended to be a poor wet little cuckoo so that Hera held him to her breast, and then he turned back into Zeus and forced his love on her?'

'Great. That's exactly the kind of line Penny would fall for – a poor little damp cuckoo. I'd better tell her to watch out. He wouldn't go down too well in the age of Time's Up, would he, your Zeus?'

'What is Time's Up?'

'You don't want to go there.' Dora didn't relish explaining this tricky concept to a fifteen-year-old inhabitant of a tiny Greek island. 'Your Zeus, he always seems to be having his wicked way with something, from swans to cows.'

'You do not understand,' corrected Ariadne. 'Zeus did not make love to a cow. He turned her into a cow so his wife would not see her.'

'I know the type.'

She glanced round the olive grove, wary that its owner might appear and chuck them off. 'Oughtn't we to get moving?' she suggested.

'The goddess is angry today. She has been here not long ago. Can you not smell her perfume?'

Dora breathed in. There it was again: a distinct aroma of myrtle. It was most disconcerting.

'And today she left this. She has never done this before. It is a bad omen, I am sure of it.' Ariadne produced a large bunch of fluffy white flowers from behind her back.

Dora regarded them sceptically. 'I think it's more likely these are from Mr Georgiades than the goddess Aphrodite. Ouch!' Focused on the flowers, she had stepped too close to a thorn bush and ended up with a thorn in her toe. She looked round for a rock to sit on. Instead there was a convenient stone bench about three feet long, with some faded carving on it, next to the ramshackle cabin.

Again looking nervously round, Dora sat down on it. 'Funny,' she commented as she pulled out the offending article from her big toe, 'I didn't notice this here the other day. Did you?' Ariadne shrugged. She was too concerned with the current mood of the goddess to care about benches.

Dora had no idea why, but she suddenly felt an overwhelming instinct that she should take a photograph of the bench with her iPhone.

Ariadne gave Juno a shove in Dora's direction. 'She wants to be in the photo!'

Dora shooed the goat out again. 'Sorry, Ariadne, but I just want the bench. I'll take a photo of Juno afterwards.'

Six

Penny and Nell were amazed to find about thirty people gathered on the narrow beach in front of the boathouses. Some were solid, silent fishermen with dark sun-leathered skin, one or two with impressive moustaches, their eyes permanently narrowed from scanning the horizon for changes in the weather. Their wives, even the ones dressed entirely in black, twittered round like noisy parakeets, no doubt gossiping about these strange English ladies who seemed to think they could help bring tourism to the island.

'Oh Jesus,' Nell murmured. 'I hope I've got enough food for this lot.'

Penny sniffed the air. As well as the faint tang of the sea and a slight odour of motor oil from the boats, there was the distinct aroma of baking bread. 'You can always nip over and get more bread. The answer to every party.'

After that she surprised Nell with her impressive efficiency in marshalling the troops, using mostly sign language since not many of them spoke English. First she laid out all the equipment on a table and was momentarily dispirited to see very few scrapers or brushes, but the moment she held one up, dozens more materialized out of pockets, shopping bags and in one case, the tight top of a rather glamorous lady in high heels and full makeup.

This unlikely volunteer Penny soon recognized as a type who, despite the sexy and wholly inappropriate outfit, could be found at any fundraising event of a charitable nature in the Home Counties. Bossy, loud-voiced and entirely without scruples in the name of a good cause, she was just what Penny needed. Her name was Demetria and she instantly became translator, group organizer and provider of extremely good coffee from the nearby cafe and bakery.

Soon ladders were assembled and fishermen with scrapers sent up them, while their wives held onto the lower ends and chatted enthusiastically.

'Oooh,' Nell breathed, 'it's just like that scene in *Mamma Mia* where the women leave the men up the ladders and follow Meryl Streep and jump into the harbour.'

'Which of us is Meryl?' Penny enquired.

'You are, obviously!'

Penny started doing a mock Greek dance, and then checked herself. 'Come on, I've done this sort of thing before. You have to get the work done before everyone loses enthusiasm.'

Soon she and Demetria had them all scraping and sanding away. Demetria decided no one needed to hold the ladders, so the wives had to do their bit too.

They were just beginning to flag when a kind of flutter ran through the women in the room, like the suspicion a fox might be approaching the hen house.

Penny turned to find not a fox but the lone-wolf mayor, Nikos, had arrived. This time he was in black motorcycle leathers, looking like something out of one of those sexy yet sophisticated French films by Godard or Truffaut.

'I wondered if these might be of any assistance?' he enquired in his fluent English. He held out two electric sanders and a fistful of different sanding disks.

The men up the ladders, their arms beginning to tire, fell on them with enthusiastic cries of '*Daxi! Daxi!*' which Penny was fast recognizing as 'OK, OK' and probably the most useful word in the modern Greek language.

He strode over to speak to Penny. Nell watched surreptitiously for signs of that strange intensity she was sure she had witnessed in him when he looked at her friend earlier.

'You have lost your hairband,' he observed.

'I threw it away,' Penny replied.

'Good. It did not suit you.'

'Thank you. *Efharisto.*' She tossed her head shyly.

'That is what you used to do,' he said, his eyes soft with a mixture of surprise and tenderness.

'Sorry?' Penny shrugged her shoulders, mystified. 'Have we met before?'

'You really do not remember?' His light blue eyes pinned her to the spot.

'Remember what?'

'On Zanthos. We went out together two or three times.'

A few feet away Nell listened, fascinated, pretending to mix a salad dressing.

'But we can't have,' Penny insisted. 'I would have remembered. It's not that I have had so many boyfriends I would forget.'

'Again, Penelope, that is so like you. The honesty. No – how do you say – feminine wiles?'

Nell suppressed a giggle. Feminine wiles were the last thing Penny would use.

'We went out. You and me, and your friend . . .' Nell dropped her whisk when he pointed to her. 'The last time we went to the temple of Apollo in Zanthos.' He suddenly looked almost angry. 'And you had to tell me my own history. How it was Apollo who pulled the sun across the sky in his chariot each day in Greek mythology!'

'I only got that from Moira,' Penny could feel his anguish and wanted to reach out to him. 'She's a classics lecturer now.'

Suddenly the occasion he was describing came vividly back to her. How they had innocently agreed to go to the temple with these two Greek boys, and the boys had just wanted to go to bed with them.

'But that boy was called Christos!' she suddenly remembered, her outraged virtue surfacing almost comically. 'And his friend with Nell was Spiro!'

'I remember him!' Nell piped up, the salad forgotten. 'He thought it was so funny when you talked about gods and goddesses. The only religion he knew was the Orthodox Church, which wouldn't let him near Greek girls, so he thought we English girls were fair game.'

Nikos delved into the pocket of his leathers and produced a crumpled black-and-white photograph.

It was of two young girls, one fair, one dark, the sun setting on the Temple of Apollo behind them, and two Greek boys, each with an arm round them, one pointing sassily towards the camera.

'Oh my God,' Penny breathed. 'It's us!'

She stared at Nikos. 'You're Christos!' she accused. 'Did you make that up because you had a wife and children or something?'

'I was nineteen! Christos is my middle name; I just changed it, that was all.'

'Why on earth did you keep the photo?'

Again he looked at her intently, as if it were crucial she understood.

'Because that moment was important to me. I was ashamed. Ashamed that all we wanted to do was seduce you. Ashamed maybe even more that I was so ignorant of my own culture! I was a working-class kid. My father was a labourer. I wasn't interested in mythology or history, so I never listened at school. I just wanted to leave and get a job and have money in my pocket. But I was an ignorant pig, and suddenly, because of you, I knew it! So I created a new identity. I studied and went to university and turned into Nikos, and eventually I came here.'

'And became the mayor,' Nell congratulated, smiling.

'What did you study?' Penny asked.

Nikos produced a dazzling smile. 'Classical civilization. What else?'

'Well, you'll certainly get on with Moira,' Nell commented.

'Another Greek name,' he replied.

'I thought it was Irish.'

'The Moira were the fates. The ones who decide how long your life should be, and choose the moment of your death.'

'Terrific,' Nell said wryly. 'I'm not sure I'd trust our Moira with that.'

'And you are Helen, whose irresistible beauty was the cause of the Trojan War,' he told Nell. 'And Penelope . . .' He turned to Penny, his eyes fixing on her face. 'Penelope was the wife of Odysseus, who waited ten years for him to return.'

'Don't remind me,' commented Penny, with more bitterness in her voice than Nell had ever heard. 'I'm the long-suffering wife who always does the right thing.'

'Ah, but our other friend is definitely not Greek,' Nell said. 'What is her name?'

'Dora.'

'But is that not short for Pandora?'

Penny nodded.

'Then she was the first human woman. Zeus gave her a box or urn and told her not to open it, but she did, and released all the evil into the world!'

'It's Eve and the apple all over again!' Nell protested angrily, shaking her head at the unfairness of it. 'Women are always blamed for everything bad. Anyway, our Dora's more likely to keep makeup in the box.'

One of the fishermen let out a joyous shout.

'He has finished!' explained Demetria. 'And so have Pavlos and Petros, and Andros and Manoli!'

'Goodness,' Nell grinned. 'I think maybe we'd better have lunch.' She and Demetria began to spread the food out on trestle tables on the beach.

By unspoken agreement, Penny and Nikos stayed behind.

'I would like to ask you about your life,' Nikos stared at her intently. 'Do you have a husband?'

Penny nodded.

'And are you happy with him?'

Penny had no choice but to face the reality of her own heart. 'No.'

'But you are still together?'

She nodded, and he pushed for no further explanation. 'And you have children?'

'A daughter and a son,' she laughed, then added, 'And three grandchildren!' She didn't know if she wanted to ask the next question, but knew she had to. 'And you? Are you married?'

'No.'

The answer was stark in its simplicity. 'I have had relation-ships, many of them, some good, some bad. But not the right one.' He grinned suddenly. 'Don't worry, I didn't wait for you with a broken heart, but somehow I didn't meet the right woman that I wanted to marry.'

'How long have you lived here?'

'Twenty years. I went to university in Athens and lived there afterwards, sometimes travelling to other countries. It wasn't a bad life, but when you come from an island it's hard to live in a city.'

He stared out at the dazzling blue sea, dappled with deeper turquoise, to the perfect straight line of the horizon, as if it somehow held the answer to the question neither of them was asking.

'You are doing a good thing here,' he said, as if wrenching himself back from the unanswerable to manageable reality. 'The island is dying. The young all leave. The Greek economy is shattered. The shipping which once brought wealth to Greece is now international – from Korea, or even Russia.'

It was true, Penny realized; when she was young, people had often talked of Greek shipping millionaires instead of Russian oligarchs.

'The old ways of farming and fishing are too hard for the young people. They want a different life. So we need tourists. Do you think you can make these boathouses attractive?'

'I'll do my best,' Penny smiled.

'Then you are staying in Kyri for a while?' Again his eyes fixed on her face.

'I don't know . . .' she faltered, knowing that she had been avoiding this question. 'Perhaps.'

They looked at each other for a moment in painful silence.

'One thing,' Penny rescued the situation with practicality. 'That man Xan. He said we would need a building permit. Is that true?'

'Not if the house is already lived in.'

'Are the boathouses lived in?' she asked.

'I think you could make that argument. Fishermen do sleep here sometimes.'

'I wonder why he said that?'

'He is trying to make trouble before we decide about his building plan,' said Nikos. 'There will be a public meeting. The olive grove is sacred to some.'

'Especially Ariadne's goats,' Penny laughed. 'Dora says they're in there all the time.'

'I doubt they will be welcome when he builds his mansion.'

'But can't you stop him?'

'It is a difficult question. Many of the olive trees are dead; that is why Yannis sold it to him. Also, we need tourists and he will use local labour to build it. He is being very careful to learn all the regulations. We will see how people feel. Meanwhile, I would be honoured if you came to see my house.' He smiled, a hint of teasing in his light blue eyes. 'Simply to take in the design, which is very similar to these.' He indicated the row of twenty or so boathouses that lined the cliff-side.

'I'd like that.'

'Shall we go now? You can see the possibilities for the other boathouses,' he added, with a smile she found almost irresistible.

Nell watched with interest as Penny followed Nikos along the beachside path and out of sight.

'I'll save you some lunch, then,' Nell murmured ironically. 'Right, Demetria, let's get them all to the table!'

They walked along the path between the boathouses and the sea. A few small boats were moored there, but the fishing boats that were kept here in winter were still in the main harbour. Penny felt the sun beating down on her back, incredibly hot for the time of year, yet Nikos seemed entirely at home in his leathers. He was the kind of man who always seemed at home, it struck Penny. There was a kind of peace about him in spite of – or perhaps because of – the life he'd led alone, without a wife or family.

The next cove was entirely empty apart from a large white building created from a row of boathouses. Penny looked round at the amazing setting. Your own house, right on the beach, with no one to disturb you but the odd sea bird or dolphin.

'Do you ever get dolphins here?' she asked, suddenly shy again now that they were alone.

'All the time. They come right up and dance with joy for you. When the weather is warm like this year, they call it a dolphin spring.'

'Don't you ever get lonely?' she asked.

Penny, who always thought she was a people person and liked being surrounded by neighbours, suddenly felt herself magnetically drawn to silence and the sound of waves.

'Never.' He paused and looked at her. 'At least, not until now.' He took a step towards her, and then as if perhaps remembering the husband, the children and grandchildren, checked himself. 'Besides, I have the bike. And the boat.' Penny almost gasped. Of course – it was the romantic ship they had seen with Takis, the one with the beautiful carved figurehead that made you think of pirates.

'So, Nikos the mayor –' Penny realized she sounded as if she were flirting, and was shocked – 'do you have a bit of pirate in your soul?'

'Why?' His voice was stern, but the expression in his eyes

told another story. 'Do you want to be kidnapped and held for ransom while I have my wicked way with you?'

Penny looked out to sea so that he couldn't see the response that flickered in her eyes.

'That's how they made their money, the French corsairs here on Kyri.'

'Yes,' Penny was grateful for the change of tone. 'Moira was telling us about the pirate who found a statue of Venus that the French king wanted so much, he offered him freedom. And then the king double-crossed him, so he hid it in a cave.'

'She's well informed, your friend. Olivier de Menton. And no one yet has managed to find it. That would certainly put Kyri on the map.' Together they climbed some steps and he opened the front door straight into one large single room, with a balcony hanging right over the sea.

It had the kind of simplicity that could easily have been the work of a smart interior designer, had it not been saved by one or two reassuringly down-to-earth touches. An old door painted bright teal served as the dining table.

'Doesn't your glass of wine fall off the panelling?' Penny asked with a smile.

'Yes,' he said, holding her smile with his eyes. 'But the door came from my parents' house. They didn't have any antiques or pictures, just a portrait of the pope, and as I'm not religious I preferred the door to remind me of them.'

To the left was a wall with shelving, on which were ranged about twenty wooden boats.

'You collect boats, I see.' She smiled again. 'Always good to have a hobby.'

'Thank you,' he replied, laughter in his voice. 'In fact I made them. They are *kaikia*, Greek fishing boats. I make them from driftwood I find on the beach.'

Penny picked up a boat and examined it. It was about a foot long, in driftwood painted duckegg blue with a mast and two sails plus a jib at the front, a proper wheelhouse and a ladder for the imaginary sailors to climb. It was perfect, down to the anchor chain and mooring ropes fashioned out of old string. It was beautiful in its craftsmanship and simplicity.

'I love driftwood,' Nikos explained. 'The idea that it has lived before. Perhaps been a boat already. I hate to see it wasted.'

Penny felt such a powerful answering emotion that she hardly knew what to say. She hated waste with a passion. Colin liked their huge American fridge to be full to bursting, 'in case anyone drops in', as he put it. 'It would be embarrassing not to feed them.' But no one did drop in. And every week she had to throw away mountains of expensive food, or put it in the compost heap.

'I love the idea of living simply.' Nikos stood looking out at the dazzling sea, shading his eyes from the bright sunlight. 'Just fishing and eating what you've caught.' His glint of humour returned. 'Unfortunately I'd miss lamb too much. Cooked on hot charcoal. And hummus. And *spanakopita*. Do you know what they are?'

Spanakopita. It was so recently she'd bought those for everyone in Piraeus, and it seemed a lifetime ago. 'Yes,' she replied, almost overwhelmed. 'I know what *spanakopita* are.'

'I'd forgotten,' he said, his voice suddenly dropping to a hoarse whisper, 'you've been here before.'

And without either of them seeming to move she was in his arms and he was kissing her.

The hungry fishermen descended on Nell's food like wolves on the fold, to paraphrase Lord Byron. Instead of the omnipresent Greek salad, she had tried them out on baba ganoush made of charred aubergine with garlic, lemon and pomegranate seeds. But it was her chicken with sumac and lemon that was the hit of the day. Demetria had to promise six of the fishermen's wives that she would get them the recipe.

'How did you manage to get sumac here?' asked Penny, when she slipped quietly back to join her half an hour later.

'I always pack it. What have you done with your mayor?' Nell asked, trying not to smirk.

'He isn't my mayor,' Penny replied quickly.

'No, of course, only teasing. Sumac is always useful.' She delved into her handbag. 'As a matter of fact, I take it everywhere. You can't cook Ottolenghi without sumac.'

Penny began to laugh. 'Nell, you are funny.'

'Excuse me,' corrected Nell. 'But aren't you the girl who packs PG Tips in her suitcase?'

'That's different.'

'And a travel kettle,' Nell pushed home the point. 'And walks miles to get fresh milk?'

'The day needs to start with a proper cup of tea,' Penny replied.

Nikos had now appeared and seemed to be deliberately avoiding Penny and talking to all the fishermen instead. Clear evidence of guilt, in Nell's opinion. She remembered it from office parties. You snogged your colleague in the stationery cupboard, and then pretended not to know each other so no one would guess. But everyone knew anyway.

Eventually he'd worked his way round the assembled gathering and very casually joined them. Nell studied him in this new light. He was certainly a very attractive man, especially compared to Charmless Colin.

Penny had managed to salvage a small piece of chicken with accompanying salad, pine nuts and a few ruby-coloured pomegranate seeds.

'Be careful eating those,' Nikos counselled. The flirtatious spark was back, whether he knew it or not. 'Remember what happened to Persephone.'

'What did happen to Persephone?' Penny asked, faintly ashamed that she only knew the name as the publisher of beautiful books at home.

'Hades, the god of the underworld, kidnapped her. She could only be rescued if she hadn't eaten or drunk anything while she was down there. Unfortunately he tricked her into eating six pomegranate seeds. That meant she had to go back down to the underworld for six months of every year, and only return to earth for the other six. That's why we have winter and summer.'

'So if I ate these seeds, I might not be able to go home and would have to stay here for six months?' Penny asked, her eyes on his.

'That could be one interpretation.'

Still looking at him, she slowly ate them.

Nell looked away, taken by surprise at Penny's behaviour and feeling she was witnessing something both strangely erotic and intensely private.

'Right,' she announced crisply. 'Time I cleared away these dishes and let you get on with the painting.'

By the end of the afternoon everyone was exhausted, but the boathouse doors were all painted in an array of glorious colours from bright red to turquoise, primrose yellow, Greek blue and orange, with the shutters and balconies of the floors above painted to match. Only the one owned by Demetria and her husband dared to stand out, with lime green doors and tangerine balcony and shutters.

Standing on the furthest point of the jetty, Penny stood back to take photographs. They looked amazing.

'Now all we need is to furnish them,' Penny said, trying not to feel too daunted. 'And where on earth are we going to find the furniture?'

'Have a word with Takis,' Nikos counselled. 'He's the best fixer on the island.'

'I must go,' Penny announced, seeming suddenly to lose her new-found nerve.

'Yes,' Nikos sighed, as if he entirely understood the depth of her dilemma. It was so amazing, Penny thought wonderingly, how this man could be so different from the one she'd spent the last thirty years with.

'You must be exhausted,' Nell remarked as the last ladder was stowed and they headed back to their hotel.

'Yes,' replied Penny.

'You've done a really good job.'

'Have I?' she answered quietly, and Nell knew she wasn't just talking about the painting. They were due to fly home from Athens in a few days. Would Penny be coming or not?

And Nell realized something quite mysterious, magical even, about Kyri.

The place was beginning to seem more real and vivid than home.

When they got back to the hotel, Dora was sitting on a bright turquoise sofa in the reception area deep in conversation with a rather elegant-looking woman whose back was towards Penny and Nell.

'How did it go, girls? Are your boathouses ready to photograph?' Dora asked.

'The exteriors are looking brilliant.' Penny held out her phone to show the photos. 'But we've still got to furnish the interiors.' She expected Dora to say, 'How the hell are we going to do that when we're just leaving?' But Dora didn't.

Penny was just about to ask who the newcomer was when she turned round.

'Look who's back on her feet!' Dora winked at them broadly.

'Moira!' Nell gasped, surveying the new-look Moira. She was wearing a smart black dress, and her bird's nest had been tamed and cut into a loose, shiny bob. It was little short of a miracle. 'If this is what your bug did for you, I'll come down with it too!'

'Actually,' Moira smiled, 'it's all down to Eleni, the doctor's wife. She used to be a hairdresser. She's obviously dead bored, and decided to do a makeover on me!'

'Well, it certainly worked,' Penny marvelled.

'And I've been doing lots of thinking while I was ill.'

'Right . . .' Penny and Nell chorused nervously.

'Pirates!' Moira exclaimed. 'This place doesn't make nearly enough of its piratical history. I think there should be pirate cruises, and I'm going to talk Takis into turning the beach bar into a venue called Treasure Island. It's only for a while. Just a gimmick to get some of the boat trips from Santorini to stop here and give the island some business. We can mix cocktails called Black Dog, Long John Silver and Billy Bones.'

'I wouldn't advise one called Black Spot,' Dora grinned. 'As far as I remember, that means certain death.'

'That'll go down really well, then!' Moira insisted. 'Nell, you can do the food,' she offered graciously.

Dora looked round at them as if they were mad. 'Apart from the fact you don't like alcohol . . .' she began. 'And we're going home,' she added without any conviction.

'Don't worry about that,' Moira interrupted gaily. 'Eleni's won me over with this amazing dry red from the central valley.'

'Get her,' Nell teased. 'Moira O'Reilly, wine buff.'

'Good God, this Eleni's only had you for a few days and she's turned you into a lush!'

'Actually, I think it did me more good than the antibiotics.'

'I didn't think you could drink on antibiotics,' Penny remarked.

'The doctor said that was nonsense. Maybe it's a Greek view.'

'As I was saying,' Dora continued more forcefully. 'Has everyone forgotten we're flying back soon?'

'I'm not,' announced Penny. There, she'd said it.

'I might not either,' endorsed Nell. 'I mean, I'm retired, so no one cares what I do.'

'Moira? Surely you have to get back to college.'

Moira looked round for Takis to order a drink. 'Oh, didn't I tell you? The college won't offer me another contract at my age. Lots of dons are up in arms about it, but do you know, since we got here I've been thinking, Kyri's a lot more fun than Cambridge.'

'Well, I have to be back,' Dora said grandly. 'Obviously.' For one split second she thought of admitting that Venus Green, singer and reality TV star, had dumped her after all she'd done for the bloody girl, but instantly thought better of it. Her world was so different to theirs. She needed the excitement of getting her clients onto magazine covers, even if they were tacky ones. Venus, on the other hand, thought she ought to be on the cover of *Vogue* and *Cosmopolitan*.

Moira spotted Takis scuttling through the reception area as though he was trying to hide from someone. She looked round for who this might be and spotted the louche, elegant figure of Xan Georgiades approaching the front of the hotel just as Takis dipped down behind the desk.

Xan glanced irritably round the room and, seeing no sign of Takis, approached them instead. 'Hello, ladies. I hear you're taking the island by storm.' His tone, aiming for jovial friendliness, still only managed to sound patronizing and vaguely unpleasant. 'It'll take quite a lot to turn Kyri into St Tropez.'

'Indeed,' Moira matched his tone. 'Which is why we're not aiming for anything so bloody ridiculous.'

Stung, he looked round again. 'Have you seen the owner, by any chance?'

'Out,' replied Moira firmly, swinging her new bob dismissively. 'He mentioned something about going to the beach bar.'

'Right. I'll go and look there. If he does reappear, can you tell him I'm looking for him? He's got my number.'

'Certainly.' Moira assumed all the authority of a Cambridge classics don. 'Now, if you don't mind, we were having a private conversation.'

The others tried not to laugh as Xan strode crossly out and Takis popped up like Mr Punch from behind the reception desk. '*Efharisto, kyria Moira!*'

'What does he want with you so urgently, anyway?' Moira enquired, glad that he was feeling grateful so she could bend his ear over her Treasure Island bar concept.

'The meeting tomorrow. About the olive grove. He wants me to argue that it's a good thing to build his house there.'

'And do you agree?'

'No, but I am in a difficult position. He says I shouldn't be deciding at all because I don't want his house near my bar.'

'Is that why you oppose it?' Moira enquired.

'Of course not. There are no customers for the bar anyway. I just like to see the olive grove there, where it has always been. And . . .' He hesitated. 'Let's face it. I can't stand the man. Now, let me buy you ladies a drink to thank you for covering up.'

'Well,' Nell said, chinking her glass against everyone else's, 'it sounds like we're in for some drama at this meeting tomorrow.'

Her phone beeped in her handbag, and she reached down for it. Amazingly, Willow had actually sent her a video. She pressed the arrow, and her delightful granddaughter Naomi walked towards her on hesitant, chubby little legs. These must be her first steps! A feeling of longing as powerful as any she'd ever felt suddenly swamped her. How she wanted to hold Naomi in her arms.

'Isn't she gorgeous,' chorused the others, gathering round to watch too.

Naomi turned, smiled directly into the camera, and began to wobble. A pair of thin, tanned arms with enough clanking silver chains to start a jeweller's shop instantly picked her up. 'Come to Marigold!' boomed out from off camera.

'Remind me who Marigold is?' Moira asked. 'Apart from rubber washing-up gloves.'

'The Other Granny,' whispered Penny. 'Though she doesn't like being called a grandmother, apparently. It's too ageing. Nell's got a bit of an obsession with her.' Penny began to feel suddenly exhausted. 'I need a shower before we eat. Shall we meet outside in an hour?'

Moira stood up decisively. 'I'm going to get a map and work out where everything is on the island.' She picked one up from the reception desk and strode into the pearly evening light.

The beach bar she wanted to turn into Treasure Island was along the coast to the left. It looked like you could walk there in about twenty minutes. It would be a lot quicker by boat, of course. The famous boathouses were on the north coast, facing the southern part of the Aegean. The caves she wanted to explore, where Olivier de Menton had hidden his booty, were at the far tip of the island next to the narrow channel to Ximonos, the tiny island which had probably once been part of Kyri. Beyond that was the luxurious White Hotel, which she'd read about in *Condé Nast Traveller* and whose prices she could never aspire to. It mainly catered to yachties dropping in for mojitos and to use the spa, or minor celebrities who thought they needed to escape their public.

As soon as Penny unlocked her room, she pounced on her phone. There was a message to call Wendy.

She sat on the bed and dialled the number.

'Hello darling, how are you?' Her daughter had a nice, ordinary husband and two nice ordinary children; Penny viewed both of these things as major triumphs.

'I'm fine. More to the point, how are *you*? I thought we'd have heard from you. You haven't run off with some hunky fisherman like in *Shirley Valentine*, have you?'

There was an infinitesimal pause from Penny. 'Fishermen aren't really up my street.'

'Me neither. And the Greek guy was really Tom Conti anyway. So what have you been up to on this tiny island?'

'Trying to help them put it on the tourist map a bit. How's Dad? Is he getting on all right?'

'For goodness' sake, Mum.' Wendy took up her usual argument. 'You do far too much for him. If he had an account at Harrods deli counter he'd never even notice you'd gone!'

As it happened, for once Wendy was wrong. Colin had certainly noticed Penny's absence. He had expected her to answer immediately when he called but she hadn't done so. Not only had he run out of food and clean shirts, but everywhere he went people kept on asking him where Penny was, as if *she* were the interesting one instead of him.

He stood in front of the mirror in their dressing room, looking at himself. OK, his hair was grey and receding, but he was convinced he still had an air about him.

No one would suspect he had started life in Dagenham, a joke of a place. He had done well in life, and in his view Penny had made zero contribution. She'd never earned a penny since they'd been married, she had no style and she wasn't even a very good cook. He could have done a lot better. She should be grateful enough not go buggering off to Greece with three women he hardly knew, even if they had been bosom buddies at college.

Colin wasn't just feeling grumpy, he was beginning to feel angry. So angry that his major pleasure at the moment was working out the ways that he was going to make Penny feel it when she got back.

The meeting was scheduled for six o'clock the next evening in the village square, which in point of fact was simply a large indentation in the harbourside. Dora walked along to the office for one of the ferry companies and booked her ticket back to Athens. She still found it hard to accept that she would be going alone. She then climbed up the steep hill behind the village towards the beach bar and its private cove. This was one aspect of the holiday she was really going to miss. She'd come to regard it as her own private beach, which was very nice for her if not so good for the island's tourism.

There was no sign of Ariadne to make her cappuccino, which she tried not to be irritated by; but like the princess and the pea, it was definitely spoiling the perfect morning she'd planned. She looked out at the little beach with its soft white sand and turquoise sea, sparkling and rippling in the sunlight. It was so clear that she'd almost considered snorkelling, but that would have meant getting her hair wet so she'd contented herself with hunting for shells. In half an hour she had quite a hoard of blue whelks, purple and green sea urchin shells, a small conch striped like a jungle animal and, most beautiful of all, a scallop shell just like the one Botticelli painted of Venus rising from the foam. Venus, bloody Venus; why did that name follow her around?

Her desire for a cappuccino was becoming impossible to ignore, so she piled her shells onto her towel and went off in search of Ariadne.

She had only just set foot in the olive grove when Juno the goat spotted her and danced – there was no other word for it – towards her over the dry earth dotted with occasional fallen olives. If Juno was here, Ariadne wouldn't be far away.

She found the girl sitting on the curious stone bench outside the cabin, her eyes closed as if she were sleeping or sunbathing like a lizard.

'Hello Ariadne,' Dora greeted her. 'Are you having a little doze?' She suspected Cassandra kept the girl working pretty hard.

Ariadne opened her dark eyes, a little like olives themselves. It struck Dora how ridiculous the expression 'olive skin' was, when olives were usually either green or almost black. 'I was breathing in the myrtle. Can't you smell it? It's very strong today.'

Dora sniffed loudly. There it was again, the mystifying but unmistakable aroma of that bloody blossom! She looked around. There were no flowers at all, let alone the imaginary cliff roses Xan Georgiades had tried to fob her off with, and certainly no myrtle.

'The goddess is angrier than usual.' Ariadne pointed at the furrows in the ground near them. 'She has been digging. All the earth is disturbed. It is as if she was looking for something.'

Dora couldn't imagine goddesses, especially Aphrodite, scrabbling around in the earth. Oh for goodness' sake, what was she thinking? Goddesses didn't exist in the modern world – had never existed, in fact. They were a fiction used by people to try and make sense of a scary and uncertain world. She glanced nervously over her shoulder at the cabin. She didn't want to be accused of trespassing by the owner the day before the meeting.

Quite suddenly, the scent disappeared.

'She has gone now,' Ariadne announced. 'I will come back later and see if I can help her.'

'Absolutely. I'm sure she'll be pleased. But do you think for now, you could make me a cappuccino?'

As they walked back down to the beach, Juno the goat trying at every step to join in the conversation, Dora could sense that Ariadne was genuinely unhappy. She didn't have much to do with young people but she could tell from the girl's listless demeanour and the dark smudges under her rather lovely eyes that all was not well.

'Is something worrying you? You can tell me. I'm not your father or grandmother.'

'I don't want to be stuck on this island any longer!' Ariadne declared passionately. 'I want to learn things! My father is all right, but he's under his mother's thumb, which is sad at his age. Could you try and persuade him? Maybe I could come to England and stay with you?'

There was so much sudden hope in her voice that Dora, who didn't even want the responsibility of a cat, was oddly

111

moved and found herself saying, 'I will talk to your father and grandmother. Try and persuade them.'

Ariadne launched herself at Dora and hugged her. 'Thank you! You are very kind and good.'

Dora felt she could take the credit for neither of these qualities. If she wasn't careful, she'd end up with a fifteen-year-old Greek girl coming to stay with her in London.

Seven

So many people turned up for the meeting to decide the fate of the olive grove that they spilled out from the village square on the harbourside into the cafes along the quay.

There was a table at the front with various officials ranged behind it and Nikos, dressed for the occasion in a smart suit and white shirt, officiating. Penny, watching from the back, couldn't help thinking how he seemed to emanate natural authority without even needing to speak loudly.

'Good evening, friends,' Nikos began. 'To begin with, I have asked anyone who has a serious objection to stand up and make their point. After that, Mr Georgiades will explain why he thinks the project should go ahead.' He spoke in Greek, but Cassandra was standing close enough to translate for Penny and the others.

Deep silence fell on the crowd as everyone looked round to see who would be brave enough to speak out. It almost looked as if no one was going to oppose the scheme.

Finally it fell to Takis to be brave and stand up. 'I oppose the scheme,' he announced. 'I know this means I cannot be any longer on the planning committee because I will be seen as prejudiced and so, Nikos, I give you my resignation now.'

There was a murmur in the crowd but Penny couldn't tell whether it was approval or disapproval.

'This olive grove has been part of Kyri as long as anyone can remember, providing a living for Yannis before he got too old to harvest the olives. If Mr Georgiades builds his house, part of the grove will go forever. What was a living for a poor man will be a luxury for a rich one. Surely this is wrong, my friends?'

A number of people turned to each other and nodded, and a soft chorus of agreement began.

Nikos raised a hand. 'Mr Georgiades, you have heard a significant objection. What would you like to tell us in reply?'

Xan Georgiades got to his feet. He had no sign of nerves and was clearly a practised speaker.

'First of all, I have followed every regulation to the letter. My house will not be within thirty metres of the beach. My lawyer has been authorized by the public notary. I have proved there was a dwelling there before 1923; I have employed a *mechanikos politikos*, a specially approved civil engineer to advise me . . .' Now his voice was becoming shrill with anger. 'And above all, I am building a beautiful house, a house the village can be proud of.'

'If you like big boxes,' heckled someone from the back.

Georgiades smiled. 'All Greek houses are essentially cubes, mine is just a larger cube. And I will build it entirely from local materials. And more importantly, with local labour.'

'No bloody foreigners,' added another heckler in the audience.

'Or thieves from Santorini!' seconded another. 'You could build a house in Athens for what those villains charge you!'

'And our friend Takis – who is making such a noble gesture

by resigning – talks of losing a harvest of olives big enough to be a man's living. But most of the olive trees are dead and the others dying, that is why Yannis sold it.'

Now the nodding and murmuring was definitely in agreement.

'He's winning them over,' Penny said anxiously. 'The meeting's starting to go his way.'

'What is more, the noble Takis has another motive,' Georgiades went on, taking advantage of the turn in the tide. 'He doesn't want my house on top of his bar because the work will disrupt his business. Or maybe he has plans to sell his bar – a bar with no customers – to some developer. I ask you, friends, would it not be better to let me build my house and swimming pool as a community facility which people from the village can come and use?'

This was a definite hit, especially among the mothers with children.

'Like hell he will,' Dora threw in, not even attempting to lower her voice. 'Our neighbour in Wembley promised that till he got his planning permission, and then he told everyone to get lost!'

'So, I ask you, friends – you are in need of tourism,' Georgiades continued. 'When my house is completed I have plans to spend much more time here and open a beach club somewhere on the island. That will attract plenty of tourists. Does anyone have a proper objection to me building my house?'

At the very back of the crowd, a disembodied voice shouted: 'The goddess Aphrodite does!'

Everyone turned, and a passage opened up like the parting of the Red Sea to reveal Ariadne full of angry confidence. 'The grove is sacred to the goddess and she is very angry at your blasphemy.'

Xan's response was to start laughing. Soon others in the crowd started to echo him.

'Poor girl,' sympathized Dora, 'she's only fifteen.'

'Aren't you're the daughter of our hero Takis?' Xan sneered. 'No doubt you want to keep your job working for him.'

'No, she doesn't.' This time Dora got to her feet to intervene. 'Ariadne is a clever girl. She doesn't want to work in a bar or at the hotel. She wants to go to university and study plants!'

Xan ignored her. 'So how do you know the goddess is angry with me?' he asked rudely. 'More imaginary scent of myrtle?'

'Because she left this!' Ariadne drew a perfectly carved marble hand holding an apple from her sleeve, where she'd been hiding it.

'Oh my God!' breathed Penny.

'Maybe it's all true,' Moira endorsed, hardly able to contain her excitement, 'about Olivier de Menton's Venus!'

Xan Georgiades shook his head dismissively. 'This is Greece. There are bits of statue in every farmer's field. Anyway, how we do know she didn't plant it there?'

A snigger at the back of the crowd swelled into a laugh like an aural Mexican wave until almost everyone was doubled up at the idea of little Ariadne, a village girl, finding and deliberately planting a marble hand in a field to thwart this posh Athenian's holiday home.

'He's lost them,' grinned Dora.

'Enough, enough now, *arketa, arketa.*' Nikos rose to his feet. 'Thank you, my friends. I think we must look into the mystery of this marble hand. We will postpone the decision for tonight at least.'

Xan glared at Ariadne and tried to grab the hand from her. 'Where did you get this anyway?'

Ariadne stood her ground and hung onto the carving.

'Who do you think you are?' he demanded. 'Some kind of sibyl at the Delphic Oracle? You're just a stupid little girl!'

'Thank you, Mr Rich Athenian,' Takis intervened. 'As we've already heard, she's a very intelligent young woman.' He put his arm round his daughter and shepherded her towards the hotel.

'But this is all so exciting!' Moira was already making mental plans. 'What if it really is part of the lost statue of Venus? Finding that would really put Kyri on the map! It would be the Venus de Milo all over again! This calls for a drink!'

'I think we'd better keep an eye on Moira and the retsina,' Dora winked at Nell. 'They do say converts are the worst.'

They made their way through the crowd to their usual table outside the hotel.

Moira was looking pensive. 'The thing is,' she said excitedly, 'I'm pretty sure I've seen an artist's impression of the statue, more of a sketch actually, probably done by the French king's envoy. I'll go to Eleni's tomorrow and try to find it. It was in the doctor's library somewhere.'

'It's great to see you back to normal,' Penny smiled.

'You mean, being ill might stop me boring you with classical allusions?' Moira grinned back.

They all laughed.

Moira suddenly leaned forward. 'Dora, how can you think of going back now? I know you're this big important person in PR. Even I have read about that singer – what was her name?' she appealed to them.

'Venus Green,' Penny supplied. 'She won that *Make Me a Star* programme. My daughter Wendy and I were addicted. Colin said it was a load of old rubbish. Dora is her mentor.'

Moira laughed. 'How could I forget someone called Venus, of all things?'

This time the temptation to come clean was almost irresistible. All at once, she felt she could trust these women. Maybe because they were so outside her world; but there was also something more, something shared that she wasn't used to feeling.

Before she could speak, a small, anxious figure launched itself out of the bar, almost making her fall off her chair.

'*Kyria* Dora, my father has just told me. You are leaving Kyri and going back to *Anglia*! Please, please do not go! You are the only one who believes *I* can do more than look after stupid goats and make coffee!'

Dora got up and put her arm round Ariadne. She looked round at the others. 'The truth is, Venus Green has fired me and gone to a rival agency. The PR world will have been gossiping about little else. To be brutally honest, that was the main reason I came.'

There was a pause while they absorbed this information.

Moira was the first to speak. 'Then there's every reason why you should stay on,' she announced briskly. 'Screw the lot of them.' The others looked at Moira in surprise. She and Dora hadn't seemed to get on at all. 'You can help put Kyri on the tourist map. And we'll need your PR skills if we find the statue. By the way, Ariadne – what have you done with that hand?' Moira glanced round to make sure no one else was listening.

'My father locked it somewhere safe.'

'Excellent. I can't wait to look for that sketch. What time is it?'

'After ten,' Nell replied. 'Don't you have a watch?'

'Never believed in them. I wonder, is it too late to go round to the doctor's . . . ?'

'Yes, unless it's a matter of life and death,' grinned Penny.

'To quote Bill Shankly about football, which my father did all the time,' Moira replied, 'it's much more serious than that.'

'Who the hell is Bill Shankly?' Dora asked, increasingly bewildered.

'Manager of Liverpool FC,' Moira supplied.

'Ah.'

'So that's settled, then,' Moira sailed on gaily. 'You're much better off on a tiny Greek island till this girl realizes her mistake, or the waters settle in the exciting world of PR and they start to bitch about someone else.'

Ariadne was still by her side, looking imploringly up at her unlikely heroine.

'It seems it's all been organized,' Dora conceded. 'Yes, Ariadne, I will stay on Kyri and not go to home to *Anglia*.'

Before Dora knew it, Ariadne had flung herself into her arms.

The others watched as Dora patted the girl ineffectually, unused to any sign of genuine affection.

Ariadne looked up to Dora's superior height. 'Juno will be very pleased too.'

Dora glanced round at her old friends, feeling suddenly light-headed and possibly even happy. 'There you are,' she said with a smile. 'I'm only doing it to keep the goat smiling.'

The doctor was only too thrilled next morning to offer Moira the services of his library. He was fanatical about local history, and it made a pleasant change from the daily rounds of his patients.

The trouble was, Moira couldn't remember which book she'd seen it in and they ended up taking down every volume in the place.

Improbably, it turned out to be in a modern guidebook to

the Cyclades. Almost bursting with excitement, she took it back to the hotel to show the others.

'How funny,' remarked Dora. 'I read the reviews to that guide and they said don't buy this book, it's full of boring history and doesn't tell you about any good bars and restaurants.'

'Excellent,' said Moira. 'The fewer people who read it and come across the sketch, the better.'

They opened the page with the rudimentary line drawing. It was of a beautiful young woman with bare breasts, draped in exquisitely carved folds of linen, reclining on a couch and holding an apple. Even from the rough drawing, it was possible to tell that this was no ordinary statue.

Nell stared at the hand with the apple. 'It's hard to tell, but the hand did seem to look the same as that. The fingers were slightly splayed in the same way, don't you think?'

'I can't honestly remember,' Dora shrugged. 'I was so surprised by Ariadne's outburst. She's a shy little thing except when she's talking about plants.'

'I wish Professor Brinkley were here,' Moira sighed. 'He's head of classical antiquity at one of the museums in Cambridge. He lives and breathes this stuff.'

'Get him out here, then!' Dora giggled. 'The more the merrier! Takis will be thrilled to fill up his hotel rooms with distinguished professors.'

'Do you know what,' Moira beamed, 'I think I'll try.' She photographed the sketch on her phone. 'I just need a shot of the hand with the apple too. If nothing else, he can give us some advice on whether it could be authentic or not.'

They made their way back to the hotel, where Penny had stayed to talk to Takis about furniture for the boathouses.

'What kind of furniture do you want?' he asked.

'Anything I can paint, from old doors to washstands. Chests

of drawers, screens, bookcases; really anything people don't want to use any more.'

Takis nodded and tapped the side of his nose as if they were striking some illicit deal. 'I will see what I can do.'

'Takis, great! There's just one more thing.' Moira descended on him so enthusiastically that he instantly looked worried. What was this forceful English lady going to ask of him now?

'I just wanted to photograph the marble hand and apple Ariadne discovered.'

'Ah,' Takis began to look relieved. 'But be careful. I have heard a rumour that Mr Rich Athenian has been to the police to say that it belongs to him, as it was found on his land.'

'And does it?'

'Nikos insisted the Department of Cultural Antiquities be informed, so he has not been allowed to pursue his claim. In fact —' he smiled impishly — 'Nikos also said that if a statue was likely to be buried on his land, he might not be able to build on it until the matter was investigated further.'

'Do you know,' Moira beamed, 'I like this Nikos more and more. Did you say that you two met when we were here before?' she asked Penny.

Penny tossed her hair in a gesture of involuntary shyness that gave away far more than she intended. 'Yes. Nell and I went out with him and his friend when we were all in Zanthos. He'd kept a photo of us.'

'Had he indeed?' Moira surveyed her, a smile just starting at the corners of her mouth. 'I wonder why he did that for all these years.'

Nell, who had a very good idea why, came to her rescue. 'Penny and I made quite an impression on him. We were so scathing about his ignorance of mythology that he decided to go to university just to show us.'

121

'Goodness!' Moira was impressed. 'What a wonderful story. And here you are wandering right back into his life so he can demonstrate his knowledge!'

'Of course, there was also the small matter of them trying to go to bed with us,' Nell added, offhand.

'Oh well, I suppose that's something that won't happen this time,' commented Moira tactlessly.

As if to rescue the situation Penny's phone began to ring and she bent to get it, looking flushed.

It was Colin – no doubt to voice some complaint about the milk being off, or the dishwasher needing to be emptied. 'It's only my husband,' she informed her friends, with a smile none of them had seen before.

And she took great pleasure in letting it go to voicemail again.

'Penny! Penny!' Nell's voice penetrated her surprisingly peaceful sleep – possibly encouraged by the fact that she hadn't listened to Colin's voicemail.

Penny dragged herself out of the exceptionally comfortable bed and threw open the shutters, forgetting that she had been so hot in the night she'd discarded her schoolgirl nightie and wore only a pair of white bikini briefs.

An amazing sight awaited her. Just to the side of the hotel, near the entrance to its small car park, a vast bonfire-sized pile of furniture had appeared.

'My God, look at that!' Nell marvelled. 'Takis must have gone round ringing a bell like a rag and bone man to have got all that so quickly.'

Various people, Nikos included, were gathered on the quay nursing cups of strong Greek coffee, surveying the heap. Penny waved. He looked up and smiled a slow, sexy smile.

Penny, suddenly conscious that she was half-naked, ducked behind the shutters.

Ten minutes later, she was standing next to him. 'Sorry about that,' she murmured.

'Please,' Nikos grinned. 'No apologies. We are Greek. The female form is high art to us.'

'Ah, I see,' Penny replied, with mock modesty, 'that's why you wanted to get my clothes off all those years ago in Zanthos.'

Nikos bowed. 'I apologize for my uncouth behaviour.'

She was about to say 'Pity. I was rather hoping you'd repeat it,' when there was a shout from the glamorous Demetria, who'd been so helpful with the stripping and painting of the boathouse doors. 'Penelope! Come and see these things. Some of it is quite good.'

Penny, now in jeans and sweatshirt, joined Demetria. Takis had been even better than his word: there was furniture from cottages, farmhouses and even, by the look of it, a monastery. Amateur though she might be, Penny had developed an excellent eye at jumble sales, bric-a-brac shops and the occasional country auction. She could instantly see what could be salvaged, painted and turned into an attractive item versus what should go straight to the tip.

They had soon divided the pile into two distinct sections.

'I suppose the best place to paint would be in one of the empty boathouses.'

'My husband will take the things there for you. He has a pick-up truck,' offered Demetria.

'It will be a lot of journeys in a pick-up. Are you sure?' Penny asked

'He will do what he is told,' Demetria smiled.

Penny smiled back. She couldn't imagine a marriage where the woman had the power. If she hadn't been stupid enough to

123

give up work and be dependent on Colin, maybe their relationship would have been different. On the other hand, she'd seen plenty of situations where the wife contributed nothing but was still in charge.

What she really longed for was a relationship where there was some kind of equality. A bit late in the day to be thinking about that.

She looked up to find that Nikos had started to help Demetria's husband load up the stuff, and she somehow felt unbearably moved. She hadn't even needed to ask him.

She was smiling her thanks when her phone began to ring, insistently this time so that each time she switched it off it just started again. Naturally it was Colin.

She stepped away from Nikos and the others to speak to him.

'What the hell do you mean, not answering your phone?' was his affectionate conjugal greeting.

'I was in the middle of something,' Penny answered calmly. She wasn't going to let him get to her.

'When do you get home tomorrow? Knowing your inefficiency it'll probably be in the middle of the night. Don't think I'm coming to bloody Gatwick to get you.'

Penny felt her blood pressure rising and fought it. 'As a matter of fact,' she replied, 'I'm not coming home tomorrow. I've decided to stay on here for a bit.'

'What the hell do you mean? When *are* you bloody coming back?'

'I'm not sure.'

She could see Nikos watching her, as if he'd guessed who the call was from.

'What do you mean, you're not sure?' Colin demanded aggressively.

Why hadn't she noticed what a bully he was? It had taken being two thousand miles away from him to finally see it.

'It depends on how long I go on enjoying myself and feeling useful here,' she replied calmly.

'Useful? You're no bloody use to anyone.'

Nikos was smiling at her now, as if to encourage her, and somehow it worked. 'In that case you won't miss me, will you?'

'Have you lost your mind?'

'I think maybe I'm just beginning to find it. Now I'm afraid I can't talk any longer. Someone's waiting for me.' And she put the phone down.

She had never put the phone down on Colin in their entire marriage. It felt wonderful.

Of course he would get straight on the phone to Wendy, but thank God, Wendy wouldn't listen. So he'd go down to the pub or the golf club, where the entry requirements were being a misogynist and a bore, and moan to the other misogynists about what a shower women were.

Meanwhile she was on a beautiful Greek island with an attractive, apparently kind man smiling at her. Her mother would warn her that it would end in tears, and maybe it would. But her mother was dead, and for the first time she could remember, Penny felt very much alive.

'Have you noticed what's happening to Penny?' Moira murmured to Nell at breakfast the next day.

'No,' replied Nell, trying to resist looking at her phone and seeing the latest update from Marigold the non-Granny. 'What?'

'You must have noticed. She looks like the first humans must have done when Prometheus brought them fire. Amazed and excited and also a bit frightened.'

Maeve Haran

'Moira, what are you talking about?' Nell enquired crossly.

'Not another bloody cultural reference, Moira!' Dora stopped filling her plate, which already held enough fresh fruit to feed six guests. 'Have you still not twigged that we know nothing about Greek myths and care less?'

'That's a bit harsh,' Nell corrected. 'I got grade one in my Latin O-level.'

They looked over at Penny, who was standing on the quay looking dreamily out to sea.

'She's falling in love with Nikos,' Moira clarified. 'God, my college says I lack empathy with my students, but I've got a damn sight more than you two!'

'Don't be ridiculous,' Nell replied. 'She's been married to Colin for thirty years.'

'Maybe it's thirty years too long.'

Penny turned at that moment and gave them a dazzling smile. Without the hideous hairband she had stopped looking like a gauche schoolgirl; in fact, there were distinct blonde streaks in her hair from the sun, and a sprinkle of attractive freckles had begun to appear on her nose.

'It's true, she is different,' Dora agreed. She looked at Nell to see what she thought, but Nell was rummaging in her bag. 'Come on, Nell, put away the EnvyGram and think about Penny. Do you think she's fallen for Nikos?'

At that moment, Takis wandered out of the hotel's reception with the mayor a step or two behind him. Penny's whole demeanour instantly changed, as if a lightbulb had been turned on inside her. And the most telling thing was that she didn't even know.

They all stared, with varying degrees of discretion, at Nikos. He walked straight over to Penny. 'How's the furniture transformation going?'

'We're only really starting this morning,' Penny replied. 'What will happen now with the olive grove?'

'The Department will want to come and have a look. Mr Georgiades is livid. He has even offered for us to go and dig it up ourselves to prove there is no statue there.'

'It's funny,' Moira whispered, watching Penny and Nikos. 'They're talking about furniture when they really want to talk about sex.'

'Moira!' Nell and Dora chorused.

'Don't be such prudes! You're in the country of Eros, the god of sexual attraction! If he shoots an arrow at you, you have no choice but to succumb.'

'Well, I hope Eros keeps his arrows in his quiver, especially where I'm concerned,' Nell said firmly.

'Oh, I don't know.' Dora looked across at Takis, who was rearranging the tables and chairs on the hotel terrace. 'Our host here has rather a taking twinkle, don't you think?'

A little later Penny joined them, still glowing from her encounter with Nikos.

'I forgot to show you,' Moira suddenly said. 'With so much going on.' She winked at the other two. 'Here's the drawing from the doctor's library.'

There it was: the statue of Venus, reclining on a couch, holding the golden apple in her hand. Penny looked at it intently while Dora studied it over her shoulder, then had the sudden brainwave to photograph it on her phone.

'It's very beautiful,' she said. 'You can tell the quality of the workmanship even in this basic drawing. No wonder the king wanted it.'

Not only was it beautiful, Dora couldn't help thinking, but there was also something vaguely familiar about it that had nothing to do with the hand holding the apple.

Perhaps she'd seen a copy of it in a museum somewhere. The only thing was, Dora wasn't really one for museums. The only Venus in her life had been all too real, the little bitch. Dora put her phone away, trying not to think about Venus Green, who she had probably become much too fond of, and who was now being represented by Dora's greatest rival.

Eight

Penny began the furniture restoration with a chest of drawers, standing at the front of the room so that the rest of the helpers could see how she did it.

She'd chosen an attractive piece with two small top drawers and two large ones, with simple round handles, on charming curvy legs which gave it a slightly French look, like a saucy can-can dancer.

The hearts of the helpers seemed to plummet a little when she produced more sandpaper after the marathon session sanding the boathouse doors.

'Don't worry! You only need to sand a little bit and then you can use this! My secret weapon!' Demetria translated with much emphasis and many hand gestures. Penny produced three bright yellow cans shaped like outsize lighter fuel containers, proclaiming that they were 'LIQUID SANDER – replaces sandpaper'. The message was clearly getting through as they started to clap.

The tins, rather scarily, boasted a large skull and crossbones and the message POISON: FLAMMABLE. 'Be careful how you use them,' Penny warned. 'They're pretty stinky, so can someone go and open the boathouse door?'

One of the women pushed the newly painted red door wide open to find all their menfolk were standing staring outside, as if they wanted to know what was happening but somehow felt this was women's work.

'Off to the *kafenion*, the lot of you!' shouted Demetria. She turned back to the assembled women and pointed at the liquid. 'Useless lot! If any of you wants to get rid of your husband, put it in their ouzo and they probably wouldn't notice the difference.'

The audience began to cackle as Penny, wearing rubber gloves, opened the tins and distributed paint brushes.

'Where on earth did you get that?' Nell enquired. 'Surely you didn't pop that in your suitcase along with the PG Tips, just in case liquid sander was useful on your Greek beach break?'

Penny looked faintly embarrassed. 'Nikos got it for me. He does quite a lot of DIY, apparently.'

'Really?' Moira enquired archly. 'Is there no end to that man's talents?'

By the end of the day they had painted the chest of drawers in olive green, an old door in teal to be used as a table top like the one Nikos had in his studio, a book case in bright yellow and a kitchen cabinet in duck-egg blue. Moira had excelled herself by repainting a damaged screen picturing the nymph Io disguised by Zeus as a cow.

'I must say,' Dora remarked, impressed, 'that's a very pretty cow.'

'Yes,' Moira grinned. 'I think that's what Zeus thought.'

At the end of the day, Penny arranged the new furniture in the boathouse. It looked surprisingly effective, except for the very plain divan bed.

'I know,' Penny decided finally. 'We'll use Moira's pretty cow as a headboard.'

They pushed the just-dried nymph to the top of the bed and somehow the whole room instantly came together.

Moira, usually immune to her surroundings, was forced to see decoration in an entirely new light. 'You know, Penny, you really have a talent for this.'

'I agree,' seconded Dora. 'You've taken a featureless space the size of a garage and turned it into something that wouldn't be out of place in a loft in Shoreditch.'

'As long as the loft was by the seaside,' giggled Nell.

'The seaside!' Penny exclaimed. 'We need something nautical.' She looked round, hoping to spy something of a seafaring nature, but couldn't see anything appropriate. 'I know,' she concluded. 'I'll go and borrow a couple of Nikos's boats.'

'I thought he was in town with Takis?' Nell pointed out, trying to hide a smile.

'He told me he never locks the place anyway.' Penny could see the trap she'd fallen into as her friends exchanged frankly knowing glances at her familiarity with Nikos's boathouse.

'Go and get these boats, then,' Dora instructed, grinning.

Ten minutes later Penny came back with two boats and arranged them on the bookcase.

'These are beautiful,' admired Dora. 'Just don't tell me he carves them himself.'

'They're made from driftwood. He likes to take things that nobody's using and bring them back to life.'

'What was that I was saying about appropriate metaphors, Dora?' Moira winked.

'Moira, stop it!' Dora protested, convinced that Penny must see the parallel with herself, but Penny was avoiding her glance. Dora decided she'd better change the subject.

'Penny, you really must put this on Instagram. I'm sure some hipster would kill to stay here.'

'We need Willow to help us,' Nell offered. 'She's brilliant at that sort of thing.'

'Send her the photos then,' said Dora.

'Do you really think so?' Penny asked anxiously.

'Yes!' they all insisted. Dora added, 'We do. You are genuinely talented at this, Penny. Now for once, believe in yourself!'

'All right then. I'll send them to your daughter and we'll see what she thinks. I have to get the owner's approval, though.'

'Penny, why do you think all these people have spent the last two days covering themselves in sawdust and paint,' Dora demanded, 'if they don't want us to help them rent out their empty properties?'

An hour later, Ariadne leapt onto Dora as she came back into the hotel reception area.

'*Efharisto, efharisto, kyria Dora!* My father has persuaded my grandmother to let me go back to school! I can learn about botany and biology and may be clever and go to university – and it is all thanks to you!'

Dora, possibly the least touchy-feely being on the planet, experienced an unexpected welling of the eyes which she attributed to a passing speck of dust. 'Excellent!' she replied crisply, untangling herself from Ariadne's embrace. 'Juno the goat will miss you.'

'Now you will be the voice of the goddess!' insisted the young girl passionately. 'She will be pleased that you spoke out in my defence.'

'OK,' Dora replied, suppressing a smile. 'So are you starting school straight away?'

'Yes. At once. The headmistress says it does not matter that it is halfway through the year. She says I'm a smart girl and she didn't think I should have left in the first place,' Ariadne continued excitedly. 'My grandmother says that is because she's scared her school will close down if she doesn't have enough pupils.'

'Good old Cassandra,' murmured Moira. 'Always happy to put the boot in. Anyway, girls, I'm happy too because this means Takis will be looking for staff at the beach bar, and I am going to volunteer!'

They all looked at her in amazement. 'Moira! A week ago, you were teetotal!' pointed out Nell.

'Not any more!' Moira asserted. 'Anyway, I hate that expression. It makes me think of those temperance sayings.' She pursed her lips and adopted a theatrical posture. 'The lips that touch liquor will never touch mine!' she announced in a dramatic tone. 'I just didn't like the taste. Now I do. And with a bit of luck, I can turn the bar into a success at last!'

'But you're a classics don from Cambridge!' protested Nell. 'You can't be a barmaid!'

'Why the hell not? Cambridge doesn't want me any more. Besides, I've always wanted to be a barmaid. All that pulling pints.' She gave a demonstration. 'Excellent for the biceps.'

'I'm not sure how many pints you'll pull in Takis's beach bar!' Dora shook her head. Ariadne was still standing with them, looking slightly sad.

Dora suddenly swept the girl into her arms. 'Sorry, Ariadne, I haven't made enough of your news. Let's clap her, everyone, to celebrate that Ariadne is giving up the goats and the bar and going back to school!'

They all put their hands together, while Ariadne looked a little embarrassed but mostly delighted.

'Congratulations.' Moira patted her awkwardly. 'Dora's always telling us what a clever girl you are.'

Beaming now, Ariadne bounced off to the kitchen.

'Well done,' Penny whispered to Dora. 'She really appreciated that.'

Dora grinned round at them all. 'I expect the goddess moved me!'

Whether or not it was the goddess prompting her, Dora laid the clothes she was going to change into later for dinner out on the bed and slipped into jeans and her supermarket plimsolls. There was something bothering her, a little detail that had stuck in her mind about the olive grove, and she was just going to have to go there and check it out. She passed through reception and glanced at the cubby hole for the key to Xan Georgiades' room. It wasn't there. That meant he was either in his room now, or he always carried it with him.

Ten minutes later, she was clambering up the hill behind the hotel. Even in her enthusiasm to get to the olive grove and back in time for dinner, she couldn't help noticing how amazingly beautiful it was tonight. The sea had a phosphorescent shimmer about it, making it almost green rather than blue, the colour of Murano glass, and the faintest mist blurred the horizon. The sun was sinking fast in the sky.

She quickened her steps, almost colliding with Juno the goat.

'Bloody animal!' She rubbed the ankle she had slightly twisted trying to avoid her. 'Why do you like me so much? Do I have a scent of male goat about me?'

She stroked the rough fur on Juno's neck, and Juno rubbed against her enthusiastically.

'Look, Juno, I am Pandora Perkins, the scariest PR in

London, and I am not, I repeat *not*, a goat, either male or female. Now move!'

Juno refused to budge a centimetre, while Dora's shoulders sagged as she thought how inappropriate her 'scariest PR' tag sounded now. Who did she scare these days? Who did she even represent? She had become far too involved with the career of Venus Green, and her other clients had quietly dropped off. She'd always worked solo anyway and now she wasn't working at all. The impact of that suddenly hit her like a speeding train and she had to sit down, which Juno took as encouragement to come and playfully butt her.

Dora had her own flat and some savings; not that much, but some. A few years ago she might have sold her business. She'd even had offers. But that was hardly going to happen now.

She found she'd arrived in the olive grove, and stared round her. Something seemed different, although she couldn't put her finger on exactly what it was. She breathed in deeply. No scent of myrtle tonight. That was rather a relief.

She picked her way through the trees towards the tumble-down house that had belonged to old Yannis.

And then she realized.

The unusual marble bench that had been here last time she'd visited – the one she'd sat on with Ariadne – had gone.

Suddenly breathing fast, Dora got out her phone and looked at the photograph of the missing Aphrodite. The figure was reclining on a couch that was incredibly similar to the missing bench. Could the figure of the goddess have been split from the marble section she was lying on? Both sections would be immensely heavy. Or had Xan found the statue in two parts and, perhaps unable to move either unaided, hidden one part by leaving it in plain sight until he could think of a way of removing it?

If the statue of Aphrodite really was here, it would be incredibly valuable and also worthy of extraordinary historical interest. The Venus de Milo had been found on a neighbouring island and was possibly the most famous statue in the world! Maybe he'd hidden it because he thought it would stop his home going ahead, or – and Dora felt this might well be his intention – he could sell it on the black market in antiquities. That would certainly pay for a few extra bathrooms. Once the idea would have seemed ludicrous, but it was common knowledge here that, with the economy so bad, lots of people dealt in stuff they had found and not told the authorities about.

Darkness was descending fast as it always did, and she really ought to go back and think what to do next. Would anyone believe her incredible idea when she told them?

A sudden sound of dry soil shifting made her look round anxiously. She stepped back into the shadow. She could see the light of someone's cigarette glowing at the other side of the grove, coming towards her. She just had time to duck underneath a protective cypress branch as Xan Georgiades appeared and began to unlock the door of the house. Could the statue be hidden inside?

After only moments he came out again, this time holding a powerful torch. What the hell was she going to say to him about why she was here? He began to walk round the perimeter, shining the torch into every possible hiding place. Should she just step casually out and bluff? As she tried to work up her nerve to do it, there was a shout and then a curse as the torch was knocked violently out of his grasp and fell to the stony ground, shattering the bulb.

'Fucking animal!' Xan kicked out at Juno, who had followed her heroine into the darkness of the cypresses. Juno's response was to butt him so hard he fell to the ground, landing only feet from Dora's hiding place.

'I'll have you turned into goat curry, you fucking moron of an animal!'

The temptation to giggle welled up in Dora like hiccups. She was saved again by Juno, who walked casually over to Xan and pissed all over his feet.

This was too much for Xan and he rolled away, aiming one last kick at the goat, then hurried back through the olive grove.

Dora ruffled the coarse fur on the goat's neck again. 'Thanks for that, Juno. And I wonder what we make of him? A bad lot, I suspect, don't you? Never trust a man who wears tweed in Greece, my old Dad might have said.'

Gingerly she emerged from under the cypresses and stopped. As well as the overpowering smell of goat's piss, the aroma of myrtle wafted unmistakably through the olive trees.

Penny had a message from her daughter on her phone, and wondered whether to ring her back now or leave it till the morning. It would inevitably partly concern Colin and she didn't know whether she was up to it.

She sat at the small dressing table and began to brush her shoulder-length hair. It was definitely going blonder in the sun. She stared at her face. Her mother had told her that since she wasn't pretty she would have to be nice or interesting. She had never managed interesting; maybe that was why she'd gone for nice. But nice had meant a lifetime of Colin, who probably couldn't tell her from an automaton as long as the fridge was full. In fact, if she stayed away much longer he would probably start browsing the net for one of those creepy sex dolls with blank faces and all orifices available, and write Penny off altogether.

But was she behaving any better? Penny breathed in and hid her face in her hands. What were her feelings towards Nikos? Wasn't he the real reason she had extended her stay, much as she might be enjoying painting furniture and getting the boathouses ready to rent out?

Wendy had joked about Shirley Valentine falling for a hunky Greek fisherman, but wasn't that just what she was doing? Was she just as deluded as Shirley, thinking she actually meant something to him?

She'd certainly had significance for him in the past, but she suspected that had been more to do with his disgust at his own ignorance than any passionate feelings towards her. She was a symbol of his decision to change. She thought of the dog-eared photograph he'd kept all these years. Maybe getting her to fall for him now would feel like some kind of payback. No, because she didn't think Nikos was a shit, but it could still be a milestone marking how far he'd come.

'You are *not* going to go to bed with him!' she told herself firmly. 'Under any circumstances!'

Feeling morally armed against his charms, at least for the moment, she rang Wendy.

'Mum, how are you?' Wendy demanded. Her daughter had inherited Penny's niceness but tempered it with a touch of steel, which, Penny suspected, made her life much more enjoyable.

'I'm having a great time,' Penny replied. 'Helping the locals paint furniture to put in these boathouses they want to rent out. Give them a touch of style.'

'Make sure you have two chairs on the balcony, painted that amazing Greek blue, plus a little table with a bottle and two glasses! We all have that fantasy about getting away. In fact, I wish I were there now.'

'How's Dad?' Penny asked reluctantly.

'Gone quiet lately. I'm sure he'll find something to moan about soon. How long are you staying?'

Penny bit her lip, refusing to feel anxious. 'I'm not sure. I'm having a really good time. Feeling useful. You know I like that.'

'Good for you. Why should men assume we're there just to look after them?'

Penny laughed. She couldn't imagine Wendy's husband Martin daring to demand she look after him. 'How are the children?'

'Milo's still looking for a job. His particular talents of archaeology, DJing and playing the delightfully named Red Dead Redemption have yet to find the right niche. But he seems happy enough. Ben is working hard for his A levels and Flossie is being Flossie, charming the socks off her teachers while doing no work at all. Look, Mum, I'd better go and finish making supper. But have a great time with your paintbrush!'

Penny thought about the conversation. That was the real world. Grandchildren. Wendy and Martin. Tom was in Hong Kong getting rich, and she rarely heard from him, but one of these days he would get married and might even come home. Then there was Colin. Her heart plummeted at the thought. Maybe it was time she did something about Colin. At least her feelings about Nikos might make that clearer.

She sighed and selected a plain, square-necked cotton dress. And then she remembered Nikos had said it suited her.

And she smiled.

Nell brushed her hair and chose a taupe linen top to wear. It was crumpled but OK. And it wasn't as if anyone was going to be noticing. She was about to put her phone in her bag. Baby Naomi was her screensaver, from one of the few photos without Marigold. At the last moment she decided to leave it in the room. No one would need her for the next two hours anyway.

She sat down, feeling overwhelmed with sadness. No one needed her, ever. That was the honest truth.

There was a knock on the door and Penny's cheerful tones penetrated her wave of depression. She felt suddenly grateful for this odd assortment of friends.

Picking up her key and bag, she answered the door.

'I was thinking,' Penny said on the way down. 'If we are staying here for a bit longer, maybe we could see if Takis could do a deal on our rooms. It's nowhere near the season yet, so you never know. I've got a bit of money left from my legacy but obviously I only budgeted for our original plan.'

'Same here. I think that's an excellent idea. After all, we could always offer to do the washing up!'

They both laughed, remembering how this had been a real fear for them last time they were in Greece, with so little to spend it was amazing they got by at all.

'*Kalispera*, ladies!' Takis greeted them with a theatrical bow. 'May I offer you a drink from my humble establishment before your dinner?'

'I'd be delighted,' Nell bowed back. 'As a matter of fact I'd like to try to some raki.'

'Raki?' Takis echoed, stunned. 'But that is a Turkish drink.'

'Raki,' Nell repeated firmly.

'Not Greek ouzo?' Takis's face took on a wounded air.

'I have a reason,' Nell explained. 'My daughter Willow used to play this song over and over again. It said something about sipping down raki and reading Maynard Keynes and I always promised myself I would try some.'

'And who is this Maynard Keynes?'

'He's a British economist.'

'We certainly need those in Greece. Invite him over.'

'I would, but sadly he died in 1946.'

'That is a problem. And you other ladies?'

'I'll join Nell with the raki,' Moira grinned. 'There's an old saying you shouldn't drink raki alone.'

'Or at all,' Dora sniffed. 'The stuff's 40% proof! White wine for me. Where do you get all this information, Moira?'

'Too many years in libraries.'

'Wine for me too, thank you,' Penny agreed.

'Takis,' Penny asked, hoping he wouldn't be insulted, 'with all that's been going on, we've found ourselves staying longer than we planned and instead of going home, some of us would like to stay on for a while.'

'How many?' he asked.

'Who's up for staying in Kyri a bit longer?'

Nell put up her hand instantly. Then Moira, and eventually Dora as well.

'Of course; and you can have a special rate!' Takis said delightedly. 'I will give you my business rate. And you are helping the island! I should let you stay as my guests.'

'No, no,' Penny insisted firmly. 'A business rate would suit us fine!'

They sat down at their usual table looking out at the harbour. All around them the everyday life of the island unfolded. Old men chatting on the bench at the side of the quay, kids playing football, fishing boats coming in after a day at sea; a few smart yachties showing off with cocktails on their deck; an Orthodox priest in his black robes, huge beard and tall hat hurrying along, trying not to be tempted to join members of his flock sitting down for a drink. And just below, the white sand beach fringing a glorious aquamarine sea.

'What do you most like about Kyri?' Penny suddenly asked them.

'The fact you always know tomorrow will be sunny,' Dora smiled. 'And the feeling of sand between your toes down at the beach bar.'

'That's two,' pointed out Moira. 'The friendliness of the people. They'll do anything for you. Look at the doctor and his wife putting me up for a pittance. Can you imagine that at home?'

'The sound of flip flops,' giggled Penny.

'Greek yogurt for breakfast with honey and walnuts!' added Nell.

'The peace of the place.' Dora closed her eyes and felt the last rays of sun on her face. 'I've never known anything quite like it.'

'That's three now,' Moira corrected. 'I love the fact that it's so reasonable here. I mean, this hotel, for example. You never feel like you're being conned. And now he's going to give it to us even cheaper!'

At that moment Takis arrived with their drinks. He handed out the wine and then the raki. 'The Turks call it Lion's Milk,' he told them. 'Medicine for soothing the mind and for healing the heart.'

'That'll suit me then,' Nell commented as she took the drink.

'Do you have a heart that is hurting, lovely Helen?' Takis demanded, so quickly that the others stared at him.

'Only because I miss my baby granddaughter,' Nell replied, amused.

'Ah, I see,' Takis smiled back delightedly. 'And here are the menus for tonight.'

'Well, well, lovely Helen,' teased Moira. 'You clearly have an admirer there. I wish it were me, because then he might let me do what I want with the beach bar. But, first things first: who's up for coming with me tomorrow to see where these pirates had their lair?'

'I'd love to,' volunteered Dora instantly. She'd just had a thought she wanted to follow up.

'Great,' Moira said, surprised. 'Anyone else?'

'Nell and I really ought to get on with the boathouses,' Penny explained. 'Now we're being subsidized by Takis. I hope you won't mind?'

'Not at all,' Moira grinned. 'With Lovely Helen out of the way I can work on Takis about Treasure Island. But first I need to see the Pirates' Lair.' She looked at the row of small boats touting for customers to take on boat trips round the island. 'Which of these do you think is likely to actually know anything about their history?'

Penny raised her glass. 'You should ask Nikos. He has a boat of his own, and no one knows the island like he does.'

'I might do that.' Moira picked up her raki. 'To Nikos, mayor of Kyri, practically perfect in every way!'

'I thought that was Mary Poppins,' Dora drawled, her face still directed towards the setting sun.

'Isn't having your face in the sun very ageing?' Moira enquired.

'I'm past caring about any of that crap.' Dora shrugged her low-cut dress so that a bit more of her elegant cleavage appeared.

'You could have fooled me,' Moira giggled just as Takis was passing with another order. 'Takis, one question.'

Takis skidded to a stop. 'Are you enjoying your raki, *kyria Moira*?'

'Very much. It tastes like vintage paint stripper. Your

esteemed mayor, Nikos: how does he afford to have a boat and a lovely house on the beach? What is his secret?'

'He used to be a – how do you say it – an accountant.'

'An *accountant*?' Moira almost choked on her raki.

'Yes. He worked for big global company, travelled all over the world, made lots of money and came back here to live simply with the rest of us. Good plan, no?'

Penny sipped her wine, feeling suddenly foolish. There was so much she didn't know about Nikos.

'Do you think he would take me out and tell me about the pirates who ruled the roost on Kyri?' Moira enquired.

'I think he would love nothing more,' Takis grinned. 'Especially if Penelope is interested in pirates also. Do you want to hear tales of the wicked French corsairs who terrorized the island and took our women as captives, faithful Penelope?'

'Please don't call me that!' Penny burst out.

The other three stared at her. Penny sounded genuinely upset.

'Just because Penelope waited ten years for bloody Odysseus to deign to come home doesn't mean I'm like her! In fact, I shouldn't think my mother had ever heard of the woman when she called me Penny!'

'Calm down, dear.' Moira patted her ineffectually. She'd never been any good with student outbursts, or any other strong emotion, but she certainly hadn't expected this from Penny.

'I thought I was called Pandora after Pan's People,' Dora interjected. 'Not some stupid nymph with a box! Do you remember them on *Top of the Pops*?'

'Of course I do!' Nell squealed. And to the embarrassment of the others she jumped up and started to wiggle her hips and wave her arms in some half-remembered and highly unsuitable dance routine. 'I used to copy their every movement! It was because of them I wore stripy leggings for three years, long after anyone else wore stripy leggings!'

Penny sipped her wine and looked visibly calmer. 'Sorry about that, everyone. I'm a bit wrought up. I was talking to my daughter on the phone and it made me feel that – unlike bloody Penelope – I'm being a bit irresponsible staying here.'

'Do you want to stay here?' Moira asked instantly.

'Yes.'

'Well, there's your answer. You've got to learn to do what you want! Now are you coming on this pirate trip or not?'

'Would it be helpful if I did?' she asked, feeling stupid after her outburst.

'Penny, stop it!' Moira demanded. 'Another simple question. Would you like to come or not?'

'Of course I would!' And she began to laugh.

'I'm glad we've got that settled. I think your life could be greatly improved if you were a bit more selfish,' Moira observed. 'Look at the Greek gods. They did exactly what they wanted all the time.'

'And didn't that create rather a lot of problems?' Penny replied, laughing. 'Nymphs being turned into cows, people having their liver eaten by eagles, that sort of thing?'

'Well, there was that,' Moira conceded. 'A toast, everyone!' She grabbed her raki. 'To Penelope, who has had enough of waiting for men, whether they're called Odysseus or Colin!'

Penny raised her wine triumphantly. 'I'll certainly drink to that!'

Nine

Nikos was delighted to take them, especially when he learned that Penny was one of the party.

The following morning, they all trooped down to the harbourside and climbed on board his black-hulled, double-masted *caique* with its romantic dark-red sails. To complete its engagingly ruffian image, the bare-breasted figurehead smiled down at them from her commanding position on the prow of the boat. To Moira's delight, there was even a crow's nest high up in the rigging.

Takis and Cassandra had followed them down to the quay. Cassandra handed over a basket full of lunch and Takis a cool bag chinking with bottles.

'This is getting better by the moment,' commented Dora.

On the quay, the children and old men waved them goodbye. Watching them, Nell felt oddly touched that they had been accepted so readily in Kyri. She waved back, then nudged Dora. 'Look who else has come to say goodbye!'

Dora pushed her sunglasses onto her head and squinted at the quayside.

Amongst the old men stood Xan Georgiades, staring at the

departing craft. His face was blank, yet Dora sensed irritation if not open hostility. She saw him speak to Takis and could almost bet he was asking where they were going.

After Takis had turned back to the hotel, Xan still stood there watching them.

A sudden thought occurred to Dora. If Xan had found the statue and hidden it, and she was pretty sure he had, it wasn't impossible that he had hidden it in the caves, as generations of pirates had done before.

Moira, meanwhile, was staring up at the crow's nest. 'Pity we don't have a Jim Lad to send up there and look out for any enemies,' she joked.

'All you'll see round here are day trippers and the occasional cruise passenger, I'm afraid,' Nikos laughed as he instructed the youth who'd come to crew to untie the mooring ropes. 'All the pirates are long gone. It's hard to imagine an island as small as Kyri being the hub of the Levant, but that's what it once was.'

'But why?' Dora couldn't imagine tiny Kyri being the hub of anything.

'We'll go and see the caves and I'll show you.'

Nell settled herself at the front of the boat and boldly took off her blouse to reveal a smart black swimsuit underneath. 'Are you going for a swim?' Moira asked.

'You must be joking.'

'Wait till we're near the caves,' Nikos shouted. 'The sea there is amazing.'

Dora, more of an indoor spa person, looked out at the Aegean Sea in May and shuddered. 'Rather you than me.'

'I'll let the ladder down and you can climb off the back,' Nikos laughed. 'You won't even have to get your hair wet!'

For the moment Nikos was using the engine. They steered

out into the open sea, where the waves had white crests, and they all felt the movement of the boat as it dived up and down in the lively swell.

'Not feeling sick again, Moira?' Dora teased.

'That was nearly a week ago!' she countered. 'And anyway, that was food poisoning.'

'God, is that all it is?' Nell marvelled. 'It seems so much longer.'

'Give the ladies a drink, Andros,' commanded their captain, and a bottle of white wine appeared which he delicately poured into plastic cups. It was even nicely cooled.

Round the next headland the conditions changed completely, protected by the landmass of the island. Nell peered over the side as they puttered gently in towards the shore, mesmerized by the beauty of the water. There was every shade of blue, green, turquoise, aquamarine, and even flashes of sudden iridescence like the inside of a mother-of-pearl shell.

Nikos guided them into a secluded bay, surrounded by high cliffs of golden stone, dotted with bushes and shrubs – and even, Dora laughed to see, the occasional goat. Presumably not Cassandra's.

As they nudged their way towards the shore they passed a series of rocks, some of which had large round holes in them. 'That is where the pirates moored their ships,' Nikos informed them.

'Those actual holes?' Moira demanded excitedly.

'Those actual holes. This bay was one of their favourite haunts. When we stop I'll show you why. Drink up, ladies – from here on we're in the small boat,' he winked at them, looking faintly piratical himself in his striped t-shirt, the light blue of his eyes contrasting with the permanent deep tan of the year-round sailor. 'Now we will go and see the famous pirate caves.'

Still perched on top of the cabin, Nell took a rare selfie to send to her daughter. She smiled into the camera, the dazzling blue sea behind her, then checked the photo self-consciously, finding she had Penny peeping over her shoulder. 'You look amazing!' Penny cried. 'How do you get your hair that gorgeous shape when you've just been out in a boat?'

It was true. Nell did look good. She had picked up a light tan, and her dark hair was gleaming in the sun.

Nell grinned. 'I had a Brazilian wrap! It cost eighty quid and was worth every penny!'

'I thought that was something you had on your pubes!' interrupted Moira, staring at Nell's nether regions.

'That's a Brazilian wax, when they take off the lot. For aspiring porn stars, or Essex girls on reality TV.'

Listening from the other side of the deck, Dora winced at the mention of reality TV.

'So what is a Brazilian wrap, then?' Penny persisted.

'No idea exactly what they do,' Nell giggled. 'But I think it involves formaldehyde.'

'Isn't that what they preserve your appendix in?' Penny asked. Colin had kept his proudly on top of the telly until Wendy knocked it over accidentally-on-purpose when she was fifteen.

'The very same.'

'Goodness!'

No more conversation about hair treatments was possible, as young Andros had nimbly threaded the mooring rope through the hole in the nearest rock. Then he and Nikos helped them down into the small blow-up boat they had been towing behind them.

'We had one of these when we went on holiday to Devon,' Nell informed them. 'Me and my brother had to blow it up with a bicycle pump. It took hours!'

'I'm glad you and your brother didn't blow up this one,' Dora remarked, stepping into it gingerly.

'Thank God you've given up those stupid stilettos,' remarked Moira.

'Yes,' Dora grinned. 'I am now the proud owner of a pair of plimsolls.' She flashed her foot at them.

'My God, look at that!' Penny pointed at the water over the rock formation many feet below as they approached the entrance of the first cave. 'It's like an impressionist painting!' They all stared down. The water was a blaze of not just blue but green, bright turquoise, yellow and even rusty red.

'It's because of the minerals in the rocks underneath,' Nikos explained. He steered the boat through a natural arch in the rock and they found themselves in a vast cathedral-like cave, with other smaller natural chambers leading off it. At the far end was another arch leading back out into the bright sunlight of the Aegean.

'That was why it was a favourite with the pirates,' Nikos explained. 'They had an escape route. They could get straight out to sea through that arch. They would rob the Turkish, or sometimes the British ships, and hide their spoils here. They didn't rob the French ships because they came from France themselves. That was why they were allowed to get away with it. Until, in the seventeenth century, the king of France decided they were too much of a risk and started hanging them.'

But Dora wasn't listening. She felt her heart speeding up and found she was unconsciously holding her breath. She was holding her iPhone as if to take a photograph and had surreptitiously put on the light instead. As she directed it into the second cave, she thought she could see something that had been stashed there.

Silently, Dora pondered what to do. She'd always hated water. The very idea of scuba diving made her feel like being stuck in a lift.

Of course, she was probably wrong, and she would look very stupid if she made the suggestion that Xan Georgiades had found the Venus and hidden it here.

She would have to look more closely.

'It's so fascinating in here,' she said enthusiastically. 'Would it be OK if I swam?'

They all stared at her, stunned.

'Dora, are you feeling quite well?' Moira asked.

She was saved, if that was the word, by Nikos. 'I am sorry, Pandora, it is not such a good idea. There are currents. And the water is very, very cold.'

Dora nodded, fighting her disappointment, yet overcome with relief at her deliverance. She liked Nikos. He seemed a calm man, and yet a surprising one. She might even trust him with her suspicions.

A few minutes later they were back in the glorious sunlight and Dora was asking herself if she was mad. What was it to her if Xan had found a statue and hidden it so that he could go ahead with his holiday home?

Yet, try as she might not to think about it, she found she did care about the fate of the lost Venus.

'*Kyria* Moira! *Kyria* Moira!' The sound of someone shouting penetrated Moira's pleasant on-deck snooze as they headed back in to the harbour. Takis was standing on the quayside dancing about like a bear on hot coals. 'You have a visitor!'

Moira gathered up her stuff, unable to immediately imagine who on earth her visitor might be.

'It is a venerable gentleman,' Takis enlightened her. 'He seems extremely distinguished.'

'Could it be your dad?' enquired Penny.

'I doubt it. He was a schoolteacher who drank himself to death in 1973.'

'Oh Moira, I'm so sorry,' Penny apologized, deciding that perhaps this explained both Moira's social oddness and her desire to show off. 'I wonder who it is, then.' She said goodbye to Nikos and thanked him profusely for taking them. 'It's been so amazing to see all round Kyri in your beautiful boat.'

'I would take you any time,' Nikos replied, and the look in his eyes told her he meant it. 'Perhaps next time just us,' he added softly so that the others wouldn't hear.

'I'd like that very much,' replied Penny, trying not to blush.

They didn't have long to wait for the solution to the mystery. A curiously dressed man in an ancient white suit with matching long white hair, who nevertheless managed to give off an air of great distinction, walked towards them.

'Hello, Moira dear,' he greeted her, his small eyes dancing with merriment. 'Thought I'd give you a bit of a surprise and just turn up! I hate tedious arrangements.'

'Professor Brinkley!' Moira gasped. 'But I only got in touch with you the day before yesterday!'

'Nothing like a bit of spontaneity at my age,' he replied, squeezing her hand. 'You might be dead if you don't do things at once. What's to keep me in Cambridge anyway? I'm emeritus now, you know.'

'What's emeritus?' whispered Dora. 'Is it a condition, like dementia?'

'I think it's a posh word for retired,' Nell replied.

'Besides,' their new visitor continued gleefully, 'what a wonderful mystery! This hand of Aphrodite with the apple! Most exciting thing I've heard in years. Now, my dear, I want to hear the whole story.'

They made their way back through the crowded quayside, past babies in buggies, the eternal little boys with footballs, a few tourists stopping for an early evening drink in the cafes watching the day trippers return from their boat trips.

'Then really, you'll have to ask my friend Dora,' Moira winked. 'She was in on it from the start. She even smelled the goddess's perfume!'

'Did she indeed?' He beamed at Dora. 'Then you are extraordinarily honoured. Shall we sit down and share a libation?'

'Hey,' Moira protested, 'don't say you believe all this goddess nonsense? What happened to good old academic scepticism?'

'Over-rated, dear Moira,' he beamed. 'But I would genuinely like to hear the story from the start.'

'Are you staying at the hotel too?' Moira asked him.

'Certainly. It seems a charming place. I can hardly believe that as a lifelong scholar of classical Greece, I had never before visited this island. It is entirely delightful.'

'But too well kept a secret, which is part of their problem here,' Moira sighed. 'So why don't we all go and get changed, since we've been on a boat all day, and meet again in an hour for drinks and dinner and tell you all you want to know.'

'Perfect,' Professor Brinkley beamed. 'I'll spend the time looking in on the archaeological museum.'

'I'm not sure there is one,' Moira hesitated.

'Nonsense. There's always an archaeological museum. Even if it's in somebody's front room.' He hurried off with the enthusiasm and energy of someone twenty years younger.

Dora, unable to resist dressing up for male company,

however ancient, reappeared in a silver minidress more suited to someone half her age and ordered everyone a glass of raki.

'Goodness,' pronounced the professor, 'how deliciously wicked! And you must all call me Karl. It's unfortunate, but it is my name. My father was an enthusiastic communist. I would have preferred Odysseus, or even Hermes, but there you are. Now let me get you all clear. When I get interns at the museum, I always ask them to say a line about themselves and why they came to join us.'

They look at each other, stunned, as Takis brought the menus.

Professor Brinkley cast his eye over it and instantly replied that he would have the grilled halloumi, followed by *sheftalia* cooked on charcoal coals and a bottle of Mythos beer. 'We have a very jolly Greek restaurant near the museum where I have lunch every day,' he explained as the others hesitated and argued over their choices.

'Right. Back to you girls.'

Penny took a deep breath. 'I'm Penny Anderson. I'm a housewife from Surrey and I think I came here to get away from my husband.'

The others stared.

'I'm Helen Winstanley and I'm a retired doctor's receptionist. I came because it sounded fun.' Nell paused and bit her lip. 'And, to be honest, because I'm lonely.'

Moira paused a moment. 'I'm Moira O'Reilly, as you know, and my college has told me I've got to retire, damn them!'

They all looked expectantly at Dora, waiting for her to announce that she was London's scariest PR.

'I'm Pandora Perkins, and three weeks ago I was dumped by my biggest client, a celebrity ironically called Venus Green. I came here to get away from the flak.'

'Never heard of her,' replied the professor briskly. 'The ancient Greeks knew that kind of fame never lasts, and think, if she hadn't done it you would have missed meeting the goddess in the grove. Now, tell me how it happened.'

Dora laughed and ordered some wine for the table. She would need it.

She explained how it was really Ariadne who knew about the goddess, and she was convinced that Aphrodite visited regularly and that there would be a powerful scent of myrtle whenever she did – and yet no myrtle plants were visible.

'And you believe that Aphrodite really did come, as the girl suggests?' he asked gently.

Dora sighed. 'To be honest, I've no bloody idea. My rational brain says it's ridiculous, but I did smell the myrtle. And then there was the hand with the apple, which the owner says was planted there to stop him building his holiday home.'

'And do you believe him?'

Dora looked around her furtively. There was no sign of Xan anywhere. She leaned in and dropped her voice. 'I think the man who's bought the grove found the Venus and has hidden it somewhere. Maybe in one of those pirate caves Nikos showed us.'

'But why would he do that?' Penny asked.

'Two reasons. So that he can go ahead with his holiday house, and maybe also because he wants to sell it.'

'But surely you can't sell a famous statue?' asked Nell.

'Well, actually,' the professor interrupted thoughtfully, 'I'm afraid you can. The curator of the museum was just telling me. Apparently, smuggling antiquities out of Greece used to be run by organized crime, along with drugs and guns. Now, with the Greek economy gone to pot, everyone's at it!' He took a sip of his wine. 'A couple of years ago, two farmers were sent to prison for trying to sell a statue they'd found for ten million euros.'

'Bloody hell,' Moira marvelled. 'I had no idea!'

'There are six thousand Greek islands, and only eighty staff in the Department of Cultural Antiquities. It puts de Gaulle and his comment about not being able to rule a country with two hundred and forty-six cheeses somewhat in the shade, doesn't it?'

'But how do you smuggle six-foot statues?' Moira persisted.

'I'm afraid to say, the curator says they break them up. Then, often, they hand most of it to a collector except a vital part they hold back – often the head – and demand more money for it.'

'Now that,' Moira raised her glass and finished it in one gulp, 'is not acceptable!'

Conscious of how much they still had to do, Penny and Nell got up early the next morning, even sacrificing Cassandra's cakes, and went straight to the boathouses on the rather rickety bikes they'd been lent by Takis. Fortunately the bakery next door was open and they were able to pick up a coffee and a *bougatsa*, which turned out to be a delicious Greek pastry filled with custard.

'This should keep us going,' Nell grinned as they got out their paintbrushes. They had finished the first two boathouses and were starting on the third, with the invaluable help of Demetria. Demetria was enjoying herself so much that she and her husband had decided to open a B&B of their own.

'Now I see how you ladies do it,' she grinned. 'Turning a load of old junk into antiques. Very clever.'

By the end of the day the upstairs room was almost finished, and they just needed an attractive headboard. 'We need Moira to paint us another one,' Penny said. 'How about that old door with the curved panelling?' she suggested, pointing to a recent donation.

They tried slipping it behind the bed. Somehow it worked brilliantly, the dark stain of the wood showing up perfectly against the crisp white bedding Penny had put on just to try out.

'Penny, you really are amazing,' Nell congratulated her. 'I wouldn't mind sleeping in that myself!'

Penny grinned. How different it was here, where people made her feel good about herself, from how she felt at home.

At just that moment Nikos put his head round the door, looking slightly disconcerted to find both Nell and Demetria there as well.

Demetria took pity on him. 'And what can we do for you, Mr Mayor?'

'I'm sailing over to Ximonos, the small island round the bay, to drop something off tomorrow and I wondered if you'd like to come, Penelope? The farmer over there said he had some small pieces – paintings and such – you might find useful for your redecoration project.'

Penny could see Demetria and Nell exchange a smile and pretend to be busy fiddling with the door while secretly watching her response.

'That sounds great,' she replied, trying to sound brisk and businesslike. 'What time?'

'About nine? It's not too busy in the harbour then.'

'He didn't want Takis and the whole village seeing you,' teased Nell, as soon as both Nikos and Demetria had disappeared.

'I'm sure you're making too much of it.' Penny shook her

head. 'As he said, we're just going to pick up some bits and pieces for the boathouses.'

'Like hell you are,' Nell whispered when Demetria had left the room. 'Faithful Penelope, I think you probably ought to face facts. Nikos is falling for you. What are you going to do about it?'

Ten

'Guess what!' Moira was almost jumping up and down with excitement when they arrived back at the hotel on their bikes, exhausted and sweaty. 'The boathouses have had their first booking!'

Penny was delighted but absolutely mystified. 'But how? We haven't even advertised them yet.'

'Demetria had the brainwave of putting the photos on the island's own website, and bingo! Two adults plus a baby are arriving on the ferry today!'

'A baby!' Penny immediately went into panic mode. 'I didn't think about babies. What will we do about a cot?'

'Don't people bring their own?' Nell asked, trying not to be irritated that this had all happened when she'd already sent the photos to her daughter Willow and asked for her help in marketing the boathouses.

'Demetria will find one,' offered Cassandra, who had been listening.

'I'll paint it for you with some nice Greek myths,' offered Moira.

'Couldn't you stick to nursery rhymes?' Nell suggested. 'Probably safer.'

'Considerably safer!' endorsed Professor Brinkley, who had just emerged from reception with Dora on his arm – where, to the surprise of all, she looked rather happy.

'Karl here has been telling me fascinating facts about Venus,' Dora announced enthusiastically. 'Not only was she the goddess of sex and love, but also prostitution! She was born from the foam after Saturn castrated his father and the blood fell into the sea. And wait for this – myrtle, the flower I keep smelling in the olive grove, is a Roman symbol of the fanny. Especially the clitoris!'

Cassandra stared at Dora. 'Who are these Fanny and Clitoris?' she demanded. 'Are these your British gods?'

'*Definitely* stick to nursery rhymes!' Nell collapsed in giggles, all her annoyance about the photos forgotten.

Demetria, efficient as usual, produced a wooden cot no longer needed by the wife of a farmer whose children, to her great sadness, had left to look for work in Crete and Santorini.

Moira painted it with the cow jumping over the moon, spent an hour drying it with her hairdryer, and delivered it to them at the boathouse with the help of Demetria's husband in his pickup. 'There you go,' she grinned. 'Though the cow could easily be Io, the poor girl Zeus turned into a heifer to avoid his wife's wrath.'

'I prefer the Hey Diddle Diddle version,' Penny laughed. 'What have you got there?' She indicated a carrier bag bulging with bottles.

'On my way to the beach bar! Come round later and you can test out the piratical cocktails.'

Penny and Nell busied themselves with making up two beds

with white linen they had ordered online from Athens, vacuuming diligently and checking that there were enough pots and pans for the guests to self-cater.

'What about a welcome pack?' Nell suggested. 'I always like one of those. It means you don't have to dash straight off to the shops.' They phoned Dora and asked her to pick up some basics which, when she delivered them, turned out to be a rather Dora-like selection consisting of hummus, pitta and olives, coffee, tea, a large slice of Cassandra's cake plus two bottles of white wine.

'*Two* bottles of wine and no milk?' queried Nell.

'Nine out of ten mothers prefer it. Fact,' Dora asserted. 'How about flowers? Shall I go and pick some?'

'OK, but no myrtle,' Nell grinned. 'We don't want to attract any passing goddesses. It might scare the baby.'

Dora came back five minutes later with pale pink oleander, some orange crocosmia and a striking splash of purple bougainvillaea. Nell and Penny had to agree it looked stunning. 'I did a flower-arranging course,' Dora confided. 'We were told every arrangement needs a gatecrasher – a clashing flower that makes the whole thing work.'

'I would never have put you down for a flower arranger,' Nell admitted.

'I got fed up with paying a fucking fortune to trendy florists every time I organized an event!' Dora replied.

'She's full of surprises, isn't she?' Nell whispered as she left.

'I know. Who would have thought Pandora Perkins, scary PR, would learn flower arranging? Or get on so well with a classics professor who won't see seventy again?'

They put the flowers in the middle of the painted teal dining table that had been a door in its previous life, and looked around. 'Do you know what, Nell?' Penny sighed with deep satisfaction. 'This place looks bloody amazing!'

'It does, doesn't it! Let's go down to Treasure Island and celebrate our talents!' Nell put an arm round Penny, and they went out to look for their bicycles.

'I know it's a lot to ask,' Professor Brinkley asked nevertheless, adding a charming smile which managed to have a hint of boyishness despite his years. 'But I really would love to see this famous olive grove sacred to the goddess Aphrodite.'

'OK,' Dora agreed. 'We'll get Ariadne to come too. She's the unofficial guardian of the goddess. And she's the one who found the hand with the apple.'

Ariadne was only too delighted to take them so they set off, a colourful group, the professor in his crumpled white suit, Dora in velvet and plimsolls, led by Ariadne, and with the unshakeable Juno guarding the rear.

'I see we have protection,' the professor laughed.

'She's in love with *kyria* Dora,' Ariadne explained, laughing.

'And who could blame her?' he replied, bowing, managing to sound sweet and funny rather than creepy, which was quite a skill, Dora decided.

They climbed up the disused mule track, pushing aside branches of yellow broom and breathing in the wild thyme under their feet, the only sound that of cicada and distant goat bells. The air was so clear you could almost bottle it.

'You almost feel you were going back thousands of years,' Dora whispered.

'That's what makes Greece so special,' Professor Brinkley acknowledged. 'We all feel its history belongs to us.'

Dora resisted the urge to say that what Greece usually made

her think of was *Mamma Mia*. Besides, even she was beginning to get a sense of its rich mythical past.

They had reached the tumbledown house, and Dora paused a moment to take a piece of paper from her pocket. 'Once when I came here there was a kind of bench by the side of the wall. I sat down on it with Ariadne. Do you remember?' she asked the girl. 'It seemed to me to look a lot like the couch Venus is lying on in this drawing.'

'And where did the drawing come from?' asked the professor.

'Moira found it in a guidebook. It's supposed to have been done by a French envoy to show the king of France in the seventeenth century. Apparently this pirate found the statue of Venus and offered it to the king in exchange for a pardon. Then he discovered the king intended to hang him, so he hid it instead.'

'How very exciting,' replied Professor Brinkley.

'And this was where I found the hand.' Ariadne indicated an area of earth that had been recently disturbed.

'But you felt the goddess visited here often?' the professor asked gently.

Ariadne glanced at him to see if he was mocking her, but he seemed unusually serious.

'Yes. Whenever I could smell the scent of myrtle, I knew she had been.'

'Oh for Christ's sake,' a man's voice exploded behind them, 'you're not still listening to this girl's demented claptrap?'

They whirled round to find Xan Georgiades only a few feet away. Dora got the distinct impression he might have followed them.

'She wouldn't be the first to still believe in the old gods,' the professor said evenly. 'Half the shrines you see by the roadside used to be dedicated to Apollo or Demeter before they were conveniently commandeered by the Orthodox Church.'

'And who the hell are you?' Xan demanded rudely.

'Karl Brinkley, Emeritus Professor from the Museum of Classical Antiquity, Cambridge.'

'So you've started bringing in fucking experts!' exploded Georgiades.

'As a matter of fact,' Dora replied calmly, 'he's a personal friend of ours.'

'I remember you.' He pointed a finger at Dora. 'You were the troublemaker at the meeting who encouraged this crazy girl in her crazy visions.'

'Have you ever heard of St Bernadette of Lourdes, Mr, er . . .' interrupted the professor.

'Georgiades. Of course I have, but that was a load of clap-trap too.'

'Then what exactly is your explanation for the hand holding the apple, Mr Georgiades?' Professor Brinkley asked politely.

'And for the marble bench outside your cabin that has somehow disappeared?' Dora added, not politely at all.

'Why don't you just go back to your museum – stuffed, no doubt, with stolen Greek artefacts – and leave us alone!' shouted Xan, refusing to answer her question. 'And may I remind you that whether or not I build a house here, this is still my land!' His long aristocratic face, with its high domed fore-head and drooping moustache, hardened into a look that made Dora think of feudal landlords who could throw their troublesome tenants into an impenetrable prison; or, even better, stick them down an oubliette where they would drown in its stinking waters.

'Charming man,' commented Professor Brinkley as they

marched silently back through the grove towards the mule track.

'Isn't he?' agreed Dora. 'Come on, let's go and celebrate the fact he hasn't had us shot, or horsewhipped us, with a visit to Treasure Island!'

The view from the top of the hill was so amazing that the professor made them stop for a moment and look at it. 'I have to do this in Cambridge sometimes to remind myself what an incredible place it is. No matter how wonderful your surroundings, you stop seeing them – but just look at that!'

The small bay unfolded beneath them, its waters a bright turquoise, shading into aquamarine where the sandbanks made it shallower and a dark deep blue out towards the horizon. The sand on the small beach looked white and tempting and promised to be so soft you could almost feel it between your toes. The cliffs encircling the bay were golden stone saved from crumbling by clumps of sea holly and wildflowers. The warm, waxy scent of *angeliki*, with its tiny white flowers, hung heavy and sweet in the air. They breathed it in and smiled in deep contentment.

'Makes me want to run down and jump straight into the sea!' laughed Professor Brinkley. 'But I'd probably break my leg doing it at my age.'

'Nonsense!' Dora insisted. 'You look as sprightly as one of Ariadne's goats. Why is she wearing a bell, by the way? She doesn't usually.'

'She broke into Mr Georgiades' house and ate everything he keeps there. He was very angry. My father says she has to wear a bell so we know where she is.'

'That goat has very good taste,' murmured the professor. They had just reached the beach bar.

It was unrecognizable from Dora's last visit.

'*O Thee mou!*' Ariadne whispered respectfully, looking round in awed amazement.

'What's she saying?' whispered Dora.

'OMG, is how I think my students would translate,' replied Professor Brinkley.

'She's certainly got a point!'

Moira had managed to transform six plastic chairs and a drop-down canteen van into an exotic island paradise. The bar was swathed in palm branches and she had tacked straw door mats from the little supermarket together to provide an authentic-looking covering for the van itself. She had painted a large map of Treasure Island complete with an X marking the spot, and nailed it to a nearby tree. There was even an old chest stuffed with cheap fake jewellery which was more likely to come from Taiwan than the Spanish Main.

'Avast, me hearties!' Moira strode towards them in full pirate get-up, black eye patch and even a fake parrot on her shoulder. 'What'll be your pleasure this fine afternoon?'

'Moira!' Dora shrieked. 'You look amazing. Where on earth did you find the parrot?'

'I borrowed it from the wildlife museum. I am supposed to be using it to inform the primary class about *Aves Psittaciformes*, the common parrot! I have to convince Takis – and more seriously Cassandra – that it's worth spending a few euros to get the boat trip visitors to stop here for a drink. As I've said to Cassandra, they need to try something!'

Dora looked at the list of colourful cocktails behind the bar, next to the rows of garish-looking liqueurs in various dazzling hues.

'This may be a mistake, but I think I'll try a Billy Bones.'

'Good choice!' Moira slipped behind the bar and filled the cocktail shaker with five or six ingredients, plus ice, and shook it enthusiastically. She poured the resulting mixture into a bulbous wine glass, adding a slice of pineapple and a pink umbrella.

'Dare I ask what's in it?' Dora enquired.

'Quarter ounce of rum,' Moira grinned. 'Half of amaretto, quarter of cherry brandy, another of peach schnapps, some orange bitters plus a dash of pineapple juice, another of blood orange, half a lime and some coconut cream!'

'Bloody hell. I'll be prostrate. Where did you learn how to make it?'

'I'm following the barman's bible – one of sour, two of sweet, three of strong, four of weak – apparently you can't go wrong with that.' She turned to the professor.

'So, Karl, what'll you be having?'

'I'll try the Black Spot for my sins, and let's hope I live to tell the tale.'

Moira deftly mixed a deadly-looking concoction that seemed to involve most of the bottles on the shelf, including a lethal dose of blackberry liqueur.

'Thank you.' He eyed it dubiously. 'And will you be having one yourself?'

'Don't mind if I do. I think I'll try a Long John Silver.'

'Far be it from me to spoil the party,' he shook his head, 'but I thought you were teetotal.'

Moira swigged from a bottle of coconut rum in a convincingly piratical manner. 'That's before I discovered the demon drink.'

Karl and Dora took their cocktails down to the water's edge and found a comfortable rock from which to survey the idyllic surroundings. 'I must say, Moira's much more fun now she's fallen off the wagon. I used to duck behind the potted palm when I saw her coming at parties. But where did she get all the booze?'

'From Takis,' Dora replied. 'He's got some dodgy Albanian supplier who gets it all cheap, no questions asked, and very probably nicked from a cruise ship. That man could wangle contraband out of God Almighty. Look at that.' She pointed. 'One of the boat trips seems to be coming this way.'

A largish motor vessel from the neighbouring island, pop music blaring, stuffed full of girls in tiny bikinis and well-oiled men with embarrassing spray tans who looked as though they'd already had a few, was heading straight for the beach, where it deposited about forty enthusiastic revellers.

Soon they were all knocking back Moira's exotic cocktails. Neither Ariadne nor Dora had ever seen a tenth as many customers at the beach bar before.

'How did you manage it?' Dora enquired when she went up for a refill.

Moira grinned. 'Don't tell Takis, but I offered them the first one free as long as they had a second. Then I adjusted the price to cover them both, so everybody's happy. The boat captain's promised to make us a permanent stopover!'

At the top of the cliff they suddenly glimpsed a furious Xan Georgiades arguing heatedly with a delighted-looking Takis, who almost skipped down the path towards them.

'*Kyria* Moira, your name means fate in Greek, and it was a good fate for me when you came! Thank you, thank you, good lady. At last my little bar might make me some money!'

Moira smiled back. This probably wasn't the moment to remind him of the small fortune he'd shelled out on the liquor in the first place.

Later that afternoon, Penny and Nell were waiting on the quayside for their boathouse guests to arrive. 'Right, here comes the ferry. Do you think it's a bit OTT of us to be waiting here rather than at the boathouse?' Penny asked anxiously.

'Not at all,' Nell reassured. 'We're the equivalent of those little old Greek ladies who used to meet every boat. Besides, it's quite complicated to get to the boathouses, and we can make it seem easier.'

The huge ferry drew in and started to lower its stern ramp onto the quay for cars and trucks to come on and off. Foot passengers were already filing down the gangway at the side.

Penny held out a sign saying 'Mrs Williams', the name in which the booking had been made.

Most of the passengers turned out to be locals who came off the boat very swiftly, and after a minute or two Penny and Nell began to wonder if the new tenants had missed the boat. Then a young woman in huge sunglasses emerged, pushing a buggy.

'Oh my God,' Nell squealed, 'it's Willow!'

She began to run up the gangway and folded her daughter in a tight embrace. 'Willow! Darling! Why didn't you tell me you were coming, and why the hell did you book in the name of Williams?'

At that precise moment, a thin blonde emerged into the sunlight behind Willow. She looked like a rock chick preserved in aspic, wearing skin-tight white jeans and more silver than Cleopatra.

'Oh sweet Jesus. It's only bloody Marigold,' Nell murmured, so softly only Penny could hear.

'Well, actually . . .' Willow sounded both embarrassed and apologetic. 'It was Marigold who made the booking, and only told me afterwards. She thought your idea with the boathouses had real potential, and as Ollie's off on some banking jaunt we ought to jump on a plane and take an actual look.'

She gestured round to the beach, the tamarisk trees and the bright Greek sunshine. 'Plus, all this is pretty tempting.'

There was no mention of coming to see her, Nell noted. 'But why didn't you at least let me know?' she asked.

Willow dropped her voice. 'I'm sorry, Mum. You know what Marigold's like. She sort of took over, and she was paying. The thing is . . .' She hesitated, looking even more embarrassed. 'I think Marigold reckons she might be good at doing up boat-houses herself.'

Nell made herself banish the thought that she'd quite like to kill Marigold. It was wonderful to see Willow, whatever the reason she'd come. Although if bloody Marigold thought she was going to take over the boathouses, she could take a running jump.

Nell hugged her daughter. 'Never mind, it's just great to see you.' She bent down to say hello to her granddaughter, who was just waking up and wondering where she was after the plane journey – and whose was the face that loomed towards her. Suddenly unnerved, she started to cry.

Marigold didn't waste a second but swooped down and plucked her out of the buggy. 'Naomi, poor little love, come to Mari.' She stroked the chestnut tuft of curls on the child's head possessively as if the baby were own. 'Everything's going to be all right. We're in Greece and we're going to stay in a lovely house right near the sea. Maybe we'll see a mermaid!'

Nell felt like telling her they were called nereids round here, but decided it wasn't worth it. She felt a sudden pressure on her back, and realized it was Penny offering sympathy.

'Right,' Penny said brightly. 'Let's sort out your luggage. You may find the easiest way to get around during your stay is by bike. We can arrange a baby-carrier attachment, I'm sure.'

One look at Marigold's white jeans, not to mention her

appalled expression, told Penny this was not likely to be a popular option.

'Fine, we'll call you a taxi. Why don't you go with them, Nell? I'll follow on by bike, since we won't all fit in.'

'This is all rather impractical, isn't it, having to travel so far to the town?' Marigold complained frostily as they all clambered into a cab. 'You didn't mention that in the advertisement.'

Nell decided it might be wise not to say she hadn't actually seen the advertisement, and had been absolutely stunned when anyone had booked.

She tried to distract them by pointing out the minuscule churches, the purple bougainvillaea that covered all the houses, the olive groves with goats sheltering underneath the trees and the tiny roadside shrines, but Marigold continued to look irritated.

Ten minutes later, they arrived.

'But this place is in the middle of nowhere,' Marigold objected. 'What if we need nappies? Or baby milk?'

Nell had been about to say that to a lot of people, the peace of the place would be the appeal, but again she held back. It would only be a red rag. Instead she produced the tourist map from the hotel and handed it to them. 'Here you are in this top corner,' she began. 'The island is only half a mile wide, so you're actually very near everything. Just round here is the beach bar run by the hotel. And there's the harbour, just ten minutes by taxi or a lovely journey by bike.'

Marigold stared at the map angrily. 'It feels like we're marooned on a desert island.'

Fortunately Penny arrived at that moment and rushed over to help them unload. 'This is so exciting! You are the very first people to stay here,' she smiled. 'The locals call them *smyrnata*, these places – they used to be where the fishermen kept their boats in winter, that's why they're right on the water.' She began to help carry their bags, while Marigold held the baby in her arms.

Marigold stood in frosty silence surveying what some people might call a picturesque spot set in deep peace, but clearly she saw as the back of beyond.

'There's a bakery just round the corner,' Penny explained, correctly interpreting Marigold's thoughts. 'You can get delicious pastries and even a takeaway cappuccino.'

'That's something, I suppose,' she acquiesced. The implication being that the location certainly needed compensations.

They climbed up the white stucco staircase at the side of the apartment, with Nell in the lead.

Once inside, Nell waited for Marigold's judgement.

'Oh, Mum,' Willow enthused, 'you've done a terrific job. It's cosy and hip at the same time!'

Nell couldn't help glowing with pleasure. 'It was mostly Penny. She got all the fishermen's wives doing the sanding and painting.'

'Yes, but *teal?*' Marigold enquired in tones of shock bordering on horror, 'with primrose yellow?' Her copious silver bracelets jangled in endorsement of this glaring error of good taste. 'And that sofa looks like some old divan with cushions on it.'

Neither Penny nor Nell rushed to inform her that that was precisely what it was, Chelsea Harbour being rather inaccessible from the island of Kyri.

'Our friend Moira has painted a cot specially for Naomi,' Penny enthused, changing the subject.

'We won't be needing that,' Marigold shrugged, 'we brought our own.'

Who's 'we'? Nell wanted to shout. *How dare you speak for my daughter in that silly fake Cotswolds drawl of yours, you stupid cow?*

Marigold finally handed the baby back to Willow so that she could examine the welcome pack. 'Wine. Good. But it isn't even cold, and I suppose it'll be revolting anyway. You could have left us red at least.'

Penny took one look at Nell and announced it was time they left. 'Would you like us to order a taxi to pick you up later?' she offered.

'I'm tempted to come back with you and book into that little hotel on the harbour,' Marigold threatened. 'At least that looked convenient.'

Penny and Nell exchanged horrified glances. Before they could answer, the knocker sounded on the newly painted front door.

'God,' Marigold shook her head. 'Nosy neighbours as well. No doubt it'll be hell to get rid of them.'

Nell went down to answer the door to find that Nikos, who lived round the next headland, was on the doorstep, smiling.

'Is Penelope with you? I have been hunting for her everywhere.'

'Yes, she's upstairs with our first guests, who have turned out to be my daughter Willow, her baby and her mother-in-law, Marigold. Come up and meet them.' She dropped her voice and added, 'We need a knight errant. You could help us get away before I kill the woman and Kyri gets on the map for all the wrong reasons!'

'Ah, of course; I will do my best. Sadly, though, I brought my bicycle rather than a white horse.'

At the unexpected arrival not of a nosy neighbour but a charming and sophisticated gentleman, Marigold's entire demeanour transformed from petulant older woman to helpless ingénue. It was quite a performance, as Nell remarked to Penny when they were alone later on.

'Marigold,' Nell said, a fake smile pinned on her face, 'this is our good friend Nikos, who is not only mayor of Kyri but lives just round the headland from you.'

'If there is any way I can be of help,' Nikos bowed, instantly taking in the nuances of the situation, 'please do not hesitate to ask me.'

'I can't tell you how reassuring that sounds,' simpered Marigold, subtly turning her entire body to face him. 'We are here with a small baby and entirely without transport. It goes without saying that we had no idea how remote this place was.'

'Actually, Marigold,' Willow attempted to interrupt and was ignored, 'it did say that this was one of just a few converted boathouses.'

'Villages usually have village shops,' replied Marigold dampeningly.

'Just hand me your list,' Nikos smiled, this time mainly at Willow, to Marigold's obvious irritation. 'And who is this?' He smiled at baby Naomi.

Here Marigold found herself in a dilemma so obvious that Nell almost laughed out loud. The last thing she wanted to own up to was being a grandmother.

'Our granddaughter,' announced Nell, laughing. 'Marigold and I are the two grannies, though obviously Marigold must have been a child bride.' She beckoned to Willow. 'And this is my daughter, Willow.'

'Welcome to Kyri, and thank you for supporting our newest venture. Your mother and her friends have been magnificent in their efforts on our behalf.'

He looked round for Penny and smiled a slow, sweet, intimate smile which made Marigold bristle with irritation.

'And where is your husband, Penny?' she asked in a sugar-coated voice. 'Colin, isn't it? Such a successful businessman, I assume he couldn't take the time off. Will he be joining you soon?'

'Not for the moment,' replied Penny, looking her in the eye. 'Now, we must go. I hope you have everything you need. Anyway, you have my number.'

'Penelope.' Nikos caught her arm as she was about to leave, while Marigold raised her perfectly plucked eyebrow. 'Don't forget the boat trip. I'll pick you up from the quay at nine.'

'I'll be there,' Penny replied, brisk as a gym teacher, not wanting to give Marigold any more ammunition for bitchy gossip.

'Oh my God,' she whispered to Nell as soon as they left, 'you weren't exaggerating! She's an absolute shocker. I only met her for a moment at home and she seemed okay, but she's a nightmare when you get to know her!'

'I'm so glad you think so!' Nell grinned. 'She's ghastly, isn't she? She had a moment in the Seventies when she was a bit of an It girl, called herself a model, hung around the King's Road with the smart set. Convinced poor old Ted, though. Old and rich and adores her, even though she treats him like something the cat brought in. They live in the fake Cotswolds with a house full of fake flowers. How the hell she dares to criticize our decorating!'

'But why does Willow spend so much time with her? I mean, she seems such a sweet girl.'

'Willow found it hard to forgive me for having the affair that broke up my marriage.' Suddenly Nell found herself on the verge of tears. 'And of course she's right. It *was* bloody stupid. I find it hard to forgive myself.'

Penny had just started to climb onto her bike. She put it

down, and came and hugged Nell. 'Look, I don't know what happened, but I know this. Most men do it because they can, but you're not like that. If you had an affair, there had to be a good reason.'

Nell looked at her intently. 'Just as there'll be a good reason if you have an affair with Nikos.'

'Yes,' Penny replied, holding her gaze. 'Thank you for seeing that.'

Eleven

At nine in the morning, Penny noted gratefully, the quay was almost deserted. It was too early for the boat trip captains to have arrived or for any tourists to be walking up and down deciding which trip to choose. Takis and Cassandra were still busy in the hotel and – thank God – it was far too early for Marigold.

She waited at the end of the landing stage, watching the sun sparkle on the sea and feeling it warm her skin into a delicious sense of well-being. Not to mention that she was about to spend the day alone with Nikos for the first time.

She wondered for a moment if she needed to be nervous. Did he take her eager acceptance to be some kind of invitation? As soon she saw his piratical boat rounding the headland, red sails billowing in the brisk morning wind, she knew he didn't. Their understanding was too deep.

Nikos smiled and threw her a rope. 'All ready?'

'Absolutely,' smiled Penny.

'Let go of the rope and climb aboard then. You'll have to be my second in command.'

Penny saluted and threw him what she hoped was a saucy sailor's grin.

'If you look like that,' Nikos threatened, 'I might have to come over and kiss you, which is maybe not a good idea with all Kyri watching.'

'There's no one on the quay,' protested Penny.

'That's what you think. Our every move will be dissected in the butcher's along with the lamb chops, I promise you!'

'We'd better get a move on, then!' Penny was shocked at herself. Where had this light-hearted, flirtatious person come from?

'So,' she asked as they left the shelter of the harbour, 'where are you taking me?'

'I was going to take you to the famous blue grotto, but it's on the exposed side of the island, and I don't like the look of those clouds.' He pointed at the curious flat-topped cloud arrangement. '*Cumulonimbus incus,* named after the anvil in Latin; you can see how much it is shaped like a blacksmith's anvil? Not a good sign. We will keep our eyes on it carefully. Instead we are going to a sheltered bay with my favourite beach on the whole island.'

'Aye, aye, Cap'n. What would you like me to do?'

'I want you to hold the tiller while I make some adjustments.'

'Fine.' Penny sat down and took over steering, not confessing that on dry land Colin told her she couldn't tell her right from her left. Colin wasn't here. It suddenly struck her that it had been such a short time since she'd arrived here, but already she seemed like a completely different person. The truth was, she wasn't missing Colin at all, and with every moment that passed she felt less guilty about her choice in staying here. She missed Wendy and the children, of course she did; but Tom never kept in touch anyway. Like father, like son. Oh dear, she did hope not.

She felt the wind whip her hair across her face and realized she must have changed the angle they were sailing at. Without being told, she corrected their course to the original direction, feeling proud of herself as she did. She was beginning to see that by his continual chipping away at her self-confidence, Colin had kept her dependent. He had made her think that without him she would be even more hopeless. But perhaps it wasn't true. She had become more confident and competent after only a few days here, two thousand miles away from him.

The thought struck her, scaring her suddenly, that though Colin hadn't been in touch, he wouldn't just give her up – or worse, let her give him up. There would be a fight at some point, and she would need all her new-found confidence and competence to survive it.

They were now mid-channel and the waves were higher, not protected any longer by the shoreline. The boat dived and righted itself, almost like a rollercoaster. She'd always hated rollercoasters, but she was enjoying this. It made her feel alive.

'Well done,' congratulated Nikos. 'It isn't easy to keep the course in this swell. You're a natural sailor. What other talents do you have? Can you weave wool, by any chance?' He laughed down at her. She could see herself reflected in his blue sunglasses, happy and laughing and actually quite pretty.

'Why on earth?'

'Your namesake, Penelope. Odysseus was away so long, everyone tried to persuade her to marry again. She had hundreds of suitors. So she said she'd choose one when she'd finished weaving a shroud for his father. But at night she unpicked it so that it was never completed.'

'Clever Penelope. She must have loved him.'

'I too have waited a long time because I loved someone,' Nikos said softly.

Penny held her breath. Was he telling her he loved her? Surely she had to be imagining it. How could a man like Nikos be in love with her, gauche, plain Penny, who, as Colin pointed out, hadn't even earned anything since they'd been married?

'You always put the world's value on yourself,' Nikos added, reading her thoughts. He had to shout because the wind was getting up. 'But that is not the only value that counts. Kindness counts, and generosity of soul. You have a generous soul, Penelope.'

She didn't have to answer, to her immense relief, because they were coming in to a small bay and Nikos gently took over the tiller. 'There are rocks underneath, just here as we turn. They protect the bay and make it a haven that few people know about. I am hoping we will have it all to ourselves, you and I.'

Penny felt a wave of desire and apprehension, confusingly tangled together.

Nikos threw down the anchor and began to fill the small boat they towed behind with the things they would need on shore.

Penny stared down into the sea. 'I've never seen water as clear as this. I can even see the shells on the sea floor.'

'Do you want to swim ashore?'

Penny hesitated, thinking of how she would look with her hair all wet, maybe eye makeup running, and then stood up, took off the linen shift dress she was wearing over her swimsuit, and dived in.

The beauty of the underwater world somehow added to the unreality of this whole experience. She could see purple sea urchin shells, the pointed perfection of a tiny topshell, the whorled beauty of a whelk, and yet when she put her hand down to pick any of them up they were swept away.

She got to the beach at the same time as Nikos and helped pull the small boat up onto the shore. The sun beat down on them, as hot as if it were summer.

'It's amazing!' Penny looked around her at the empty white sand beach, curving gently round the empty bay, the sea a dazzling aquamarine. 'You could be in the Caribbean!'

Nikos carried their stores over to a sheltered spot at the side of the cove and began to look for stones to put round a fire he wanted to make to cook their lunch. Penny watched, fascinated, as he produced kindling and matches and even a metal grille to put over the flames.

'Robinson Crusoe would have found his kindling on the beach,' she teased.

'Ah, but Robinson Crusoe didn't make boats. Find me some driftwood, and I'll have a better use for it than burning it.'

'Aren't you going to catch your own fish?'

'As a matter of fact, I have brought lamb from the supermarket, and vegetables from my garden. And here is another thing Robinson Crusoe wouldn't have had.' He produced a cool box and handed her an ice-cold Mythos beer. 'Now go and find that driftwood!'

Laughing at her own wickedness to be happily drinking at eleven, Penny walked along the beach looking for wood swept in by the sea. Instead her eye was caught by shards of green glass, washed to a frosted opacity, their sharpness blunted by the tumbling of the waves. A few yards further were two more, this time cobalt blue. Feeling suddenly excited, she looked for more. Nikos had told her that Kyri was on the popular sea route from Crete to Athens, and here was the evidence. Not sunken treasure, but bottles thrown overboard and broken up by the sea into these jagged pieces, which over time had acquired a beauty of their own. To her delight she found a tangle of old rope in a faded shade of greeny-blue and extracted a long piece of string, which she used to deftly bind up her pieces of glass until she had made a rough necklace. When she had ten or so pieces, she tied the string round her neck and headed back to Nikos.

'What, no driftwood?' he asked. 'What happened to Robinson Crusoe?'

'He found this precious jewellery instead,' she laughed, pointing to her necklace.

Nikos put down his fork and stared. He got to his feet and walked towards her, a look of immense tenderness tinged with loving pride in his eyes. 'My Penelope, only you could take broken glass and turn it into something beautiful.' He swept her into his arms and kissed her.

In the moment his arms were around her, she felt a vibration in the pocket of the dress she had slipped back on. Her phone. And she had the strongest intuition who it would be. It was as if her husband somehow knew what she was feeling and was determined to sabotage it. But she wasn't going to let him. She took the phone from her pocket and, without even looking at it, tossed it into one of the bags.

'Don't you want to answer it?' asked Nikos. 'Maybe it's something important.'

Penny smiled. Of course, it could be Wendy or Tom or something wrong with the children; but she didn't think so. Only Colin's timing would have been so spot on. She didn't want to be that Penny any more, always keeping everyone happy, never thinking of herself. She wanted to be like Penelope, who had waited so long for the man she loved. She was feeling strong and powerful and happy for the first time now that she had found him.

And for once she wouldn't let herself be submerged by her usual destructive thoughts. What if he was only using her for some undiscovered reason? What if she was making a fool of herself and would end up alone, her marriage in ruins?

Instead she put her arms round Nikos's neck, having to lean up even though she was tall, and pulled his head down to hers.

'I felt just like the broken glass, ignored and useless,' she whispered, using words she could hardly believe were her own. 'It's meeting you again that has made me feel strong and beautiful.'

They sank together onto the wet sand, and Penny could think only of the touch of his hand on her breast and an over-whelming desire for him to make love to her.

'Come and see the rest of the boathouses,' Nell suggested to her daughter. 'You'll meet Demetria – she's taken on a lot of the work for us. She may look like Melina Mercouri but don't be fooled, she's more like Sheryl Sandberg on speed.'

They arranged to meet Demetria an hour later. Naomi slept peacefully in her sling while Marigold, to Nell's relief, sun-bathed on their balcony.

The next-door boathouse was the one where Moira had suggested a beautiful old door for a headboard behind the bed.

'What a clever idea!' Willow snapped away with her camera. 'I'd never have thought of that, but it really works.'

'We didn't have a lot of choice,' laughed Nell. 'All the furni-ture in the boathouse was donated by the village, and we just painted it.'

'Like the teal dining table that Marigold hated so much?'

'Exactly!'

Willow looked round, taking in the painted chest of draw-ers, the floor-length indigo curtains with their tie-backs made of fishing nets, the screen painted by Moira with a nymph being chased by a satyr which screened off the bath; the old wooden cupboard brought back to life with each panel adorned in a different shade of green; and how with all the quirky objects, the place still looked spare and stylish.

'Did you do this, Mum?' she asked, genuinely impressed.

'Some of it. I really enjoyed it, actually.'

'And this was why you wanted to stay on?'

'We feel useful here. They really need tourists, and there's something about Kyri that makes you want to get involved. It's a very special place.'

'More special than Sevenoaks?' she teased.

'Sevenoaks is fine, a bit suburban maybe. The thing is –' Nell realized she hadn't even admitted this to herself – 'I was feeling at a bit of a loose end once I'd stopped working at the surgery, maybe even a bit lonely.'

'Oh, Mum.' Willow slipped her arm round Nell, and Nell, practical, efficient Nell, had to fight back tears. She hadn't meant to make Willow feel guilty. 'Why don't you get in touch more? We'd love to see you.'

'I often want to, but you seem to be . . .' She hesitated, real-izing she had to tread gently here.

'. . . At Marigold's rather a lot?' Willow supplied. 'Ollie says the same, and she's his mum! She does rather take over your life. The thing is, she can't bear to be alone, ever! Ollie says it's because she was quite a wow when she was young, in all the gossip columns, and she can't accept being on the sidelines because she isn't young any more.'

'That sounds very astute of Ollie. Especially about his own mother.'

'Maybe I should be a bit more astute about you.'

Nell took the plunge. She didn't get many chances these days. 'I know you're still angry because of what I did, screwing up the family, just being selfish and stupid. But believe me, I've paid too.'

'Mum, that was years ago!' Willow shook her head. 'I just thought you weren't really interested, that you didn't want to be a grandma. I mean, you do look very young. Younger than Marigold, actually, even though she spends more on beauty products than Kim Kardashian!'

Nell felt laughter and tears bubble up at the same time. 'Darling, I don't care whether I look a hundred – well, maybe not a hundred. I'd *love* to be a grandma!'

'Then we'll have to see what we can do,' Willow grinned. 'Wrestle Naomi from She Who Must Be Obeyed and remind her there are two grannies in this family!' She looked round again. 'You do have a talent for this, you know. I can't wait to put it all on Insta. We need to find you a project at home. Unless you're intending to stay in Greece permanently? With what's happening with the EU, I wouldn't blame you.'

'Maybe I'll do a blog or vlog or whatever its name is, and call it The Other Granny. I bet that would hit a nerve!'

'Absolutely! My friends are always talking about the rivalry between the grannies, checking up on Instagram to see what the other one's doing with the grandchildren and whether it's more exciting than with them! Worse than sibling rivalry, apparently.' Both of them laughed. 'And where did all this interior design savvy come from? I always thought you were a fifty shades of taupe person.'

'To be honest, most of the ideas were Penny's.'

'What, boring goody-goody Penny? Penny in the Alice band?'

Nell thought of this morning, when she'd looked out her window and glimpsed Penny climbing alone onto Nikos's boat, and smiled.

'People aren't always what they seem, you know. Me included.'

'Come on, we'd better go and rescue Naomi from Marigold. She's probably breastfeeding her by now.'

'She doesn't!' Nell replied, shocked and repulsed.

'No,' giggled Willow. 'But I do sometimes have to remind her, politely of course, that Naomi is *my* baby!' She reached out her hands. 'Come on, old Mum, let's have a hug.'

Nell hugged her back, feeling blissfully happy. She didn't grudge Penny her Nikos. Seeing more of Willow, and holding her little granddaughter in her arms at last, would be more than enough for Nell.

Dora finished putting on her makeup and checked herself in the wardrobe mirror. She had on her bronze off-the-shoulder number and, with her satisfyingly suntanned skin, decided she looked pretty good. She'd always tanned easily, and one slight benefit of getting older was that your tan seemed to last longer.

She got down her Mulberry shoulder bag and began to transfer makeup, hairbrush, wallet and room key into it. She didn't know why she was going to all this trouble, since she was only having dinner with Karl. Still, he might be old but he was fascinating. He'd been involved in digs in Egypt, Syria – he'd almost wept when he described how beautiful Damascus used to be, the city of roses – as well as helping find Viking hoards closer to home in Staffordshire.

Downstairs she said good night to Cassandra, who was on reception, and handed over her key. They had decided to eat at a small restaurant round the bay rather than the usual one on the harbour.

Dora, always exactly ten minutes late, which she had decided was the required time to be cool without being rude, looked round the restaurant. It was charmingly chaotic, with a few wooden tables and chairs on one side of the narrow road to the harbour and others right on the beach. It had a play area put aside for children where numerous small people were bouncing up and down noisily. Dora decided Karl must have opted for the beach, probably to get away from the children, when an attractive older man with short, immaculately cut hair, wearing a smart pale blue suit, stood up and addressed her from an adjoining table.

'Karl?' she demanded, her jaw almost dropping at how different he looked.

'Professor Karl Brinkley at your service, ma'am,' he bowed.

'What have you done to yourself?'

'I decided if I was going to have dinner with a beautiful woman, I ought to make a bit of an effort. So I went to the barber. Greek barbers are the best in the world, you know. So then I had to get out a clean suit.'

Dora surveyed him critically. She had rather liked the shambolic professor look, but the twinkle was still there, thank goodness. 'You look like a superior Italian lounge lizard,' she announced.

'I take that as rather a compliment for a Cambridge professor of classical antiquity.'

'Emeritus professor,' she reminded him, laughing.

'Ouch,' he replied with an engaging grin. 'Emeritus professor. Shall we sit down?'

She was about to sit next to him, when he shook his head. 'Sit opposite,' he suggested as they sat down at a pretty table under a huge mulberry tree with a glorious view of the beach. 'Then I can admire the view.'

'But the sea's in the other direction,' she pointed out.

'Precisely,' he replied with his twinkly smile.

'Thank you, kind sir.' Dora pretended to bat her eyelashes, thinking of a silly magazine article she'd read that said you sit next to a friend and opposite a lover. How ridiculous.

The chaotic charm of the place ran to home-made pottery plates, water jugs and beakers instead of wine glasses, and a menu written out by hand. They ordered aubergines roasted with tomatoes and the local soft cheese, followed by *sheftalia*, spicy meatballs flavoured with fresh coriander, for Dora and *kleftiko*, slow-roasted lamb shanks, for Karl.

'Did you know *kleftiko* literally means "stolen meat"?' Karl asked. 'It used to be illegal for poor people to own animals so they stole a sheep and cooked it in a hole in the hillside with lots of fresh herbs for maybe twelve hours, so deep the smoke wouldn't show and the smell of roasting meat wouldn't give them away. That's why it's so delicious.'

Dora surprised herself by finding she was really interested. 'It's fascinating to learn about a culture through things like that. Ariadne – she's the girl who found the hand of the statue – knows how every herb can be used for healing, because that was what they used before they had doctors and drugs. Did you know, if you scratch yourself you can use lavender? And that rose petals can reduce swelling?'

'Aren't we the folklore experts?' he laughed. 'By the way, I was talking to a colleague in Athens. These stolen statues are much bigger business than I thought. It's got so common here that they even had an advertising campaign to tell people why dealing in antiquities is stealing, and terrible for Greece as a country.'

The waiter was just arriving with their food. 'Tell you what –' unconsciously Dora's voice had dropped to a whisper – 'tomorrow I'll take you to the caves. I haven't given up on the missing Venus yet, I promise you.'

'Good,' he grinned back. 'That's why I came, after all.'

The meal was delicious. Dora abandoned all thoughts of calories and ordered a baklava for pudding, followed by two thick Greek coffees accompanied by fragrant slices of lemony Turkish Delight dipped in icing sugar.

'Shall we push the boat out and have a glass of Greek brandy? Metaxa is supposed to be pretty good,' Karl suggested.

Dora laughed. 'No, no, you must try Ariadne's recommendation. Not Metaxa but Mastiha!'

'What on earth is that?'

'A local spirit made from the resin of the mastic tree. It tastes like ouzo, but with a slightly resinous flavour. According to Ariadne it's also useful for acid reflux, heartburn, indigestion and ulcers!'

'Sounds just about perfect after three courses and Turkish Delight. Waiter! Two glasses of Mastiha please!'

The waiter looked momentarily nonplussed. Clearly this was not your everyday request.

'While we're waiting I'll nip off to the ladies',' Dora smiled. 'If I can find it!'

'Excuse me, madam, ladies' toilet is down the road a little. I am very sorry,' the waiter told her apologetically. 'Ours not work and we share with cafe nearby.'

'Never mind. Send out a search party if I'm not back in five minutes. No, maybe make it ten.'

The shared ladies' wasn't too far away and Dora made the most of the tiny mirror to adjust her makeup and tidy her hair. As she was putting her brush back in her bag she picked up the tones of an urgent conversation taking place just outside. Even though she couldn't speak Greek there was something about it that made her stand stock still. One of the voices was familiar, but she couldn't quite place who it belonged to.

Without emerging into the lighted street, she glanced surreptitiously round the wall that separated them.

Two men were standing with their backs to her. The first managed to look both rich in a flashy sort of way – the sort of man you saw coming off the yachts that occasionally docked in the harbour – and also somehow untrustworthy. Maybe it was the unnecessary dark glasses, or the way he kept looking up and down the street for no apparent reason.

The second was Xan Georgiades.

He looked up just at the moment Dora was ducking back into the toilet, and for a fraction of a second their eyes locked. Pandora Perkins, the scariest PR in London, felt her chest tighten uncomfortably and her breath begin to come faster.

It was an unfamiliar emotion she recognized as fear.

Next day, Nell spent a delicious afternoon playing with her granddaughter on a shady rug on the balcony, with the waves lapping gently beneath, while Willow and Marigold sunbathed. Marigold, typically, wore a Heidi Klum bandeau bikini that Nell recognized with a jolt of envy as being the one she'd wanted herself, until she saw the £275 price tag and settled for a £7.95 version from Primark.

'I hate strap marks,' Marigold had announced as an explanation for why she had paid nearly £300, 'they're so unsexy. Besides, I used to know Heidi a bit.'

Nell ignored this attempt to show off and concentrated on tickling Naomi's tummy, while Willow appeared not to have even heard.

'So where is your friend Penny today?' Marigold asked Nell. 'Not out with the sexy mayor, I hope?'

'I have no idea,' responded Nell, ignoring the spiteful tone that was creeping into Marigold's voice. 'Probably painting furniture or doing something helpful. She usually is.'

'She's hardly that much of a saint. I saw the look they exchanged, as if they wanted each other on toast. Why is that husband of hers letting her stay on here anyway? Colin, isn't it? Nice man.'

'You only met him for five minutes in Harrods, Marigold,' Willow reminded her.

'I'm an exceptionally good judge of character,' her mother-in-law insisted.

'When did you meet them?' Nell asked her daughter. 'You didn't mention it.'

'I still had baby fog. Penny remembered me, actually. I was looking for the ladies' and she pointed it out.'

Nell grinned. 'That sounds like Penny. She'd always know where the ladies' was even if you were on Jupiter.'

'I still don't know what he's thinking, letting her gallivant off to a Greek island,' Marigold commented bitchily.

'Marigold, for goodness' sake,' Nell tried to keep her temper for Willow's sake, 'we are in the twenty-first century. Why did Ted let *you* come?'

'That's quite different.'

'Because you've got him firmly under your thumb, that's why,' Willow commented jokily, not looking up from her book.

Marigold cast a venomous glance at Nell. Her biddable

daughter-in-law was behaving quite differently in her presence. Almost rude.

'I just wonder if he has any idea what's going on out here and whether someone ought to have the courtesy to let him know, that's all.'

'Marigold!' Willow snapped her book shut this time, making her mother-in-law jump. 'For goodness' sake! This has nothing to do with you. You don't even know them.'

'I don't think that's the point. If Ted were teetering on the edge of infidelity I would want someone to tell *me*, I can assure you.' Willow fought back the image of chubby, submissive Ted on a precipice of temptation and decided it would be a jolly good idea if he fell in.

'Anyway,' Marigold continued, with a smile so deliberately fake it would have scared the fishes under the deck, 'why don't we all go out to dinner tonight? I'm not one for staying in –' she couldn't resist getting a dig in as well – 'and there's nowhere to shop for supper nearby anyway. And I'd like to meet your other friends. You could invite the mayor along too,' she added innocently.

'What about Naomi?' Nell asked Willow.

'Naomi'll be fine,' Marigold answered for Willow. 'I used to take Ollie to nightclubs in a basket and he just slept under the table. He was the youngest member at Tramp and Annabel's. If anyone objected, I just checked him with my coat and gave the attendant a big tip. It made him the easiest baby.'

'I bet that's why he hates going out so much,' Willow giggled. 'I've never met anyone like Ollie for a night in with the telly!'

Marigold ignored this jibe and decided that Nell was a thoroughly bad influence.

'I'll talk to everyone and let you know.' Nell replied

politely. She didn't know if she could bear a whole evening of Marigold.

'Penny, what on earth are you doing?'

Penny was sitting staring out at the sea, her usually cheerful face a blank, cutting cotton wool buds in two.

'Oh, this,' she replied absent-mindedly. 'I'm doing it for the environment. Haven't you seen the photo of the seahorse with its tail wrapped round a cotton wool bud?'

'No, Penny,' Nell said gently. 'Why are you really doing it?'

Penny's face became a picture of anxiety, 'I don't know what to do. Do you think I should tell Colin?'

Nell sat down next to her. 'Tell Colin what exactly? That you've fallen in love? Have you talked to Nikos about the two of you? What his intentions are, so to speak. Is this a holiday romance or would you want to leave Colin and live with him here?'

'Oh God, Nell,' Penny almost wailed. 'I don't know . . .'

'OK,' Nell continued, 'let's look at it another way. If you hadn't met Nikos again, would you be perfectly happy with your life at home?'

'No. But I would have gone on putting up with it, because that's what I do. That's my problem – I put up with things. But now I've seen an alternative, a man I don't need to put up with, someone who cares about me, amazing though it is.'

'You may hate me for saying this, but I think you need to have a conversation with Nikos before you take it further. I had an affair with someone who saw it as just fun, and it completely wrecked my life. I think you're different, and so is he. But you need to know what you're dealing with.'

Penny stopped chopping up the cotton buds and smiled.

'You're right. There's no point telling Colin until I know what my choice really is. Thank you.'

Nell's face twisted into an ironic smile. 'This would make my daughter laugh. Me giving marital advice! It's taken her twenty years to even talk to me. And how about this for a diversion? The ghastly Marigold would like us all to meet up and go out for dinner. And you'd better watch out. I rather think she's got her eye on your handsome Nikos.'

'Well, that would be one solution to my problem,' Penny laughed. 'I'm game if you are.'

Unusually for Dora, she got dressed without even thinking about what she was going to wear.

She was feeling stupid about the way she'd reacted to Xan Georgiades and his dodgy-looking friend. The man could be anyone, and Georgiades was just naturally resentful of her because she'd interfered at the public meeting by supporting Ariadne. It was equally ridiculous to feel nervous about showing Karl the cave where she thought there could be something hidden.

They didn't even have to draw attention to themselves by hiring their own boat from the quay. As long as they found one that had a small blow-up motorboat that went right into the caves, they should be able to see what had caught her eye last time. Tomorrow she'd take Karl down to see if they could detect anything suspicious.

Unless, of course, someone had moved it.

Twelve

They all gathered round a long table, laid for nine. It was a glorious night and the last rays of sunset still illuminated the harbour, outlining the fishing boats against a sky streaked not just with pink but yellow, grey, blue and orange.

'It's such a beautiful place,' Nell sighed. 'Such a pity the tourists all flock to Santorini when they could discover all this.' She gestured round at the beach and the tamarisk trees.

'Is that what you'd want?' Moira countered. 'So many cruise ships they have to ration them?'

'They could send one here, surely that would help,' Nell persisted.

'The town is thinking of allowing that,' Nikos said quietly. He was dressed casually in white chinos and a crisp cotton shirt that Penny loved because it brought out the light blue of his eyes. 'That, or allowing an airport.'

'But that would be terrible!' Penny protested. 'Just look at what happened to Zanthos when they got an airport!'

'What snobs you all are,' Marigold sneered. 'What's wrong with cruise ships and airports?'

'Nothing, of course,' Nell agreed. 'It's just that Kyri is such a special place.'

'Bloody boring, if you ask me,' Marigold shrugged. 'It could do with a bit of rowdy nightlife. A few stag parties would liven the place up.'

'There you are, Nikos,' Penny giggled. 'You could make Kyri the stag party capital of the Cyclades!'

'OK, everyone,' Takis beamed round. 'Nice to see the generations!' He patted Naomi on the head, and to Willow's surprise she didn't cry. He twisted his rubbery features into a Mr Bean smile which reduced the baby to such an attack of giggles that she got hiccups. 'What will you have to drink?'

'An ouzo for me,' volunteered Nikos, turning to Penny to see what she wanted.

'Me too,' instantly seconded Marigold, favouring Nikos with such a seductive smile that he glanced behind him to see who it was directed at.

'White wine for me, Takis,' Penny requested, trying not to laugh at Marigold's less than subtle technique.

'And me,' Dora nodded. 'What are you having, Karl?'

This time it was Moira's turn to smile. To her, he was still Professor Brinkley. 'A Mythos, please. They have so much of archaeological interest here. I'm sure they could get the upmarket tour operators interested.'

'Bloody hell, I can just see it,' Marigold shook her head. 'All those *Guardian* readers with their guidebooks and their crochet. Give me Club 18-30 anytime.'

'Aren't you a bit old for that, Marigold?' Nell asked naughtily.

Takis had come back with their drinks and the menu.

'What fresh fish have you got?' Nikos asked.

'Calamari! Straight from the sea today. Caught by my

nephew, Christos. He isn't much good at fishing, but he always catches the squid!'

'Not for me, thanks.' Moira shuddered. 'I don't think I'm ever going to eat anything with tentacles again.'

'My God, no!' Nell sympathized. 'But just think – if it weren't for your food poisoning, we'd never have discovered Kyri.'

'And how long are you planning to stay?' Marigold asked, her eyes fixed on Penny. 'I mean, you'll have to get back to real life soon, surely?'

For no apparent reason Dora, Nell, Penny and Moira all began to fall about with laughter. They didn't need Marigold to ask them something they were already asking themselves.

'What on earth are you laughing at, you mad bitches?' Marigold demanded.

'It's just that for some reason,' Nell eventually explained through her giggles, 'Kyri has turned out to be more fun than Sevenoaks!'

'Is there any development over the status of the olive grove?' Professor Brinkley asked Nikos, once sanity returned and they had ordered their food.

'I have approached the Department of Cultural Antiquities many times,' Nikos sighed. 'But they tell me it is becoming so common for criminals to find artefacts and sell them that there is little they can do.'

'So, is that it for the lost Venus?' the Professor enquired.

Dora listened intently.

'Maybe,' Nikos looked momentarily defeated. 'For the moment, at least. I have no powers to take it further without the Department.'

A loud crash made them turn. Ariadne had dropped the tray of their drinks she was carrying. 'You cannot abandon her!' she accused, her face as pale as any marble statue.

Takis rushed out and started to pick up the debris. 'Ariadne!' he commanded. 'This is not the time. Help me with this mess.'

Still white-faced with anger, she bent over the broken glasses and started to pick them up.

'I will replace them instantly,' Takis apologized.

'Don't worry,' Dora whispered to the professor. 'Tomorrow we'll go on a boat and I'll show you where I think she could be hidden.'

Ariadne, whose hearing was sharpened by years of listening out for goats wandering off to distant parts, lifted her head fractionally and looked at them.

'I'm so sorry you can't get anywhere with the authorities,' Penny said softly to Nikos. 'I know how frustrating that must be.'

'It is,' he replied, his eyes softening. 'My power means so little, it seems. Thank you for understanding.'

Marigold watched the interchange intently. Suddenly she grabbed the baby back from Nell, on whose knee she had been sitting happily. 'Aren't you at least a little shocked by your friend's behaviour?' she whispered to Nell in an almost-audible tone. 'I mean, she has a perfectly nice husband at home. And here she is making a spectacle of herself. At her age, too,' she added spitefully.

'I'm really not sure it's any of my business,' Nell replied crisply. 'And it certainly isn't any of yours.'

'Oh, really?' Marigold reached for her bag, got out her purse and slapped down a ridiculously large amount of euros. 'I'm not sure I should be colluding in this. There are certain things one should take a moral stance about. I find I'm not hungry after all. Here's our contribution. Goodnight!'

Marigold swept off towards the taxi rank by the harbour.

'I'd better follow her, Mum,' Willow apologized. 'I know she can be a pain in the arse, but she is Ollie's mum. I'm sure she doesn't mean it.'

Nell watched the departing figures. 'And good riddance,' she muttered to no one in particular. 'Now we can start to enjoy ourselves.'

The next morning, Dora and Karl met in a cafe by the harbour and looked at the small row of boats offering day trips round the island. They waited deliberately for the popular ones to leave and headed for a rather dilapidated vessel whose skipper looked as if he'd be happier in the bar than on a boat. His fisherman's jersey had more holes than a string vest, and his eyes were distinctly rheumy and red from a hard night's drinking.

'Really?' asked Karl dubiously, eyeing the better-maintained little boats leaving the harbour. 'Are you sure?'

'Really,' asserted Dora. And then, softly, though it was unlikely the skipper spoke much English, 'He'll be happy to go wherever we want him to, and there are no other passengers to get in the way.'

In that she was mistaken. At the last minute, Ariadne emerged from the hotel and ran across the quayside, jumping aboard just as they were leaving.

'I'm coming too,' she announced, her sweet face with its almond eyes set in unusual determination. 'It was me the goddess spoke to!'

While Dora looked shocked, Karl made room for her, adding with his usual twinkle: 'I rather think you heard us discussing our little trip last night.'

'If you are looking for the goddess, I need to be with you,' Ariadne insisted.

'You know,' Dora said gently, 'she is actually a statue, not a real goddess?'

The girl didn't answer and stared at the horizon instead.

As they motored towards the open sea, Dora couldn't resist glancing behind her.

'You know,' Karl pointed out in his quiet way, 'you really shouldn't keep looking behind you. It makes it seem as if you're doing something you shouldn't be. Besides, I think you can be pretty sure that in a place as small as Kyri, everyone will know exactly what everyone else is doing.'

'You may be sure *he* will know,' Ariadne stated matter-of-factly. 'The rich Athenian the goddess hates. He keeps a glass in his bedroom to look far away. I have seen it when I cleaned there.'

'Well, there's your answer,' Karl laughed, and he turned back towards the quayside and waved.

Their captain decided it was time to take control. '*Oriste*, my friends. Where is it you would like to go today?'

'I would like to see a little of the coastline in that direction,' said Dora, pointing the opposite way from the caves.

'Aha.' Karl tapped his nose in confirmation. 'Confuse the opposition, eh?'

'But there is nothing of interest that way, *kyria*,' the captain protested. 'That way, only the beaches that have suffered from debris being thrown from many yachts.'

'Ah,' Dora announced self-righteously, 'but I am extremely interested in the topic of pollution by plastic.'

Even Ariadne got the giggles at this.

'*Kyria* Dora,' she stated through her laughter, 'you are beginning to sound like your friend Penelope!'

After they had tutted at a beach where the blue edge of the waves was not created by nature's palette but made of minuscule pieces of blue carrier bags, which Dora photographed enthusiastically on her phone, they set off back in the direction that really interested them.

'So where exactly is this cave where you saw something suspicious?' Karl enquired in a low tone.

'We follow the other boats to the popular pirate caves, and it's a little further on,' Dora explained.

They stared down into the gin-clear water, where little troupes of striped tiger fish darted ten feet below.

At the first lot of caves, the occupants of the earlier boats were diving merrily in or climbing carefully down ladders, their snorkels on their heads. Dora wished she were braver, that she didn't view snorkelling as a terrifying endurance test. And as for scuba diving! It was her idea of hell.

They passed the landmark rock that stood alone in the sea with a natural archway, too small even for a boat to pass through, nosed round the headland and motored towards a gaping hole in the cliff, where their skipper slowed and threw down an anchor. 'Now you swim,' he announced.

'Swim?' almost shrieked Dora.

'Come, I will show you,' Ariadne giggled, searching on the floor of the boat for a mask and snorkel tangled among the ropes. 'I am a good swimmer.' She leapt joyously over the side, leaving Dora, in her off-the-shoulder Ralph Lauren swimsuit, to climb gingerly down the ladder.

'I'll keep an eye on the boat,' offered Karl. 'Make sure it's still here when you come out.'

'Karl,' Dora instructed sternly. 'If I can do it, so can you. It's important!'

Reluctantly, Karl stripped down to extremely baggy trunks and dived over the side.

'Don't go away!' he called to their skipper, who laughed as though the idea were a huge joke.

Once in the cave, Dora tried not to panic. As long as she could see the sunlight at the cave mouth, she told herself, she would be all right. If she looked down she could see the pattern of the currents on the sand of the seabed, as clear as the sharp lines of a woodcut. Above her, the rock was striped in greys and yellows by thousands of years of buffeting by stormy seas. Dora could appreciate its beauty while at the same time battling with terror.

Was this the right cave, anyway? Her certainty began to ebb away like the receding tide. And then she saw the side passage leading off to a smaller cave, and knew it was the place after all. 'There!' she shouted. 'I saw something in there!'

Ariadne, braver than the other two, instantly dived down and out of sight as Dora held her breath.

'Are you all right?' asked Karl, sensing her fear.

'Fine, but I'll be better when we're back on the boat.'

Ariadne seemed to be out of sight for far too long, and Dora felt her chest began to tighten with panic when the girl's face appeared above the water. Dora knew at once that the cave was empty. 'Perhaps I missed it,' Ariadne began. 'I got a bit scared. I will go again.'

Dora pulled herself together. She couldn't let Ariadne take the risk. 'Let's go back to the boat. I probably imagined it.'

They swam gratefully towards the light. When they came out of the cave mouth, they looked round for the boat.

It was nowhere to be seen.

'Oh my God, the boat's not here!' Dora gulped in air and water, making herself accidentally choke, and gasped dramatically for breath.

'Calm down, Dora,' instructed Karl.

He forced her to lie on her back and float. 'Floating stops you swallowing air and helps calm the panic,' he explained to Ariadne. 'She'll be all right now. I'll go and investigate.'

He swam further away from the cave, grateful at least for calm seas. As luck would have it, the other tourist boats had already left, so there would be no one to call for help. The risk would be if there was a current or rip tide not visible to the eye. He looked up at the cliffs beyond the caves. There would have to be some way of climbing them.

To the left of the cave, the sea was completely empty.

He swam slowly, keeping himself very much under control, round a small headland to the left.

There was the boat!

Their skipper had moored out of sight of any prying tourists and helped himself to a large slug of ouzo, the evidence of which was still in his hand as he snored happily away.

Karl swam up to the boat and climbed up the rather rickety ladder at the back, strode across the deck and whipped the bottle out of the sleeping skipper's grip. 'For God's sake, man, what the hell do you think you're doing?'

The captain woke in a daze to find he was being berated by an angry, white-haired old man with an expression like thunder, and rubbed his eyes. Surely Zeus was just a legend?

Furious though she might be, Dora had never been more grateful to see anybody when the boat appeared in the cove.

Ariadne shinned up the ladder, full of youthful energy, and held out a hand to help Dora.

'Is she all right?' asked Karl anxiously.

Ariadne grinned up at the professor. 'I think she's just disappointed about the goddess.'

They refused the beers the captain offered them on the way back – though Dora would have dearly loved to accept – on the grounds it would encourage him.

'So,' Dora said, looking round at the other two as they motored towards the quayside, 'maybe it wasn't the statue after all. But what the hell do we do next?'

*

203

'I've done something rather stupid,' Moira confessed to Nell, when she bumped into her in the little supermarket behind the hotel.

Nell put down her shopping basket, which contained a large container of still water and a rather delicious-looking sandwich plus some mosquito repellent, a plug-in anti-mosquito device with little blue tablets and a packet of those coil things you burn which the Italians call *spirale*.

The only mosquito on the island had had the discrimination to bite Marigold and she was making the most ridiculous fuss about it. If Nell couldn't reassure her that it wouldn't happen again, she'd started talking about moving to the hotel. And Nell couldn't stand that.

'What have you done?' This was rather intriguing, as Moira was about as given to self-analysis as Donald Trump. In fact, the Donald was probably slightly more prone to diffidence than she was.

'I've offered to cook a meal for thirty people.'

'Why?'

'The boat-trip man who brings all the tourists to the bar wanted to throw in an al fresco supper.'

'And you agreed?' Nell asked incredulously.

'It was part bribe, part threat. He said if I couldn't, there was a bar the other side of the island he might start taking them to instead.'

'I see.' Nell kept a straight face. 'Do you have a signature dish? Something you could stretch a bit with bread and salad?'

Moira folded her arms unhappily across her chest. 'Do I look like the kind of person who has a signature dish? I lived in a Cambridge college for thirty-five years. We had food laid on. OK, it was terrible, but at least it was there.'

'What about Cassandra? Surely she'd help?'

'Cassandra's cross with me. She thinks the whole Treasure Island thing is too much of a risk. I keep telling her it's just an experiment to lure some boat trips, but she's still cross.'

'Takis, then. He owns the bar, after all.'

'He's going to visit his son on Zanthos.'

'Ah. How about a barbecue?'

'Brilliant idea! Will you help me, Nell?'

Nell had, of course, worked out where the conversation was heading.

'I mean, you wouldn't want to waste that Prue Leith course. And you did wow the fishermen with your sumac.'

'OK,' Nell agreed. 'On one condition. You keep an eye on Dora. I think she's got a bee in her bonnet about finding this missing Venus.'

'What's wrong with that?' Moira shrugged. 'We're in the birthplace of western civilization, and Dora is interested in finding a Greek statue instead of trying to get D-list celebrities into crappy magazines. I'd say that was progress.'

'Yes,' Nell replied dubiously. 'But I have a bad feeling about it. Professor Brinkley said there can be big money in smuggling things out of Greece. I just hope she's not taking risks.'

'Life is about risks, otherwise you might as well be dead,' Moira stated.

'Well, get you, Ms Greek philosopher,' Nell replied. 'You'd better start keeping a notebook. The thoughts of Moira O'Reilly, retired classicist.'

'Less of the retired, if you don't mind. My mind is still extremely active.'

'Not, unfortunately,' Nell reminded her, 'when it comes to thinking of recipes.'

*

It was probably stupid to feel she needed an excuse to see Nikos, but to just descend on him out of the blue and demand to know if he loved her was something Penny couldn't contemplate. She'd never been good at being direct, anyway. What would Colin have done if she'd ever asked him if he loved her? She could just imagine it. He'd have looked at her as if she'd lost her mind and then bark, 'I married you, didn't I?'

The scene suddenly struck her as both totally accurate and acutely painful.

As she went to find her bike Kyri's daily life unfolded all around her. The children playing football on the beach, the old men in their usual position at the end of the harbour poised like old maids on the concrete wall, gossiping. The sun pouring its liquid gold over the aquamarine sea. The ferry arriving and disgorging lorries loaded with building materials or watermelons, a local woman with a vast checked shopping bag and finally a thin stream of tourists.

It was almost lunchtime and a couple caught her eye sitting at a table by the water's edge. They were probably in their seventies, he white-haired, in a check shirt, she with shoulder-length hair in that forgiving colour somewhere between blonde and grey, nicely styled. She wore white jeans and a pretty top. For some reason Penny thought they might be Scandinavian.

But that wasn't the most noticeable thing about them. It was that they shared a kind of affectionate peace. They didn't seem to be talking but not – as with some couples you glimpsed in restaurants – because they had nothing to say. Penny sensed it was more because they didn't need to. Being in each other's company after many years together was enough.

Out of the blue, Penny's eyes began to blur. She would never have that. But then, with Colin she never *could* have had it. She couldn't think of a single happy evening they'd spent eating out, just the two of them, with a fraction of the peace this couple seemed to have.

She thought about home, and suddenly her decision to stay on here seemed extraordinary, outrageous even. To have just abandoned her husband, her daughter and her grandchildren on what must seem like a crazy whim. She thought about her usually tidy and sparkling home. Would Colin have tidied or washed up a single thing? What was he thinking anyway, that he had made so little protest? Wasn't she worth protesting over?

She parked her bike and leaned on the harbour wall, staring out to sea. Just next to her two little boys were fishing, no different from her own son when he was young, or her grandson. Suddenly she missed them all passionately, all her certainty undermined. Was she just being some stupid Shirley Valentine?

She had to know.

The little boys looked at her in surprise as she jumped onto her bike and started to ride with furious speed along the narrow coast road that circled the island.

She was in such a hurry that she didn't notice a figure come down the staircase at the side of one of the boathouses as she passed on her bike and stare after her.

She arrived at Nikos's house ten minutes later, propped her bike up outside and knocked on his door before she had time to lose her nerve.

Nikos opened it wearing a cotton wrap with a red karate-style belt. The sight of his soft, dark chest hair made her remember what it meant to feel genuine desire. 'You look more like a samurai than an upstanding mayor of a Greek island,' she teased, hoping he couldn't see how much she wanted him, in case he felt it was too overwhelming.

'That's good, seeing as most mayors of Greek islands are bald, paunchy and given to making long speeches about the vital importance of sewers and drainage. Believe me, I have personal experience. Come in.'

His smile of welcome was so heartfelt she couldn't help but return it.

'So what are you doing still in your dressing gown – I assume it *is* your dressing gown – at this time of day, Your Worship?'

'I am making a boat. And what is this Your Worship? Do you not save such greetings for God?'

'It's what we call mayors in England. I don't think the British talk directly to God.'

'What a strange place your country is.'

'Can I see it?'

'Of course. What would you like to see?'

Penny started to giggle. 'The boat, of course.'

'Ah. It is over here at my work table.'

Penny marvelled again at how simply Nikos seemed to live. There was no TV screen dominating his large white-walled living room. It was as if the sea, seen through a vast window of plate glass, was enough of a diversion.

He smiled, reading her thoughts. 'You are thinking that Nikos, he lives like a monk, no screens to seduce him from his pure simple life, but the truth is I have a smartphone and also a laptop hidden in the cupboard.' Feeling silly, Penny remembered that Nikos was the one who had made sure the island had modern communications. This time it was his turn to stare out at the dazzling sunlight as it danced across the blue waters of the Aegean. 'It is true that I have tried to simplify my life. When you have spent so many years as I have in meetings and hotel rooms from Copenhagen to Calcutta, living here with only water as your companion can be very calming.'

Listening to him, Penny realized again how little she knew about his life. 'What about real life companions? Relationships? Did you never want to marry and have a family?'

Nikos smiled ruefully. 'Of course. I would have been mad if I had pined for a dream of a fair-haired English girl all my life. I have been in love and been loved back, but it has not always been by the same person. Perhaps like some medieval troubadour, I have the crazy fault of longing for the unattainable.'

'How sad.' She picked up the boat he was working on and studied it. Both in its simplicity and the wealth of loving detail, it was a thing of beauty. 'And what if you could attain it?'

They stared at each other for a long moment. He took a step towards her just as there was a loud banging on the door.

'Ignore it.' He took her in his arms, and she felt the exciting brush of stubble on her face as his lips searched for hers.

The knocking persisted, even louder than before. Eventually Nikos tore himself away and threw open the door.

Marigold stood on the top step, and pushed past Nikos to address Penny. 'Is your friend Nell here with you?' she demanded, trying to disguise a smug smile. 'She doesn't seem to be answering her phone. You'd better tell her it's her grandchild. I don't think she's at all well.'

'Right,' Penny threw a look of despairing apology at Nikos, 'of course I'll look for her at once.'

She was on her bike, pedalling as fast as she could towards the hotel, before she started to wonder how the hell Marigold had even known she was there.

Thirteen

Nell was busy talking to Takis and Moira over a delicious lunch by the harbour.

Cassandra, having heard that Moira was going ahead with the lunch for thirty without her, was trying to outdo her in advance. She had persuaded Moira and Nell not to order their usual Greek salad, which was delicious enough, and instead laid before them a veritable feast: various pastries straight from the oven, succulent lamb meatballs, deep-fried courgette fritters, *dolmades*, plus the usual tzatziki, hummus and taramosalata.

'Good God,' Nell whispered, 'how many of us does she think there are?'

'I'm sure we'll manage,' Moira eyed up the food greedily. 'We can always go and throw up and start again, like the Romans did.'

'Thank you, Moira.' Nell made a face. 'Just as I thought we'd cured you of the classical references. Come on, Takis!' she commanded, as he arrived with wine and water. 'We need some help eating this lot. Sit down and join us. It's not as if you're exactly run off your feet.' She indicated the empty tables around them. 'Anyway, we want to consult you.'

Takis sighed, looking round at his restaurant with its pretty painted tables and chairs, crisp white napkins, each with a red rose in a vase decorating it, the bright blue sea a perfect backdrop. 'Yes, we could certainly do with a few more customers. If it wasn't my family working here I'd have to close down, and I don't know what I will do when Ariadne leaves.' His rubber face looked suddenly stricken until he forced himself back into his usual good humour. 'Anyway, thank you ladies for trying to help. What can I do for you?'

'Nell is worried about Dora.' Moira, tactful as usual, jumped in with two feet. 'She thinks she's getting involved in something potentially dangerous.'

'The statue, you mean?'

'Yes.' Moira piled her plate high with everything in front of them. 'Although, if you ask me, the real danger to Dora is ending up as a carer for my lovely old mate Karl Brinkley.'

'Moira, honestly!' Nell tutted. 'I've no idea if they'll end up together but Professor Brinkley hardly needs a carer, and frankly I can't imagine a more unlikely candidate than Dora.'

'You mind my words.' Moira popped an entire *spanakopita* into her mouth.

'That was amazing,' admired Takis. 'Maybe we should have *spanakopita* eating contests at the beach.'

'Anyway . . .' Moira eyed the pitta bread, deciding what to put on it next, 'do you know of a dodgy-looking rich bloke, smart clothes, always wears sunglasses, even at night, seen hanging round here lately who Dora thinks might be the kind of person in the market for an illegal statue?'

Takis sipped some wine and considered the question. 'I know someone who sounds as you describe. But he owns a place on Santorini where you can buy expensive garden ornaments only.

Greek urns, sun dials, fountains and, yes, statues, but nothing of real value.'

Moira raised a meaningful eyebrow at Nell. 'Interesting. I think I'd better go and have a look.'

Before Takis could discourage her, they were interrupted by the arrival of a red-faced and flustered Penny.

'Nell! Thank goodness I've found you!'

'I'm not that hard to find. I haven't even been anywhere.'

'You haven't got your phone on.'

'No. I left it upstairs. Everyone I want to talk to is already here.'

'It's Naomi. She isn't well, apparently. Marigold came looking for you.'

'And where were you, anyway?' Nell asked, as yet unbothered by the news. 'I thought we were supposed to be painting more furniture today.'

Penny shook her hair in her usual gesture of extreme embarrassment. 'I was at Nikos's house.'

'I see.' Nell sipped her wine, instantly understanding the situation and why Penny was so embarrassed. Bloody Marigold must have seen her pass and barged in because she was jealous. Typical. Naomi being ill was probably just an excuse. That woman really was too much. 'Well, I think we can work this one out pretty easily.' She gestured to a spare seat at the table. 'Marigold isn't getting enough attention, and is trying to create a drama with herself at the centre. I'm sure Naomi's perfectly fine. Come and join us, by the way, the food's delicious.'

Penny sat down, visibly relaxing, and Takis poured her some of the wine.

'Isn't it glorious here?' She looked out at the sun sparkling on a shimmering sea, and smiled at the sound of children laughing as they ran along the silky white sand. Here and there, gorgeous young women bronzed themselves on white plastic sunbeds sipping mojitos from the pop-up bar, while the men sat in the shade drinking cold beer and surreptitiously checking their phones.

'Thank you,' Takis said simply. 'It is a beautiful place.' He sighed gustily. 'If only we could get a few more visitors.'

Nell stood up suddenly, a wave of guilt assailing her. 'Maybe I'd better get my phone. Just in case.'

Her room had been tidied and the bed made, probably by Ariadne, and her phone sat on top of the crisp white duvet cover.

There were three messages from Willow, each more agitated than the last. Oh God, thought Nell, Naomi really is ill. She instantly called her daughter, trying to remain calm.

'Mum!' Willow replied after only two rings. 'Can you come straight over? Marigold thinks Naomi is really quite ill but you know what she's like, always overreacting to things. Can you come and see what you think?'

'Of course,' Nell grabbed her bag, 'I'll get a cab now.'

The others were still sitting sunning themselves at the table.

'Actually,' she admitted, making a face that Penny immediately understood, 'Marigold could be right. Apparently Naomi is a bit off-colour. I'm just going to lend a hand. Could you put mine on my bill, Takis?'

'On the house, madame,' he bowed.

'Takis, no!' Nell shook her head, smiling. 'That's no way to do business. We know you like us. I want to pay. See you later, girls!'

Penny stood up. 'Do you mind if I come with you? Just in case you need moral support.'

'Of course. You can distract the dreadful Marigold.'

There was a cab waiting hopefully outside the cafe two doors along, and they climbed in. Ten minutes later they were running up the staircase at the side of the boathouse.

Nell wasn't prepared for the sight that waited for her. Willow, pale as a shadow, was walking backwards and forwards over the white-painted floorboards while Marigold, for once looking normal and human, anxious even, was holding Naomi in her arms.

'Nell, thank heavens you're here,' Marigold greeted her. 'I'm sure there's something not right with her. She was just coughing and wheezing and now she's been all floppy like this for the last hour. She doesn't want to eat and she isn't even crying!'

Nell didn't think she was the mother of the year herself, but she could see there was something worrying in the way Naomi's little body drooped in Marigold's arms.

'We didn't worry at first. I thought it was just a cold,' Willow explained anxiously. 'There was someone on the plane who kept sneezing right next to us.'

'Maybe you'll be able to comfort her.' Marigold handed the little girl to Nell.

A jolt of overwhelming love laced with maternal terror ran through Nell. This definitely wasn't right. 'We need to call the doctor at once. He was very good with Moira. I'll get his number now.' She passed the baby over to her daughter.

It seemed an eternity before the phone was answered and the doctor's wife, Eleni, was on the line. 'I am afraid he is out on a call, but I will get him to come as soon as he can.'

Knowing he was on his way calmed them all until the little girl erupted into a sudden coughing fit, followed by a worrying wheezing sound. Willow, desperate to do something, went to stand on top of the steps to beckon the doctor in as soon as he arrived.

Fortunately he wasn't long.

'Bronchiolitis,' he said with reassuring certainty after examining her. 'It is a common lung infection in small children, though more usual in winter. You say you were next to someone on the plane. I see it often but this is more severe, the way she is so limp and unresponding. At her age, she should be in hospital.'

'Do you have a hospital?' Nell demanded, trying not to panic.

'No, I'm afraid she will have to go to Santorini. They have a brand new hospital there. I will arrange everything.'

'How will we get there?' Willow asked anxiously.

'Nikos,' said the doctor. 'He has the fastest engine in Kyri.'

Penny and Marigold avoided each other's eyes. Under different circumstances they might have laughed.

'I will call him now,' the doctor announced. 'He will come at once when he knows it is an emergency. It will be quicker than organizing a helicopter. Sometimes, strangely enough, they take longer to come.'

Nell bit her lip, trying to keep calm, at the word 'emergency'.

Nikos had obviously answered at once. 'Just go down to the jetty at the end of the boathouses and he will pick you up in ten minutes,' the doctor told them reassuringly.

Moira chose that moment to call and ask if everything was all right.

'No, actually,' Nell replied. 'Naomi has to go to hospital in Santorini. Nikos is picking us up from the quay outside in ten minutes.'

Moira thought quickly. Santorini was the location of the mysterious statue seller. 'Do you mind if I come too?'

Leaving no time for a polite refusal, Moira ended the call and grabbed a bike from the harbour. She'd have to find out whose it was later. She rode so fast that she got to the quay near Nikos's boathouse before they did.

'At least the sea is calm for the little one,' Nikos said, smiling reassuringly as they climbed aboard. Penny was grateful that he gave no sign of the intimacy between them. The engine was already running and they headed out to sea. She couldn't help briefly thinking how painfully different this trip was from their last. Perhaps it was a wake-up call, sharp reality intruding into a misty dream, dispelling it with the worry of Nell's sick grandchild.

'Funnily enough,' Marigold announced, recovering her usual insensitivity, 'I've always wanted to go to Santorini.'

'How long will it take?' Willow asked Nikos.

'Just over two hours if we're lucky.'

To their general relief, the gentle up and down movement of the boat seemed to soothe Naomi and she fell asleep in her mother's arms.

'Tell me if she's too heavy, darling,' Nell offered.

'There is a bed in the cabin,' Nikos suggested, avoiding Penny's eyes. 'Perhaps you would be more comfortable to lie down with her there?'

That left the awkward quartet of Penny, Marigold, Moira and Nikos.

'So, Nikos,' Marigold demanded archly, 'does having a pirate ship make you feel like a pirate? I can see you with a black patch, taking beautiful captives to your cabin.'

'As I'm the mayor, I think I would be in charge of catching pirates rather than being one.'

'But you can't even catch whoever's stolen this famous statue!' she accused playfully, looking up at him through heavily mascaraed eyelashes.

Moira exchanged a 'God, she's awful' look with Penny.

'We don't even know if there was a statue at all,' Nikos replied crisply.

'Moira's sure there is, aren't you, Moira?' Penny couldn't help replying. 'Ever since she read about the corsair who found a statue of Venus and was going to take it to the French king but then hid it instead, it's been a holy grail.'

Nikos looked suddenly as stern as a statue himself. 'Tell your friend these things are better left to the authorities – that they should not get involved.'

'Have you met my friends?' But she saw Nikos was in earnest, and stopped making jokes.

'Maybe you could make everyone some coffee?' he suggested. Penny took the hint and persuaded Marigold to come and help her.

'Is he getting all Greek?' Marigold enquired. 'I was only joking about the pirate thing.'

'I think he's just concentrating on arriving as quickly as possible, because of Naomi. Maybe it's best if we stay down here.'

'What, in this glorious sunny weather? Seems such a waste.' Marigold tossed her blonde hair. 'OK, we'll stay down here.'

Nell was sitting at the end of the bunk bed, with Willow and Naomi lying next to her. Penny started to make coffee.

'I expect you know your way round the boat pretty well by now,' commented Marigold. Before Penny could even reply, she added, 'You do think Naomi's going to be all right, don't you?' Anxiety suddenly shredded her brittle manner. 'Oh God, it was my fault we came to Greece at all! Willow wasn't sure you'd want us, but I insisted it looked such fun.'

'The doctor seemed to think it was a good hospital,' was all Penny could think of to offer as reassurance.

'Penny . . .' Marigold began, and then seemed to lose her nerve. Her hand went up to her face, silver bracelets jangling.

'Yes?'

'I did something stupid, mean possibly.'

'Oh?' Penny wondered what was coming.

'I told your husband about you and the sexy mayor.'

Penny stared at her. 'What the hell do you mean?'

Marigold looked at her feet in their silly silver Converses. 'I sent him an anonymous message. I know,' she shrugged, as if it were some minor social faux pas like forgetting to answer a party invitation. 'I probably shouldn't have, but I felt it was unfair on the man, the way you were acting. He probably won't believe it anyway,' she added limply.

Nell, sitting on the bed, leaned forward incredulously. 'Marigold, you utter bitch, are you actually saying that you told Penny's husband she was getting involved with Nikos? And you didn't even have the courage to tell him who you are?'

Marigold turned her head away pettishly. 'I said I was sorry.'

Behind them, the baby began to whimper and cough again.

'Can you all stop being so bloody selfish?' Willow demanded.

'Sorry,' Penny apologized.

'I don't think it's you who should be apologizing,' Nell commented in a low voice. She turned to Marigold. 'When did you generously pass this information to Colin?'

'The day before yesterday.'

Penny pretended to make the coffee, trying to process this information. What would Colin have made of it, and what had the bloody woman actually said? Maybe she was right, and he hadn't believed it. He probably thought no man would fancy her anyway. But what on earth was she going to do now that he knew?

'We can see Santorini now, if you want a look,' Nikos called down.

'I'll stay here with Naomi,' Willow said angrily. 'Why don't you all go up? Some fresh air might do you good.'

On deck, they all stood watching the picture-postcard beauty of the famous island with its blue-domed churches, pretty jumble of painted houses, white windmills and bright splashes of pink and purple bougainvillaea.

Penny was surprised to find they had to negotiate their way past a giant cruise ship, with another queuing behind it.

'Aren't they vast?' She stared up at five storeys of windows and balconies. The ship resembled a floating hotel more than any vessel she'd seen before.

'Tourism is a strange thing,' Nikos shrugged. 'Santorini is capping cruise visitors at eight thousand a day. They have more than two million tourists a year! All crowding the tiny streets, standing on each other's shoulders to see the sunset, which is admittedly a dramatic one. And we don't even have eight hundred a week.' He looked back to the cabin. 'How is the baby? There will be taxis on the quay which will take you straight to the hospital. I will moor the boat and join you.'

He found a mooring, jumped neatly off onto the wooden jetty and tied up the boat, then held out his hand to help them all off. Willow went first with the baby, then Nell, Marigold and last of all, Penny.

What should she tell him?

There was no time anyway, as they ran from the quay and found a taxi.

The hospital was amazing. They had expected an unassuming little clinic. Instead it was an architectural gem with a modern façade of white-painted pillars that echoed ancient

Greek buildings. They rushed into the more humble emergency wing and were seen more quickly than if they had been at home, which amazed them given the state of the Greek economy.

'The treatment is to put the infant in a tent of humidified and heated oxygen,' the doctor informed them gently. 'At her age it is the best treatment. The steam passes through the bronchial tubes and clears them out.'

'How long will it take?' Willow asked anxiously.

'Perhaps a week, but two of you can stay with here if you wish.' He indicated a pull-out bed under the examining table. 'We are used to having fathers and mothers.'

Willow reached out a hand to Nell. 'Will you stay with me, Mum?'

Nell felt her heart lurch. Willow actually needed and wanted her. She put her arms round her daughter. 'Of course I will.'

'I really don't know why they wouldn't let me in,' Marigold complained to Penny and Moira in the white and pristine waiting area. 'I am the child's grandmother as well as Nell.'

She and Moira and Penny were still stuck in the busy reception area. 'Perhaps it's the gods punishing you for bad behaviour,' suggested Moira innocently.

'I expect they have some bureaucratic rule about numbers,' Penny offered.

'In Greece?' Marigold replied sourly. 'I'm going off to get a coffee.' She didn't offer one to Penny or Moira.

'Tell you what,' Moira announced as soon as she was out of the room, 'I'm off to the posh garden centre. If I stay near that woman any longer, I may kill her. Why don't you come too?'

'I'd rather hang round here for a bit,' Penny replied. The truth was, she wanted to call her daughter Wendy at the first opportunity and see if anything more had happened with Colin.

'Oh yes,' Moira grinned. 'I'd forgotten. Nikos is going to be here. And Marigold. That's nice. The two of you will be hanging round both hoping for the golden apple for who's more beautiful. I should really stay and join in to make it a fair contest.'

'Moira, don't.' Penny suddenly felt overwhelmed by emotion.

'Sorry. I was never very tactful. You're the winner, obviously.'

'Oh God, Moira.' Penny collapsed onto a plastic chair. 'It's all such a mess!'

'That's the nature of relationships,' Moira said, patting her ineffectually. 'That's why I've never had any. Stuck to the gods and kept well away. But it strikes me that the gods did exactly what they wanted, and it had a way of working out in the end.'

Penny attempted a smile. 'Perhaps you should write a book. *The Greek Gods' Guide to Modern Living*. Books like that are very fashionable at the moment.'

'That's better,' Moira grinned. 'You'll be all right, Penelope. You're stronger than you think. I'll go and distract the ghastly Marigold. Maybe I should take her with me to the statue man. She'd probably scare the shit out of him with one wink of those Dusty Springfield eyelashes of hers!'

Then she asked, 'Would you rather I waited too?'

'No, no, go off. It's fine.'

When Moira had gone, Penny slipped out into the tiny patients' garden they had passed on arriving at the hospital. It was a peaceful spot, newly planted with pink oleander and the usual purple bougainvillaea, with a small white wall high enough to sit on all round the edge of the flowerbed. No one else was there.

'Wendy?' she blurted as soon as her daughter answered. 'Oh darling, it's so good to talk to you!' She realized instantly that this emotional reaction would probably seem odd to her down-to-earth daughter. 'How's everyone?' she continued in a more normal voice.

'We're all fine,' Wendy replied. 'Pissing with rain, so we're trying not to think about our wicked mum who's abandoned us for the sun and sea, and what's that other word? Oh yes, sex, on a sunny Greek island.'

Penny felt herself flush uncomfortably, and was glad her daughter couldn't see her.

'Martin is his usual self with comments like "Oh is the dish-washer full?", then leaving his dirty plates on top. Milo is mostly on Planet Game. Ben is making cards for his A level revision and then losing them. Flossie is mostly on Instagram making weird faces and using filters that make her look like a cross between Cara Delevingne and the creature from outer space. I, as usual, am wonderful in every way.'

Penny took a deep breath. 'And Dad?'

'Oh, Dad. The same. He makes Martin look like a new man, which I assure you is quite something.'

'Has he said anything lately about me being away?'

'I haven't seen him much . . . ow, Floss . . . hang that coat up, it's dripping all over the hall!' Penny could suddenly picture Wendy's busy and endearingly chaotic family life, where she was the lynchpin and lodestone of all around her, and felt a painful stab of nostalgia for that moment in time when you were needed and wanted.

'Are you getting guilty? Don't. As I said before, it's good for him. Besides, last time I went round he was behaving weirdly.'

'Weirdly? How?' She tried to keep the panic out of her voice.

'Well, you know how he gets his assistant to even help him send an email? He was actually sitting at the computer looking stuff up.'

'What stuff?'

'It could have been easyJet, or it might just as easily have been porn. He covered it up when I went in the kitchen and switched the PC off at the mains even though he would have lost anything he was looking at.'

'He always does that,' Penny agreed. 'He doesn't know how to log off properly. What made you think it was easyJet?'

'It looked like he was writing things down so unless he was taking notes on different porn positions, which I think rather unlikely given his gammy knee, it could have been flight times. Maybe he's planning a surprise visit. Anyway, what have you been up to? Go on, make me green with envy.'

'Mostly painting furniture for the boathouses, so we can rent some more out. Why don't you take a look on the Kyri Island website? You can give me some advice.'

'You sound like you're having lots of fun.'

'Yes, I am. Except that Nell – you remember my friend Nell – her baby granddaughter has been taken ill and is in hospital.'

'Gosh,' her daughter commented in a tone of envy, 'so your friends' families are out there too. You didn't mention that.'

'I don't think Nell knew they were coming.'

'Mmmm,' commented Wendy.

'Darling?'

'Yes?'

'If you see Dad on the easyJet website, can you let me know?'

'I have to say I can't see him just jumping on a plane and travelling all that way to surprise you, but you never know.

223

Come to think of it, he hasn't asked me to stock the fridge up, but he might be planning to stay at his club in London. I know, radical inspiration – why don't you just ask him?'

After they rang off, Penny thought about it for a moment. Should she just ring Colin and ask him straight out if he was planning to come to Kyri? She decided against it. Colin wasn't an imaginative man, and if he hadn't already thought of it, it might give him the idea.

Moira disappeared while Penny went back to look for Nell and Naomi.

When she went back she found Nell alone. 'Thank God Marigold has persuaded Willow to go and get some food. It's just me and Naomi,' Nell greeted her.

They both stared at the small plastic tent full of oxygenated air with the baby, naked and defenceless, lying on her back like a china doll in a toy shop.

'She looks so tiny and vulnerable,' Nell almost choked. 'But this is the best treatment, apparently, and at least they aren't filling her full of drugs.'

Penny hugged her friend. 'It's so great she has you with her. And they do seem very efficient here.'

Nell smiled, looking much calmer. 'I know. Thank God we came.'

'Would you mind if I went after Moira? I'm a bit concerned about her going alone.'

'Of course,' Nell smiled a small, sad smile. 'Willow, and unfortunately Marigold, will be back soon. An excess of grandmothers, you might say.'

Penny grinned mischievously. 'Could I hazard a small bet? Ten grand, say? That Marigold will not offer to stretch out on a two-foot-six camp bed with no en suite bathroom?'

Once Penny had gone, Nell sat as close as she dared to her

granddaughter. 'Darling Naomi,' she whispered. 'I love you so much, and we're going to have such fun together when you're better.'

She sat back, overwhelmed by a powerful feeling of love and fear. The baby was so still and the hospital so quiet that the whole thing had an air of a dream about it, and yet Nell knew it was all too nightmarishly real. She found herself longing for one of those busy, noisy children's wards at home.

Usually when you were in a hospital you felt safe, that the decisions were in the hands of the experts. But Nell suddenly felt that here, today, the responsibility for her baby grand-daughter was down to her.

'Well,' Moira said when Penny found her at a bus stop outside the hospital, 'at least we get to see what all the fuss is about Santorini, and why queues of cruise ships are so keep to deposit all their tourists here.'

'So where is this garden centre?' Penny asked.

'In the capital. It's about sixteen kilometres away, but obvi-ously there's a bus.'

'That sounds a long way. I hope Nell will be all right.'

'Stay if you want,' Moira shrugged. 'I don't mind going on my own.'

'No, it's OK. I'll come.' Penny felt that this was an important moment for Nell, and didn't want to intrude.

'According to my map the road is mainly through the middle of the island, not one of those terrifying coast roads where they threaten to kill you round every bend.'

Despite Moira's efficiency, they got off at the wrong stop and had to climb the last bit through a rather scrubby vine-yard, past various scavenging and underfed cats. Finally they had a moment to stand on high ground and look at the view.

It was indeed stunning. Thousands of bright white houses tumbled down the hillside, making Penny think of a birthday cake she'd once made covered in white glacé icing that she'd been so proud of until it collapsed spectacularly before cutting. Up above, they could see the famous domes of Agioi Theodoroi, painted in that unique Greek blue so bright and deep it rivalled the colour of the sea below.

And then they plunged into the narrow main street and were sucked into a moving mass of thousands of tourists, clutching phones and cameras, like some vast tech-armed amoeba, all heading upwards.

'What's the big deal?' Moira asked a passing young woman in a crop top, as they tried to squeeze into the crowd like the Tube at rush hour. 'Is it the Sermon on the Mount? Or Zeus, perhaps, swooping down from Mount Olympus as a golden eagle?'

The girl looked at Moira oddly. 'It's just the sunset. It's a big deal here.'

Moira looked at her watch. 'But it isn't sunset for at least two hours,' she replied, puzzled.

'Yes, but the bars with the best view get full really early.'

'If you don't get a seat you miss the whole thing,' endorsed her friend.

'I can see that would be tragic,' nodded Moira. 'Happy snapping!'

They pushed their way upwards, grateful to lose the sunset-seekers as they turned off a side road in their eagerness to be able to move again.

'Bloody hell,' reminisced Moira. 'It's worse than the Isle of Wight Festival, and that had Bob Dylan and The Who.'

Now they found they were in a different stream altogether, apparently heading for the domed church.

'Is it me,' Penny whispered, 'or are we in the middle one of those mass Moonie weddings?' They stopped to let about fifty Chinese brides and bridegrooms pass them, all of them grinning wildly.

Finally they reached the spot everyone seemed to be heading for: a special platform put there by some enterprising wedding planner, where brides and grooms could stand with the perfect view behind them.

'Instagrammer heaven,' one of the camp followers kindly informed them. 'Everyone wants that for their wedding photo.'

They turned down a left-handed alley. Almost at the bottom of the next hill, where the houses were less white and even a bit shabby, they glimpsed a sign that read in both Greek and English GARDEN ORNAMENTS & STATUES.

The place seemed to be entirely unoccupied, but the gate was open, so they walked in and started to wander around. There was certainly a diverse selection of objects, from twee little statues of girls in what looked like nighties to life-size copies of the Three Graces, plus an extensive selection of nymphs and satyrs with the odd Pan to vary the flavour. There was a larger than life-size representation of Ares, the god of war; a wide selection of Venuses ranging from the coy to the overtly sexual; large and small urns, some filled with red geraniums; and a magnificently enormous fountain that wouldn't have been out of place in Rome.

But there was no sign of the couch upon which their own goddess disported herself.

'May I help you ladies?' A young man appeared, wearing a white t-shirt and faded blue jeans. He was deeply tanned, with shoulder-length curling blond hair.

'Adonis to the very life,' Moira commented to Penny in a low voice. 'Thank you. We are looking for some garden furniture.'

'Ah, then you are in the wrong area. This is only statues, furniture is down here.' He led them down two more sections, to an area full of candy-striped awnings and smart off-white canvas sofas.

'I was thinking of something a little more solid,' Moira remarked, looking round. 'A stone bench, perhaps.'

'Ah!' The young man brightened and offered them a dazzling smile. 'We do have one of those.'

Moira and Penny exchanged excited glances as they followed him to yet another area.

'Is this the kind of thing you'd be interested in?' He pointed to a simple stone bench with an attractive carved pedestal at either end.

'Very nice.' Moira tried to hide her disappointment. 'But not quite what I was looking for.' She wondered whether to show him the drawing, but that might be dangerous if he revealed it to his sunglasses-wearing employer. 'Would you mind if we had a little wander on our own?'

'Of course, take your time. Could I get you a cold drink? Coca-Cola? Water?'

Moira accepted and turned to Penny to find that she was sitting on the stone bench, clearly preoccupied about something else. She guessed something was up when Penny issued a gusty sigh.

'Are you OK, Penelope?'

For the briefest moment Penny wondered whether to admit how worried she was about Colin's curious behaviour, why he hadn't contacted her recently, even when he'd got Marigold's message; but Moira was not the most sensitive of relationship counsellors. The thought suddenly struck her that if Marigold had sent an email, Colin might never even have opened it.

Penny got to her feet. 'I don't think it's here.'

Moira stared thoughtfully at the young man's departing back. 'Look, if there are Cokes there has to be a fridge, and that means a hut or an office of some kind. Why don't you engage Adonis in some meaningful conversation, while I go and look?'

They waited for the young man to return.

'There you are, ladies, two ice-cold Cokes.' He handed them over. 'You certainly need one today, it is so hot.' He breathed out, wringing the bottom of his t-shirt for imaginary sweat and showing off his toned abdomen at the same time.

'We are renovating some properties on Kyri – I wonder if you could show me how the fountain works.'

'Kyri is a shithole,' scoffed the young man rudely. 'They could hardly afford a fountain there.'

'Is it for sale or not?' Penny asked in a tone of barely controlled anger.

'*Lipame,*' the young man bowed. 'I'm sorry, *kyria*, that was not polite. Let me show you now.'

They walked towards the large fountain while Moira pretended to study a tasteful cherub apparently strewing flowers for an imaginary deity.

'Do you sell many statues?' Penny asked.

'To the villas, yes. These boutique hotels, they only like everything modern, as if they could be anywhere instead of here in Greece.' He almost spat on the ground.

'So, tell me,' she asked, feigning fascination with the operation of its intricate systems, 'how does the fountain work?'

His reply almost made her laugh out loud. 'As a matter of fact, you just turn on this switch.' He pressed a button and water began to swirl down from the top of the fountain, gather in some hidden container and reappear again a few seconds later. So much for centuries of mechanical development.

Moira skipped noiselessly through the garden furniture to the remaining part of the site, which was out of sight round a corner. There were two huts here. The newer one had a simple pay terminal and old-fashioned till, plus a stool for Adonis and some sheets of plastic, presumably to swathe the more expensive furniture if it rained. Nothing more.

The other hut was made of greying wood, in dire need of a protective sealant if it was to last much longer. This was filled with gardening equipment. Moira assumed the business must double as a maintenance service for rich and absent owners. She was about to give up when she noticed a large pile of wood at the far end. Not so strange, as Greece could be surprisingly cold in winter, but there was something about the arrangement that seemed odd.

She carefully removed a few logs at the base, experiencing a kick of disappointment. There was nothing out of the ordinary. She was just about to give up when the pile began to topple so quickly that she had to move out of the way to avoid being injured.

Underneath was a tarpaulin which covered a six-foot-long object exactly the right size to be the marble bench. It was too securely fastened for Moira to open it without a knife, not a thing she generally carried. She swore under her breath.

Beginning to panic that Penny would soon run out of ways to hold off the blond Adonis, she quickly photographed the shape of the hidden object and began to feverishly replace the logs.

Minutes later, she inspected her handiwork. Was the arrangement the same as before, or could an experienced eye easily tell it had been interfered with? She had often read about feeling sick in the pit of your stomach, and for the first time she understood what it meant.

As fast as she could, she closed the hut door and half-ran back up the hill. Penny was still valiantly engaging the young man in conversation.

'Moira, listen to this,' she greeted her. 'Yorgos here is studying classical civilization.'

'That's great,' Moira congratulated, so lost for anything more to say that she added: 'Why are so many Greek men called Yorgos?'

The young man laughed. 'I have read that a third of men in Greece are called Yorgos, though I do not know if it is true. Certainly half my family are. But I am in the only one with fair hair.' He swung his shoulder-length locks proudly.

Moira grabbed Penny's arm. 'Come on, Penny, or we'll miss the sunset!'

Yorgos laughed again. 'You are too late. You will get nowhere near the good places to watch it.'

'Ah well,' Moira pretended to look devastated. 'Maybe we'd better go and drown our sorrows instead.'

'How did you get on?' Penny demanded as they walked away.

'I'm pretty sure I found it! Under a wood pile – but all tied up in a tarpaulin so, blast it, I couldn't take a photo.'

'Oh God, Moira! What the hell do we do next?'

Fourteen

Nell sat in the silence and emptiness of the hospital watching her baby granddaughter intently. It was so quiet that it felt almost as if they were the only two people left in the world.

Nell told herself not to be so dramatic. Ollie, the baby's father, was due any minute and Willow and Marigold had gone to the airport to meet him. Soon Naomi would be surrounded by well-wishers.

The truth was, she would love another cup of coffee to stop her eyelids from drooping and to be frank she needed to pee, but she couldn't risk leaving her post here at the baby's side. All this time she'd been unable to see her grandchild, while Marigold held her in her arms, and now here she was, on her own with her at last.

She studied the tiny bare feet and the perfect hands and the slight movement of the baby's chest as it moved up and down, breathing in the warm, oxygenated air.

An overwhelming love, stemmed for so long, suddenly flooded through Nell and she had to hide her head in her hands for a moment.

When she looked up almost a minute later, she was aware

that something was different. The chest seemed to be somehow static and there was no longer a slight flutter in the baby's eyelashes as she breathed in and out. Nell jumped up, panicking.

'I won't be a moment, darling,' she whispered to Naomi and she ran to the door. There were no nurses visible at the nurses' station. 'There's an emergency on the first floor. The nurse was called away,' a young woman with a camera slung round her neck informed her. 'I think someone's had a heart attack.'

'OK, thanks,' she blurted, looking round for a staircase. She ran up two at a time to the floor above, where a group of medical staff were indeed in the process of pulling screens round a figure on the bed.

'I'm sorry to burst in when you have an emergency but it's my baby granddaughter. She's got bronchiolitis and it seems to me she's stopped breathing,' she gasped, hoping somebody spoke English and could understand what she was saying.

A senior-looking woman doctor nodded to a very young-looking nurse and issued instructions in rapid Greek. '*Daxi*. We can handle this. Go and see what the situation is with this baby.'

The young woman led Nell to a lift and they both stood tensely waiting until the doors opened on the ground floor.

'This way,' Nell took her arm.

Naomi lay absolutely still under her covering of transparent plastic. Nell could feel the tension rise in the nurse as she lifted the mist tent and saw that there was no response in the tiny figure lying inside. Her panic transmitted itself to Nell with the speed of a contagion. For a second Nell felt rooted to the spot, then she jumped up.

'I'll get the doctor,' she said, and started to run up the back stairs.

Thank God there was the same doctor in the first ward at the top of the stairs. 'I'm sorry, but you must come,' Nell blurted. 'My granddaughter has stopped breathing.' The young nurse, who had arrived via the lift, was only a step behind Nell. She nodded in confirmation.

The doctor calmly signalled to a member of her team to take over and followed Nell back down the stairs. She leaned over the baby, her ear to Naomi's tiny mouth.

'I have seen this before,' she said with the same reassuring authority. 'We will give her adrenalin, and then change the mist to nebulized salbutamol.'

She lifted Naomi carefully from her tent and carried her away.

At the door she turned to speak to Nell just as Willow, Ollie and Marigold rushed into the room.

'Oh my God,' cried Willow, half collapsing, 'what's the matter with Naomi?'

'She needs different treatment,' the doctor announced in a tone that managed to be both kind and authoritative. The woman had an extraordinary face, somehow neither young nor old, quite lined, but with a warmth that seemed to embrace all human beings. 'She will be all right. Do not worry. But give your mother an embrace. It was she who spotted there was something wrong.'

Willow threw herself into her mother's arms and wept. 'Thank you, Mum.'

Ollie knelt down by her side. 'Nell, we can't begin to tell you how grateful we are.'

In their anxiety the two of them looked suddenly so young, almost too young to be parents.

'Oh my God, if you hadn't been here . . .' Willow began.

'But I was,' Nell said simply. 'And I always will be.' She pulled her chair up next to her daughter. 'I just thank God we all have each other again.'

Relief engulfed her so powerfully that she had to close her eyes and push out the terrifying thought of what might have happened had she not managed to find that doctor.

But she had.

'I love you, Mum,' said Willow humbly. 'And I can't even begin to thank you.'

No one noticed as Marigold silently left the room.

Penny and Moira picked their way down the narrow road, empty now, since the entire island seemed to have gathered at the top of the hill to watch the sunset.

'I hope everything's OK with Nell and Naomi,' said Penny. 'Do you think we should go to the hospital?'

'Too many cooks, I'd say,' Moira replied. 'Wasn't the dad due to arrive? Let's go to the harbour and look for Nikos.'

The subject of Nikos brought a twist of panic. What was Colin up to? She wondered if she should try Wendy again, maybe get her to seriously look for him; but then she'd have to admit to Wendy why it was so important.

'Are you OK?' Moira enquired. 'Not worrying that Adonis back there will go and tell his boss about the weird English ladies snooping around?'

'I hadn't thought of that. Do you think he was suspicious, then?'

'He did seem to rush off to get his mobile, but that could have been to access the football results or check how fabulous he looked on Facebook. I suppose it was odd that we were looking at statues when we don't even live here. Not the kind

235

of thing you can take home and give Auntie Vera for her birthday.'

Despite the crowds at the top of the hill, the harbour was packed with even more tourists in the cafes, souvenir shops and a row of pleasure craft. Nikos's boat was moored slightly away from the rest. He was standing in the covered cabin area, apparently deep in thought. When Penny waved, he smiled and waved back.

'I must admit,' Moira said, laughing, 'he's quite attractive as mayors go.'

'Stay there and I'll come and get you,' he shouted, heading for the steps at the back of the boat.

'How is the baby?' he enquired as he held out a hand to help Penny onto the blow-up dinghy. 'Should we wait here, or go back to Kyri?'

Penny's smile softened at the concern in his voice. Colin wouldn't have even entertained the thought.

'I don't know. I think I'd better call Nell,' she said once they were aboard. She sat down and got out her phone.

'Glass of wine?' Nikos asked them. 'I have some opened in the galley.'

'Fabulous,' Moira thanked him. 'What did I say about him being more attractive than the average mayor?' she whispered to Penny.

'Nell, oh thank goodness,' Penny exclaimed when her friend picked up. 'How is Naomi?'

Nell burst into tears.

'Oh my God, Nell, what's happened?'

'It's going to be all right. There was this terrible moment when I saw she'd stopped breathing . . .'

'. . . and it was Mum who noticed and raised the alarm,'

intervened Willow, who had clearly grabbed the phone. 'Ollie and I just haven't got words to thank her.'

'Do you want to stay on for a while?' Penny asked once the phone was back with Nell.

Nell paused, not sure how to answer. Her instinct was to say yes, but she didn't want to intrude.

'We can't do without her now,' called Willow in the background. 'She's our guardian angel.'

'Ooh,' Moira giggled as soon as they'd put the phone down. 'I bet Marigold won't be happy about that. Talk of the devil, look – there she is on the quay, waving.'

'Nikos,' Penny asked suddenly. 'Do you think we could leave now? As in *now*, now?'

'Whatever you want,' Nikos replied, smiling to himself. In under two minutes they were turning the vessel round to leave the harbour, with Marigold standing fuming on the quayside.

'Well that'll serve her right, the old boot.' Moira clinked her glass with Penny's.

'It certainly will,' Penny responded with a grin.

'Penelope.' Nikos shook his head in mock disapproval. 'This is a side to you I have never seen.'

Penny smiled back impishly. 'Maybe I haven't seen it myself,' she replied. 'And don't worry about Marigold. She'll probably commandeer a cruise ship.'

Moira got out her phone. 'I'm just going to text Dora that we may have found the base of the Venus.'

'*Kyria* Dora, a word,' Takis murmured to Dora when she arrived at the cafe for her early evening drink. It was market day and the cafe was full for once, mostly with fishermen moaning about regulations and prices in loud, voluble voices.

'Of course,' replied Dora. 'What can I do for you?'

'It is Ariadne.' For once his rubber face looked deeply serious. 'She is only fifteen.'

They glanced over at Ariadne, her almond eyes shining in her pretty round face.

'Yes?' Dora reassured. 'I'm not trying to lure her away to a life of reality television and tawdry glamour, if that's what you think.'

'It is not that. She is talking about looking for the statue in a cave. *Kyria* Dora, it is not safe for her to be doing this.'

Dora nodded. 'I agree.'

'She will not listen to me, it is you she respects and looks up to. She told me the other day that her life had been as dull as a two-hour church service until she met you.'

'Goodness,' laughed Dora, taken aback. 'I can't say anyone's ever told me that before. I will definitely have a word.'

She studied Ariadne from across the cafe. She was such an unusual girl, with her seriousness of purpose and her amazing knowledge of botanical life – so untypical of your average phone-obsessed teenager. She was like a girl out of time.

Ariadne, suddenly aware of her gaze, grinned at Dora, and Dora smiled back. Was it her innocence that so touched Dora? Her utter belief that the goddess Aphrodite had appeared to her and chosen Ariadne to uncover the mystery of her disappearance? And yet there was nothing of the mad visionary about her. She was as down-to-earth as the next girl. Dora must in future be careful what she said in front of her, and certainly ban her from further expeditions which could put her at risk.

She sipped her glass and breathed in the warm, scented evening air. What a delight this place was, and how warm and generous its people. If only they could just have a few more tourists. And yet, the irony of course was that with a real influx of visitors, the place might well lose its unique charm.

She saw Professor Brinkley emerge from the hotel doors and look around him.

'Karl!' she shouted in such a loud voice that the fishermen stopped jabbering and looked at her with admiration, wondering what would be her next move.

He made his way through the crowded tables and joined her. 'Busy tonight,' he remarked.

'Yes. Takis said he's almost run out of ouzo. Now look, Karl, what are we going to do about this statue? There must be something.'

Karl sighed. 'Very little I can think of. We need more evidence. Even a photograph of the damn thing would be a start.'

They turned to find Ariadne staring at them. 'I came to ask the professor what he would like to drink,' she said defensively, and then added: 'The goddess will be angry if we just abandon her statue.'

Before Dora could think of a reply her phone beeped, making her jump and causing Karl to fall about laughing. 'You're supposed to be the media hotshot,' he informed her, 'and I'm the old buffer, but at least I don't jump when I get a text. How did you survive as a publicist in the unpleasant world of the Twitterati?'

Dora turned away, trying to block out the thought of being fired by Venus Green for this very reason: her incapacity to exploit social media. To think in the nurturing world of Kyri, she hadn't even remembered it for days. 'My God,' she exclaimed, 'it's Moira texting from Santorini. They think they've found the base.'

'Great idea to share that with the entire restaurant,' Karl agreed. 'Maybe you should leave a note at reception announcing it to your friend Mr Georgiades.'

'Ariadne.' Dora was suddenly serious. 'I'm sorry you heard that. Please forget what I said.'

'You have a very loud voice, *kyria* Dora. It's a good thing none of these fishermen know what you're talking about.'

'Sssh, Ariadne,' Dora replied crossly.

'No. Not until someone finds the goddess.'

It was getting dark when Nikos dropped them back to the harbour, and there was no sign of Dora.

'She must have gone to bed already,' speculated Moira. 'Are you up for a late supper?'

Penny shook her head. 'Too much excitement. I'm going up, but I'm sure Takis will join you if you need some company.' And indeed, there he was, walking towards them with his usual friendly smile.

'See you in the morning.' Penny hugged her. It was amazing how close they'd all become, after such a shaky start to this trip.

Penny had hardly opened the door when her phone rang. It was Nell.

'How is everything there?' Penny asked.

'Really good. Naomi is responding very well to the new treatment. She may be allowed home tomorrow. Ollie has been looking for flights. They'd rather be in their own home as soon as it's safe. But Penny . . .'

Penny could hear the anxiety in Nell's voice. 'Yes?'

'What is happening with your husband after that bitch Marigold contacted him?'

Penny flopped down onto the bed. 'The weird thing is, nothing. He seems to have disappeared.'

'How, disappeared?'

'Wendy hasn't seen him for days. And he hasn't asked her to fill the fridge, which he usually does.'

'Where else do you think he could be?'

'I need to try his club again – he sometimes stays there.'

'What a strange world of women filling the fridge and men staying in clubs. I don't get much of that, being single.'

'Lucky you. But what I'm really scared of is him turning up here.'

'Do you think he would?'

'I don't know. He's a control freak who's gone silent. Oh God, Nell, I feel quite sick thinking about it.'

'Come on, Penelope, you're stronger than you think.'

'You don't have a furious husband to face.'

'We'll all be behind you, remember that.'

Penny smiled. It was true. Here on Kyri she wasn't alone.

When Nell got off the line she put a call in to the Piccadilly Club and asked if Colin Anderson was staying.

He wasn't.

'Shit,' Moira suddenly exclaimed, helping herself to a veritable Everest of Greek yogurt. 'Is it Wednesday?'

'Indeed it is,' agreed Takis, eyeing her helping with mixed feelings.

'Then it's my supper for thirty tomorrow night. Oh Jesus, how did I get myself into this mess? To me beans on toast is a gourmet dinner. Is Nell back yet, Penny? I really, really need her and she's not answering her phone.'

'She told me last night she might be back today, but I imagine it depends on the baby.'

Moira gobbled her yogurt and headed for the little super-market to try and find a bribe that would persuade Nell to help her.

After fifteen minutes of fruitless searching, she came across a mother-of-pearl shell in a beautiful shade of opales-cent blue. Clutching her prize, she headed for the harbour to meet the boat in case Nell was on it. To her enormous relief, she was among the passengers.

'Nell!' she shouted as her friend started to walk down the gangway towards the harbour.

'Moira,' Nell replied in surprise. 'That's nice of you to come and meet me.' It then dawned on her what Moira's real motive was likely to be, and she burst out laughing. 'Nothing to do with your feast for thirty?'

Moira looked sheepish and handed over the shell. 'I got you this. A keepsake of our time on Kyri.'

'Thanks, Moira,' Nell took the shell, and examined it care-fully. 'Marvellous colour. Just like the sea here each morning. Pity it doesn't come from Kyri.' She turned it over, revealing a large sticker bearing the legend 'Made in Indonesia'. Still, the thought was there. 'Let me take my bag back, and we can go and see what they've got in the market.'

Half an hour later they were filling a basket with glossy black aubergines, huge fleshy red tomatoes, courgettes and red onions.

'You do have a charcoal grill down at Treasure Island, don't you?'

Moira nodded.

'I think the answer is a lot of barbecued meats, and then we can load their plates with chargrilled vegetables, my special salad with watermelon, olives and feta, and enough pitta to feed a regiment. Why don't you go to the baker now and order it?'

Moira nodded. 'I love you, Nell!'

Nell grinned. 'And I've got the shell to prove it.'

Later on, they all gathered to eat together at the cafe on the beach. It was later than usual and the sea was suffused in pearly pink light, the afterglow of the sunset.

'Is everything all right with Naomi now?' Dora enquired as they sat down at a rather rickety-looking table right on the sand. Never having had children, or even a pet, she couldn't imagine what it would be like for a baby to suddenly get ill.

'So much better they've taken her home,' Nell smiled.

'I hope the awful Marigold has gone too?' Moira added.

'Do you know, I have no idea. I assume she must have gone with them. She's well pissed off with me,' Nell smiled with satisfaction. 'She resents me for getting the credit for noticing Naomi had stopped breathing. It should have been her who was the heroine of the hour.'

'They must have been so grateful,' Penny slipped an arm round her.

'*I'm* the one who's grateful.' Nell felt the tears threatening again. 'I've finally been forgiven.'

'Surely your daughter couldn't have held a grudge all that time?' Dora asked, startled.

'My affair meant the end of our marriage and as Willow sees it, her sense of security. She spent a lot of time with her father, and apparently he never failed to say it was my fault. So maybe she had a point. I can't tell you how wonderful it feels to finally be forgiven.'

Penny looked away and stared out to sea. How would

Wendy and Tom take it if she told them she was in love with Nikos?

'Now come on, everyone, what I want to know,' Moira said doggedly, 'is what we're going to do about this statue? Takis has been letting us live here cheaply on the grounds we are helping Kyri, but are we? I was thinking, Dora, you're in PR. Should we try and get some publicity for the story? You know, "Hunt for New Venus de Milo" type of thing?'

'The trouble with that is, all we have is the hand and your drawing of the statue. I'm not sure it's enough to dangle in front of the press.'

'I wish to God we'd had time to remove the tarpaulin in Santorini,' Moira said. 'I think the guy may have been suspicious as it was. What do you think, Karl?'

'To be honest, Dora's right. We need more evidence,' Karl replied.

'We haven't been as much use to the island as we hoped,' mused Nell.

'Are you secretly pining for Sevenoaks?' Moira asked. 'And what about Treasure Island? Now a major tourist attraction!'

Nell laughed and looked around her. The sun had just sunk behind the horizon and the waves lapped peacefully only feet away from them, as shimmering and opalescent as the shell Moira had given her. 'It's probably pouring with rain in Sevenoaks. Kyri is magical. I just wish we could do more, that's all.'

The next day at breakfast Moira, always the most direct of them, approached Takis, who seemed for once not to be dashing around but looking unusually anxious. Moira hoped it wasn't because he had business worries exacerbated by them staying in his hotel so cheaply. 'We were all talking last night and concluded we've been as much help to Kyri as four spare pricks at a Greek wedding.'

'No, no,' Takis's long mournful face attempted a smile. 'You have raised our spirits and given us a goal. That is very important.' He noticed the bowl of breakfast she was carrying. 'Of course, you could eat less yogurt!'

'I'm such a pig!' Moira looked instantly mortified. 'It's just that it's the food of the gods!'

'Don't worry. It comes from my mother's goats. Speaking of goats, have any of you ladies seen Ariadne?'

Moira shook her head.

'She has not been seen all morning.' The deep lines of his face seemed deeper than usual.

'Maybe she's gone to the grove of the goddess. She loves it there,' suggested Dora.

Takis looked momentarily relieved. 'Maybe you are right.'

'I'm getting ready for the feast at the beach bar so I'll look on the way,' Moira offered.

'Thank you.'

'I'll come,' Dora instantly seconded. 'And so will Karl.'

'I will as well,' Penny added. She'd never seen Takis look so worried.

'Couldn't she be off with the goats somewhere?' Dora suggested. 'Or looking for some wonderful herb or other?'

'The goats are all penned up. Nobody has seen her at all this morning.'

They finished breakfast and headed up the track towards the olive grove. It was another beautiful morning, early enough that the sparse numbers of tourists had not yet arrived on the ferry. The sun was beating down from a cloudless blue sky and the sea glinted invitingly through the olive grove.

'Have you taken the supplies for the feast over already?' Penny asked.

'Yes. Wonderful Nell asked Nikos to give her a lift. We couldn't fit it all on our bicycles.'

From the crest of the hill, they started to walk down towards the beach below.

'It is an amazing spot,' commented Dora. 'How many olive trees do you think there are?'

Karl looked round. 'Fifty or sixty. Old ones, too, from the look of the trunks. They've probably stood here for hundreds of years.' He looked up into the silvery leaves, where the olives were already beginning to ripen. 'It will be a tragedy if any of this goes.'

Suddenly Dora grabbed his arm and stopped him.

'What is it?'

'The scent! Just breathe it in!'

Karl took a deep breath. 'What is it? Quite pleasant and fresh, with a faint tone of something aromatic, like eucalyptus.'

Dora stared at him. 'It's myrtle. It's the scent of the goddess.'

'OK, I'll believe you. Where are the flowers?' He looked around him. 'What do they look like, anyway?'

'They're small and white, with fluffy stamens with yellow dots on the end. But there aren't any anywhere near, that's the whole point.'

'Don't be ridiculous, Dora.' His voice was every inch the calm rationalist from Cambridge University.

'OK,' Dora challenged. 'Explain it. You wanted to meet the goddess. If Ariadne were here she'd tell you you've just missed her.'

For once Karl could think of absolutely no answer.

'I know!' Dora became suddenly as stiff as a board. 'I think I know where she might have gone.' She turned and started to run back up through the olive grove. 'We need Nikos! I hope to God he's still down at Treasure Island. Come on, Moira!'

'What the hell has got into Dora?'

'I think she may have had a mystical experience.' Karl shrugged. 'Let's try and keep up.'

They followed the suddenly fleet-footed Dora, still wearing her supermarket plimsolls, as she led them through the trees and down the path to the beach below.

Fifteen

'Nikos!' Dora shouted. 'Wait!'

Nikos stopped pulling up the anchor and watched Dora's approach. There was something in her voice that had alarmed him, especially coming from the cool and cynical Dora. It spoke of panic and held a disturbing edge of hysteria, as if she were only just holding herself together.

He caught sight of Penny just behind her and attempted a look of interrogation, but Penny just shrugged. She had no more idea than he did.

'It's Ariadne,' Dora gasped, now out of breath as well as nearing hysteria. 'I think she may have gone back to the caves on her own to have another look for the statue. She overheard Karl and me saying that proof was needed or nothing could be done. You have to understand –' she started to wade through the shallow water to the boat, ignoring her long skirts dragging against her thighs – 'Ariadne feels personally responsible. Like a priestess, almost. Since she found the hand, she thinks Aphrodite is speaking directly to her.' Nikos helped her up the ladder at the aft of the boat and she collapsed onto the warm wooden floor. 'And after today, I don't blame her.'

'Stay there while I bring the boat into the jetty for the others. What you need,' he smiled reassuringly, 'is a Metaxa.'

If Dora hadn't been so upset, she would have felt that Penny was bloody lucky. Nikos was not just attractive but kind, a quality her friend's husband Colin seemed to totally lack. He climbed down into the cabin and steered the boat into the small wooden pier next to the boathouses.

Penny jumped in next, wondering for a moment if Marigold was still in residence at the boathouse and whether she would have been watching the drama unfold from her balcony.

Karl followed, and they set off.

'Where is it you think Ariadne would be looking?'

'The Corsair caves. The large one, with the entrance at the front and back.'

'OK. Penelope, could you get Dora a brandy? The Metaxa is in the galley. It will calm you down.'

'How would she have got there?' Karl asked Nikos, looking out at the blue and glassy sea.

'If she wanted to be quiet about it, she could have gone by kayak,' Nikos suggested thoughtfully. 'That way she wouldn't have to get one of the tourist boats, which would be expensive and they'd probably gossip. We'd better look out for a kayak moored somewhere.'

They all fell quiet, scanning the inlets and beaches for any sign of a kayak.

After a silent and tense fifteen minutes they arrived at the caves with the holes in the rock, where the corsairs had moored their small, swift ships so that they could hide any booty in the caves and still escape through the hidden back route to the open sea.

'No sign of a kayak,' said Dora, anxiously glancing round.

'Which cave are we looking for?' asked Nikos, tying up the

boat in the very hole the corsairs had made three hundred years ago.

'We'll need the small boat to go right inside the big cave. It's off that, to the right.'

They climbed carefully down the ladder into the inflatable craft, as Nikos tried to hold it steady.

The whole cave was illuminated by bright sunshine revealing the extraordinary colours of the rock beneath: blazing bright blue with dashes of yellow and rust red, like some wild impressionist painting. For a moment Dora's claustrophobia threatened to make her turn round and rush back to the boat, but a faint sound penetrated her consciousness like the freezing needles of a cold shower.

'There!' she almost screamed. 'In that cave on the right.'

Nikos wasted no time in diving straight overboard and swimming fast towards the smaller cave, his waterproof phone tucked into his shorts' pocket in case he needed to use it as a torch.

There was silence for what seemed to Dora and Penny an eternity, and then a shout from Nikos. 'She's here! Her foot is stuck in the rock. I'll try and release it.'

Another silence, and the sound of a sudden scream, which made Dora clutch Penny's arm in a painful grip.

And then Nikos appeared, holding Ariadne in his arms and kicking with his legs. Karl leaned down and helped him transfer the almost fainting young girl into the boat, where she half collapsed.

'I came to take look again because I know you thought you saw something, Dora. But he has taken her away!' The poor girl was almost in tears, feeling she had failed her goddess.

Dora took the shivering body into her arms, and began to gently rub the ankle that had been trapped.

'Let's get her back to the boat,' Nikos said. 'I've got a blanket in the cabin.'

He started the motor and they were soon back on board with Ariadne safely encased in an incongruous Royal Stewart tartan rug.

'I am so sorry . . .' she began

Dora hugged the slender body to her again, as Penny watched, fascinated. She had never seen Dora so emotional. 'You are a good, brave girl. Braver than all the rest of us. The goddess would appreciate that.'

Ariadne looked at her, her dark almond eyes beseeching. 'Do you think she would know?'

'Of course she would,' Dora stated baldly. 'That's why her scent was in the olive grove.'

Ariadne's taught body visibly relaxed. 'Then I haven't failed her?'

'Not at all,' Dora reassured.

'Your father has been so worried,' Penny added. 'He will be so relieved to see you.'

'Not angry with me?'

'Of course not.'

After that she fell asleep, still in Dora's arms.

When they reached the harbour, Takis and Cassandra both stood waiting. They carried Ariadne gently inside the hotel to her bedroom.

'Thank you! Thank you!' Takis repeated over and over. 'Sometimes I wish this statue had never been heard of!' His sad face suddenly brightened. 'But we have some good news. Three of the boathouses have been booked for next month! Somebody in England has been showing many pictures of them and how wonderful and peaceful they are!'

'It has to be Nell's daughter, Willow!' Penny explained

happily. 'She promised Nell she would put lots of stuff on Instagram to thank everyone for how kind they've been over the baby.'

She got out her phone and opened the app.

Don't go to Santorini with a million other people! Willow had posted. Go to the undiscovered Greek island of Kyri! With its beautiful beaches and friendly people, you will get a welcome you'll never forget!

'Well, Mr Mayor, what do you think of that?' Penny demanded, laughing.

The smile in Nikos's eyes was so tender, it almost melted Penny where she stood – but Nell was right. She had to tell him what Marigold had done, and find out where they stood.

'You have helped Kyri a great deal,' Nikos told them. 'Painting those boathouses and finding the furniture brought everyone together. There are a lot of plans to open bed and breakfasts. This interest on Instagram will be very useful. Most people on Kyri are not very up to date about the means of modern communication.'

'Them and me both,' muttered Dora.

'I still put my money on the printed word,' added Karl with an engaging grin.

'Of course you do. That's because you're a Cambridge professor,' replied Dora with an answering smile.

The feast was in full swing when they climbed down the hillside. The tourist boat guests, the men in hideous brightly coloured swimming trunks that would have been more at home in St Tropez and the girls in minuscule bikinis were necking equally garish cocktails and piling their plates with salad and meat.

'I must admit,' Karl commented, 'it smells damn good!'

'I love the look of that salad with feta and watermelon,' confessed Penny. 'I must ask Moira for the recipe.'

'She'll have no idea,' Dora said. 'I bet it's all down to Nell. Hey, Nell, we're not trying to con a free lunch, we just wanted to tell you that Willow has been brilliant!'

Nell smiled delightedly. 'Has she, how?'

'Thanks to her we've got three more bookings. Takis is thrilled.'

'That's wonderful. And it means Naomi must be all right, too. Willow is something called an "influencer". Companies actually approach her to plug their stuff for money! She's got thousands of followers.'

'It sounds a bit like Jesus,' Karl smiled. 'He would have been good on Instagram. Lots of pictures of miracles, like feeding the five thousand and turning water into wine.'

'Karl, don't be naughty,' teased Dora. 'Anyway it's really good news.'

'You can have some lunch if you wait ten minutes,' Nell offered. 'This lot are about to set sail. I hope they don't fall into the deep blue briny. They've had so many cocktails I doubt they'd even notice!'

They all watched the hedonistic diners, who had each paid thirty euros for a day of gentle debauchery.

'Do you remember when we were like that,' Dora whispered to Nell, 'able to drink all day and party all night?'

Penny noticed Nikos standing alone and went to join him, no longer able to hide her anxiety about her missing husband.

'Nikos, could I have a word with you alone?'

'I can think of nothing I'd like better.' He gave her one of those looks that had made Marigold reach for her mobile. 'Let's go and have a drink at my house, where we can be private.'

They left the others to it and summoned a taxi from the

rank. For a moment his hand touched hers and she felt a shock of electricity course through her body; but he did not, rather to her relief, reach and take it in his.

Ten minutes later they were climbing the stone steps at the side of his house. He unlocked the door and led her to the wide balcony at the front overhanging the sea. She leaned over and looked out to the horizon. It was the deep blue of lapis lazuli.

'Have you ever dived off?' she asked him as he came back with two glasses of wine.

'Ah,' he smiled, 'so there's a risk-taker hidden in faithful Penelope?'

'It just looks so tempting.'

'The answer is no. Sadly there are quite a lot of treacherous rocks hidden beneath the waves. Like life, perhaps?'

'Nikos,' she said suddenly before she had time to lose her nerve, 'Marigold has sent an anonymous message to my husband that you and I are getting involved.'

'And is he coming here to kill me?' he asked with the faintest trace of a smile.

'No way,' Penny replied with spirit. 'Colin is a control freak. He'd be more likely to kill me. But he has disappeared from home.'

Nikos put down his drink and pulled her into his arms. She melted against him, forgetting all about her controlling husband and all her everyday concerns.

'You are a good person, Penelope. And you deserve a good man.'

Penny screwed up all her courage. What did he actually mean by that?

'I love you, Nikos, and I want to leave my husband and come and live with you. Is that what you want too?'

She looked at him intently, hardly able to believe she had dared to say the words at last.

'Yes, Penelope.' He leaned down to kiss her. 'It is.'

He leaned down to kiss her. Just as their lips touched, the doorbell jangled loudly, making both of them jump – as if, like the ghost of Banquo in Macbeth, Colin had indeed appeared to claim her back.

Nikos let her go and primed himself like an athlete on the starting block for the trouble ahead.

'Yes?' he almost snarled as he opened the door.

It was Marigold in a slinky, see-through kaftan, loaded with silver and a seductive smile, carrying of all things a blue Le Creuset cast-iron pot.

'Hello Nikos,' she purred. 'I saw how early you left this morning and thought you would be too exhausted to cook. This is my speciality Moroccan chicken with dates and aubergines. Even if I do say it myself, it is rather delicious.'

From the balcony above came the distinct sound of muffled laughter.

Marigold looked upstairs suspiciously as the giggling became louder. Penny, buffeted by worry about her husband and overwhelmed with relief that Nikos had told her he loved her, had found the vision of Marigold bearing casseroles too ridiculous to resist.

'I see,' Marigold said, tight-lipped. 'You seem to have company already.' And she turned stiffly away, revealing from behind that she had forgotten to put on her underwear, still clutching the casserole like some kind of protective talisman which could save her from the awful humiliation of the situation which, being Marigold, she utterly refused to accept.

*

255

Nell sat in the silence of the garden next to the cafe, glued to her phone. 'Goodness,' she suddenly said to no one in particular, 'I hope that's a good idea!'

'What's a good idea?' Moira asked, intrigued.

'It's Willow. She's done a whole blog on Kyri.'

'Surely that has to be a good thing, doesn't it? We've already had three bookings because of her. Surely we ought to be grateful?'

'You don't know what she's blogged about now. It's headed "Hunt for Greek Island's Own Venus de Milo!" It's all here: finding the hand in the olive grove, the mysterious scent of myrtle, even the drawing of the statue you found in that old book! She must have taken a photo of it when she was here. I must admit, she writes wonderfully well. It all sounds like a Miss Marple. She even mentions the eminent Cambridge professor who's come to investigate.'

'Karl will be flattered. How many people read this thing?'

'She has thousands of followers,' Nell replied proudly. 'It's wonderful, isn't it, the modern world, how an ordinary person can earn a living just because of technology?'

Moira, who hated technology with a vengeance, looked doubtful.

'Of course, she usually does it on interior design, or babies.'

'I'm sure no one will take any notice, then,' Moira commented hopefully.

'I don't know ... It's just the sort of thing newspapers get interested in on a slow day,' said Nell. 'They do ring her up sometimes wanting to follow up things she's done. Maybe we ought to warn Dora and Karl.'

'And I think I'd better go back to Santorini and see what's under that tarpaulin,' Moira sighed, not sounding at all enthusiastic.

They found Dora and Karl wandering along the beach. Dora was looking for shells and Karl was carrying them in his Panama hat, which was almost full of purple sea urchin shells which Dora planned to take home, plus various whelks and one that Dora insisted was called an angel's wing.

'You two look like an ad for investment in a prosperous retirement,' teased Nell, until she saw the look of sudden anxiety cross Dora's face at the very word 'retirement'. Nell could only suppose it made her think of home and work.

As it turned out, Nell was right about the interest in Willow's blog. A few days later, she got a call from an English-language newspaper in Athens wanting to hear every detail of the missing statue. Willow had given them her mother's number, thinking people in Kyri would be delighted at the attention for their tiny island.

'Well, it's done now,' Dora concluded when Nell told her of the call over dinner. 'And it means if Xan Georgiades has hidden it, and I am pretty bloody certain he has, then he'll have to get rid of it damn soon, and I doubt now it's out in the open he'll be able to sell it for anything like he was hoping. But I don't trust him as far as I could throw him. I think we should take it in turns to watch him.'

'Isn't that a bit impractical?' Karl asked. 'Not to mention a tad over the top?'

'Why? There are five of us, and we're staying in the same hotel. It should be easy. We'll just have to have a rota.' She looked at him piercingly. 'Do you care about this statue or not? Ariadne risked her life for it – the least you lot can do is share watching Xan Georgiades.'

'I think the myrtle's got to her,' Moira murmured to Karl when Dora left them for a moment.

'You mean she's the new priestess to the goddess?' he grinned.

'I hope not,' Moira replied, attempting a saucy look, which had the effect of making her look like a gargoyle. 'Priestesses have to be celibate.'

'La, Dr O'Reilly,' he replied, fluttering his eyelashes, 'what can you mean?'

The next day Moira decided the fewer people who knew about her planned visit to Santorini the better, so she waited in the supermarket staring at sandwiches till a small crowd of passengers gathered on the dock, and then quietly melted into the queue for the ferry that came every other day.

This time she knew exactly where she was going, and as it was thankfully a long time till the famous Santorini sunset, no one had even thought of bagging their place and the streets were just about manageable. She glanced down at the harbour. One cruise ship was just arriving, with another hot on its tail. She'd better hurry.

In fact, it was so early that the garden statue yard wasn't open and she had to look for an area where the fencing that enclosed it was breachable. Eventually she found a low and rather unstable stone wall next to it, and was able to climb in. She waited a moment, holding her breath for an alarm to go off, but there was only the sound of a lone bird trilling away in the tree above her.

She swiftly made her way to the place where the tarpaulin had been. Thank God – it was still there.

She quietly moved the pile of logs surrounding it until the whole thing was uncovered, and then began to tackle the knot in the rope that secured it. It would have been easier and quicker to cut the rope, but that would make it obvious that it had been tampered with.

As she finally managed to pull it undone, she laughed at the idea of Dr Moira O'Reilly, recently retired academic, becoming part burglar, part spy. Still, she had to admit there was a certain exhilaration lacking in her previous library-dominated existence.

And there it was: Venus's stone couch with its two supporting pillars, beautifully carved in Parian marble and quite amazingly well preserved. Moira could hardly breathe with the excitement. She'd done it!

She stood back and photographed it from five or six angles on her phone, had the wit to send the shots to Dora, then quickly pulled back the tarpaulin, retied the knot and began to pile the logs back around it, all the while half-expecting someone to come and ask her what the hell she was doing.

She looked round only once. Somewhere in front and to the right, near the hut, she thought she heard a noise; but there seemed to be no one there.

When the last log was replaced, she made her way to the place she had come in. The wall started to crumble as she put her weight on it at the other side of the wire, and she found herself tumbling into the scrub beyond. Luckily the fall was cushioned by a patch of bright blue flowering borage. As she picked herself up she remembered Pliny's claim that borage was the famous 'nepenthe' mentioned in Homer which, mixed with wine, induced forgetfulness. She picked a bunch to try it out.

There was still no one about.

She tried to look as natural as possible as she made her way against the crowds, feeling like the infuriating person going the wrong way to the Tube at rush hour. Eventually, to her relief, she arrived at the harbour and found a cafe. There were two hours to kill before the ferry came, and even then she'd have to go via two other islands to get to Kyri.

Feeling suddenly ravenous, she ordered a Greek salad with warm pitta, plus olives and hummus and a large glass of red Demestica wine. She looked around her with enormous pleasure. She had accomplished her task, the sun was shining, the sea was its usual dazzling blue and the crowds around her seemed to have only one aim in coming here – a selfie of the famous blue-domed church with themselves in front of it – so the cafes were remarkably peaceful.

Although her bag was on the floor, she had taken the precaution of putting the long strap round her ankle for safety's sake. Despite her extensive travels, there was some of her mother buried deep in Moira, who believed that all foreigners were actually thieves out to rob the innocent visitor.

She was happily sipping her red wine when she noticed in the corner of her vision a scooter wending its way along the harbour path. Not an unusual sight, as scooters were popular with tourists (who quite often fell off and had to be airlifted home on their insurance), but this one was going surprisingly slowly. Her Greek salad had just arrived when the scooter suddenly speeded up and headed in her direction.

With lightning precision it homed in and the passenger, unidentifiable due to his helmet with the visor down, leaned skilfully over and scooped up Moira's bag, pulling her off her chair as he did.

The cafe owner rushed up to help her and enquire if she was all right. '*Bastardos!*' she shouted, shaking her fist at the departing thieves. 'It is usually only in the summer we are plagued with these vermin! I am so sorry, *kyria*, do you need a doctor?'

Moira got tentatively back to her feet, watching the scooter as it disappeared into the harbourside crowds. It could be just random bad luck. As the bar owner said, there were plenty of crimes like this in high season. Suddenly the sun, which had been temporarily obscured by a tiny cloud, broke out again and caught an inch of golden curl protruding beneath the shiny black of the helmet.

Moira smiled to herself as she sat back down at her table. Too bad for them her phone was on the table. And anyway, she'd sent the photos to Dora already. She sat and sipped her wine, but somehow had no appetite for the delicious-looking salad.

Dora was standing at her window overlooking the harbour with her phone in her hand, apparently watching the everyday life passing beneath, when Karl came into the room to see if she wanted to join him for a drink.

'She's only bloody done it, Karl!' She greeted him with a beam that suffused her whole face with happiness. 'Look!' She shoved her phone in his face. 'It's the couch that the reclining Venus rests on!' She took the pirate's crude sketch out, a copy of which she kept with her at all times. 'There it is. Venus is reclining on a couch supported by two marble pillars. She is leaning on one elbow, sublimely unaware of her nakedness, which is swathed in beautifully carved linen, holding the apple – our apple, the one that is in Takis's drawer downstairs – that Paris has awarded her in her other hand, the apple that causes the Trojan War. Aren't you excited?'

'Not as much as you,' he smiled fondly.

'It's the most exciting thing that's happened to me for years!' Dora announced. 'We *have* to find the statue now!'

The room phone rang, making them both jump – it was such a rare occurrence in a world of mobile technology.

'Dora, it's me, Moira. Did you get the photos?'

'Absolutely. They're amazing. Well done you, you're a heroine!'

'Great. Rather interestingly, my bag's just been stolen.'

'Oh, Moira, no! That is so annoying!' The thought suddenly struck her. 'Not with your phone in it, I hope to God.'

'I rather think that was the point, but actually it was on the cafe table with my ferry ticket. And I'm pretty sure I caught a glimpse of our friend Adonis's golden curls under the helmet.'

'Oh my God. You see how right we are to monitor Xan Georgiades. If they're going to this much trouble to keep the couch, they must also have the statue. And somehow or other, they've got to put them together.'

'And get the hand from Takis's drawer,' Moira reminded.

'Moira! You're a genius as well as a heroine. We'd better get him to move it somewhere safer. Karl, isn't this exciting? Don't you feel a bit Indiana Jones? I mean, you're an archaeologist, for God's sake!'

Karl studied her, his eyes suddenly serious. 'Be careful, Dora. I love your wild enthusiasms, but as Takis very sensibly pointed out, this could be dangerous. And as Indiana Jones famously commented, most of the archaeologist's work takes place in the library.'

'Yes,' Dora grinned. 'But it's a good thing he didn't stick to that, or it would have made for very dull movies!'

Penny was due to meet Nell downstairs for breakfast before they went over to the boathouses to prepare them for the new bookings. The owners often came and watched so that they could pick up the knack of styling the rooms to appeal to hip modern guests.

But today she had no appetite. She was getting seriously worried about Colin. She had assumed that if he wasn't at home, he would just have moved in to his club to have white-coated servants do all the servicing she usually did.

She decided to check once more with Wendy.

'Hello, irresponsible mother and granny,' Wendy greeted her with a laugh in her voice.

Penny felt a weight lifted off her chest at the sound of her daughter's usual calm briskness. She was delighted to her core to have produced such a capable woman who took life so easily.

'Still looking for Dad? I'll go round and have a look for any clues. Maybe he was looking at easyJet. The golf courses in the Algarve are very nice at this time of year, I hear.'

'Yes,' Penny nodded. 'I suppose he could have done that.'

'It'd be just like him, you mean. I'll go round and see what I can find.'

'I love you, Wendy.'

'And I love you too. Enjoy yourself, for God's sake! You're on a beautiful sunny Mediterranean island and it's pouring with bloody rain here!'

She and Nell enjoyed a slice or two of Cassandra's wonderful cake (obligatory, or she gave you a filthy look) and a nice strong coffee before heading out to the boathouses.

'We have to be grateful to your Willow for getting us these bookings, and apparently loads more coming through, but she's really fluttered the dovecotes with her blog about the statue. Have you seen Dora's rota? We all have to watch out for Xan Georgiades leaving the building.'

'What, and follow him?' They made their way towards to the supermarket to pick up some soap and toilet paper.

'I suppose so,' Nell replied. 'Everyone's really excited about the bookings. And Demetria's a force to be reckoned with. She's getting people all over the island to do up their empty buildings. All Willow needs to do is keep getting the customers.'

Penny put a giant pack of loo rolls into her trolley. 'Do

thank her, won't you? I'd been feeling guilty that we'd got people's hopes up on the island and weren't delivering, and now we are!'

'I will, I promise,' Nell agreed. 'You know one thing?'

'What's that?'

'We all thought this holiday was a disaster and that none of us had a thing in common any more. It's Kyri that's brought us all together.'

Penny smiled. 'Yes, it has. And do you know, I really needed that, a purpose. I was actually a lot lonelier than I'd admitted, even to myself.'

She stopped her trolley, struck by the thought she'd been so lonely even though she was married. Impulsively she put her arms round Nell and hugged her, ignoring the raised eyebrows of the Greek shoppers.

'I'm so glad we came, aren't you?'

Nell grinned. 'And it's all down to you for organizing it.'

'No time for loneliness here,' Penny grinned back, and they headed for their bikes.

As they crossed the cobbled space between the supermarket and the harbour's edge, Xan Georgiades emerged from the hotel, looked around him and walked quickly round the corner. A few minutes later Dora emerged from reception, dressed entirely in black: a black polo neck, black leggings, black plimsolls and sunglasses.

It took all Penny and Nell's strength of will not to start giggling, especially when she headed off in the wrong direction. 'I see Dora's got into the role,' Nell whispered.

'Oh dear.' Penny suppressed a giggle. 'She looks like she's going on a *Vanity Fair* photo shoot.'

'We ought not to laugh.' Nell shook her head. 'It'll be our turn next.'

'Do you think we ought to follow him?'

'What, and fell him with a pack of Andrex? I suppose we could just stroll round that way and meet the path from behind the hotel.'

They were quite grateful when there was absolutely no sign of the man in the road behind the hotel, or the one going up the hill to Plaka.

'What about the underground garage?' suggested Penny.

They were still discussing it when a grey Mercedes streaked past them at high speed.

'Could you fit a six-foot statue in that car?' Nell queried.

'Only if you chopped her up,' replied Penny, and they both stared at the speeding Merc.

Feeling like James Bond, Nell rang Dora and told her the news.

'Damn bloody hell!' was Dora's reaction. 'Well done, though, girls. See you later.'

They carried on to the boathouses and began their work. There was something very relaxing, Penny found, about putting soap into soap dishes. Was her problem that she was too domestic? Was that why Colin had lost interest in her – and maybe Nikos would too?

'Hey, what are you thinking about?' Nell interrupted her thoughts. 'Your face went suddenly sad.'

'I was wondering if I'm too much of a housewife. Is that why Colin doesn't value me?'

Nell stopped dead and looked her in the eye. 'He doesn't value you because he's a prat. We're your friends and we know you're brilliant. Talented and lovable. So sod Colin!'

'But where the hell *is* he, Nell?' Penny sat down on a newly made bed. 'I don't know where he's gone. Wendy went and checked, and he's just disappeared off the face of the earth. He isn't even at his club. That's the first place I looked. Nell . . .'

'Yes?' Nell stopped folding towels and arranging soap and gave Penny her full attention.

'You don't think he could have committed suicide?' Penny suddenly blurted.

'Colin?' snorted Nell. 'People who commit suicide usually feel the world would be better off without them. Your Colin thinks the world's bloody lucky to have him! This is just control, Penny. He doesn't want you to be here enjoying yourself without him, so he's trying to spoil it.'

'Do you really think so?' Again Penny felt a weight suddenly lift off her. She wanted to go out onto the boathouse balcony and breathe in the peace and beauty that surrounded them.

'What's the betting he'll wait till you're really happy with Nikos and stage some dramatic entrance to claim you? I can just picture a helicopter . . .'

Penny couldn't help smiling, even though her heart thudded uncomfortably at the thought. 'Sorry to disappoint you, but Colin's much too mean! It'd be more like a push bike. I love you, Nell.' She gave Nell another hug, so grateful to have such a good friend to share her worries with.

'Come on,' Nell suggested, grinning. 'Let's open that wine. I can always get them another bottle.'

They took their glasses out onto the balcony, which jutted dramatically right out over the sea. Penny looked down the row of twenty or so boathouses they had helped to paint. 'Sad, in a way, that all these had fishing boats in them, and now they're empty.'

'Yes,' Nell replied briskly. 'But it's the modern world, and now they're going to be B&Bs and we're the clever people who're helping them.'

'So we are,' beamed Penny. 'Tell you what. A toast. To us! The mad old boots trying to help put Kyri on the map!'

'Excuse me,' Nell corrected. 'To us! The sexy, clever, resourceful women who are determined to help save a Greek island!'

They clinked glasses and smiled at each other.

Two doors down, Marigold, also on her balcony, smiled as well, but in an altogether more malicious manner. She reached for her phone and texted a message to a mobile number in the UK:

Dear Mr Anderson: It really is time you did something about your wife.

Sixteen

They all sat at the little restaurant on the beach. They had invited Takis along too, although he said he couldn't stay long.

'So –' without asking anyone, Dora took the lead – 'what are we going to do about Georgiades? I *know* he has the statue somewhere.' She turned to Takis. 'Where is the hand with the apple at the moment?'

'I have locked it away. Ariadne likes to get it out sometimes and talk to it. Poor girl – I do not have the heart to stop her. She cares so much about this goddess of hers.'

'Don't you have a safe?' asked Dora incredulously. 'I mean, what about the money you make from the hotel?'

'Kyri is a not a dangerous island. I have not heard of one single burglary. People here do not even lock their doors.'

'That's amazing,' marvelled Dora, thinking of her triple-locked front door at home. 'I expect I'm being paranoid, but could you go and look now? Make sure Ariadne has left it under lock and key? It's just that Xan Georgiades has started behaving rather oddly.'

'Of course, ladies. I will go now and look. Go ahead and

order; I will have the kleftiko. And do not touch his wine. It is like goat's piss. My advice is, stick to beer.' He produced the lovely rubbery smile that transformed his face from ugly to charming.

'Right. We will.'

They all placed their orders and requested five Mythos beers, which they drank enjoying perhaps the loveliest time of the day on this lovely island. The last rays of the sun gilded the tops of the tamarisk trees and the beginning of a pink glow gave the whole landscape a magical air. The sea beyond was calm and as opalescent as the inside of a shell. Improbably a family of ducks swam past, rendered in the palest dusty pink.

They sighed in collective enjoyment, then began to laugh. 'Get us,' Nell pointed out. 'We're so old, the beauty of the landscape means more to us than going partying. Whenever did that happen?'

'Years ago,' Penny commented. 'I used to love staying up, but now the idea of a nightclub till 4 a.m. sounds like medieval torture to me.'

'How about you, Dora? Surely there's a lot of partygoing in your business?'

'Fortunately they're mostly after work, and I can get home and have a pasta from Tesco Finest and devour a box set.'

'You don't have one of those TV dinner trays, do you?' The thought of glamorous Dora with a TV dinner had the others in fits.

'As a matter of fact, I do,' announced Dora grandly.

'So do I,' confessed Penny. 'It's even got a bean bag attached for stability.'

'Me too,' Nell giggled. 'Though I did resist for quite a long time. I couldn't bear the image.'

'I've always eaten in college,' Moira chipped in. 'At least I used to, until they decided I was too old.'

'Well, I usually go to the pub,' said Karl. 'The mainstay of British culture.'

'That's because you're a man,' asserted Penny. 'If you don't have someone to make it for you at home, you just go and find someone who will!'

'Now, Penny,' Dora said tactlessly, 'don't judge all men by your husband!'

She regretted it when she saw the sudden look of extreme anxiety the comment caused.

'Speaking of men,' Karl commented, 'I see our friend Takis running rather urgently along the beach.'

By the time Takis reached them, he was hardly able to talk because he was so out of breath. 'It's not there!' he burst out. 'The hand of the goddess has been taken from the drawer it was locked in!'

'Did anything else go?' asked Karl.

'Nothing at all. They knew exactly what they were looking for!'

'And we all know who took it. He's obviously going to sell the statue, or he wouldn't need the hand.'

'You can't be sure it's him,' Nell pointed out.

'Him or someone who works for him. Adonis, maybe, since he was up to stealing my bag,' Moira said angrily. 'Fortunately I didn't have much in it.'

'I don't think it would be wise to approach him directly,' interrupted Karl.

'Why?' Dora asked. 'What do you suggest?'

'Approach the middleman. Say we are interested in buying the statue.'

'But he'd recognize us. Even you, probably.'

Karl grinned, his blue eyes, still bright and almost boyish, alight with delicious mischief. 'We need someone else. Someone he won't suspect. Like my mate Stelios.'

'A sting,' said Dora delightedly. 'Just like in *Butch Cassidy*! Or was it that other film with Paul Newman?'

'Ladies and gentlemen,' interrupted Takis anxiously, 'this is not a joke. This man could be dangerous.'

'We know, Takis,' Nell reassured him. Takis just looked bewildered. These ladies had been wonderful, and he didn't want them taking risks just for a statue.

'So anyway,' Dora asked suspiciously, 'why do we need this Stelios? I thought he was the man who started easyJet.'

'Not that Stelios, obviously. Stelios Stavropoulos. He owns a small gallery in Thessaloniki. Antiquities are his speciality. You will love him. He reeks of the old Levant.'

'Is that an aftershave?' Nell couldn't resist enquiring.

'Don't be naughty, Nell,' said Moira pompously. 'The Levant was the name for the eastern Mediterranean. It used to be the biggest trading centre in the world.'

Their food arrived. 'So what will this Stelios do?' asked Dora.

'The way it works is this,' Karl expanded. 'Even if you dig up a Greek statue – our Venus, for example – you can't go to some collector and say, "Look old chum, I found this lady in my olive grove. How would you like to give me ten million euros for her?" Apart from anything else you might get ten years in prison.'

'So what do you do?' Penny asked.

'You have to somehow make her legitimate. Lots of artefacts get shipped all round the world before they ever get offered for sale. A clever middleman will know which ports will give you an export licence – probably for a small consideration. So she

271

gets shipped from port to port until she's got a paper trail of export licences. Then she will be lent, free, to some small gallery in Munich or even Japan, and then you can say she has had an exhibition. She is getting even more respectable. They call it "seasoning". Finally you make up some story that she was bought by some young aristo on his Grand Tour, and by now she's as respectable as the Queen Mother, and bingo – you get you get your ten million. It's a risky game, but the Department of Culture here hasn't got enough people to investigate. That's why we need Stelios.'

'And how do you know all this stuff?' Dora asked, actually quite impressed.

'The man in the local museum told me all about it. The authorities all know, but there are six thousand Greek islands and who knows how many Venuses, so what can they really do?'

'Well, he's not having ours!' Dora announced, suddenly sounding like Boadicea. 'How soon can this Stelios get here?'

Karl bowed. 'He's coming tomorrow. I've asked Nikos to pick him up from Ximonos so that he won't be seen coming off the ferry right under Mr Georgiades' nose.'

'You're really quite smart, aren't you?' Dora acknowledged.

'Archaeologists can be sexy too, you know,' replied Karl. 'I thought I might dress up as Indiana Jones for you. I'm sure I could find a hat like his in the supermarket.'

'What about the whip?' she replied archly.

'You might have to use your imagination for that.'

Takis looked from one to the other and saw how much they were enjoying themselves. 'So this is why they say the English are mad.'

*

272

Nikos decided that the best time for Stelios's arrival would be the early morning, when Kyri was at its quietest. So the only audience for the event consisted of an old man inspecting the ground for cigarette butts, two very thin cats, and Andreas, the baker, who had come outside for a quick escape from his heat-blasting ovens.

In fact, a rather weary Nell, Dora, Penny and Moira were ranged discreetly behind Dora's curtains in her room at the front of the hotel to get a first glance at the saviour Karl had selected to find their missing goddess.

The boat docked at the pier and a large man in a floppy black hat and trench coat, tied unflatteringly round the middle, stepped out of the boat onto the quay. He looked round him and, for reasons known only to himself, began to laugh uproariously.

'By Jupiter,' said Moira, 'Karl's hired an escaped lunatic!'

'And he'll certainly blend into the background without being noticed,' Nell added drily.

They charted Stelios's progress across the square towards the row of small shops, which were the only places open at this time of the morning. He stayed inside so long that they began to lose interest and want to return to their beds.

'What on earth is he doing?' Dora had persisted longer than the others in her vigil at the window. 'He's taking so long he could be ordering enough bread to feed thirty.'

'Maybe he's going to throw a welcome cocktail party,' suggested Nell naughtily.

'I very much hope not, as he's supposed to be asking questions discreetly.'

'Discreetly!' Nell persisted. 'I doubt if he could even spell the word.'

'I expect that's exactly what he's doing,' Dora said firmly,

273

wanting to support Karl's choice, which on the surface did look rather peculiar to say the least.

As still Stelios showed no sign of appearing, they all departed back to their beds.

Stelios was, in fact, following his usual habit of talking to the little people. He bit into a hefty chunk of warm bread from the loaf he had just purchased from the baker.

'*Nostimo!* Fantastic, my friend!' He breathed in the warm scent of new-baked bread.

Andreas was at the back of the bakery loading dough into the roaring flames of his oven, sweat rolling down his back into his dirty vest. Clearly this wasn't the moment for confidences. Stelios bought another loaf and decided to come back later.

Next door, the lady who ran the gift shop was beginning to open up.

'*Kalimera, kyria.*' He bowed extravagantly.

The owner was famous for her boot face, but there was something about this engaging bear of a man that got through her defences.

'Are you looking for anything in particular?' she enquired. 'A sarong for a lady? A beautiful necklace?'

'Alas, *kyria*, I have no lady in my life. I am as celibate as an Orthodox priest.'

'Not celibate at all, then. Our priest has children all over the parish!' she replied caustically. 'Perhaps I can interest you in one of these?' She pointed to some small marble statues of Greek gods and picked up a carving of Ares, the god of war. 'The crafts-manship is extraordinary. Look at the expression on his face.'

'Ah,' Stelios smiled engagingly, 'but I am a peaceful man. What about Ares' sometime wife, Aphrodite? Do you have a statue of her?'

'Looking for sex, are you? You won't get much here. All the girls are virgins.' She thought for a moment. 'You might try those English ladies. The English are sex mad, everyone knows. Nearly as bad as the Swedes. And at their age they'd be grateful.'

Stelios decided to steer the conversation into less dangerous waters. 'And what about the other Aphrodite? This statue I read about in the Athens paper?'

'A load of nonsense, if you ask me,' she replied crisply. 'Probably doesn't even exist.'

'Then how do you explain the hand with the apple?'

'The rest was probably broken up by a tractor. These statues are everywhere.' She paused in dusting her stock and thought for a moment. 'Everyone thinks that Georgiades man is involved, but there's no evidence. He's a good customer of mine.'

Stelios's antennae started to buzz. He couldn't imagine what the man could possibly want from a gift shop full of cheap tat that probably came from China anyway.

'I had this old map of the island from the Corsair days. Genuine, my husband said it was. From the seventeen hundreds, when this place was really big. They said it was once the richest island in the Cyclades, imagine that! It cost two hundred euros!' she announced with the satisfaction of knowing she'd bought it for a hundred.

She paused reverently. This had probably been her biggest sale of the season, and Stelios could easily imagine why it might be useful to someone wanting to hide a statue. 'He comes and goes a lot in that Mercedes of his, but that's hardly evidence. Maybe he's bored after Athens. He's quite thick with the man who carves boats in the street round the corner. He's a strange character. You might try him.'

Stelios glanced around. He ought to buy something in recognition of her time. It could, after all, be for his mother.

'Buy this,' she grinned, pointing to a miniature set of table and chairs, painted in bright Greek blue, the chairs with woven seats just like the originals found in a thousand Greek cafes. 'They're better quality than the rest of my stuff.'

They were, he had to admit, very charming. He could imagine many a tourist taking them home as a memento of a pleasant holiday. Far better than the usual ouzo in a bottle shaped like the Acropolis, bought on holiday and never touched again. Pity Stelios didn't have a proper home at the moment to display them, but lived at the back of his gallery. He'd never been one to put down roots.

'Certainly I will.'

With tender care she wrapped them first in tissue and then in gold-embossed hand-made wrapping paper, finishing with a gold bow, as if the simple table and chairs were some priceless purchase.

'Thank you.' Stelios bowed again. 'I will put them on my mantelpiece to be forever reminded of my time in Kyri.'

He didn't mention the fact that he'd only been here less than an hour. Next he headed for the cafe and downed two black coffees and three *koulouri*, the sesame-flavoured bagels that had been part of his childhood in Thessaloniki.

The shop belonging to the man who made boats was just opposite, down a small side road. Kyri was getting busy now, with hopeful tourist boats arriving at the quay offering day trips to the caves and beaches. Buses stopped outside the cafe, and soon the ferry from Santorini would deposit more visitors.

Stelios replaced his beloved hat on his head and pushed open the door.

On the first floor, Moira, Penny and Dora had gone to get dressed, but Nell was glancing out, so it was she who watched Stelios's progress across the square towards the street where the boat man, like Nikos, carved his replica boats out of driftwood. What struck Nell was the sheer physicality of the man, an energy that almost seemed to burst from his large frame. She liked the way he stopped and talked to every passer-by, even the children, and had a smile perpetually on his lips. With his abundant black curly hair and ready smile, he struck her as a large woolly bear, and she felt a tear come to her eye. What would it be like to have a man like that to laugh with and protect you?

Angrily she brushed the tear away. For more than twenty years she had lived without a man in her life, and why should she be attracted to this one just because he looked as if he could crush her in a giant embrace?

The words from a Joni Mitchell song invaded her head, about being drawn to those ones that ain't afraid. God almighty, was she going to start living her life according to the thoughts of the great Joni? Start looking at clouds from both sides now, and wishing she'd been at Woodstock?

There he was, kissing the hand of the ancient lady who begged outside the bank. Most people walked straight past! And now chasing a football with a tiny five-year-old before sweeping him out of the path of some idiot on a scooter. And all the time, laughing.

She watched him exchange a word with the line of tourists in the bus queue, some of whom, being city-dwellers, looked at him as if he were mad, before he ducked into the boat man's shop.

'*Yassas!*' Stelios greeted the man sitting perched behind the counter, a knife in his hand.

'You're in early,' was the grudging reply.

'I like to be up with the lark,' Stelios replied, his voice brimming over with good humour. 'May I look around?'

'Help yourself. This is a shop, after all.'

Stelios walked slowly round the gallery, examining each boat in detail. From the traditional Greek *caiques* to the small pleasure craft, the loving detail of each was extraordinary. He had even captured the faded paintwork and worn ropes of vessels owned by fishermen who didn't have the money to keep them pristine.

'I like to make sure they're accurate,' grunted the man behind the counter. 'I used to come here every year as a child . . .'

'From Athens?'

The man nodded. Stelios wondered how soon he could introduce the topic he really wanted information about.

'Have you always carved boats?'

The man laughed. 'I used to be in banking.'

'Quite a change.' Stelios went on examining the boats.

'After the crash. I had enough of cheating the little people.'

Stelios looked up. 'I met someone else here from Athens. A Mr Georgiades.'

The man looked up from his carving suspiciously. 'Where did you meet him?'

'In the bar of that expensive hotel. I forget the name.'

'The White Hotel?'

'That's the one.'

'People talk a lot of shit about him round here. But I'll say this for him. He cares about boats. He likes that one you're holding best. In fact I made two and he bought the other himself.'

Stelios examined the boat in his hands. It was a small caique, the kind that might be used for shallow sea fishing, with a wheelhouse on deck and cabin below.

'Is he thinking of taking up carving as well?'

The man laughed. 'He says he'd like to own one like it one day. His parents rented one every summer, so he likes to be reminded of exactly what it was like.'

'Interesting. He didn't strike me as the sentimental type.'

'He's not. He remembered them taking on board a heavy weight, some giant fish, a shark or baby whale or some such thing, and wondered if he'd dreamed it. Asked me if it was possible.'

'And could you? Take a heavy weight on a boat like this? Wouldn't it capsize, or do you think it was all his imagination?' Stelios gave one of his biggest grins. 'You know, the one that got away – even in your dreams – is the really big fish?'

'You could if you got the weight in the right place,' the man replied. 'Before the fish stocks got diminished, fishermen round here would take on tons of squid and tuna. I told him I thought it would be OK.'

Stelios examined the boat. 'My friend, it's a thing of beauty. If you don't mind I'll buy it myself!'

'Help yourself.' The man looked up and stared. 'As I said, it is a shop, after all.' He wrapped the boat lovingly and put it into a carrier bag.

'*Yassas*. And thank you.'

The man watched Stelios carry the bag to the door and open it. Stelios gave him a cheery wave as he walked down the street.

The man shrugged and went back to his carving.

Penny was in one of her worrying jags when it suddenly seemed that everything might come crashing down around her. Nikos could change his mind about loving her, and she might find there was no money left in her bank account from her legacy. She had worked this out very carefully, but she hadn't budgeted for staying so long in Greece.

They were due to be introduced to the flamboyant Stelios in half an hour, in Karl's room rather than down in the bar, because his connection with all of them needed to be discreet. Penny decided to go down to the cash machine on the corner next to the bus stop and double-check her balance first.

Kyri town was in its busy pre-dinner mood. Little boys were still kicking a football on the quay, jumping up and down with glee if they managed to hit one of the family of ducks who had taken over the harbour as their home. Teenagers frisked among the tamarisk trees on the beach, engaging in flirtation disguised as noisy volleyball. Ancient diners were ordering the Greek version of their Early Bird Specials. Noisy tourists were kidding themselves that they were having 'one last drink' before getting on their boats back to other islands. Takis was chalking up the menu that Cassandra was busy cooking in the kitchen. From the window above, Penny saw saw Nell waving down at her. Penny took it all in with almost overwhelming affection as she walked towards the ATM. She was right that her personal account was worryingly low, but at least she knew there was plenty in the joint account. Discreetly she inserted her red Santander card – only to be told there were no funds in the account. Colin had removed all their money!

Cold panic gripped her. Had he transferred it to his sole account, or taken out a large sum to pay for a flight and hotel somewhere? It would have been so much easier if he was still working. She could have just rung his business partners. But these days he was a free agent, dabbling in investments or deals as they came along. She wondered for a moment about ringing the bank, but they probably wouldn't tell her where he he'd been making withdrawals. If only she had his password she could look online, but he'd never wanted her to have it and she'd never made a big issue out of it. It somehow summed up their relationship. As usual, he had all the power.

Dejectedly she walked up the back staircase, to Karl's room. She could tell which one it was from the noisy laughter. So much for complete discretion.

The others were already assembled. Naturally Dora had brought a bottle of wine and six glasses, and some snacks snaffled from the bar.

'So, Stelios,' Karl enquired jovially, 'what have you discovered so far?'

'The poor man only arrived this morning,' pointed out Nell.

'Stelios works fast, don't you, old man?' Karl commented.

He was answered with a loud guffaw.

'Well, that was certainly discreet,' pointed out Dora. 'It probably woke Georgiades from his early evening nap!'

Stelios grinned round, undeterred. 'Friends, I have discovered two interesting facts today.'

Karl looked delighted. 'I told you he was a quick worker.'

'First, your friend bought an old map of the island, a genuine one, with all the Corsair caves marked on it.'

'We could have told you that,' Dora replied witheringly. 'I'm still sure he knew the caves well enough to hide the statue there and then remove it before we could prove anything. The fact that he bought a map is neither here nor there.'

'You may be right.' Stelios shrugged engagingly. 'And then he bought a boat virtually identical to this.'

He produced the boat from the carrier bag. It was about a foot long, with a faded pale blue hull and wheelhouse. The mast and jib were the same colour, but peeling, as if they took the brunt of the seawater. There was an anchor line at the front and a painter for mooring.

'She looks as if you could almost sail in her,' Moira admired.

'It's just like the ones Nikos carves,' Penny pointed out.

'Except this one is very like the one Georgiades sailed in as a child,' Stelios said. 'In fact, exact in every way, except that it's miniature. He was asking the shop owner if it could take on a heavy weight. He said he remembered them taking on a shark or porpoise, and was that possible?'

'Or a statue,' Karl mused.

'Precisely my thought,' nodded Stelios.

'Except that Georgiades doesn't have a boat,' Dora replied dampeningly. 'If he did, we'd have seen him in it.'

'Unless he was keeping it hidden somewhere,' suggested Stelios with a grin.

'But they don't have sharks round here,' Moira threw in irrelevantly, ignoring the crushing looks from the others.

'Now all we have to do is find out where he keeps it,' said Karl. 'And what better man to do it than Stelios?'

'I also need to start putting it about that I'm interested and I have a very rich buyer. Apparently your friend likes to hang out in the bar of the White Hotel, Kyri's only luxury establishment.'

'Where's that?' Dora asked, amazed she had missed anything that smacked of luxury.

'On the tip of the island,' Stelios informed her. 'Opposite Ximonos.'

'And near the caves,' Dora realized.

'Time you went and rediscovered your taste for martinis, then,' Karl suggested. 'As long as you remember the advice from Dorothy Parker.'

'I'm afraid that escapes me,' Stelios replied.

Before Karl could reply, Dora whipped in first: '*I like to have a martini, Two at the very most, After three I'm under the table, After four I'm under my host.*'

'I will remember that carefully,' Stelios grinned. 'Especially as the host is a rather large German. I have been thinking . . .'

'A dangerous development,' teased Karl.

'A glamorous lady who is working for the buyer as some kind of assistant might help me get information. My undoubted charm doesn't work on some people, amazing though it may seem to you. Especially fat Germans.'

'Who would you suggest?' Karl enquired. 'Who he would least recognize? Not Dora obviously. Our friend certainly knows who she is.'

'Moira?'

'I know, I know,' Moira pouted. 'No one could describe me as glamorous. And it can't be Penny, because he knows her too. I think Nell is probably the one he's seen least.'

They all looked at her. 'Could you disguise yourself enough to fool him, do you think?

She smiled back mischievously. 'I'll see what I can do.'

Seventeen

'Let's go down by the water and have a paddle,' suggested Penny. It was almost dark, and yet the pink after-sunset glow seemed to last for hours in Kyri. She thought of home, and how Wendy had said the rain hadn't stopped for what seemed like weeks. But the thought just made her feel anxious.

'What's the matter?' asked Moira, not usually the most intuitive of the group.

'It's my bloody husband. He's gone missing, and I keep thinking he'll turn up here.'

'Maybe he's been reading the Odyssey. Odysseus stayed away ten years before he returned to faithful Penelope. Perhaps he wants to keep you on tenterhooks.'

'He's certainly doing that.' She laughed at the unlikely thought of Colin reading Homer.

'You should laugh more,' Moira advised. 'You look pretty when you laugh.'

'I keep thinking maybe I should go home.'

'But what about Nikos? I thought you were serious. You look serious. Wouldn't you stay here with him?'

Penny thought of the other night when he had told her he

loved her. Why did she have so much difficulty in accepting that he meant it?

'You need to believe in yourself for a change,' Moira told her with surprising sternness. 'You have so much to offer. And so far it seems to me you've wasted it on someone who probably isn't capable of appreciating it. If it wasn't for you none of us would be here. You should be proud that you've brought us back together.'

Penny felt so moved by this, she was almost speechless. As it happened she didn't need to reply because they were suddenly set upon by an irate Demetria, looking more like one of the Furies than her usual elegant Melina Mercouri image.

'Penelope,' she shouted, so angry she could hardly speak, 'and other lady! It is bad news! Very bad news! Somebody is telling lies about our beautiful boathouses!'

She got out her phone and showed them the Kyri Island website that Nikos had set up. There was a large review of one of the boathouses, claiming that it was dirty, noisy and unsafe for children. There were even photos to back it up. Demetria was right. This could be a disaster.

'Let's go down there right now!' Moira suggested. 'Obviously it's the fault of the people who're staying there.'

'That is part of the mystery!' Demetria said angrily. 'They are empty until the new guests arrive.'

They ran from the beach, pausing only to dry their feet on the pathway. Moira was in such a rush that she just stuffed her sandy feet into her canvas shoes and half-dragged Penny behind her. 'Hurry, it won't be light for long.' They borrowed bikes from the communal pile – another of Nikos's schemes – and pedalled towards the boathouses, with Demetria following behind in her little car on account of her ridiculously high heels.

Armed with the bad review, they collected the keys and ran

off to inspect the row of boathouses that they had all worked so hard to make perfect. They checked each open-plan seating and kitchen area, plus every bedroom. All were immaculate, with shining basins and showers and beautifully folded towels, plus spotless kitchens and bedrooms that could easily have graced a luxury brochure.

'What we really need is an iPad so we can see the images on this review better,' said Moira. 'I don't suppose anyone's got one?'

A huge grin lit up Demetria's features as she produced one from her voluminous handbag. 'I bought on internet,' she explained. 'Cheap because someone have it before me. Also –' another infectious grin – 'I am allowed it as expense now I am big businesswoman!'

They studied the photos on the larger screen of Demetria's iPad.

'Where is that exactly?' Moira demanded angrily. They held the iPad screen out in front of them, but it was difficult to identify the individual property.

'And as for noisy,' Moira protested, 'listen! There's complete and utter silence.'

'And how can you say it's dangerous for children?' Penny fumed. 'We make it absolutely clear where the property is. Of course it's on the water! You can see the set-up in all the pictures we put up. Plus it's a boathouse, for God's sake!'

Moira looked at the other two. 'If it's not any of these boat-houses, then which boathouse is it?'

The truth suddenly dawned on them. Moira clutched Penny's hand.

'It's Marigold's!' they chorused. 'What the hell are we going to do about that woman?'

*

Stelios had spent all of the previous evening sitting in the bar of the White Hotel, drinking martinis and shooting off his mouth about the rich buyer he represented who was interested in buying the statue of Venus, no questions asked, if it existed at all. Having pricked their interest and, he hoped, spread the word about, he planned to go again tonight – only this time with Nell, as the glamorous assistant of the secretive would-be buyer.

'But how would they know if the buyer was genuine?' enquired Karl.

'Don't worry, my friend,' reassured Stelios, with one of his trademark grins. 'I am used to dealing with shady rich people who want to acquire antiquities because their gut tells them they have to possess them at all costs. They pretend it's all above board, even to themselves, when they know perfectly well the object has been stolen. It is a game I am used to playing. I can convince your friend all right.'

'Good, good.' Karl slapped him on the back. 'I knew we had found the right man in you!'

But Stelios wasn't listening. He was staring behind him, his mouth like a heron's beak when it spots a minnow in the stream below. Karl turned, and instantly saw his point.

Nell had just walked into the room. She wore an oyster pink Chanel jacket in bouclé wool with the signature black braid round the collar, over a pale silk blouse and tight black pencil skirt. Her dark hair was beautifully arranged into a French chignon. Black eyeliner lined her lids in a fabulous, seductive sweep. And to complete the ensemble she wore huge Chanel sunglasses.

'Nell!' shrieked Dora. 'Where did you get that jacket? I've wanted that all my life!'

'Oxfam in the King's Road. Eighty quid. Charity shops in

posh areas are the ones to go for designer bargains. Do I look OK?'

They all lined up to admire her.

'You look amazing!' congratulated Penny.

'Stunning!' seconded Dora. 'Audrey Hepburn in *Breakfast at Tiffany's* to the life!'

'Who knew you had legs?' marvelled Moira.

'And such wonderful legs!' agreed Penny.

'I'm channelling my inner Leslie Caron. You don't think I'm more Cruella de Vil?'

'No!' they all insisted.

'Wait for this.' She pouted her lips, twitched her shoulders into the tiniest slouch and looked around her haughtily. 'Monsieur Stelios, *êtes-vous prêt?*' she demanded with just the right degree of bored impatience.

'Wow,' Dora demanded, 'a French accent! Where did that come from?'

'I went to finishing school in Paris. It's never been useful before. Do you think it's a little *de trop?*'

'I think it's perfect. What do you reckon, Stelios?'

But Stelios was already standing, looking totally bewitched, holding his arm out for her to take.

'*Enchanté, madame,*' he bowed with a twinkle in his eye. '*Allons-y!*'

Next morning Moira set her phone to wake early. It was her Treasure Island day, and thirty thirsty tourists would be turning up eager to eat and get even more sloshed than they already were. Thank heavens Nell had agreed to help – if she hadn't got too trolleyed by martinis with Stelios in the White Hotel the night before.

She showered and got dressed in clothes that to an untutored eye would have seemed remarkably like her pyjamas. Then she went to knock on Nell's door, just in time noticing the Do Not Disturb notice hanging on the doorknob.

It was stupid, she knew, but the sign felt like a snub. The kind of snub geeky, awkward Moira had experienced hundreds of times as a child. Other children might have complained about not being picked for teams. Moira had never been picked for anything – birthday parties, friendships, gossipy sessions lying on beds, school discos. Here on Kyri, for the first time in her life, things were looking different. The others seemed to accept her as one of them.

Telling herself she was being ridiculous for minding the stupid sign, she grabbed her basket and various shopping bags and ran to the shops to fill them with meat, pitta, salad, pineapples, lemons and mangoes, hoping fervently that Takis would have remembered to deliver the liquor. The glasses and straws would be stored ready behind the bar.

As she passed the hotel again on her way to the beach she slipped in to reception to check. Ariadne was behind the desk, looking calm and pretty.

'Is Takis around?' Moira enquired.

'Gone down to the beach with your bottles,' was the re-assuring reply before Ariadne turned back to advise a new arrival on the times of boat trips round the island. 'Be sure they take you round the pirate caves,' she counselled, with a knowing wink at Moira. 'They're the most famous thing on the island.'

She passed the gift shop, and got a wave from the lady who ran it. The young woman working in the supermarket, just laying out her wares to entice any tourists in off the ferry, said '*Kalimera, kyria* Moira.' Moira smiled to herself. She really did feel part of Kyri's everyday life. She was just walking past the usual group of old men sitting on the concrete edge of the flowerbed where they always congregated, when a thought came to her. She would buy them a coffee.

She doubled back to the hotel and approached Cassandra, who raised her eyes to heaven at the thought of more work. Yet she could tell Cassandra quite liked the idea too. 'As long as it doesn't get to be a habit. I don't want those good-for-nothing old fools hanging about like yowling cats.'

'I'll tell them,' grinned Moira. She put down her basket and carried the tray with coffee pot, milk and paper cups back out to the square.

'*Kalimera sas*,' she greeted them. 'Morning all!'

'*Kyria*,' shouted a white-haired man in French beret, with a distinct twinkle in his eye, 'If you want to find your Aphrodite you should ask us!'

Moira's spirits soared. Generosity was being rewarded. But when she asked him more he suddenly began to laugh and put a finger to his lips, rocking backwards and forwards like a lunatic. Was he just having her on?

'*Kalos!*' chorused the other old men as they drank their coffees. '*Poli kalos!*'

'Very kind,' thoughtfully translated an aged gent with a long bushy beard.

'Tell them to take the tray back to the hotel after, or Cassandra will kill me,' she informed the English speaker.

She picked up her basket again and headed up the path towards the olive grove. So much had happened since they'd first arrived. Almost unconsciously Moira realized that for the first time she could remember, she was genuinely happy. As she walked through the olive grove she stopped for a moment. Was that myrtle? Was the goddess telling her to listen to the old men? Bloody hell, she was as bad as Ariadne.

What had happened to academic rigour? It was probably some kind of hysterical reaction. Freud would no doubt have a name for it.

Moira laughed out loud. Academic rigour could get stuffed!

Down at the bar, she was relieved to find a row of bottles already laid out on the counter. She began to merrily chop fruit, even successfully managing to put some music on the sound system. She wouldn't have exactly chosen Status Quo, but at least they were upbeat.

Half an hour later Nell arrived, looking slightly more dishevelled than her usual neat appearance.

'Hey,' Moira greeted her. 'How was it last night?'

Nell grinned. 'I'll tell you later. Dora has demanded a re-enactment this evening. In her room, in case you-know-who gets wind of it.'

'Isn't it stupid?' The morning had gone so well, Moira felt strong enough to confess her weakness. 'I thought that Do Not Disturb notice was just for me. I felt really hurt.'

'Put your knife down,' Nell commanded. 'Come here.' She opened her arms and gave Moira a hug. 'You're my *friend*!' And Moira, who didn't even cry at funerals or at the end of *Love Story*, found a tear blurring the corner of her eye, and wiped it into the nearest Tequila Sunrise.

'I just had a hangover, that's all. Mr Expensive Garden Centre kept buying me martinis, but don't worry; I minded my Dorothy Parker. And as it happens I've got a pretty hard head, so he didn't get anything out of me, though believe me, he tried.'

'I can't wait to hear. And by the way –' Moira shook her head at the outrageousness of what she had to reveal – 'we need to talk about Marigold.'

But just then they glimpsed the tourist boat on the horizon, with its cargo of half-cut hedonists heading steadily in their direction, and there was no more time to talk.

Even though it was only the seven of them meeting that evening, Dora had risen to the occasion with chilled white wine from the downstairs bar, olives with feta, mini *spanakopita* and home-made hummus spread on pitta bread. She stood at the door as if she were greeting guests at a Sloane Square cocktail party.

'Hello, darling people.' Dora embraced Nell, then Stelios. 'How was it? I couldn't sleep thinking about you!'

Moira, who was in the next room and had heard Dora's snoring, could have disputed this, but just grinned.

'Tricky!' Nell and Stelios chorused together.

'I never want to do anything like that again in my life!' Nell added with feeling. 'That garden centre man is cleverer than he looks. Stelios was great – sounding like a real expert in buying antiquities.'

'I *am* a real expert in buying and selling antiquities!' Stelios pointed out with dignity.

'Not for ten million euros!'

'We bargained him down to eight,' Nell said.

'Oh, that's OK then,' Penny joked, looking anxious all the same. 'I just hope this isn't too risky, that's all.'

'I think these people are stupid rather than dangerous,' Nikos tried to reassure her.

'But Xan Georgiades is rich. He's got a lot to lose. Couldn't that make him dangerous? Takis thinks so. He was terrified of Ariadne getting involved. What do you think, Karl?'

Karl had been quietly listening. 'I think Penny has a point. Besides, you can't keep this game up much longer.'

'Too right,' Nell agreed. 'They want us to show them the money. Then they'll give us proof of the statue being genuine.'

'The hand!' Moira blurted. 'I bet they'll show you the hand!'

'We've got to find the statue,' Penny insisted. 'That's the only answer!'

Moira suddenly remembered that morning's incident. 'One of the old men, the one in the beret who's always sitting in the square right by the harbour. This morning he said we should ask *them* if we want to find our Aphrodite!'

'The old men!' Stelios repeated, looking angry with himself. 'Why didn't I think of that? They sit there all day and night watching everything that's going on, and nobody notices them! They're invisible, just part of the scenery. I'll go and talk to them now!'

'No,' counselled Nikos. 'The square is full now. We should wait till Georgiades goes out tomorrow, and then go down and talk to them.'

'Nikos is right,' Karl agreed. 'You don't want him seeing you out of the window.'

'Tomorrow it is,' said Stelios. 'In which case, Dora, I think I'll have another drink.'

Penny was on watching duty first, and she was finding it hard to stay awake. Partly because she'd had rather too much to drink last night, when the evening had turned into something of a party, but also because rather than watching the front with all its interesting comings and goings, she was in charge of the back. She had put her phone on to Radio 4, which amazingly you seemed to be able to get here, and was listening nostalgically to some politician being bullied by John Humphrys, when there was a sudden movement below. She shut Humphrys up with all the ceremony he afforded his victims and stood up. Yes, a grey Mercedes with Georgiades behind the wheel emerged from the garage and sped off up the hill towards Plaka.

It was eight a.m. Was it too early to rouse Stelios? She decided it was important enough to go ahead.

She knocked on his door.

'Yes?' came the muffled reply from within.

'The coast's clear!'

'Right. OK. Good.' Then total silence, as if he'd instantly fallen back to sleep.

Penny decided to go down to breakfast. Even the most eager of the old men would hardly be in the square by this time.

The usual mouth-watering array awaited her. Fresh fruit salad accompanied by yogurt from Cassandra's famous goats, with or without glorious Greek honey. There were scrambled eggs and various combinations of ham and cheese beloved of the Germans and the Dutch. Not too much, though, since the number of guests was still lamentably few.

'Morning, Penny.'

She turned to find she'd been joined by Moira, in one of her original outfits that looked as if it had been rejected even by Help the Aged.

Moira happily began to load her cereal with half a goat's worth of yogurt, then stopped, her face suddenly troubled. 'Penny . . .' she began.

Penny put down her spoon. 'Yes, Moira?'

'How much longer do you think we're going to stay?'

'Until the question of the statue is resolved maybe.' Or until Colin appeared on the horizon, though that was a fear she wasn't going to mention to her friends.

None of the others had showed up, so she decided to go for a walk and think.

Penny headed out into the bright sunlit square. She liked this time of the day when everyone was opening up, good-humoured and full of hope that somehow, today, a cruise ship would appear in the harbour or flocks of tourists suddenly descend from the ferry instead of staying on board and visiting the next island.

This time she didn't head for the beach and the boathouses, but down a narrow lane towards the back of the town. She'd rarely been this way and found herself turning a corner and walking slap bang into a donkey, which was as surprised at the encounter as she was.

'Hello, old man.' She patted its muzzle until its owner emerged from one of the house with a hod of bricks. She thought for a moment of challenging him, but the donkey wasn't thin or badly treated and it seemed acclimatized to its lot. She was obviously getting used to Greek ways.

'*Kalimera*,' she nodded, and flattened herself against the wall for the donkey to pass.

Another few streets deeper into Kyri town she came across the entrance to a little Orthodox church, the kind found in their thousands in every town and village in Greece, some so tiny you could hardly get inside.

There was no service on, so it was dark and pungent with the scent of incense and recently lit candles, so strong they almost choked you. But it was more than that. Penny could feel in the air such an intense wave of hope battling against the despair of everyday life that she had to stand still. She could just make out the tiny *tamata*, votive symbols shaped like metal hearts or limbs, pinned under an icon of the Virgin Mary, each hoping for a miracle, and the forests of candles, each lit for some unrealized hope or dream.

'Can I help you, *kyria*?' The guardian of the chapel emerged from the gloom, smiling helpfully and holding out a shawl. She looked disappointed that Penny wore neither shorts nor bare arms that would need covering up.

'Thank you, no,' Penny replied, backing out, unsure of what she was looking for. She headed instead for the local museum. This was also in the back streets, but housed in a rather impressive mansion that had once belonged to a corsair captain in the days when Kyri was a powerful force in the eastern Mediterranean.

She looked dutifully through the explanations outlining the difference between corsairs – privateers licensed by the French king to attack any enemies of France, England naturally included – and how they differed from the Captain Sparrows, good old fashioned pirates, who sang 'yo-ho-ho and a bottle of rum' and keelhauled their unfortunate victims. She wondered if it was the same treacherous king who had offered freedom to the corsair in exchange for their statue of Aphrodite and double-crossed him so that he buried the statue in revenge.

She looked carefully at all the exhibits, thinking how sad it was that Kyri, once so rich and important, was now so reduced that the locals' children had to leave to work elsewhere. The small changes they'd helped make with the boathouses and Willow's blogs seemed rather insignificant, and she wished there was something bigger they could achieve before they left.

On the first floor was a series of paintings – the usual icons, the portrait of an unpronounceable local saint, some scenes from the Bible. On the wall at the end was one that made her laugh out loud.

It was Faithful Penelope, but not as she was usually portrayed, especially by the soppy pre-Raphaelites, with great tragic eyes and billowing hair, endlessly staring at the horizon in the hope of spotting her wandering husband.

This was something quite different. A medieval painting of Penelope on a barge, gaily tipping her persistent suitors overboard with a bargepole and a serene smile of satisfaction.

'She was a strong lady, Penelope.'

Penny jumped. She hadn't heard the curator approaching.

'Do you think so? Some people think she's a bit pathetic.'

He laughed uproariously. 'Not at all. She was strong. And clever. We have a copy of that picture in the guidebook, if you would like to buy it?'

'I would indeed. What a great museum.'

'Thank you. I'm afraid you will probably be our only visitor today.'

'Then I'd definitely better buy the guidebook.'

She walked back, clutching the book. When she got back she'd tear the picture out and put it up on her wall to remind her of strong Penelope!

Moira insisted on joining Stelios as he went to look for the old men, rather against his better judgement, but he began to realize that refusing Moira's company would take more strength of purpose than he possessed; in fact, probably an armoured tank. So together they approached the gaggle of old men seated on a low wall right at the far end of the harbour. There were about six of them, a couple wearing shorts and baseball caps, one in a jaunty striped top, another who looked very ancient indeed in sober navy and finally the chatty one in the beret. They sat there all day, in the shade of the tamarisk trees, providing a chorus on the activities unfolding in front of them, the stupidity of tourists, the meanness of the cafe owners who didn't offer them free drinks and, Moira suspected disapprovingly, the level of attractiveness of every woman who passed.

Their memories might be less than sharp, but they still recalled that Moira had bought them all a coffee yesterday and greeted her effusively.

'*Kalimera, sas!*' she replied equally enthusiastically. 'And this is my friend, Stelios Stavropoulous.'

They looked him over critically. 'Too old for you, *kyria*,' pronounced one.

Stelios made a great play of looking wounded. 'Now, gentlemen,' he greeted them in Greek, 'I'm sure very little escapes you that happens on the island. My friend here says we should be talking to you about where to look for the missing statue of Aphrodite.'

They all burst into laughter.

Moira surveyed them sternly. She hoped this wasn't all a wild goose chase.

'Perhaps if your friend purchased some ouzo, our memories might be usefully jogged?'

'Ouzo?' Moira replied, shocked. 'It's eleven o'clock in the morning!'

Stelios elbowed her unsubtly. 'Of course!' He smiled all round. 'And where can the best ouzo be purchased for unjogging memories?'

'From the wine shop round the corner,' instantly replied the man in the beret. 'None of that supermarket rubbish they call ouzo, when it is no more than a donkey aiming his piss in a bottle!'

'Of course, of course,' bowed Stelios obsequiously. 'I will purchase some right away.'

He linked his arm with Moira's. 'The more ouzo the better, in my view,' he whispered.

'But then they'll all just talk gibberish.'

'You insult the drinking capacity of our nation! Besides, I'll get the wine shop man to water it down a bit. They won't be able to tell. Pick up some nibbles from that deli while we're passing. Nothing that will get stuck in false teeth, mind.'

Moira pushed open the door of the deli, feeling somewhat flummoxed. She had no idea what snacks would get caught in false teeth. She settled on some harmless-looking olives with chunks of feta cheese, and some chilli-flavoured Doritos. She wasn't quite sure of the wisdom of these but they were all she could afford, having only a small amount of money with her.

She met Stelios coming in the opposite direction with a bottle of ouzo and some small borrowed glasses.

The ouzo was duly poured, circulated, and a toast raised to the health of all, which Moira imagined must be quite important at their age. Stelios had just asked again for any news of Aphrodite, when their beret-wearing friend began to seriously choke on a chilli chip.

'Oh dear!' apologized Moira. 'I knew those Doritos were a mistake.'

Stelios began to hit him energetically on the back.

'Be careful you don't kill him!' advised Moira stoically. 'At least, not before he tells us what he was talking about.'

'Get some water, then!' Stelios instructed. 'There's some in that jug!'

Moira poured some into a glass, held the man's head back and poured it down.

'Not like that!' Stelios grabbed the glass from her. 'In sips.'

After five or six attempts, the old man finally began to stop coughing and look normal.

'Ouzo!' he cried plaintively, as if it were mother's milk.

Stelios added a little to the glass of water and handed it back to him. Gradually he became a more normal colour.

'Georgiades,' he finally announced. 'Rich Athenian bastard.' He made sure every eye was on him before he came up with his final revelation. 'He rents a boathouse. Go to the end of the bay and then past the headland. There is a small inlet, hidden from sea view. You will find it there.'

Stelios pumped his hand. 'Thank you!'

'Be careful,' the beret-wearer added as an afterthought. 'He is not a good man.'

Moira and Stelios walked gleefully back towards the hotel. 'Congratulations, Moira. This was all down to you. Now we are getting somewhere.'

When they got back to the cafe outside the hotel, Dora, Karl and Nell were all sitting round a table, looking deathly serious.

'Somebody tell a joke!' Stelios greeted them, 'We have some news at last.'

'What's the matter?' Even Moira, not the most attuned to human emotion, could tell something was wrong.

'Have you seen Penny?'

'No, why? She went off for a walk earlier.'

'Takis says there is someone upstairs, waiting for her. In her room.'

Moira considered this for a moment – and then it dawned on her. 'Oh my God! It must be Colin, the horrible husband!'

Eighteen

'I suppose one of us had better go and look for her,' Nell said glumly. 'It would be awful if she walked in not knowing.'

'I will,' offered Moira.

They looked at her in surprise.

'I mean, it was Penny who invited me on this reunion when I wasn't really your close friend; I was just the swot who lived on the same floor.'

'Maybe we should all go up to her room with her,' Nell suggested. 'To show this creep where to get off.'

'Good idea. Or give her the option of not coming back at all,' suggested Dora. 'And we'll deal with him for her.'

Moira picked up her key and started to leave.

'Moira ...' Dora began, looking uncharacteristically hesitant. 'You know you're our friend now!'

Moira found she couldn't stop smiling as she headed off to hunt for Penny.

'And when you find her, tell her we're all behind her!' Nell shouted.

Ten minutes later Moira found Penny emerging from a back

street, clutching a guidebook to the architectural museum, looking surprisingly happy.

Penny held up the guidebook. 'I've been round the museum. Karl would be impressed with me,' she grinned. 'What's the matter? You look like you've eaten a cup of cold sick!'

'I came to look for you. You've got a visitor waiting for you in your room.'

Colin.

A combination of dread and sickness, mixed in with a kind of relief that it had finally happened, swept over Penny. What on earth was she going to say to him?

'Do you want some moral support? I'm happy to come up with you,' Moira offered. 'In fact, we all are. Or Dora's offered to tackle him for you, if you prefer.'

Penny's fear began to evaporate. She wasn't alone.

When they got back to the harbour, Dora, Karl, Nell and Stelios were still outside waiting for her.

Stelios jumped to his feet. 'Stelios Stavropolous, at your service,' he announced with a bow. 'People always tell me I'd make an excellent bodyguard.' Penny considered his bear-like appearance and could quite see why, although the permanent twinkle in his eye rather undercut any capacity to intimidate. 'I could wait outside in the corridor, if you prefer.'

'Thank you, but I'm sure it'll be all right,' Penny assured him. 'Just knowing you're all here is enough.'

'Open the window as soon as you get into the room,' Dora counselled. 'Then you can shout for reinforcements. And remember: you're a wonderful woman, and he's a lousy shit!'

Penny decided to take the stairs up to her room rather than the lift. She stood outside the door, got out the key and breathed in deeply, then put it in and turned it.

The figure lying on the bed rolled over and smiled.

'Wendy!' Penny screamed, half fainting with relief. 'Darling! Why didn't you tell me you were coming?'

Wendy got up and gave her mum a big hug. She was tall with attractive rust-coloured hair cut into a long bob, warm brown eyes, freckled skin and a large smiling mouth.

'It was all a bit sudden. Martin got some time off work, and I thought what better way to use it than let me visit my gypsy mother on a sun-drenched Greek island?'

'I'm *so* glad to see you, darling!' Penny found she was close to tears.

'Well, don't cry about it, then. Tell me all about what you've been doing. We thought it was so wonderful you had your own money for once and could do what you wanted.'

This instantly made Penny think of Colin.

'Has there been any sign of Dad?'

Wendy shrugged. 'We think he's gone to Portugal. Forget about him. He's probably trying to spoil your time here because he can't bear the idea of you being independent.'

'Is that what Martin thinks too?'

'Don't get Martin started. He thinks you ought to have left him years ago.'

Penny hugged her again. 'It *is* lovely to have you here!'

'It's lovely to be here. Can we get something to eat? It was a really early flight, and good old Ryanair don't exactly run to free breakfasts. Last thing I ate was a croissant at Jamie's Italian at six a.m.'

Penny linked arms with Wendy and led her down the corridor to the lift.

'This seems a sweet little hotel. I wondered if I could share your bed?' She looked quizzically at her mother. 'Unless there's another occupant?'

'Of course there isn't!' Penny replied, thinking of Nikos and how she was going to explain their relationship to her daughter.

The others must have heard from Cassandra or Takis that it wasn't Colin waiting upstairs, since they had tactfully disappeared to give her some time with her daughter.

'What a great location!' Wendy looked around her. 'Right on the harbour, so you have the fun of watching all the boats come in and out, but far enough back that it's quiet.'

'Yes, we've been very happy here,' Penny agreed. 'The owners, Takis, his mother Cassandra and daughter Ariadne are absolutely lovely.'

'Ariadne! What a wonderful name,' Wendy smiled. 'Does she carry a ball of string? Poor girl – I expect everyone asks her that, thinking they're being smart-alecs who know about Greek mythology.'

'It's just an ordinary name here.' Penny found a quiet table on the corner in the shade. 'Everyone you meet is an Adonis or an Achilles.'

'How funny!'

Takis emerged at that moment carrying a tray, and Penny called to him. 'Takis, come and meet my wonderful daughter Wendy!'

A huge smile cracked Takis's face. 'I am so glad to meet you!' he grinned. 'Your mother and her friends have done so much to help our island. Penelope, you must show your daughter the boathouses. But first, what will you have to drink, ladies?'

'I am more concerned with eating, thank you,' Wendy replied. 'I had a very early flight and I'm starving!'

'I will get you a menu at once,' Takis promised, and disappeared back inside.

'I like him. He's got such a funny face!'

'He's the kindest man on the planet.' Penny looked round,

but there was still no sign of the others. As soon as Takis came back with the menus they both ordered some meze plus a Greek salad and a glass of wine, and some warm pitta bread.

'My mother will be so excited to hear that Penelope's daughter is staying with us as well!' Takis enthused as he scuttled back to the kitchen.

'How great that they appreciate you so much,' Wendy commented.

'I know. It's nice to be appreciated.'

'Especially after Dad.' They both giggled.

'Oh, it *is* good to have you here!'

Takis arrived with the salads, with an extra-wide smile to see them looking so happy.

'You must take your daughter on a tour round the island. I am sure Nikos would be delighted to take you.'

Penny looked up at him, but he had a poker face with no hint of any implications.

'Who's Nikos?' Wendy enquired.

'A friend of ours here,' Penny replied stiffly.

'Aha. I knew there was somebody from the tone of your voice when you rang me up. Is he tall, dark and handsome? I suppose, being Greek, he's bound to be dark.'

Before she'd had a chance to reply, Moira bounded up to them with the air of a startled sheepdog.

'Wendy, this is my old college friend, Moira,' Penny introduced her. 'This is my daughter Wendy.'

'So not your horrible husband at all,' Moira blundered with her usual tact. 'Takis told us it wasn't.'

'Wendy's come on a surprise visit,' interrupted Penny, trying to signal her not to go there.

'It certainly was that.'

Wendy looked at her curiously.

'We're going to go on a tour of the island,' Penny continued, trying to steer them into safer waters. 'What do you think I should show her?'

'Oh, you must see the Corsair caves,' enthused Moira. 'They're the most significant thing about Kyri. You can tell her it was the caves that made this such an important place in the seventeenth century.'

'*Was* it an important place?' Wendy glanced round her. 'It hardly seems like it now.'

'I know it's hard to believe, but Kyri was the hub of the whole eastern Mediterranean,' said Moira with a flourish.

'You sound so proud of the place,' Wendy smiled.

'We are, aren't we, Pen?' Moira slipped an arm round Penny. 'We've sort of adopted it.'

'How long are you planning to stay?' Wendy asked.

They both jumped guiltily. Wendy noted the response with interest. They clearly felt they ought to be going home, but didn't want to.

Takis was back with their wine. 'I will call Nikos,' he said tactfully, 'and see if he can take you ladies on a tour.'

'Why doesn't Penny call him?' Moira enquired, ignoring Takis's warning look. 'He's more likely to take us if she asks him than you do!' she blundered on.

Wendy, acute as ever, stored this interesting information away and got stuck into her salad.

Just as they were finishing, Dora and Karl appeared. Seeing that Moira was there already, they came up to join the group.

'This is my wonderful daughter, Wendy!' Penny informed them meaningfully. 'She was in my room waiting to give me a surprise!'

'Ah,' acknowledged Karl, sagely nodding.

'Takis was right, then . . .' began Dora.

'Yes, Dora,' Karl interrupted swiftly.

'He has just phoned Nikos to see if he can take us round the island.'

'But you should see the boathouses first,' Dora suggested. 'Your mother was absolutely amazing with the boathouses,' she told Wendy enthusiastically. 'She has a real flair for design!'

'I know,' agreed Wendy. 'She should believe in herself much more.'

'She was brilliant. Her and Nell. Where is Nell, by the way?'

'I think she's worried about being seen with us, after the other night.'

'Ooh,' Wendy commented. 'How fascinating. What happened the other night?'

She could see from their faces that they didn't know how to answer this. 'Aha – a mystery. Even better. Don't feel you have to tell me. I have just escaped dreary reality and my demanding children for some sunshine. I am happy to lie around like a basking seal with earphones on. I shan't give your game away.'

Takis descended on them, all smiles. 'He asks if you could go round to the jetty near the boathouses at three p.m., and he will be happy to take you.'

'Oh good,' Penny smiled. 'That gives us plenty of time to show you round a bit.'

'And avoid Marigold,' Moira agreed. 'If you can.'

'Who is Marigold?' asked Wendy.

'The most dreadful woman you could imagine,' Moira replied.

'Now, Moira . . .' Penny began.

'She is, and you know she is. You're too nice, Penny. Always were. Though, thinking about it, that is the only reason I'm here today.' She turned to Wendy. 'I wasn't really part of the magic circle, you see. It was Nell, Dora and your mum. But she still asked me to come. And think about it, Karl – if she hadn't, you would never have met Dora.' Dora and Karl exchanged tender looks. 'Oh enough, enough! Karl's my old mate from Cambridge. I've been teaching classics there ever since.'

'And will she let us forget it?' Dora quipped. 'No chance of a classical reference is overlooked. Moira makes sure we know our nymphs from our dryads, don't you, Moira?' she asked affectionately.

'We need to borrow a bike to get round to the boathouses. They have a free system here that Nikos devised. He's the local mayor.'

'I must admit he sounds very intriguing.'

'Right.' Penny stood up quickly. 'We'll see you later, everyone. Where's Stelios, by the way?'

'Who's Stelios?'

There was a brief silence before Karl replied, 'A friend of mine. He owns a gallery in Thessaloniki.'

'Karl is Director of Classical Antiquity at a museum in Cambridge,' Moira explained.

'Gosh, what a clever bunch you all are! I'll have to listen and learn,' Wendy grinned.

'I very much doubt that,' said Karl. 'Sunbathing with your headphones on sounds much more instructive.'

They agreed to meet up later, and Penny and Wendy went off to find bikes.

'Hmmm,' Wendy breathed as they rode along, 'bliss! Just feeling the sun on your shoulders and knowing it's probably still raining at home . . .'

They rode past the first two boathouses to find Marigold out on her step, apparently polishing her door knocker.

'*Ciao*, Penny,' she called out, 'and who's this?'

'My daughter Wendy.' Penny wasn't going to offer anything but the bald facts.

'Off to see Nikos again? I'm sure he's waiting for you.' Marigold managed to make this short statement sound as if Nikos would be wearing a thong and tied to the mast for Penny's personal gratification.

'What a weird woman,' commented Wendy. 'She looks like the type who says she and her daughter are best friends and do everything together because she can't accept she's not twenty-one any more.'

'She is. Only it's my friend Nell's daughter she's best friends with, and it drives Nell mad. We've been getting some wonderful reviews on the island's website for the boathouses – and then Marigold posted a really nasty one, saying it was dirty and dangerous. With photos. When we went round to have a look we realized it was actually her who'd been doing the posting.'

'What a cow! Why did she do that?'

'For some reason she seems to be jealous of Nell, and wanted to ruin it for us. Apparently she used to be a bit of a rock chick.'

'And is still trying to be,' Wendy commented.

'Anyway, she's used to being the centre of attention and can't bear anyone else to be.'

'She's just a jealous old bag.'

They had arrived round the corner at the small pier where they were due to meet Nikos. He was waiting on board, waving at them. Wendy took a good look at him and liked what she saw. He was wearing jeans and a plain navy t-shirt, free of football or any other logos. He struck her as about the same age as her mother, with close-cropped greying hair, stubble that was halfway between designer unshaven and the beginnings of a holiday beard, and penetrating light blue eyes, unusual in a Greek man. They were softened at the moment by a welcoming smile. There was nothing remotely pretentious about him.

'Hello there,' he greeted her with a smile. 'You must be Penny's daughter.' He held out his hand and shook hers. His handshake was firm and strong. Another good sign; Wendy had a horror of men with grips like wet fish. 'Welcome aboard.'

Wendy looked at the vessel admiringly, from its beautifully painted figurehead to the glossy dark hull and red sails. 'What a fabulous boat!'

'Thank you. You must sit at the front and get some sunshine. That's what everyone from England comes here for.' He held out a hand to Penny, and Wendy caught the brief, loving look that flashed between them. After that, it was the way they *didn't* look at each other, almost as if they didn't dare, that told her the most.

The trip round the island was fascinating and beautiful, and she could see why her mother had lost her heart to this place. And quite possibly this man.

She found herself studying his face as he concentrated on manoeuvring them round a tricky headland. The question she wanted to know was – did he feel the same about her mother?

As Wendy let the sun warm her heat-deprived skin, she thought about the reality of the situation. How would her father react? His recent behaviour had been strange in the extreme. Would her mother ever have the strength to stop letting him control her and choose a life that might bring real happiness?

They would miss her, of course. She was a part of the children's lives, but they had all grown up enough not to need the ministrations of a grandmother. And sensible Wendy could see the attraction of lovely Greek holidays for them all. Unless of course there was a Mrs Nikos? Where her mother was concerned, Wendy had a strong protective streak. Maybe she should ask a few subtle questions and find out.

When she opened her eyes, Penny was standing at her elbow with a glass of white wine.

'Nikos thought you might like this. In his experience we Brits like sun, sand and Sauvignon.'

Wendy laughed. 'How very true.' The thought struck her that her own father would no more think of a nice gesture like this than he would stand on his head with his trousers round his ankles.

'He also wondered if you wanted to swim? We could stop in one of these little bays, and you'd have the sea to yourself. You don't have to dive off if you don't want. There's a little ladder that you can climb down at the back.' She knew Wendy's one vanity was her hair, and she might not want to get it soaking wet.

'Perfect. You will not be surprised to know I have my bikini on underneath.'

'That's my girl!'

Penny went back to the wheelhouse while Wendy stripped off. 'The ladder for me, please!' she told her mother. 'Are you coming?'

'Why not?' Penny took off her dress and climbed down gingerly after her daughter.

They swam together in the gloriously clear water, which was blue yet so transparent that you could see shells on the sea bed.

'Do you remember how I used to collect shells when I was little?' Wendy asked. 'Nothing as exotic as the ones here. Kyri is a very special place. I can see why you might not want to come home.'

'It's not just the landscape,' Penny explained as they swam towards the shore. 'It's feeling useful, trying to put Kyri on the map. All the other islands are popular – Santorini too much so. Sifnos is famous for its food, Ios for partying . . . and somehow Kyri got left behind. And the people here are so kind and eager. We've all felt really at home here.'

'So you're going to stay?'

Suddenly Penny looked lost and unhappy.

'Has Nikos asked you to?'

'Yes he has. But I'm not sure he means it. I've been a memory to him: a kind of symbol of how much he's changed. I'm not sure it's me he loves – boring old Penny who's always trying to please everyone. I've never been pretty or interesting.'

'You only feel like that because Dad's undermined your confidence. You'll never know till you make a choice. I think Nikos is a good guy. And I think he loves you. And as for all this bollocks about not being pretty – you've never looked prettier! In fact you're making me quite jealous!'

Penny laughed out loud, reflecting on how much she loved and admired her daughter. She is brave and wonderful partly because of me, Penny told herself. Even if it was because Wendy had defined herself in opposition to Penny's inability to stand up for herself.

'Or happier,' Wendy added, as they swam back towards the pirate ship. 'You haven't asked my advice, but I'd say go for it, Mum.'

Back at the boat, Nikos helped them aboard. 'So, to the famous caves,' he announced, steering the boat to the next headland.

Penny went below to change out of her wet swimsuit. Wendy decided to seize the moment. 'Have you ever been married, Nikos?' she asked, pulling a t-shirt over her bikini.

'No, never,' he grinned, instantly aware of the direction of the conversation. 'Which is considered very strange in Greece. I've had long relationships and almost tied the knot, but somehow it never happened. Does that make me a bad bet?'

'Better than having a wife you forgot to mention,' replied Wendy, always one to put her cards on the table.

'Don't worry,' he replied. 'I'm what the Americans call baggage-free. So, now I have a question for you. What is the situation with Penelope's husband?'

'My father, you mean?' She liked his directness; it echoed with her own. And he wouldn't be asking unless his intentions were serious.

He nodded.

'He's never really valued her. And now if he loses her he'll probably only realize too late what he's lost. And even then, he'll find a way of blaming her.'

'You think she'd be better off without him?'

'Yes.' Wendy looked him in the eye. 'I honestly do.'

'Good,' smiled Nikos, as if she had answered something that had seriously worried him. 'You don't know how relieved I am to hear you say that.'

Wendy went back to her perch at the front of the boat. She had a strong feeling that Nikos would turn out to be a good thing.

'Where is Stelios?' Karl enquired as they met for their usual early evening drink.

'For that matter, where is Nell?' added Dora.

'I think he's feeling sorry for her because she's still staying in her room to avoid detection,' Moira suggested.

'She can't stay there forever,' Dora shrugged, trying to catch

Takis's eye. 'Takis, sweetheart,' she smiled seductively. 'How about opening a bottle of prosecco?'

'Dora, behave,' Karl objected. 'They'll never sell the rest, and it will cost them a fortune.'

'I'll drink it,' Dora said. 'No, I won't – I'll take it up to poor imprisoned Nell.'

'Are you sure poor imprisoned Nell isn't up there enjoying the company of charming Stelios, and might not welcome an interruption?' he suggested.

'Everyone welcomes interruptions involving prosecco,' Dora commented blandly.

'*I* wouldn't,' replied Karl.

'I'll try and bear that in mind. Takis, two more glasses, please. And some of that delicious pepper hummus Cassandra makes. Oh, and some pitta bread. And maybe some olives.'

'Tell them we'll meet them at the cafe on the beach,' suggested Moira. 'That should be safe enough. We're always the only people there.'

'All right. Say in an hour?'

'Giving you time to knock back the prosecco and neck the hummus and olives?' replied Karl.

'Exactly,' agreed Dora at her most imperious. She made her way towards the lift bearing the Prosecco on a tray as if it were some kind of divine offering.

Moira and Karl looked at each other and grinned. 'She'd make a good goddess,' winked Karl. 'Let's you and me have a beer.'

Takis brought them two green bottles of Mythos. Moira shook her head. 'You really can't get away from myths in this country. Even on the beer bottles!'

'Well, ancient Greece was pretty influential,' Karl reminded her.

'The cradle of western democracy.'

'And they invented cynicism.'

'And stoicism.'

'What a country!' They toasted the land of their hosts by drinking their beers in record time and ordering another round.

Dora knocked sharply on Nell's door, then waited thirty seconds in case there was any funny business going on in the bedroom. But when she entered she found Nell sitting chastely on a chair by the window and Stelios stretched out on the bed with his hands behind his head, regaling her about one of his more extraordinary clients.

'He came in one afternoon, this old guy, didn't even look particularly rich. Arrived in my shop in and told me he wanted to buy everything every last little thing. Just as if he were walking into Harrods!'

'He was probably an escaped lunatic,' Nell replied.

'No, he was absolutely genuine. A Russian millionaire.'

'Ooh, prosecco,' cried Nell gleefully. 'How absolutely lovely!'

'I think Nell is being too cautious hiding up here,' pronounced Stelios.

'We thought you could come down to the beach cafe as soon as it's dark,' Dora told them. 'Anyway, Stelios, what are we going to do? Nell can't hide up here forever. What did you find out?'

'That Xan Georgiades has a boathouse beyond the final headland. And he keeps a boat there that he never even mentions.'

'My God! That's it, then. What are we going to do?'

'I don't know,' Stelios confessed. 'I have the body of a lion and the courage of a mouse. That was why I was lying on the bed, thinking.'

Nell was standing by the window drinking her prosecco. Suddenly she froze.

'What's the matter?' demanded Dora.

'It's him! He came out of the underground garage and stared directly up at me.'

'You're absolutely sure he saw you?' asked Stelios.

'One hundred per cent.'

'That's it, then.' Stelios knocked back his prosecco in one gulp. 'Whatever we do, we'll have to do it tonight.' He jumped off the bed with an agility that was surprising in a man of his proportions. 'We'll leave Nell to get dressed in privacy.'

'Where will I meet you?' she asked nervously. There was something immensely reassuring about Stelios's presence.

'We'll be just outside, don't worry,' he smiled.

Dora detected the tenderness and concern in Stelios's tone, and glanced at him in surprise. She hadn't realized things had progressed so far.

'Dora,' he said, suddenly firm and decisive once they were in the corridor outside Nell's room, 'I don't think Nell should be involved tonight. It's too risky for her. The man is ruthless and he has seen her now.'

Dora remembered the frisson of fear she had felt when Georgiades stared at her with those cold aristocrat's eyes not so long ago.

'The trouble is,' he continued, 'will she listen? Please try and convince her. She has already been through a lot with her granddaughter – and now she has the chance of happiness at last.'

It was on the tip of Dora's tongue to say that happiness might also lie in having someone who cared about you as much as Stelios clearly did, especially when you'd been alone as long as Nell. She wondered if Nell had any idea, and how she would react if she did.

How exciting. This holiday was certainly turning out to be full of surprises.

Nineteen

'Right,' demanded Dora in her best Boadicea tones, 'what are we going to do? I think Stelios should go and look at this boat-house because he knows where it is. And Karl can go with him to make sure it's the right bloody statue!'

'Stelios says he's scared,' pointed out Moira.

'So am I,' seconded Karl. 'I may be old, but I still enjoy life.'

'Well, you'll have to get over it,' Dora continued mercilessly. 'I don't like heights but I've made myself go up the Eiffel Tower.' Before Karl had time to argue that he didn't think that was at all the same thing, she continued, 'Now, if it is the statue, how are we going to transport it?'

There was a silence.

'I know!' Nell offered enthusiastically. 'Demetria. She can get the old fishermen involved.'

Karl shook his head. 'Considering our age, this is beginning to sound like the Hatton Garden jewel heist.'

'Didn't they get caught?' Moira asked tactlessly.

Nell ignored her. 'If we had the fishermen standing by with the van we used for picking up furniture, they could carry the Venus between them and we could cover it in blankets. Kyri was big in the Greek resistance, almost as famous as Crete, so Cassandra told me. I'm sure they'd be up for it. The honour of the island.'

'And what will we do with it, once we've got it?' Karl enquired stoically.

'Take it to the main square,' Dora commanded. 'Unload it next to the hotel, where it's busiest. He can't get it back from there – too many witnesses. And Kyri can have her Venus back.'

'You sound bloody efficient, I must say,' conceded Karl. 'Especially since you won't be going.'

'Come on, the two of you,' she encouraged. 'Stiffen the sinews and all that.'

'How are we going to get there?' Stelios asked. 'It's quite a hike. Is there even a road?'

'No idea. We need Takis. Moira, go and get him down here for a moment,' instructed Dora.

'When did you get to run things?' Moira asked resentfully. 'You wouldn't know Aphrodite from a hole in the ground.'

'And that's exactly where she's been,' Dora snapped. 'Somebody has to take charge, or he'll move the bloody thing again.'

Moira went off, harrumphing, into the starry darkness. Fifteen minutes later she was back with Takis.

'Moira has explained your daring exploit,' he said seriously, looking like Mr Bean Goes to War. 'I am all behind you. There is a small road that meets up with the coast road about half a mile beyond Nikos's house.'

'I'd better go and look for Demetria.' Nell jumped up. 'I'll call you when I know about the fishermen and the van.'

'Nell, you must not,' intervened Stelios. 'It is too dangerous!'

'Stelios,' Nell replied angrily. 'I'm not some precious little flower that needs protecting!'

Stelios and Karl exchanged a look of male sympathy. If chivalry was dead, it was because women saw it as part of the patriarchy.

'When we go in, how will we know that Demetria is ready with the van?'

'I'll flash my phone light three times,' Nell suggested. It all felt to her like Five Go to Rescue a Goddess. She was interested to note that she felt no fear at all.

Demetria was at her usual amazing best. 'I will send a message to the fishermen that we will pick them up in half an hour in the van. Lucky for us, the moon is new. Come – let us get the van now.' She said something in rapid Greek to her husband, who simply shrugged. Clearly he was used to doing what he was told.

Once they had the van, Nell called Stelios and gave him an update. According to Demetria, about twelve fishermen had already volunteered. All they had to do was pick them up from a meeting point.

'The whole bloody village is getting involved in this venture.' Karl shook his head.

'The more the better,' Dora insisted. 'Safety in numbers.'

'You don't really think he's dangerous?' pooh-poohed Moira.

'The rich are always dangerous if you threaten to take their money,' pronounced Stelios.

They all waited another ten minutes until Nell phoned again to say they were on their way. When they got to the road behind the boathouse, they would hide the van somewhere discreet and signal three times with Nell's phone.

'Oh my God,' Nell suddenly blurted, 'I hope my bloody battery's got plenty of charge left.'

'Karl, you and Stelios had better get started,' Dora commanded. 'Takis, drive them as near as you can, or the van's going to get there before they do.'

'My car's in the garage under the hotel. I'll get it now.' He sprinted off at once. A couple of minutes later he was back.

'Right,' Stelios took a deep breath, 'I suppose we'd better get on with it.'

'Take care, old man.' Dora leaned down and kissed Karl. 'And remember: in the end, it's only a statue. Not worth getting killed over.'

'Now she tells me,' he said with a grin.

'Don't go in till you get the signal from Nell that the van's ready and the fishermen are standing by,' Dora reminded them.

'We do have brains, you know,' Karl replied, nettled. They climbed into Takis's car, and he sped off down the narrow coast road.

'Now we have to hope Karl and Stelios know what they're doing,' Moira commented.

Demetria was as good as her word. Once they had the van, they drove about a quarter of a mile to a small chapel with the familiar dome and shrines all round it. A gaggle of whiskered fishermen, none of whom knew a word of English apart from possibly 'squid' or 'seabass', stood excitedly chattering outside. They shook Nell's hand in the manner of children embarking on a school trip.

Oh God, Nell thought, I hope this is going to be all right. A wave of anxiety rose in her at the realization of how many people they'd involved without any guarantee of their safety.

A grey-bearded man called Apostolis, who wore a cap and fisherman's jumper and seemed to be the leader, rapped out something indecipherable, and deep silence fell as they all climbed into the van.

'His father was a hero of the resistance,' Demetria confided with a wink. 'I think Apostolis has decided this is his moment to grab a share of fame.'

Twenty minutes later, after lumbering over a small road rutted with potholes, they arrived at a spot north of the boathouse and parked in a small grove of tamarisk trees.

Nell felt for her phone. She climbed silently out of the van and walked round until she had a clear view of the boathouse. Then she looked for the light on the phone. Typically she couldn't find it, and swore to herself about how much she hated technology. Magically the light suddenly came on.

She flashed three times, and held her breath.

Twenty

'Stelios!' Karl grabbed his arm as they made their way towards the isolated boathouse. 'Had you thought? It'll probably be locked.' The usually jaunty Karl looked as white as whey, which had the effect of making Stelios feel braver.

'Of course,' he grinned, producing a small tool kit from his pocket, 'I imagined it would be. As a dealer in antiquities, many people think I am only one step away from being a criminal anyway.'

Karl would usually have spent a happy hour arguing the case that he was among them. In his view, antiquities should remain in the country of their discovery, rather than being sold to rich foreigners for their private collections. Stelios would, of course, have countered that the museum Karl had spent his life working for was stuffed with antiquities pilfered from Greece and other historic settings. But tonight Karl was much too scared.

Stelios turned the door handle. 'Locked. Inevitably.' He selected a tool similar to a small bradawl and began to fiddle with the lock until there was an audible click.

'Open your eyes, Karl,' teased Stelios. 'We're in!'

As quietly as a cat stalking a bird, Stelios began to push open the door to the large ground floor, where fishermen would pull up their small craft to protect them from winter storms. He shone his torch around the entire space, about thirty feet by twenty. It was entirely empty apart from some lengths of rope, a couple of buoys and some blue nylon netting covered in seaweed.

'It's not here!' he whispered furiously. 'Karl, go and look down the far end and double check.'

Suddenly a much more powerful flashlight illuminated the boathouse.

'Thank you for stating the – er, bleeding obvious – as your compatriot Michael Caine might say,' said an infuriatingly calm and contemptuous voice, with only the slightest foreign inflection. 'You are too late, I'm afraid. The statue is in fact on board the speedboat moored just outside. We are planning to take her to a watery grave where she can sleep soundly with the nereids. I have had enough of this stupid business.'

'Georgiades,' Karl begged, 'you can't! She could be the most important discovery this island has ever had. She could bring flocks of tourists just to see her. She could outshine the Venus de Milo!'

'Why should I care about any of that? The people here wouldn't even let me build my house, all because of this stupid statue.'

'Or maybe because they loved their olive grove,' added Stelios.

'*Vlakes!* Peasants! My building would have been the most beautiful on the island.'

'Helped along by the eight million euros for the statue,' pointed out Stelios.

Georgiades ignored him. 'There will be no evidence for that.

It was a stupid idea anyway. I am a businessman, not a burglar. Wish her goodbye now, you stupid little men.'

Karl hoped that Nell and the fishermen might have seen the flashlight beam and guessed something was up. Maybe they could do something – if only he could keep Georgiades in the boathouse for long enough.

'Wait!' he began, thinking desperately of some way to hold things up.

'Too late to increase your offer now,' Georgiades sneered. 'Besides –' he turned to Stelios – 'I knew you were a fake from the start. You and your English lady friend, pretending to be French. It was only that idiot from Santorini, led by his prick as usual, who talked me into even hearing you out. And now I really must go.'

He swept grandly out and ran down the beach towards the water. But before he could get there, three whiskered fishermen materialized out of the darkness, tripped him up and proceeded to hold him down.

'Take the statue!' he shouted from his prone position on the beach to the driver of the speedboat. 'Follow your orders!'

But once again he had been forestalled. The fishermen knew their business, and two of them had swum out and swiftly disabled the speedboat's outboard engine. It simply sputtered, then stopped altogether.

The driver of the boat, whom Stelios recognized as the garden-centre owner from Santorini, dived overboard and swam frantically away. The fishermen watched him, smiling broadly.

'Next stop Heraklion!' one of them shouted.

'We'll find him round the bay in an hour. Exhausted or dead,' shrugged the other.

'But how did you know to come to the beach?' Karl asked,

amazed when Nell and the other fisherman arrived in the boathouse.

'You sent a recording on your phone!' Nell informed him. 'You're the hero of the hour, Karl!'

'Am I?' Karl was bewildered.

'Has anyone called the police?' asked Stelios grumpily, feeling that Karl was getting too much of the credit.

'Nikos is coming with them now.' They saw a solitary car with a flashing light on its roof making its way along the bumpy path.

'*Ho makarios Theos!* Blessed God! Not often you see that on Kyri,' marvelled one of their rescuers, clearly thrilled to be involved in Kyri's biggest drama of the decade.

There was a sudden shout from the man in the sea, only just audible. He had clearly got into difficulties already.

'Shall we take the boat out and pick him up?' the fishermen asked Stelios respectfully.

Stelios stared out to sea for a moment. 'I think you'd better. Tempting to let him drown, and I'm sure the goddess would approve; but perhaps not humane. Go!'

Georgiades, just behind them, took advantage of the diversion to make a run for it, moments before the arrival of the police. He dashed with impressive speed towards the tamarisk grove and pulled a powerful motorbike out of its green depths. With a thousand-cc roar, it tore off in the opposite direction as its rider held up two fingers in a V-sign of angry defiance.

'Shit!' yelled Stelios. 'We lost the bastard.'

'There is nowhere he can go,' Nikos shrugged. 'Do not concern yourself. He will be caught. It is a pity we only have one policeman here. But there is usually no trouble on Kyri.'

Meanwhile the one policeman was busy taking the man from the boat, breathless and dripping, into custody, while shouting down his phone to the station to summon reinforcements. He bundled the prisoner into the police car with the help of the strong, silent fishermen, and drove off.

Stelios and Karl looked at each other, and then at Nikos. 'What are we going to do with the statue?'

Nikos shrugged. 'That is a good question. If she goes to the police, they will just hand her over to the authorities.'

Stelios grinned. 'We have the van and the manpower. Let's take her to where she ought to be.'

'Where's that?'

'Where the people of Kyri can appreciate her! In the square in front of the hotel, as Dora suggested. She can be like the Statue of Liberty, greeting everyone who arrives on the island.'

'Except that she's lying down with a tempting smile, rather than extending an arm of welcome,' pointed out Karl.

'Well, she is the goddess of love. Maybe Kyri can become famous for sex rather than food or sunsets.'

'I'm not sure about that,' Nikos said doubtfully. 'Anyway, let's take her before the policeman comes back.' He turned to the assembled fishermen. 'Come on, friends – we are going to bring the statue from the boat. Can one of you bring the speedboat and drive it up on the beach? As far as possible without damaging it? Hey, what the hell – the boat belongs to Georgiades. You can damage it as much as you want!'

With not a shred of argument, two of the old men calmly dived into the sea and swam out towards the boat.

'That's Andreas for you,' one of the others commented proudly. 'Eighty-three, and he swims every day of the year, even Christmas. He's stronger than men half his age.'

'Particularly me,' admitted Karl ruefully.

'I thought you Cambridge men were always stripping off and waving your bits at ladies from the river bank?'

'You mean Parson's Pleasure in Oxford. That was banned years ago, and a good thing too!'

They all watched as the impressive Andreas and his companion climbed easily aboard the boat, tinkered with the engine, then turned it round and drove it back towards the shore.

'Bravo, Andreas!' called Stelios, hugely enjoying himself.

At that moment, Nell, who had retreated to the van for fear she would be in the way of any arrests, appeared back on the beach – directly in the path of the speedboat. Without hesitation, Stelios threw himself on top of her and rolled them both out of the way.

'Are you all right?' he asked, with so much emotion in his voice that Karl's suspicions were confirmed: Stelios was in love with Nell.

'I'm fine,' Nell replied. 'Have you hurt yourself at all?'

'Only my dignity,' Stelios smiled.

'My dear,' Karl said generously, 'you should have come earlier. Stelios has been the hero of the hour. Nikos has agreed that we should take the statue and erect her in the square next to the harbour.'

'Won't she get stolen again?'

'No,' insisted Stelios. 'The people of Kyri will respect her.'

'And I will arrange for her to go to the Archaeological Museum at night,' Nikos added.

Andreas and the others tenderly carried the statue from the speedboat to the van, where Nell created a cosy nest of blankets to protect her from being knocked against the walls. They slipped her carefully in.

One of the fishermen mumbled something to Stelios that made him laugh out loud.

'What did he say?' asked Nell.

'Roughly translated, that he is extremely glad she is in two parts. But he said it with a little more emphasis.'

'I'll bet he did! I must admit, she looks very happy there,' commented Nell with a grin.

'If you'd been buried for four hundred years, only to be dug up and threatened with being dumped into the deep waters of the Aegean, you might like being wrapped in a nice warm blanket too.'

'Poor lady. I've just had a thought,' Nell exclaimed. 'Ariadne will be over the moon. She's the one who most wanted her goddess back.'

'Let's go and get her, then,' Stelios said. 'Come on, Karl. Climb in the front with Andreas.' He turned to Nell. 'At least you're not in the path of his driving this time.' He slipped a quite unnecessary arm round her.

'It's not me that you need to hold on to,' Nell commented wryly. 'It's the Venus.'

Unfortunately, Stelios seemed to have gone temporarily deaf.

A quarter of an hour later, they arrived in the square and began to unload the marble couch.

Stelios, Nikos and Karl toured round the square looking for the ideal position, while Nell rushed off to get her friends. They wouldn't want to miss this for the world.

The spot they finally chose was right outside the hotel, next to the stone wall of a flower bed, where the goddess would get a good view of the harbour and there would be space for a crowd to gather – just as it was already doing.

The fishermen heaved the statue onto the couch where she had once lain for centuries, smiling with an extraordinary sensuality and holding the apple that had eventually caused the Trojan War. Her hand had been thoughtfully restored to her by the people who wanted to sell her to the highest bidder.

By now Moira, Penny and Dora had all hurried to the scene with Nell. Along with Stelios, Karl and Nikos, they stared at the Venus in silence.

All the abuse she had suffered had hardly damaged the sheen of her shining white skin, fashioned from the best Parian marble. Three or four small dents in the smooth line of her shoulders served only to give her a vulnerability that made her seem almost human, but the imperious set of the rest of her body, commanding mortals to watch in awe, tinged with desire, was pure goddess.

Her other arm lay along the back of the couch, supporting her long neck below a perfect oval face, straight nose and eyes looking not at the viewer but slightly to one side. The smile that had lit up the face through the centuries was confidently seductive. A swan-like neck and perfect shoulders led the eye down to her gloriously naked breasts, the sexy whisper of a pot belly, with an immaculately carved linen cloth, clinging and almost transparent, even though it was made of stone, covering her most private parts.

She was the goddess Aphrodite almost brought to living flesh, although this Aphrodite had lived for thousands of years, her smile inviting and delighting generations of worshippers and admirers.

'Isn't she amazing?' said Nell in a hushed tone, almost as if she were in church.

'She's all goddess, isn't she?' Moira replied. 'Wouldn't it be great to go round seducing mortal men and having fun starting wars?'

They all looked at her. 'Moira, I didn't know about this secret desire to go round creating sexual havoc!' laughed Dora.

'Come on, Dora, it's exactly what you do!' Moira countered.

'Why else would you wear all those body-con dresses made for eighteen-year-olds on the pull at the disco?'

'For a start,' Dora replied grandly, 'my dresses are made by Azzedine Alaïa, and they are strictly for grown women.'

'Because only grown women could afford them,' put in Penny with a grin.

'True, they are expensive,' Dora conceded. 'But wear one of those and you could seduce anyone on the planet.'

'Even an old guy, too weak to put up a fight,' pointed out Moira naughtily.

'If you mean Karl –' Dora glanced across the square, and found he was watching her rather than the statue – 'I assure you, there's plenty of life left in him yet.'

Moira was about to reply when a figure shot out of the cafe and flung herself into Dora's arms.

'Thank you, thank you, thank you, you have brought back the goddess!' She clasped Dora's hand and kissed it reverently. 'She will bless you forever more!'

'And what about the people who *really* found her – Stelios, Karl and Nikos . . .' reminded Moira.

'And me,' added Nell sternly. 'And Demetria, and an eighty-three-year-old superman called Andreas. And Andreas's fellow fishermen, names unknown.'

But Ariadne still stared adoringly at Dora. 'I have a question to ask.' She hesitated, blushing and suddenly tongue-tied.

'What is it?' Dora asked gently.

'Have you heard of the word *koumbara*?' Ariadne's dark eyes had taken on a new intensity.

'*Koumbara*?' repeated Dora, savouring the syllables slowly. 'No, I don't think I have. Is it something you sing with a guitar?'

'That's *kumbaya*, you nitwit,' corrected Moira.

'It means godparent,' Ariadne persisted shyly. 'Someone

who helps and advises you, and keeps you on the proper road in life.'

'I can see why no one has ever asked me to be one, then,' joked Dora.

'But I am asking you now. Dora, will you agree to be my *koumbara*? Could I come to London and live with you for a little while? Please.'

There was a note of desperation in Ariadne's voice, as if she could only flourish if she got away from the daily demands, well-meaning though they might be, of a family business where home and work, leisure and constant demand, were inextricably tangled until she felt suffocated by their web.

Dora glanced over at Karl, who had clearly been listening, and raised one eyebrow a millimetre. Karl's gaze softened as he looked across at her, and he replied with the tiniest of nods.

So it's got *that* far, thought Moira, who was a lot more perceptive than people gave her credit for.

'Of course I will be your *koumbara*,' announced Dora, and held Ariadne tightly in her arms. The warmth of the girl's slight body brought out a streak of protectiveness she had never felt before. Here was someone who trusted Dora with her whole future – and she would do her best to enable it.

Penny, watching from the cafe terrace, wanted to cheer. Dora had never in her whole life experienced the kind of love that meant pain and sacrifice as well as joy and fulfilment. From now on, she would. Nell, so newly restored to contact with her own daughter, rushed forward to congratulate them both.

And Moira, who had lived a life of eccentric independence within the strange institution of a Cambridge college, found she was actually envying Dora. She wouldn't mind being a *koumbara* herself. Not that anyone was likely to ask her.

'Shall I come with you to ask Takis and Cassandra?' Dora offered, understanding how difficult this might be for Ariadne. The girl smiled gratefully.

'Before you go,' Nell interrupted, 'Ariadne, could you take a photo of us and the statue for me to send to Willow?' She handed over her phone, and they all posed round the statue and smiled.

'Let's see,' demanded Moira as soon as she'd finished. She grabbed the phone and studied the photo. 'Actually, we don't look bad for a bunch of old broads!' She passed it round to the others.

'God, my hair,' protested Dora. 'It looks like one of Joan Collins's wigs!'

'You look gorgeous,' reassured Nell. 'And Penny, you look rather stunning, you're all brown and freckled!'

'Me?' asked Penny, startled. 'Do I really?'

'Yes,' Nell repeated firmly, 'you do!'

Penny took the phone and studied it. 'I do look OK, don't I?'

'More than OK,' said Nell. 'You look gorgeous!'

'What about Aphrodite?' Dora decided they'd heard quite enough about Penny. 'How does she look?'

They all contemplated the statue.

'She'd never make Page Three with those tits,' commented Moira.

'Moira!' Nell replied, scandalized. 'This is the age of Me Too and Time's Up. You can't talk like that.'

'Aphrodite wouldn't have time for any of that crap. She was always off seducing people. Ares, the god of war, for a start.' Moira grinned. 'And he was her half-brother!'

They were about to go back to the hotel when a bearded Orthodox priest emerged from the crowd, bristling with so much anger that even his beard looked cross.

'Who is responsible for this disgraceful display?' he demanded, pointing at the statue. 'Do you not remember the Ten Commandments? "Thou shalt have no gods before me"? And I find this pagan statue being displayed as if it were a holy saint? I am going to find the mayor instantly!'

'Shall I tell him it was the mayor who helped put it here?' asked Nell naughtily. She looked at Penny and winked.

'Or get him to explain why the scent of myrtle so often accompanies her?' giggled Dora. 'That would probably give him an apoplexy.'

'I still don't know what to make of that.' Nell bit her lip. 'But I do think there was something – I don't know – magical?'

'I do too,' agreed Penny.

'Yes, but Christ knows what,' added Dora. 'Oops – that expression seems a bit inappropriate, given the circumstances.' They all began to giggle.

'We obviously all imagined it,' insisted Moira doggedly, refusing to laugh. 'Group hysteria. It's a well-known phenomenon.'

'Let go a bit, Moira!' Nell teased her. 'What happened to the laid-back cocktail-maker of Treasure Island?'

'Reality hit her,' Moira replied sternly. 'Now that we've found the statue, what are we all doing here?'

The question was like being pushed into a freezing swimming pool on a gorgeous summer's day. They all looked at each other helplessly.

Dora was the first to recover. 'Well, I for one am going to break the news to Takis and Cassandra that my new god-daughter is coming to stay with me in London. Moira's quite right. I will have to start making plans for going home.'

Twenty-One

In the privacy of her room, Nell studied the photographs Ariadne had taken of them with the Venus of Kyri. They were of excellent quality, and everyone looked proud and happy. She would send them straight to Willow, and also to that English-speaking paper in Athens. Maybe they would pick it up. Surely finding Aphrodite had to be a good story, even on a strong news day.

She looked through the photos again. They had all become such good friends, caring for and helping each other as well as the island. Coming here had been exciting, fulfilling and even healing. They had discovered a completely different way of living from the one they had at home.

But Moira was right. She would be sad to leave Kyri, but now that she had Willow back in her life, and the joy of being a grandmother to look forward to, she knew she would have to go.

The thought of Stelios flashed into her mind. He was fun and he made her laugh, which hadn't happened with a man for a very long time; but she didn't think it was any more than that.

She thought about Penny and Nikos. Now that *did* seem serious. Except for the small question of her missing husband. Nell had been divorced so long, she didn't know what the current situation was. Could a husband refuse to give you a divorce? She seemed to remember a story in the papers of a husband who'd done just that. Oh dear, poor Penny! But at least her lovely daughter Wendy was still here, though she'd gone to spend some time at the spa in the White Hotel.

Penny herself was sitting in her own room, thinking roughly the same thing. She was scared. Nikos seemed to love her, but he hadn't repeated the invitation to stay with him. Her instinct told her that he could be trusted – but what if it was all some kind of fantasy? There was something of the romantic in his character, the knight in shining armour. What if he had needed to rekindle a romance from long ago, but had come to realize that was where it should have stayed?

She felt suddenly cold and vulnerable, her new-found confidence seeping away. She wished Wendy was back from her spa. She was so wonderfully reassuring and down to earth. 'Just ask him,' she would probably advise. As if it were as easy as that.

And where the hell was Colin?

And then there was the question of leaving Kyri, the place that had become more real to her than her own home. And the people who lived here – Takis, Cassandra, Demetria, even Andreas the fisherman – had become closer and more important to her than her actual neighbours.

Leaving would be an almost unimaginable wrench.

Moira too was in an unusually soul-searching frame of mind. She realized that her life until now had both protected and narrowed her. It had fed the life of the mind, and she would never regret a single moment of learning and teaching about the classical world; but it had been at the cost of wider experience. And here she had tasted that. If anyone in her college had heard that Dr Moira O'Reilly was running a beach bar catering specifically for booze cruises, they would have laughed in disbelief. But she'd done it. In this short time, she'd changed from being a teetotal bore who took the joy out of any situation into someone who could be the life of the party.

And it was all thanks to Penny for inviting her. Moira was, she knew, about as sentimental as a brick wall, but somehow she'd come to care about Kyri and its inhabitants, and even more extraordinary, they'd come to care about her. Back home people were all so busy, staring at their phones, dashing for deadlines. Dashing, dashing, dashing, with no time for anyone or anything. It was only when you were away from it that you noticed life didn't have to be like that. Kyri might be slow, but somehow it was never dull.

She felt a sudden swell of pride. How many times in your life did you help save a statue that had been created two hundred years before the birth of Christ?

Later that evening, for no reason she could think of, Nell changed into her prettiest dress and added a pair of dangly earrings. This climate certainly suited her. Her skin had been burnished into an attractive olive that, together with her large brown eyes, gave her a Mediterranean look that would have astonished her steadfastly British parents.

Her phone beeped. It was Willow. Her amazing daughter had already updated her blog with the headline BRITISH HEROINES DISCOVER VENUS OF KYRI, illustrated by the photos of them standing with the statue.

She was about to text a reply when her phone actually rang. This was such a rare occurrence that she jumped. Breathlessly, she pressed the Accept button.

'Mum, Mum,' shouted Willow. 'I've just had the *Daily Post* on the phone! You know how much they love stories about ladies beyond the first flush of youth!'

'You mean old bags like us?'

'Exactly! Anyway, a journalist on the paper follows my blogs – you know how desperate they are to be first with something – and she's picked up the story about you and the Venus, so you may get a call. The woman's called Delilah.'

'Of course she is,' Nell laughed.

'I got the impression they might be planning something big.' Willow was almost bursting with excitement. 'I so wish I was still there! Good luck, and keep me in touch!'

'Did you give her the others' numbers too?' Nell asked. She had a horrible vision of this Delilah getting hold of Moira in one of her un-PC moods.

'Only Dora's. I didn't have the rest.'

'OK, I'll warn her. How is Naomi?'

'Completely better. Missing her granny,' replied Willow.

Nell's heart turned over. Of course it wasn't true, but it might be when she and Naomi saw much more of each other.

'Are you ready to go home?' Dora asked Karl.

'I think I am,' he replied, watching her. 'I even quite look forward to it. Except that we live in different cities.'

'It's only an hour from King's Cross,' Dora pointed out. 'It's not like we're on different continents.'

'I know it's highly unlikely, but I don't suppose you'd consider coming to live in Cambridge?' Karl asked, suddenly serious.

'Or you move to London?'

'I'm not really the London type.'

'We do have museums in London, you know,' Dora teased. 'There's even quite a big one stuffed with classical antiquities stolen from Greece.'

'You're not exactly a habitué of the British Museum, then?'

'Once, on a school trip. That was enough.'

'My life is in Cambridge.'

'And mine's in London. Especially now I've promised Ariadne she can come and stay.'

'You can learn English in Cambridge too, you know. They even have quite a good university, I gather.'

'God,' Dora laughed, with a hint of bitterness in her tone, 'we sound like that Gershwin song. You know the one, I say "potato" and you say "potahto" . . .'

'Don't, Dora,' he said, reaching out for her. 'Remember how that song ends.'

'They decide to call the whole thing off,' she said crisply.

'You're wrong,' he brightened, the lyrics suddenly coming back to him. 'They decide to call the calling off off and compromise because they love each other.' He pulled her firmly into his arms. 'And that's what we should do.'

'I'm not very good at compromise.'

'I'll teach you. First lesson, close your eyes when I'm kissing you. I don't want to see that sceptical expression.'

Dora did as commanded. It was a very nice kiss.

'Am I being selfish?' he asked when she opened her eyes. 'Forget where we live. Am I too old for you?'

'Young men are dull,' Dora laughed. 'They always want to talk about themselves. And they want sex all the time. My Grandma used to say, "Better to be an old man's darling that a young man's fool."'

Karl roared with laughter. 'I'm not sure that's entirely complimentary.'

'Anyway, stop being unselfish. I don't care if I'm too young for you. You make me laugh, and I didn't think I'd ever meet a man who did that. I'm not complaining, and despite what my friends all think, I'd make a wonderful carer.' She smiled sweetly at him. 'I'd just hire someone else to do it.'

'You would, would you?'

'I'd make sure she was nice, though. Much nicer than me!'

'Pretty?'

'I'm not sure you're allowed to ask that kind of thing now.'

'Ah well. Nice will do.'

Dora's phone beeped with two new messages. One was from Nell, warning her about Delilah from the *Daily Post*; the other was from Stelios, inviting them all to come and celebrate.

'That sounds fun,' Dora smiled. 'Look, I'll just call this woman now so that she doesn't spoil the fun later.' She took out a large purple ring file. 'I know, I know,' she laughed, 'a Filofax, symbol of the Aspiring Eighties. I prefer it to my phone. Probably why Venus Green sacked me.' She flipped expertly through it, dialled a number, and adopted a loud London voice. 'Delilah, darling. Pandora Perkins here.'

'Pandora!' shrieked the woman. 'Where have you got to? Everyone's been gossiping about the way you disappeared. You're not in rehab?'

'No, I'm on a Greek island. That's why you wanted to speak to me. I'm one of the heroines who found the Venus.'

'Oh my God, *you're* the Dora she was talking about? That couldn't be more amazing because . . .' At this point, the line went as dead as a five-day-old story.

Dora dialled again, but unusually the connection on Kyri

seemed to be down. 'We have to hope that's the end of her. Actually, I might turn my phone off and claim it was a problem on the line.'

'Is that being a good PR?' Karl enquired.

'No, but it means having a good evening. The story will keep till tomorrow. Come on – let's go and join Stelios.'

Stelios was sitting with Nikos at a large table on the terrace, just next to the Venus, clearly in an expansive mood. They were both staring at the statue's glowing white limbs in deep admiration. Under candlelight, she seemed even more lifelike than by day.

'What period would you say she was?' enquired Nikos.

'Hellenistic,' Stelios replied. 'I'd guess 200 or so BC. I don't think she's Roman, even though the couch has a Roman look to it.'

'What would she be worth?'

'Beyond price.'

They suddenly burst into a passionate argument in their native Greek.

Penny, the first to emerge for the evening, was wondering if she should leave them to it, when Stelios noticed her and produced one of his trademark roars of delight. 'Penelope! Faithful wife to Odysseus, ignore us stupid men. We were just arguing over the Venus. I say she should stay here in Kyri, where they can look after her, while Nikos here insists the Minister must decide. Look what happened to the Venus de Milo, my friend. She ended up in Paris, in the Louvre.'

'That was three hundred years ago. Besides, it's the law.' Nikos smiled tenderly at Penny.

'Come on, we're Greek. We don't believe in laws,' declared Stelios.

'I thought we invented democracy,' Nikos countered.

'The Minister will probably find out anyway,' said Nell, who had just appeared beside Penny. 'That paper – the *Athens Times* – has got all of us on the front page with the Venus tomorrow! I've just had a call from them.'

'That was quick,' Stelios marvelled.

'The power of social media,' Nell shrugged. 'Newspapers get half their stories from the internet these days. Plus, of course, I sent them the picture.'

'Did you hear that, Takis?' Stelios shouted. 'The lovely English ladies are going to make Kyri famous!'

Takis dropped what he was doing behind the bar and dashed over, boiling over with excitement. He began to wring Penny and Nell's hands so hard they had to shake them afterwards. 'But this is such good news! At last Kyri will be on the map! Forget Sifnos with its food and Santorini with its cruise ships! It will be Kyri the tourists want to visit at last. Nikos, we must build her a temple where she can be safe and happy, and not have drunken louts lean on her and pretend to kiss her on the mouth!'

'Do they really do that?' asked Penny.

'Yes! I have seen them!' insisted Takis in outraged tones.

'Hello, Mum.' Penny whipped round to find Wendy behind her.

'Hello, darling, how was your spa?'

'The spa was great. I don't think I've ever had my toes and fingernails match before. But the hotel was gruesome. Everything was so white that I kept on bumping into things. You couldn't tell where the furniture ended and the wall began. It was like staying in an overheated igloo full of pretentious people. Ugh!'

'You missed all the drama!' Penny stepped back to reveal the Venus a few feet in front of Wendy.

'Oh my God! You found it!' She hugged Penny and Nell. 'What heroines you are! And what's happened to the wicked Athenian?'

'Disappeared to evade capture,' said Nell.

'We sent out a search party,' Nikos explained, 'but we suspect he's managed to get off the island.'

'They only have one policeman,' Stelios added, trying to keep a straight face.

'Willow's already blogged about it. There's even some journalist on the *Daily Post* interested!'

'Evening, all,' Karl greeted them as he and Dora emerged from the hotel.

'Karl, is that some joke implying Kyri's one-man police force is worse than Dixon of Dock Green?' asked Nell.

'No. Is he?' Karl replied.

'He's lost Georgiades,' Penny explained.

'Good riddance, if you ask me. I wonder if he was actually committing a crime?' Karl mused. 'The world of antiquities is so murky.'

'Quite a lot of countries would be guilty,' Dora chipped in. 'Our own, for a start, with the Elgin Marbles.'

'Now don't start that old chestnut.' Karl shook his head.

'We Greeks don't think it is – how do you say it – an old chestnut,' Nikos grinned. 'We would still like them back.'

'Quite right, too,' stated Moira, who had just emerged from her room.

'Moira!' chided Karl indignantly. 'How unpatriotic!'

'Is it patriotic to go round stealing other people's culture?'

'But that was what the British did best!' Karl reminded her with a grin.

A loud noise from above put an end to this conversation, one which Moira and Karl had clearly often had before.

'A helicopter!' exclaimed Dora as they all gazed upwards. 'Kyri's fame is spreading fast. Do you think it's a billionaire coming to try and buy the island?'

Only Nikos noticed that Penny, standing next to him, had paled and looked almost as if she might faint. They'd joked about Colin making a dramatic entrance in a helicopter, but it had been just that, a joke. Now she suddenly wondered if it might indeed be him, arriving with immaculate timing to spoil their moment of triumph.

Moira, who had also joined them, had no interest in helicopters, and was studying the latest arrivals on the evening ferry instead. She was so taken with the sight of a huge woman with a tiny husband laden down with luggage, looking as if he might at any moment collapse under the weight, that she didn't at first notice the inappropriately dressed businessman type who followed them. She soon got bored with the large lady and focused on the man instead. What caught her eye was his defining greyness. He wore a grey suit with a grey spotted tie; his neatly cut hair was grey and receding; he even wore grey glasses. There was something about him that reminded her of a worm, and Moira wondered idly whether, if you cut him in half, there would be two of him. Not a pleasant prospect, she decided.

There was also an air of just-confined irritability about the man, as if at any moment he might explode over the smallest inconvenience. She hoped he wasn't staying at their hotel.

Her attention was diverted by the helicopter again. She assumed the occupants were going to the White Hotel, it being the only upmarket hostelry on the island. With luck the angry worm was going there too, though he certainly didn't look hip.

To her surprise, the helicopter seemed to be descending somewhere at the back of Kyri town.

'I bet it's the amphitheatre,' Karl said. 'That's a big enough space for it to land.'

'Since when do you know how much space helicopters need?' Dora teased.

'Karl's right,' Nikos backed him up. 'The amphitheatre is surprisingly big.'

'I'd better get some drinks in,' Stelios grinned. 'We may be in for some fun, and it looks like we've got a ringside seat.'

He disappeared into the hotel reception, and emerged almost immediately with a bottle of white wine.

'That was quick,' Dora remarked admiringly.

Stelios winked. 'I know where Takis keeps his emergency supply.'

They sipped their wine and watched the approach of a short, bearded man with an exceptionally long lens on his camera, followed by a harassed-looking woman in white jeans and stilettos and behind them – clearly the VIP – a blonde in sunglasses and a long, clinging bodycon dress that left very little to the imagination.

'Oh my God!' Dora grabbed Nell, who was standing next to her. 'It's only bloody Venus Green! I've got to get out of here!'

She turned round to run off, but a surprisingly strong hand on her shoulder stopped her. 'Don't be a coward,' Karl said softly. 'I fell for a strong woman. You can deal with this.'

Meanwhile, Venus had just caught sight of her.

'Pandora!' she shrieked. 'What the hell are you doing here?'

'I could ask you the same question.' Dora willed herself to be calm. 'That was some arrival. We thought you were Donald Trump, or the Pope!'

'I've been sent here by the *Daily Post*. They're doing a piece on this statue – Venus meeting Venus, or some such thing. Where is she by the way?'

'Over there. They'll be taking her off to the museum soon. She sleeps there for the night, in case of vandals.'

Venus Green took off her sunglasses and studied the two-thousand-year-old triumph of Hellenistic sculpture.

'I didn't realize she was lying down,' she remarked pettishly. 'I thought she'd be standing up, like that statue without the arms on the album cover of *Critical Mass*.'

'You mean the Venus de Milo?'

'Does she have arms?'

'No, she doesn't.' Dora tried not to laugh. Her ex-client had never claimed to be culturally savvy.

'Then that's the one. I thought I'd stand next to your Venus for my new album cover and call it *When Goddess meets Goddess*, and the *Daily Post* could pay! But that won't work now she's lying down.'

She turned her full attention, which Dora knew from experience to be somewhat limited in scope, onto Dora and demanded: 'Anyway, where have you been? I've been sending you endless messages, and nobody knew where you were. Have you had a breakdown or something?'

Dora smiled. 'As a matter of fact, it started as a reunion of four friends who went to college together. And then we fell in love with this island and stayed on here for a while.'

'It feels like ages! I know because I sacked Barbara Ryan the day you left. Dora, she was a nightmare! I've been trying to find you ever since, to ask you to come and handle my PR again!'

'Wotcher, Pandora,' the bearded photographer threw in. 'No one can handle features editors like you!'

'Thanks, Bill,' Dora smiled, recognizing him from previous shoots. For a moment she thought about her old life, with its eternal negotiations and cliff-edge deadlines. But it seemed as remote as someone else's pressure-cooker existence, and she realized she had absolutely no interest in picking up the reins.

'I'm sorry, Venus.' She caught Karl's eye. 'But I'm moving to Cambridge.'

'*Cambridge?*' repeated Venus, as staggered as if Dora had opted for the North Pole. 'Whatever for?'

'I'm retiring. I may pick up a bit of local work for museums and stuff.'

'Are you *sure* you haven't had a breakdown?' Venus's voice was suddenly syrupy with sympathy.

'Not unless the symptoms are waking up happy and looking forward to what the day may hold,' Dora said lightly.

'Crying waste,' commented Bill, the bearded photographer. 'Come on, Venus love, better take these shots before the light goes. I may already have to add some filters as it is.'

Venus instantly went into full-on posing mode, lips out, stomach in, placing herself behind the statue and leaning over its white marble shoulder. She was employing her most effective weapon – her only effective weapon, Dora had often thought – looking into the lens as if she wanted to have sex with it.

'Did you mean that?' Karl asked, taking Dora's hand, as everyone else watched tomorrow's headline being created in front of them.

'Nah,' Dora grinned, 'just said it to get rid of her.' She saw the momentary flash of hurt in his eyes and put her arms round him. 'Yes, I meant it. When she offered me my old job back, I realized it was the last thing on earth I wanted.'

'Time to go home soon, I think?' he asked, glowing with sudden happiness.

'Yes, soon,' she agreed. 'But not quite yet.' Out of the corner of her eye she had noticed an angry grey-suited man, sweating profusely, approaching Penny's daughter Wendy.

'What the hell are you doing here?' he asked rudely. 'Why aren't you at home looking after your children?'

Wendy stiffened. 'Because my husband is generous enough to look after them so I could have a holiday,' she replied crisply. 'Some men are, you know.'

'I don't know what's happened to women,' the man continued angrily. 'First your mother ignores all her responsibilities and disappears off here on some feeble excuse. And then with absolutely no word why, she stays on for weeks!'

'You can talk,' Wendy snapped. 'Where the hell have *you* been?'

He ignored this and looked round pugnaciously as Moira and Nell began to work out what was going on and searched for Penny in case they needed to step forward and protect her.

Colin had finally glimpsed her at the edge of the crowd, talking to a Greek man.

'Right,' he said loudly, pushing people out of his way as he fought towards her. 'Go and sort out your stuff, Penny. There's a ferry to Santorini in the morning and we can fly straight to Athens from there. I've booked our flights for 11.45 tomorrow night. It all works as long as you get your bloody act together.'

Penny could see her three friends all lined up in her defence. Nikos too was at the ready, trying to catch her eye. She shook her head, both to acknowledge their support and to indicate that she could manage this on her own.

'Hello, Colin,' she greeted her husband, forcing her voice to be calm, her posture erect. What she saw was a small, sweaty man, bristling with anger and eager to find a scapegoat for his irritation. In the past it had usually been her.

She thought of all the years she had spent being slighted by him, her every opinion put down and dismissed. His eternal criticism of everything, from her driving to what kind of mother she was. Why had she put up with it all this time? It was only at a distance that she could appreciate how steadily he had undermined her self-confidence, making her feel she was a nobody.

Crossing her arms, she remembered she was wearing the silver snake amulet Dora had bought her in Zanthos. The same bracelet she'd worn when she was young and carefree, before she'd made the decisions that had shaped her life. The blue jewel in the snake's eye blinked at her, urging her to be brave, to see that it wasn't too late.

Suddenly Penny began to laugh.

'What the hell is the matter with you?' Colin demanded, looking at her as if she had lost her mind. 'Why are you bloody laughing, you stupid woman?'

'Because I find you ridiculous, Colin. You're charmless and controlling and there is no way I am going back to England with you.'

Moira and Nell exchanged a proud glance. Penny was doing just fine. They both wanted to cheer.

'Then what the hell do you think you're going to do?' he demanded nastily.

She held out her hand towards a man on the fringe of the crowd, whose dark eyes were already locked on hers. 'I am going to live with Nikos.'

Powerless Penny had found her voice at last.

'You mean Zorba here?' Colin asked insultingly.

Nikos simply laughed in his face, and put his arm tightly round his Penelope.

'How pathetic. Don't you know what a fucking cliché you

are?' Colin hissed at Penny. 'He'll dump you for some Scandinavian blonde half your age, mark my words. And don't come crawling back to me.'

'Goodbye, Colin,' Penny had the urge to start laughing again, but this time hysterically, and only Nikos squeezing her hand in support was keeping her going. 'I won't say good luck.'

Colin seemed to know when he was beaten. 'I'm going to get something to eat. I've been up since five with nothing to eat but a Ryanair sandwich, which I had to pay for.' He stomped off towards the hotel cafe.

'I hope to God he's not staying here,' Penny breathed.

'It won't matter to you.' Nikos's smile was a mile wide. 'You'll be with me, at the boathouse.'

'Well done, Penny,' congratulated Moira. 'You were magnificent!'

'Yes, Mum,' Wendy hugged her. 'I'm so glad you've finally managed to stand up for yourself and choose what you want.'

'Really?' Guilt at breaking up her family was beginning to seep in.

'Yes!' Wendy insisted. 'Tom and I are old enough to deal with it. Be happy with Nikos.'

Nell, meanwhile, was watching Colin's progress as he tried in a loud British voice to negotiate a room from a reluctant Takis, who had just told him the hotel was full – even though there were clearly rows and rows of keys behind him in the pigeonholes.

'Perfect!' Nell's face suddenly lit up with delight as she watched the scene. 'We couldn't have designed it better. Look who's decided to take Colin under her wing!'

Twenty-Two

A vision in a brightly coloured silk kaftan had descended on a bewildered-looking Colin and, like a ministering guardian angel, led him to one of the quiet tables at the far end of the hotel lobby.

Nell, eager not to miss a moment of this titanic encounter, slipped quietly into the nook by the lift shaft so that she could keep listening. Willow would kill her if she didn't relay every word.

'Mr Anderson,' announced the vision, 'or may I call you Colin? My name is Marigold and, believe me, I am very glad to see you.' She paused for dramatic effect. 'And not before time, either. It was I who sent you the anonymous messages.' She smiled bashfully, as one driven to this extreme conduct out of deep sympathy for a wronged husband. 'Your wife has been behaving outrageously.'

'That was you, was it?' asked Colin, not sounding at all grateful.

'You look exhausted. Can I get you a beer?'

He accepted this offer ungraciously. Marigold fetched him one from the honesty bar plus a glass of wine for herself, somehow forgetting to pay for them.

'What I chiefly need –' Colin's grey appearance was getting even greyer, through extreme tiredness and disbelief that Penny had dared to refuse him – 'is a bloody hotel room, and the stupid chap at reception says they're full.'

'Don't worry about that. You can stay with me. I have plenty of room.'

Tucked away in her nook, Nell almost got the giggles at the prospect of Marigold slipping into Colin's room at the dead of night as she'd tried to do with Nikos. From what Penny said, he probably wouldn't notice.

'That's kind of you.' He remembered his manners. 'Colin Anderson, nice to meet you. Anyway, my wife, the stupid cow, refuses to come home. Says she's staying here with that Greek chap.'

'Nikos. He's supposed to be the mayor here, so surely he shouldn't go round stealing people's wives.'

'Not that I'll notice,' Colin continued, not even registering her comments. 'She was a bloody useless wife anyway.'

Nell had to check herself from running out and hitting him on the head with his own beer bottle.

'How long are you staying?' Marigold undid another button on her kaftan.

'Going home tomorrow.' He looked her over for a moment, weighing up any similarity she might have to Penny. 'Why don't you come?' he invited, leering slightly. 'I have a spare ticket, if you're interested. Shouldn't be too hard to change the details. 11.45 tomorrow night. From Athens.'

Marigold thought for a moment. It was time she went back, and there was something about the wild and spontaneous nature of this idea that appealed to her. She wasn't at all sure about Colin, but she was even more fed up with Ted, and she quite liked the idea of walking off with Penny's husband. Nikos was far too attractive for plain Penny Anderson and he'd soon see there were prettier fishes in the sea than her.

Besides, she could always dump him at Gatwick. And it sounded as if he was offering a free seat.

She favoured him with one of her most terrifyingly seductive smiles. Colin, calculating how much money her offer of a bed would save him, failed to notice.

Marigold stood up. 'Let's get going, then. I'll find a cab.'

As soon as they'd departed, Nell scooted back to the others. 'I can't wait to tell Willow,' she giggled. 'Penny, the most wonderful news. The frightful Marigold has just scooped up Charmless Colin and taken him home!'

'Oh my God, talk about two people deserving each other!' Penny collapsed with laughter. 'I couldn't be happier for them! A thought occurred to her. 'Oh dear; poor Wendy and Tom.'

'I shouldn't worry. Wendy will either see her off or make her life hell. Besides, they'll probably have fallen out before they get to Athens airport. Where is Wendy, by the way?'

'Gone to pack. She's looking up flights at this very moment.'

Nell started to giggle. 'I hope she doesn't get the 11.45 from Athens. She might bump into Romeo and his new Juliet!'

The thought of her bully of a husband as Romeo had Penny and Nell in stitches.

'Have I told you how lovely you look when you laugh?' Stelios informed Nell, putting his arm round her with a flourish. 'More beautiful than your namesake Helen of Troy! Come with me and stay in Thessaloniki,' he suddenly begged. 'It is the second biggest city in Greece, and no one in Britain has ever heard of it!'

'I have to go home, Stelios. To see my daughter and granddaughter.'

'Then come and stay when you have seen them. Just for a holiday.'

She studied him for a second. 'Perhaps.'

'I do not like "perhaps". It is not a word we have in Greek.'

'Is that true, Nikos?' Nell appealed.

Nikos just laughed. 'I can see it is not a word in Stelios's vocabulary.'

Nell suddenly realized how dull her life would be without a man who didn't have the word 'perhaps' in his vocabulary. He was someone who took life by the horns and, like the books she'd so enjoyed by Mary Renault about Theseus the bull-dancer, made it dance to his own tune.

'Stelios!' she suddenly said. 'I hate the word "perhaps" too, so I shall use another one. Yes! I would like to visit the second biggest city in Greece that no one has ever heard of, but I'm afraid I can't remember its name!'

'Thessaloniki!' Stelios started to jump about like a dancing bear released from captivity. 'Lovely Helen, I know you have important commitments in . . .' He grinned wickedly. 'I'm afraid I can't remember the name of the place!'

'Sevenoaks!' Nell replied, smiling as broadly as he was. Stelios swept her into his bearlike embrace and kissed her soundly.

They were prevented from making further romantic declarations by the arrival of a large entourage consisting of Venus Green, the bearded photographer, Delilah from the *Daily Post* and various hangers-on they'd acquired at their hotel, who clearly wanted as many selfies as possible with this faintly famous person before she left.

'You'd better order six copies of the *Daily Post*, ladies,' Delilah announced, as if she were awarding them all a golden apple. 'Venus is on the front page! And I have written up the dramatic story of your search to find the statue, as well as what a great undiscovered location the island is. Kyri is about to find itself in the limelight!'

Waving goodbye like gracious benefactors, the party headed for their helicopter.

'I think she expected a curtsey, don't you?' asked Nell cheekily.

'Now how are we going to get six copies of the *Daily Post*?' Penny wondered.

'Most of their readers are dead anyway,' Moira commented.

'Thank you, Moira,' Dora replied. 'Just because she didn't interview you!'

'We can buy them at the airport,' Karl announced dramatically. 'I've been looking up flights. Your horrible husband was right, Penny. Ferry to Santorini and flying to Athens is definitely the quickest.'

'And bump into Colin at the airport?' Nell replied in horror. 'Absolutely no way. You lot can risk it if you want, but I certainly won't.'

'Nor me,' Moira backed her up.

'I think we should go the way we came,' Dora said. 'On the slow ferry that stops at all the islands.'

They all looked at her in amazement.

'But you moaned all the way!' Nell pointed out. 'You said it was the worst eight hours of your life! You criticized everything from the food to Penny's madness in booking it at all.'

Dora hid her face in her hands. 'I know. I was a complete bitch. But that was before I got to know you all. The thing is . . .' She hesitated for a moment, unsure how much of herself she wanted to reveal. 'I've never had any real friends before. I was always a man's woman. My God, doesn't that sound creepy?' She looked from Penny to Nell to Moira, all so different and yet united in the closeness they'd discovered here in Kyri. 'I love you all, and I want to make our time here last a tiny bit longer.'

'You know, Dora,' Moira added, looking embarrassed in turn, 'I agree with every word you've said. But our friendship doesn't have to end in Kyri.'

'And you can come and stay any time with Nikos and me, whenever you want!' Penny added, almost in tears as she realized they were all going and she was staying, even though it would be with Nikos.

'Stelios,' Nikos requested. 'You know about wine. Go and get some good stuff from the bar. Tell Takis I'll pay!'

Takis arrived with a dusty-looking bottle that seemed to be covered in cobwebs. 'I have been saving this for a very special occasion,' he announced reverently.

'And the fact we're leaving counts as very special?' Moira teased. 'So you want us to go, then?'

Takis launched himself at her like a missile. 'Miss Moira, you are coming back! I will go bankrupt if you are not here in the high season to manage Treasure Island. It was your idea! Your vision! Everyone thought you were crazy, but it worked! You charmed all the customers! Promise me you will agree.'

'I *charmed* your customers?' Moira asked incredulously. Moira, who had always known she was awkward and socially inept, a born outsider.

'They complained when you were not there!'

'Come on, Moira!' seconded Nell. 'Why don't we all agree that we will come back in the summer and have a drink at Treasure Island? But only if Moira is behind the bar.'

'I will reserve your rooms now!' Takis was already getting out his laptop. 'Three rooms with sea view for two, no, three weeks, in July. Before all the crowds arrive looking for the Venus of Kyri, all thanks to you!'

Stelios, who had opened the dusty bottle, handed them all a glass. 'To our own four goddesses, with thanks from Kyri.' He raised his glass.

Nikos caught Penny's eye, so that she knew which particular goddess he was toasting.

Dora wiped a tear from her eye and breathed in the night air, determined to remember the scent of sea and the evening perfume of the place she'd come to love. Out of the star-spangled darkness, Ariadne suddenly appeared at her side. Dora reached out an arm for the girl and pulled her close.

'Oh my God.' Nell suddenly clutched Moira, who was next to her. 'Breathe in, everyone! There's an overpowering scent of myrtle!'

They took a deep breath.

'Do you know,' said Moira, almost lost for words, 'I think she's right.'

'It's the goddess,' announced Ariadne. 'She's saying thank you and goodbye.'

Moira caught Karl exchanging a tolerant glance with Nikos. Clearly they couldn't smell the myrtle. So was it a special gift, given only to them, as Ariadne believed?

She looked across at the Venus, reclining seductively on her couch as she had done for more than two thousand years.

'Don't worry,' her delicately chiselled smile seemed to convey, 'what do they know? After all, they're only men.'

Acknowledgements

With enormous thanks to Ian Jenkins OBE, Senior Curator at the British Museum, and expert on Ancient Greek sculpture.

In twenty years of researching novels no one has given me as good an idea to follow up as Ian did. I hope I have done it justice.

I certainly had a lot of fun trying, and became mesmerized by Ancient Greece, and Aphrodite in particular. Coming back down to earth from such Olympian heights was quite a shock, but I am so glad I got the opportunity to lose myself in Greek culture for a while. I hope the reader feels the same.